Bayard looked up the path to where the ogre sat astride a horse, waiting like a huge metal barricade. I stood where I was, in no hurry to rejoin my companions. But as I watched Bayard stagger a little on the rocky incline, raise his sword in the Solamnic salute, and motion to Agion to help him back onto Valorous, I felt something like shame.

Shame for not lending a hand.

Not that I let that bother me long. After all, a fellow could get killed up here among the ogres and centaurs. I crouched by a stump downhill from the conflict and awaited the outcome, all set to run if the conflict turned against my protector.

Mounted now, Bayard wheeled Valorous about, and shouted out a challenge to the monster who loomed over the path ahead of him.

"Who are you who so rudely stands between us and our peaceful way across these mountains?"

No answer.

Bayard continued. "If you have aught of peace or justice in your spirit, stand aside and let us pass without quarrel or conflict. But if it *is* quarrel and conflict you desire, rest assured you will receive it at the hand of Bayard Brightblade of Vingaard Keep, Knight of the Sword and Defender of the three Solamnic Orders."

It sounded pretty, but the guardian of the pass stood where he stood, a darker form against the dark eastern sky.

Sword raised, Bayard charged at the ogre.

THE DRAGONLANCE® SAGA

CHRONICLES TRILOGY
DRAGONS OF AUTUMN TWILIGHT
DRAGONS OF WINTER NIGHT
DRAGONS OF SPRING DAWNING

LEGENDS TRILOGY
TIME OF THE TWINS
WAR OF THE TWINS
TEST OF THE TWINS

THE ART OF THE DRAGONLANCE SAGA

THE ATLAS OF THE DRAGONLANCE SAGA

TALES TRILOGY
THE MAGIC OF KRYNN
KENDER, GULLY DWARVES, AND GNOMES
LOVE AND WAR

HEROES TRILOGY
THE LEGEND OF HUMA
STORMBLADE
WEASEL'S LUCK

PRELUDES TRILOGY
DARKNESS AND LIGHT
KENDERMORE
BROTHERS MAJERE

HEROES II TRILOGY
KAZ, THE MINOTAUR
THE GATES OF THORBARDIN
GALEN BEKNIGHTED

PRELUDES II TRILOGY
RIVERWIND, THE PLAINSMAN
FLINT, THE KING
TANIS, THE SHADOW YEARS

ELVEN NATIONS TRILOGY
FIRSTBORN
THE KINSLAYER WARS
THE QUALINESTI

MEETINGS SEXTET
KINDRED SPIRITS
WANDERLUST
DARK HEART
THE OATH AND THE MEASURE
STEEL AND STONE
THE COMPANIONS

H•E•R•O•E•S
Volume Three

WEASEL'S LUCK

Michael Williams

Cover Art
LARRY ELMORE

To Terri, devoutly

DRAGONLANCE® *HEROES*

Volume Three

WEASEL'S LUCK

©Copyright 1988 TSR, Inc.
All Rights Reserved.

Random House and its affiliate companies have worldwide distribution rights in the book trade for English language products of TSR, Inc.

Distributed to the book and hobby trade in the United Kingdom by TSR Ltd.

Distributed to the toy and hobby trade by regional distributors.

Interior illustrations by Jefferey Butler and Valerie Valusek.

All DRAGONLANCE characters and the distinctive likenesses thereof are trademarks of TSR, Inc.

DRAGONLANCE and AMAZING are registered trademarks owned by TSR, Inc.

The TSR logo is a trademark owned by TSR, Inc. All TSR characters and the distinctive likenesses thereof are trademarks owned by TSR, Inc.

First Printing: December 1988
Printed in the United States of America.
Library of Congress Catalog Card Number: 88-50060

9 8 7 6 5

ISBN: 0-88038-625-8

TSR, Inc.
201 Sheridan Springs Road
Lake Geneva, WI
53147 U.S.A.

TSR Ltd.
120 Church End, Cherry Hinton
Cambridge CB1 3LB
United Kingdom

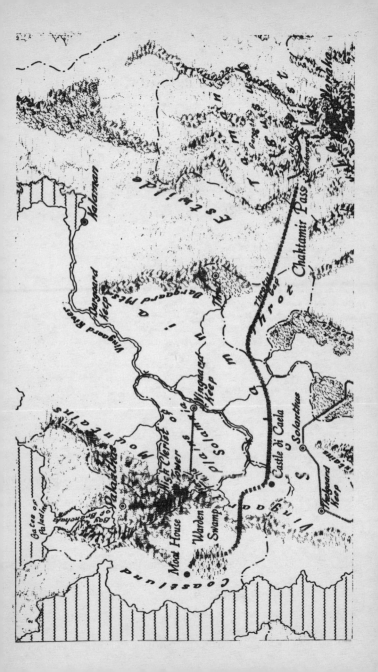

PART I

FROM THE MOAT HOUSE
TO 'WARDEN SWAMP

The Sign of the Weasel is tunnel on tunnel,
enchantment on enchantment.
He digs beneath himself, and in digging
discovers all roads into nothing.
Burrow the dark until darkness unravels,
in dark the philosophers dance.

—*The Calantina*, IX:IX

CHAPTER 1

It started on the night of the banquet I did not attend.

While the others were celebrating, I was cleaning my eldest brother Alfric's chambers, sweeping away the daily confusion of soiled clothes, of bones, of melon rinds. It was like a midden in there, like an ogre's den. Surely the missing servants were only hiding from Alfric somewhere in the moat house, and would turn up shortly.

Don't misunderstand me. It would be wrong, then or now, to compare my brother to an ogre. An ogre is larger, more lethal. Probably brighter.

Yet Alfric was bright enough to have me sweeping his quarters, soaping his windows, while he and the rest of the family sat down to supper with an honorable guest. For eight years running he had blackmailed me for the smallest of misdeeds, so that while the sons of other Solamnic Knights had spent their teens in horsemanship and falconry, I had spent mine in sweeping and dread, for reasons . . . well, the reasons come later.

Let it just be said that at seventeen I was feeling too old to be my brother's keeper.

While I stirred the dust in his quarters, Alfric sat in the great hall, at the table where Father entertained Sir Bayard Brightblade of Vingaard, a Solamnic Knight who had ridden up to our backwater estate in the glittering armor that was already the subject of song and a legend or two. To top it off, Sir Bayard was supposedly the best swordsman in northern Solamnia.

Not that I cared.

What was especially galling about our visitor was his redemption of Alfric. For it seems that Bayard Brightblade was on his way to vie for the hand of some southern nobleman's daughter in some glorified tournament, and had stopped in our rice paddy of a county as a favor to our once famous father. Bayard was taking my brother on as a squire at the advanced age of twenty-one, where half a dozen Knights had balked and refused. He would take Alfric with him, whip him into shape, and return him to Father as a man with knightly prospects.

Hearing of these prospects, Alfric had decided to celebrate: another horse had been found dead of exhaustion in the stables this morning, and once again, our tutor Gileandos had been set on fire. Arson was a hobby both Alfric and I pursued, but as usual, I had been blamed, dismissed from the hall without ceremony and supper, while a celebrity dined in our midst.

Laughter and the clatter of crockery arose from downstairs as I dusted my brother's nightstand, passing the cloth over the freshly carved "Alfric was here" on its surface. No doubt they were talking about me over wine and venison downstairs, hoping I would soon grow out of whatever I was supposed to grow out of. Brithelm, my middle and spiritual brother, had been excused from supper once again that evening for the gods knew what ancient and honorable fast, and Alfric was no doubt seated at the right hand of my father, nodding in agreement with the old man who had done his best by all of us, while Sir Bayard looked on in solemn and knightly approval.

I stewed over the festivities as I swept cinders, more bones, more feathers. But the stewing—not to mention my story—had only begun.

*   *   *   *   *

As I crawled beneath the bed to finish the sweeping before turning to the window I had to scrub daily, I heard a noise behind me in the doorway of the chamber. My first thought was that Alfric had enjoyed scarcely enough bullying for the evening, and had excused himself politely from the table in order to sprint upstairs and whale the daylights out of me for the sheer joy of daylights-whaling. I paused amidst broken pottery, empty wine bottles, several spent oil lamps, and more bones, and crouched beneath the bed.

A voice—honeyed and musical and deep—flowed out of the doorway.

"Where is everyone, little one beneath the bed? You needn't hide, for I can see through the dark, through time and stone and metal, and I know where you are. Where is everyone? I have business in this house."

Within that voice was also steel and danger. I thought of assassins, of the hired killer who speaks with a voice as sweet as a choir's, as the soft sound of the cello, even while he draws the dagger or pours the poison.

What was more, in the presence of the visitor, I swear that the lights dimmed in the chamber, that a low mist rose from the floor. The temperature dropped until the rising mist was laced with a white and bitter ice.

More frightened than when I had thought it was only my brother intending to batter me senseless, I answered in the way I thought safest, to render the least harm to the most dear.

"Look, I don't know who you are, but don't hurt me. I'm way down the line to inherit the fortune of this place, so I'm not even worth a well-planned kidnap. If you're looking for Father, he's downstairs at a banquet, but you'd probably have an excellent shot at him coming up the stairs in the wee hours of the morning. By the way, he had a hunting accident six months back, still favors his left leg, so aim toward the right.

I began to weep, blubber, and expand on the subject.

"Or if it's my brother Brithelm you're after, he's probably meditating in his room—some kind of religious holiday. Down the hall, third door on the left."

Brithelm was harmless, good-natured, and of all the family and guests I liked him the best. But not enough to place myself in the way of a would-be murderer. Quickly I continued the list.

"The only other soul on the floor is our tutor Gileandos, who won't hear a thing, since he's recovering from burns and probably from brandy by this time of night."

Through these betrayals, I stayed beneath the bed, from where I could see the intruder from the knees down, first standing in the doorway, then entering the room and seating himself in a chair by the window. His legs seemed large through the bend of the glass globe of the discarded lamp, and he wore black boots tooled with silver scorpions, as though black boots alone were not sinister enough. I raked a fortress of bones and crockery and lint about me, sliding closer and closer to the wall against which the far side of Alfric's bed rested.

"Of course, you're aware I have an older brother Alfric, too. If you'd like his entire schedule for the next several days, and a list of his favorite foods . . ."

"But, little one," interrupted the stranger, his singer's voice a lullaby, a drug. "I intend no harm to you or your family. Not unless it is necessary, of course. For it is another I am searching for . . ."

"Oh, you mean Sir Bayard. Well, if you are after his life it would be better if you came back later, after we're all asleep, after even the servants have gone to bed. That way the whole business would be cleaner, more private. You wouldn't have to kill anyone else to do whatever it is you want to do."

"Don't you listen, child?" The voice grew lower still, almost a whisper, and the air turned even colder. Outside, the nightingales ceased their singing, as though the moat house and everything surrounding it lay hush to catch the murmured words of the visitor. "Are you that in love with the sound of your own voice? I tell you that *I seek no man's life.*"

I raised myself onto my elbows, stirring up a cloud of dust beneath the bed, which I dearly hoped would hide my thoughts and trembling as well as my whereabouts.

Quietly the gentleman in black began to explain himself, as the fire in the hearth sank lower and lower.

"I have no designs on lives tonight. Not tonight, oh, no. It is only the armor I seek, little one, the fabled armor of Sir Bayard of Vingaard, renowned Solamnic Knight of the Sword, who rests here in this house this evening, or so I understand. Oh, yes, only the armor, a small price to pay, don't you think, for the continued safety of those you love so dearly?"

Well, to be honest, those *I* loved so dearly were mostly under the bed. And if I wept from fear before, I was practically weeping with joy, with relief now, there amidst the rubble. For my visitor was merely a small time thief—a burglar. A kindred spirit.

I would have crawled from beneath the bed to kiss those silver scorpions, that black instep, had I thought I served to benefit further by adoration, by thief worship. But I feared that sudden movement was still unwise. Instead I lay there, wondering what he wanted with Sir Bayard's armor.

It was only a moment before he read my silence. He stirred in the chair. The room grew even colder.

"As I said. It is only the armor that interests me, little Galen, nor should you concern yourself with what use I have for it." I thought of the fine Solamnic breastplate, greaves, and helmet which stood, poorly polished by my eldest brother, in the huge mahogany closet of the guest chambers.

The intruder was welcome to it. I had other worries.

"How do you know my name?"

"Oh . . . that need not concern you, either. I bear you no ill will."

All the while I was listening for the sound of approaching

footsteps on the stairway, in the hall.

"Well, if the armor is all you're after, it's yours for the asking. It's in the great mahogany closet of the guest chambers. Welcome to it."

"Ah!" said the voice.

"The problem is, the guest chambers are locked, triply locked—bolt upon bolt upon bolt. And my brother Alfric has the keys. I expect you'll have to break the door down or pick the complex series of locks, but the second would take too long and the first would alarm the whole house . . ."

"But my little friend, I have an alternative," he stated, musically, the worn heels of his boots visible as he leaned back farther in the chair. And in the cold air was the smell of smoke and of sweat and of old blood. "I love alternatives."

Something told me that this was no representative burglar, that I was in over my head.

Then a movement—silent, as quick as a striking adder— and a small leather bag hurtled through the air and landed by my side. I shifted uncomfortably, tugged at the drawstring. Into the dim light tumbled half a dozen shimmering stones—onyx, perhaps, or black opals. Perhaps a dark jade. In the shadows beneath the bed, it was hard to tell. They were cool and slick in the palm of my hand, clicking seductively together and against the band of my naming ring.

"For your troubles, little Galen," the voice soothed. Something in that gave me the shudders. The intruder continued.

"I shall return to this castle at midnight, at which time I expect to walk without hindrance to the guest chambers and find the armor awaiting me. From that moment on, we shall be done with each other.

"If, however, you fail to uphold your end of the bargain, or if you break the silence to which I enjoin you this night, this moment—if indeed you break that silence to anyone, or speak of me aloud to the walls of your bedchamber on this or any other night . . . I shall have no choice but to *dance in your skin*, little boy."

I ignored the threat at first. After all, I was caught up in marveling at the glittering objects in my hand, and in reckoning how much bargaining power they would get me with the merchants in the village, who despite my promises and pleas and threats had begun to deny me credit.

Upon such reckonings the gods lay heavy trouble.

For lulled by greed, I extended my hand out from under the bed so that the stones might catch better light. Green and yellow they were, with a dappling of deep red . . . And was grabbed by the black-gloved hand of the intruder.

I was startled at first, then worse than startled, as the hot pain of his grip shot up my arm like a quick-acting poison in the arteries. It seemed as though the bed was spinning above me, and dizzily I struggled for purchase, for balance in a rapidly blurring room. The grip relaxed, and just as I began to breathe readily again, a tickling and scratching on my throbbing hand took my breath once more.

For a truly real scorpion stood perched in the palm of my hand, dark amid the bright jewels, tail coiled and poised to strike.

I almost fainted, but the honeyed voice alerted me, jogged me back to my senses.

"Something tells me you aren't paying me the proper . . . attention, little man. Oh, but let me correct any misgivings on your part, any tendency you have toward underestimating me here at our first encounter. For I want a certain honesty between us. Even scorpions play by the rules, though the rules may be their own."

The creature on my arm stood deathly still, as though it was an ebony brooch. A brooch with a poison pin.

The room, the voice, the whole world seemed to focus in the clammy stillness of my palm.

"And the rules in this transaction are simple ones. Your complete cooperation. Your total silence. Your willingness to come when I call and never to question the mysteries of my workings.

"For this you receive your life daily. Of course, we shall take stock of your doings, now and then, to see if you have played by the rules or have been . . . found wanting. Death is a cozy nest, boy. You might even grow to prefer it."

The scorpion vanished from my hand. I closed my fist rapidly, spilling semiprecious stones across the floor. When the clattering died down, when the last stone had rolled to a halt under the intruder's chair, he rose, his boots glinting ebony in the firelight.

"Remember, Galen Pathwarden. The scorpion returns as quickly as it departs, as unexpectedly. But we will take stock, at midnight, in the guest quarters of the moat house. At that hour, the armor is mine. Or you are."

Suddenly the boots stood before the chair, the intruder using it as a step to rise to the sill of the window and out, down three dizzying stories into the gathering dark, the shutters of the window creaking back and forth behind him. I knew from experience that it would still be safer underneath the bed. Above me I heard movement, creaking, a servant climbing the steps to the bell tower, and soon afterwards, the ten tolls of the bell that signaled the hour.

There followed a long pause in which the air in the chambers began to warm, the sound of bird's song outside the window resumed, and I finally ceased shaking, crawled out into the light, and lay sprawled on the floor for a moment, recovering my breath amidst a litter of dark opals.

For dark opals they were, and a sizable bribe for my efforts and silence. I gathered them up, inspecting them for flaws. The Scorpion, as I decided to call him in honor of both his companions and his wardrobe, was evidently a man of his word.

Which gave me pause, naturally. For a man who keeps his word in one venue . . .

Is likely to keep it in others.

I sprang to my feet and out the door of Alfric's quarters, leaving behind me the room half-swept, the windows open, and the fireplace heavy with ashes. Down the narrow granite stairwell I rushed, touching perhaps two steps on my way to the second floor, landing heavily, off balance, then recovering in stride on my way to the door of the guest chambers.

Which was triply locked. Bolt upon bolt upon bolt.

And the keys dangling from Alfric's belt in the main hall somewhere, no doubt ringing together as pleasantly as sleigh bells while their bearer's little brother awaited midnight and the *dancing in his skin*.

I drew out my knife and began gouging at the upper lock.

* * * * *

There I might have stayed, whimpering and gouging until the hour of reckoning, growing more frantic and more defeated as the minutes passed. But luck—Weasel's luck, as Alfric called my ability to fall in a midden and come up smelling like jasmine—stepped in after a long absence.

I heard the sound of someone ascending the stairs toward Alfric's quarters. From the heavy tread and the puffing and muttering, I knew that my brother had been paying court to the wine while Father and Sir Bayard had been distracted by nobility and conversation.

Hulking like an ogre, smelling of pork and port, Brother Alfric paused, reeling, on the second floor landing. Shading his eyes with one meaty hand, he squinted down the hall in my direction.

"You again, Weasel? I just saw you on the stairway."

By the way, he calls me Weasel, if you haven't guessed. "Galen" means "Weasel" in Old Solamnic, and Alfric has other reasons—unfair reasons—of his own.

"The old gallon distemper," I explained, referring to his wine-slanted vision. "How is your guest enjoying his stay?" I continued, my voice full of sweetness and brotherly affection—as best I could imitate, at least.

But it had dawned on Alfric that I was hovering about the guest chambers door in a way that I should not be hovering. Lumbering up the hall he came, his fists clenched, promising mayhem.

"What was you trying to do to that lock, little brother?"

"I'm not here, Alfric. You just saw me on the stairway, remember? What you see before you is a resinous vision, the dregs of the wine."

I never claimed to have planned this all too well. But he stopped at that and puzzled it out for a moment. Meanwhile I scrambled to my feet, backed away from him, and kept talking.

"Brother dear, even as I speak there are mysteries milling about this moat house, endangering all of us."

It sounded good.

"Endangering you above all others. For you are to be the

squire of a certain reputable Knight whose . . . belongings may be at jeopardy this very evening."

Alfric paused in his unsteady charge, hiccupped, and stared at me in stupid puzzlement. If he came after me, he would have the stones—and probably the whole story—in an instant. Would probably drub me senseless in exchange.

My visitor would return, would find the the armor still locked away behind a door thrice bolted. Would ask for his stones back, which I would not have.

Would dance in my skin.

I kept talking, quickly, desperately, dancing through memory, through invention, through downright lies.

"Brother, only now when I was at the finishing touches to your quarters . . . there flitted a dark shape in and out of the shadows in the courtyard."

"A servant?" Alfric had stopped, panting and leaning against the wall of the corridor. His ragged red hair clung sweatily to his forehead: when Sir Bayard had sworn to whip him into shape, the noble Solamnic had admitted it was "a monstrous undertaking."

"Servants don't flit in and out of shadows, Alfric. Burglars do."

"Burglars?"

"And what is there around this backwater moat house worth the burgling?"

Alfric stared at me questioningly.

"Sir Bayard's armor, damn it!" I shouted, then lowered my voice, afraid that the noise would carry downstairs. "Coming down to get you would have raised a stir, perhaps for nothing. But I had to know that the armor was safe, especially since it had been entrusted to my dear brother's safekeeping, and if he lost it . . . well, his squirehood—*your* squirehood, Alfric—would be delayed even longer than . . . ill fortune . . ."

"And politics . . . ," Alfric interrupted, sliding down the corridor wall to a sitting position.

"And politics . . . have delayed it already."

I could not resist reminding him that a twenty-one-year-old squire was a bit grotesque, like our ancient tutor Gileandos sending flowers, sonnets, and scandalous proposals to

Elspeth, our twenty-year-old milkmaid.

"You expect me to believe that? Expect me to believe that even if there is a burglar, he could get in past them locks and all our servants and the dogs?"

"Look at our servants, Alfric. Look at our dogs. This castle is wide open to any secondstory man who crawls out of our own private swamp down the road. The servants themselves are always complaining of missing pennies, missing baubles and beads."

"Some of that's you, Galen."

"And some you. But we both know our petty thievery doesn't add up around here. There's more that slips through the cracks than slips through the cracks, if you catch my meaning."

I'm not sure he did, but his dimwitted face fell.

"About this burglar?"

"Outside before the bell struck ten."

"A dark shape?"

"Flitting in and out of the shadows, Alfric. A burglar if I ever saw one."

My eldest brother curled up on the floor of the hall, jamming his head between his knees.

"Oh, little brother! What shall I do?"

This was better. I looked at Alfric, then down to the window at the opposite end of the hall. Outside I could hear the call of a cuckoo as it settled somewhere for the night— probably in another bird's nest, where it would lay its egg and fly on under cover of darkness, as the old legends said, leaving its young to the kindness of a robin, a nightingale, one of the pretty singers who would raise the croaking infant as its own.

"All isn't lost, Alfric. After all, the armor may still be in the room."

He looked up at me hopefully, his big gap-toothed grin awash in the torchlight. I thanked the gods that the brains that ran in the family had never run after him.

"So first of all, we should check to see that the armor is there."

I looked back to the door, and in a sudden rush Alfric was on me. I was slammed against the wall and hung there, feet dangling helplessly in the corridor. A strong hand gripped my throat, another tangled less than lovingly in my hair.

"You better not be up to nothing, Weasel."

I began to weep, flatter, lie.

"Please, please, Brother, don't throttle the baby of the family! I know you're a good man, you're going to be a fine squire and an even finer Knight! Remember, Father had younger brothers, all of whom survived well into adulthood! He's come to consider that a family tradition."

Alfric took the hint. His grip slackened, and I took courage.

"Of course I'm not up to anything. No need to borrow trouble, Brother. The worry and the confusion and the running around headless will come soon enough if there's no armor in this room."

Alfric let me drop and was on his knees by the door in a moment, knife in hand and gouging where I had left off gouging.

"Alfric?"

"Shut up, Weasel." The irritating and frantic sound of metal on metal as the knife slid through the lock. I looked down the hall. Nobody there.

"Alfric, the reason you're so essential in this is that you have the keys to the room on your belt."

After fumbling with keys and locks for a while, we gained entry to the guest chambers which tonight were to house the most ingenious of Solamnic swordsman. It was the most richly appointed room in the moat house, Father being a zealot about hospitality: each wall was hung with tapestries, the enormous bed was covered with goose down blankets, and the fire blazed cheerily.

It was not a room for misdeed.

Alfric charged in ahead of me, lurching in a drunken panic toward the standing closet; I hovered behind him, thinking frantically of explanations I could summon if Sir Bayard Brightblade were to walk in the door and find us burrowing in his belongings.

Thinking frantically of how I might proceed from here.

Alfric stumbled once, grabbed the doors of the closet, and pulled. Of course they were locked. Of course the key was on the ring at his belt, and of course he had forgotten it, too, in the anxiety and wine. Inside the closet, the armor rattled like a ghost in an old story.

You can see a miracle coming for miles if you only pay attention. It all added up—the recklessness, the jostling, the heavy armor in the closet. After my brother had fumbled with the keys a long and distressing moment, one fit into the lock. With his considerable brute strength, Alfric yanked at the door, which flew open readily.

Bringing with it Sir Bayard Brightblade's extraordinarily heavy breastplate.

Which, when it made contact with my brother's head, set up a ringing that might well have disturbed my father and Bayard in their Solamnic discussions downstairs, and upstairs might have roused Brithelm from his meditations and Gileandos from his stupor.

But it did none of these. It did nothing, in fact, except lay out my brother on the floor of the guest chambers. The ringing of metal on the rocklike substance of my brother's head was lost in the ringing from the bell tower. As I said, you can see a miracle coming for miles if you only pay attention.

"Look out, Alfric," I said, quietly and in gratitude, as the eleventh bell tolled.

*   *   *   *   *

The rest was uncertainty, waiting alone in the guest chambers for the hour before the intruder returned and the armor changed hands. Outside all the birds were still silent, except for the nightingale, who sang merrily while I lingered and stewed.

I cast the red dice I kept always beside me to determine fortune. I rolled nine and nine, tunnel on tunnel for the Sign of the Weasel—great fortune, considering my nickname—though had I remembered the second line that went with the dice spots, I should have been less secure.

So I waited until the tower bell began to toll once more, steeling myself for the return of the intruder. At the seventh ring I heard something outside in the hall—down by the window, as if someone were climbing through.

The acrobatics alone were impressive.

I scuttled toward the bed, ready to dive beneath it should the Scorpion fellow be less the man of his word than he allowed. But a groaning behind me brought me up short.

There was a knot in the miracle. For my brother was waking at midnight, to the gods knew what mayhem.

That is when the helmet occured to me. It lay beside the breastplate on the floor, slightly dirty because of Alfric's lack of squirely attention, but impressive nonetheless, with its intricate weavings of inlay, copper and silver and brass.

Footsteps approached up the hall toward the guest room, as my brother stirred toward wakefulness and, of course, toward my ruin.

There was no time to deliberate. I snatched up the helmet as I rushed to my brother's side, and raising it above me, brought the whole damned artifact—visor and crown and plume, iron and copper and silver and brass—crashing down upon his forehead. Again the sound of the impact was lost in the bells. Alfric grunted and fell back upon the floor, where he lay still.

My panic subsided. My reason returned. For a long minute I stood in dismay above my brother, thinking that the murder for which I had shown promise those five years ago on the moat house battlements had now come to pass.

There was a movement at the door. I did not turn but dove toward the bed. A strong hand grasped my ankle and dragged me into the center of the room, where I lay shivering and bleating. Behind me I could hear the Scorpion lift the armor in a quick, fluid, almost effortless movement. And again came the voice—still soft, still poisonous.

"You have done passably well, little one, though the violence with which you concluded was a bit . . . untidy."

I looked around. A black, hooded figure moved to the door, the heavy suit of armor slung over its shoulder like a bundle of sticks or a blanket. Then it stopped and turned.

The red glow of the eyes shot through me like the grip that had pained and poisoned me scarcely two hours past.

"Your ring."

"I—I beg your pardon?"

"Your naming ring, little man." And the gloved hand stretched forth, palm extended. "You see, we are bound together by more than . . . a gentleman's agreement, shall we say? I would be more content—indeed, more comfortable—with some token of our transactions in hand."

"Not my naming ring!"

"Oh, but you can have the stones back, sir. They're certainly worth more than this little copper ring, and, after all, they were yours in the first place."

The intruder stood silently, gloved palm extended. Reluctantly I removed the ring, copper but intricately carved—one of a kind. It had been given to me four years ago, on the night of my thirteenth birthday when I had passed into the rather sorry manhood I had now botched up even more by dealing with some sort of armor-craving villain.

If anything identified a Solamnic youth, it was his naming ring.

I tossed the ring to the Scorpion. It disappeared with a flicker of his gloved hand.

"By the way," he murmured, "I still hold you to the rest of your bargain. Not a word of this to anyone, for on the night you speak that word I shall hear of it . . . no matter where I am. Perhaps that very night your skin will come due. Perhaps another night. But it will be soon, oh, yes, very soon." And quickly, stepping over a slowly stirring Alfric, he was out the door.

Someone—perhaps a servant—raised the alarm, and I stood there at a loss, hoping that stalwarts such as my father, such as the incomparable Bayard Brightblade, could harness the character in black boots before he slipped back into darkness with the armor and his plans for my skin. I had no idea how swift and efficient the intruder was, how the armor would have vanished, and he with it, by the time that Father, by now burdened with wine, and Sir Bayard, cold sober but burdened with Father, had climbed the stairs to a belated rescue.

CHAPTER 2

I did not know how the countryside would take it, what the farmers and peasants would say when my visitor, now disguised in the armor he had taken from Sir Bayard, began to turn the villages near our moat house into his own private fief. However, marauding never played well in the rural areas—the demands for tribute and cheeses, for livestock to be slaughtered and roasted on the spot. The demands for money and for daughters. Though for what purpose this disguise and rampage, I could not say.

The very day after the armor was stolen, peasants began to arrive at the moat house to petition my father. Each one bore his hat in hand, and each one suggested, simply and humbly at first, that "the Master do something about the troubles in our village."

The "something" suggested was usually that Father draw and quarter the offending knight, placing various parts of his anatomy "upon a platter" (what part of the anatomy depended upon the peasant's imagination).

"If the Master wills it, there's a lot of us what would like to see the culprit's head set before us on a silver platter."

"If it would not take too much of the good Master's time and trouble, the wronged people of Oak Hollow would fancy dearly the sight of those thieving fingers set in a row on a bronze platter."

"Oh, that his heart was pulsing on a copper dish beside the well in my back yard!"

And onward, as each tried to outdo his neighbor, as the simple folk descended to bodily parts I had never heard of, until I wondered what they thought about besides torture while they worked their fields.

Father listened only halfheartedly, his attention, no doubt, on the negligence of his boys. He was an old style Solamnic Knight, all stern and strict to the Code and the Measure. That any guest would be robbed beneath his roof was enough to send him into paroxysms and assure that Alfric would be placed under house arrest for his negligence—and confined to the moat house "until further notice."

Moreover, the ransacked guest was Sir Bayard Brightblade, one of the most promising Knights in northern Ansalon, whose swordsmanship and bravery (and good sense, evidently) had been rumor even as far to the north as here in our godforsaken, backwater estate in the middle of Coastlund (which was northwest of the Vingaard Mountains and southeast of nowhere). Bayard was quietly, politely stewing, no doubt vexed at the delay that kept him at our estate when he would much rather be on his way to Solamnia, where he could batter the heads of younger men in a contest for a girl he had yet to meet, if what I was hearing was true.

That was probably why I was being punished, too.

For on that night that now seemed ages ago, the black-booted intruder out the door, Alfric face down in the closet, and Father and Bayard approaching rapidly up the stairs, I was forced to think quickly.

I would draw too many questions if I stood unharmed at the scene of the struggle. Far better to blend into the scenery.

I lowered my head and ran into the oaken door of Alfric's chambers.

As a result, mine was the first body the Knights found lying in the room, the first they revived. And of course I knew nothing, and only moaned pathetically while Father rushed to my eldest brother, pulled him by the ankles into the center of the room, and slapped him awake.

It was my first real look at Sir Bayard Brightblade. And he passed muster.

Here was a man a full head taller than my father, and a good deal thinner; darker; moustached; thirty at the youngest but not forty yet; long hair, shoulder-length, in the Solamnic style of that time; a calm upon his countenance—his face like a handsome but expressionless mask, as though it were carved on a monument in an old landscape where there was nothing but rock and sun.

Bayard regarded me only briefly, then looked meaningfully at my father, who scolded me bluntly, groggily.

"Never mind the fanfare, Galen. Tell us what happened."

Alfric was still stirring below us. He groaned, and Father glanced anxiously his way. I began the story rapidly.

The two Knights heard the same story as had my hapless brother—of the flitting, shadowy shape outside the window, of my concern for our guest. That in my concern for Sir Bayard's belongings I had tried the door of the guest chambers, finding it locked, and enlisted my brother's help as he passed by.

"So it was all with the best of intentions, Sir Bayard, that my brother and I came into this room. In our concern, perhaps we did not notice the felon in question as he sneaked up behind us from a dark notch in the hallway, or . . . " and I paused meaningfully, hoping to cast a fly into Alfric's soup, ". . . or perhaps he was already hiding in your room, allowed in there by a previous oversight."

I paused, let that settle, and continued. "Whatever way, I'm not sure. But I turned for a moment at a noise in the hallway, then back to see a black-hooded form looming over my fallen brother. Whoever it was moved quickly. He was on me before I could gather myself, before I could see anything clearly.

"The next thing I know is that you're waking me and I'm lying here by the doorway and Alfric face first in the wardrobe and . . . I'm feeling a little faint now, Father."

I lay back in mock exhaustion. Alfric grunted on the floor beside me.

"I do hope," I sighed, "that my dear Brother is intact."

Intact enough to wait another decade for his squire's spurs.

* * * * *

Within the next several days, things changed around the moat house—things that I noticed from the first but the others dismissed as bad climate brought about by a sudden switch in the weather. From the moment the birds hushed their singing on the night of the banquet, there remained a certain absence in the air: where you might expect the song of the nightingale, the quarrel of jays, the flapping and gurgling of pigeons, there was now only silence, and eventually it occurred to me that even though it was still high summer the birds had gone, perhaps to a warmer climate to await the passing of winter.

Because of the time of year, we expected summer—light and heat, and the smothering damp rising from the notorious swamps scarcely a mile from our walls—but the weather was acting otherwise. In the morning we would wake to the stiffness of frost on the grounds and the trees shedding leaves prematurely. We had trouble keeping the fires lit, much less the candles, as though all light and heat were being siphoned away.

Gileandos had studied with gnomes. He almost always ignored the obvious, preferring to notice something subtle, hidden in a situation, from which he almost always drew the wrong conclusion. When he noticed the departure of birds, the sudden drop in temperature around the moat house, he blamed events on "the precipitous action of sunspots upon marsh vapors."

I recall him now, staring absentmindedly through his telescope directly into the face of the sun, so that when he turned from his stargazing he no doubt saw sunspots that were never there in the first place. He was at least sixty years old, but had no doubt been stooped and graying for years, all jewelry and combed beard and slick pomades and colognes—a dandy gone nightmarishly wrong in his declining years. But to this appearance he was adding a peculiarly haunted look of late, as the gallons of gin caught up to him.

He taught us poetry and history. Mathematics, too, until the day Alfric fainted from exhaustion in class. He also taught heraldry and rhetoric and Solamnic lore—a jack of all trades he was, lukewarm in all disciplines and running scared of sources of heat and light.

Which is why, as usual, I paid his explanation no mind, preoccupied as he was with conjecture and rumor and superstition. Instead, I cast the Calantina, the red dice from Estwilde, and received four times running the five and the ten, steam on earth, the Sign of the Viper. I consulted the books in Gileandos's library, read all the commentaries on the augury, but afterwards I knew no more of the mystery than I had before.

In the meantime everyone was worked up about the events of the banquet night. Bayard, armed only with borrowed leather jerkin, shield, and sword, was ready to set out in pursuit of the thief, if only he could locate him. He was upset at the delays to his tournament plans, but being by nature a lenient sort, he still intended to take his squire with him, even though Alfric had been caught nodding while the armor changed hands. Father, on the other hand, brooded over Alfric's part in the theft.

Father was not a lenient sort.

"Bayard, is the penalty for armorial neglect still death by hanging, or has the Order grown soft in the years since my retirement?"

I remember this word for word, set to memory as I stifled a cough from the ash and old smoke. You see, there were secret passages in the moat house, passages Father had either forgotten or never knew about in the first place, that Brithelm was too spiritual and Alfric too stupid to discover. They were there, nonetheless, perfect for a boy accustomed to escapes, to dodging responsibility and punishment. I was especially fond of the entrance to the great hall concealed handily in the back of the fireplace, from where I listened to Father and Bayard.

"Not soft, Sir Andrew, as much as *understanding* that squires or would-be squires can make mistakes." I could see him lean forward in his chair, hear the leather jerkin creak and crackle as he paused for emphasis. The armor was too short for him and would have made him look comical were it not for those gray eyes and impassive face that silenced all comedy. "No," he continued, "nowadays the Order tends toward leniency, nor am I all so sure that is wrong."

So it was not to be hanging. Very well. There were always accidents upon the road—bandits, hostile centaurs, even the peasants themselves, who for generations had not been altogether fond of the Order—something to do with the Cataclysm, Gileandos said, though the Cataclysm happened almost two hundred years ago.

The peasants had long memories, evidently.

At any rate, our local swains would welcome any excuse to waylay any Solamnic Knight who passed through their farmlands. Or so we in the castle had been told.

"I see it as a boyish error," Bayard continued, scratching the ear of one of our innumerable dogs that had crawled over to sit beneath his chair. Bayard raised his hand to underscore the point; the dog beside him, conditioned by its years in the moat house, flinched and whimpered.

"But don't forget, Bayard, that the 'boy' you speak of is twenty-one years old," Father growled, his huge hands tightening on the cane he used when the colder mornings brought back the pain to his leg, recalling the hunting disaster of last winter. "And Alfric, as you know by now, isn't the brightest of youngsters."

Bayard hid a smile politely and nodded. Father never noticed, his eyes on the floor in front of him.

"Let's face it, he tends toward being oafish and petty and not altogether pleasant. He's twenty-one, Sir Bayard, no boy, and not liable to grow out of such things.

"Had he any appeal or decency as a child, he would have been a Knight by now. Had he been a peasant, he might well have been responsible for a wife and several children."

And had he been a dog or a horse, he would have been long dead, past causing trouble.

My hiding place was too cramped. I shifted my position, but in doing so scraped my belt against stone, making a sound I could swear they had heard in Palanthas, in Pax Tharkas, at the ends of the world. I held my breath and waited.

Bayard leaned back in his chair, glanced smoothly and quickly my way. I was sure he had noticed me.

But immediately he turned back to Father, who was droning on as if nothing had happened.

"All I am saying, Bayard," the old man continued, "is that by twenty-one Alfric should have put away 'boyish error.' By his age I was a Knight of the Sword, held with a small band the Paths of Chaktamir, waded to my knees in the blood of the men of Neraka . . ."

"And those, Sir Andrew, were special times, in which special men were the actors," Bayard responded smoothly, respectfully. "I've heard tales of your doings at Chaktamir. That is why I believe that, regardless of how little promise they have shown, there may be merit yet in a son of yours. After all, blood will tell in such things."

Father reddened behind the graying red of his beard, never one to accept a compliment easily.

"Damn it, Sir Bayard, I wanted these boys to have their ticket out of Northern Coastlund, here at the swampy end of the world. Get 'em down into Solamnia, into adventure and swordplay and righting wrongs and all. My middle son's some kind of . . . monk, and the youngest has all the markings of a miscreant . . ."

Bayard glanced quickly in my direction.

"You judge them harshly because of your high standards," he suggested, but Father wasn't buying.

"And the oldest . . . a surly lump in my larder. It's enough to make an old man rampage."

"My offer still stands, Sir Andrew," Bayard replied, a bit impatiently. "A son of yours—I say now, any son—as my squire. He'll find me a resourceful teacher." He leaned back and steepled his fingers, turning ever so slightly to face the fireplace.

I shrank into the stonework of the chimney, back in the safe and ashy gloom. It was there that I suddenly had other problems. A rat, awakened or flushed from hiding by my adventures in the tunnel, scuttled across my foot and huddled, half-terrified, in the dark corner of the fireplace. I yelped, leaped, and hit my head against brick and blackened stone, showering myself in ash and cinders.

It was then, naturally, that the dog came barreling toward my hiding place, sure that he had cornered something wild and perhaps edible. I reached out with my foot, kicked the rat into the path of the oncoming dog, and scrambled up into the passageway, the sound of snarls, shouts, and last desperate squeals fading behind me as I slid into the closet of my room, changed my sooty, incriminating clothes for an innocent nightshirt, and slipped into bed, filling the late morning and the empty wing of the castle with the sound of false snoring.

*   *   *   *   *

The discussion continued in my absence, the two Knights reaching the worst possible decision.

Father was convinced that the burglar had ambushed us from inside the room, let in by Alfric's complete inattention. Despite Bayard's assertion that Alfric required understanding, Father passed sentence rapidly and angrily.

Big Brother was to seethe about under house arrest, confined within the walls of the moat house. From there, unlike the end of a rope or the depths of a dungeon, he could quite possibly savage my person with one of any number of available weapons.

For it was Alfric's opinion that I should have spoken out—should have taken the blame for the whole mishap.

Such is the ingratitude of brothers.

*   *   *   *   *

Needless to say, it unsettled me these days to hear my brother's footsteps coming up the hall. Alfric was surly, blaming me cloudily for the theft of the armor, though the wine and the blow on the head had made him hazy as to what happened that fateful night.

Haziness, however, never stayed his fist or his well-aimed foot. So I would hide for hours in the secret tunnels and alcoves, cowering in ashes and occasionally booting rats to a curious dog, for I knew that of all creatures in the moat house, I was in the greatest danger. I wore disguises, once passing quite effectively for a chimney sweep. When I was not masked or hidden, I put on the face of innocence, doubled my efforts at my chores, and kept close to either Father or Brithelm.

I always kept my hands in my pockets, so that nobody would ask what had become of my naming ring.

I was reduced to keeping company with Brithelm, and listening to his speculations on the gods. I tried not to fall asleep.

"Galen, what about the nature of prophecy?" he would ask, feeding the birds in the moat house courtyard, benign smile on his face and red hair askew over a patched red robe, looking for all the world like some outrageous scarlet fowl that had taken up with the pigeons and the ground doves.

"I don't know, Brithelm. Watch out for that trough."

At the last moment my brother stepped around certain immersion, still casting corn on the ground and whistling to himself.

"I mean, prophecy is a hall of mirrors, one reflecting on another and all reflecting back to the eye at the center of watching."

"You know, you're right, Brithelm. Don't step on the dog."

"These birds, Galen," Brithelm mused, stepping over a terrier sleeping in the shadow of the trough. The dog paddled its feet, running in dreams.

"In the Age of Light the clerics foretold disaster by following the formations of birds on the wing. Sometimes in my sanctuary . . ."

"Back in 'Warden Swamp? I've heard that it's overgrown and that a full cypress tree can grow there in a matter of weeks; the air is so humid that man-eating fish fly through it in search of their prey."

Brithelm paused, looked straight at me while he kept on

walking toward the cistern. I took him by the arm, steered him gently toward the stairway that mounted the south wall of our little run-down fortress.

"One man's swamp . . . ," he began, and laughed gently, tossing a final handful of corn toward a pursuing band of pigeons, "is another's hermitage. Sometimes in the mornings there are a dozen quail you can see in the open, little brother. They'll eat out of your hand. And there are dark things, too, but the legends magnify them.

"So birds are the most famous of auguries. Then there are leaves, the unruffled pool of water where you stare until you see beyond the reflections . . ."

Such was the time I spent in pure malarkey, while the eldest brother plotted and schemed, whined and pleaded, though he never could remember enough to fix me with the blame for anything. Still, he bent the old man's ear with conjecture. After a morning in superstition with Brithelm, I often caught Father scowling at me suspiciously from the head of the table at lunch, while Alfric scowled at me over bottles and venison from his seat of disgrace at the far end of the hall. It was like being caught between mirrors.

* * * * *

So it went, with Father angry at Alfric's negligence and growing suspicious of me, though the evidence never seemed to come in. Bayard, too, seemed to lose his good humor as the moat house hung for weeks in ominous suspension.

It was not until we heard of the killing that Father lost his temper completely.

Another group of peasants came to the moat house, a crowd this time, bearing the worst news so far. It was shortly after dawn. Bayard had already left on his daily search for the rampaging armor thief, but the peasants caught Father throwing the dogs out of his chair in the great hall so that he might hold audience in dignity.

The oldest of the peasants, a woman of eighty if she were a day, dressed in a homespun mantle against the unnatural cold, and grayed and warted like a storybook witch, was their appointed speaker. And she wasted no time, launching into her speech before the last mastiff hit the floor howling.

"It was like this, Your Knightship, and may the gods strike me and my children unto five generations if every word I speak is not the truth."

Red-faced and puffing, Father sat down, and put on his most interested look. I tried to guess where celestial lightning would first strike when the old harpy lied, as they always did, as she surely would.

"I tremble to tell this, Your Knightship, but there has been murder on your lands, murder most foul and unspeakable. Murder at the hands of one of your own order."

She was good. Father gripped his chair in outrage. Brithelm was already standing by the fireplace, and stifled a cry of dismay. On the other hand, Alfric and I remained seated. Alfric sharpened his dagger meaningfully, while I buried my nose in a book I was not reading.

I was listening all the while. But I cannot say that the old woman's lament "opened my eyes to the sad plight of the peasants," as laments are supposed to do for anyone with a speck of nobility in his soul. I knew full well that the poor led lives filled with sorrows that never touched upon ours.

In all honesty, that was the way I preferred it.

For it seemed that whenever those lives did touch ours, it set off Father, and his sons reaped the whirlwind. I slumped behind the table as the old bat continued serenely, already caught up in her story of gloom and random violence. If I was lucky it would be Alfric who would harvest the big trouble.

My oldest brother, heir to all the holdings, sat there and wiped his nose on his sleeve, unaware that he stood poised on even harder times. A bulldog, taking the silence as a good sign, crept back into the room and begged for bacon by my chair.

"It is a terrible tale I bring you," the old bag droned on. "Yesterday, as the evening came on, a man on horseback, wearing the armor of Solamnia, rode up to the house of my nephew Jaffa. You remember Jaffa, Your Knightship? The one what lost an ear to your eldest boy in that quarrel over the taxes last year? Not that I blame the lad or that Jaffa, the gods rest him, carried hard thoughts against Master Alfric!

33

'Boys are liable to swordplay,' he would say, 'and it never hurt my hearing none.'"

By Huma, she was good! I cast a glance over the book and at the bulldog trying desperately to look appealing. Alfric's attention was no longer upon his knife. He was squirming, all right. I smirked into my pages.

"Well, Jaffa was restoring thatch to our roof—thatch where the mysterious fire touched it only a month gone by."

It was Alfric's turn to smirk, to look far too revealingly in my direction. I buried myself behind the cover of the book.

After all, I had never intended for that fire get out of hand.

The old bag continued, blissfully caught up in her unfolding tale of bloodshed.

"And this knight dismounts—oh, we had heard about him, about Sir Raven, as he goes by in the villages, about the demands for cheeses and livestock and the virtue of our daughters. And still we never thought he would come our way! But does a body ever think so until evil is at his doorstep?

"Anyway, the knight asks for cheese, and I want you to know that Jaffa, who was sliding down off of the roof when the gentleman asked, was fixing to give him that cheese and give it gladly, thinking he must be one of your family or friends or somehow connected to this house. But then Sir Raven asks for Ruby, our cow, and Jaffa figures who he is and stands still."

"Still, but not defying him or mouthing at him in any way," piped a younger voice out of the crowd gathered behind the old woman. Had they arranged this beforehand?

I was eager to ask about the mysterious knight, to know if he spoke in a voice that was low and soft and dangerous. But I couldn't do that. Asking about him would reveal that I knew more than I was telling. I lifted my eyes from the book as the bulldog gave up and waddled over to where Alfric was sitting. It seemed that everyone was asking for trouble this morning.

"As the girl says: not defying him, mind you, but standing still until the knight grows itchy, asking for Ruby again, but this time not as much asking as telling, if you understand. Then he asks after Agnes, and only then does Jaffa answer him back with hard words.

"Agnes herself come to tell you that this is the fact," the old bag said, and brought forth a pasty-faced, frog-eyed blonde about my age and twice my size, the very one who had been piping up behind her like some husky chorus. Jaffa's wife or daughter? I neither knew nor cared. Whichever, the visitor would have done better to have snatched up Ruby the cow.

This Agnes took up the story where it had been left off, lumbering up to the forefront of the crowd, clutching a bloody shirt in her hands.

I confess, it was a bit too much for me.

"It's just as the goodwife says, Your Knightship," the girl whimpered, wringing the stained shirt in her heavy hands. "Jaffa just stands there. Then he drawed his knife and says to Sir Raven, he says, 'High-born though ye may be, ye'll not touch a hair of the girl.' Those was his words entirely, or may the gods blight my family unto five generations."

All of them seemed eager to put their families at stake. I could sympathize with that ploy.

We heard the rest of the story from the old woman. How Jaffa stood fast, how words progressed to shouting, shouting to blows, and blows to a quickly drawn sword slipped clumsily into the peasant's chest. After she had finished, there followed the usual weeping in front of the lord of the manor, six versions of the same story (all with the same unhappy ending), and the displaying of the helpless survivors—the old woman herself, the daughter (or wife—whatever). The peasants even offered to bring in Ruby (as the old woman put it, "the cow in question") if it would soften Father's heart the more.

Father's face reddened as he listened to the outrages. Brithelm, too, was beside himself with sympathy. Alfric twitched and kicked the unfortunate bulldog, as Father promised retribution.

"Upon my honor as a Knight," he claimed, hand on his sword, "I shall not rest until these wrongs have been righted, until the villain stands before me and receives punishment, until all those whose exploits touched upon these foul deeds are punished."

And sure enough, as the peasants left in a flood of tears and worries and *bless you, sirs*, as they were leading the bereaved Agnes and the cow in question across the rickety moat bridge that the servants were too cowed to mend or even mind, Father turned upon my eldest brother.

"Set aside that dagger and look at me, boy."

A quick glance told me that the boy at issue was Alfric, and I settled behind my book again, to listen and to enjoy.

"There is no answer to this in the duty of father to son, of son to father. Perhaps I have been too soft in dealing with you over the weeks, but the gods forgive me, I thought that nothing truly ill had come of this negligence. That indeed we were guilty of betraying the promises of host to guest, and though in the old days no punishment was severe enough for such betrayals, these are the new days, when the eye is inclined to blink at those misdeeds not . . . capital."

He rose to his feet, and somehow in the morning light he seemed to take on a little of that stature and bearing he must have had before we were born, when he was counted among Coastlund's finest before the declining years caught up with him and retired him to our little out-of-the-way estate.

He must have looked that way years ago, and by the gods, he must have been formidable! Had he asked questions then, I might well have spilled the story—told of my every misdeed with the Scorpion and even some things that happened years ago, simply because it looked as though he could see right through us and would punish us even more fiercely if we lied.

But Father was finished with questions. "That is no longer the case," he continued. "You have done a terrible thing that becomes more terrible with time. Be it negligence or worse, for deeds such as this, the Measure alone provides the answer. The Measure and the Code."

Father stared at the floor, stared ever so long before speaking again.

"I have no other choice. Would that it were otherwise, but my options have gone out." He raised his sword in the formal Solamnic salute.

"Until Sir Bayard Brightblade of Vingaard, Knight of

Solamnia, returns the thief, the false wearer of his armor, to our hands for trial and execution, I must confine my eldest son, Alfric Pathwarden, to the dungeon of these premises until we may determine a just and fitting punishment for his disgraceful actions in this matter. Within those forsaken walls, I hope my son will reflect upon his part in the crimes that have blotted the name of our family and of the Solamnic Order."

I must admit I never thought Father had it in him. I looked at Brithelm, who shrugged and cast his gaze skyward. Alfric, on the other hand, was too astounded to do anything but laugh. And laugh he did at first, shaking his head in disbelief, kicking the bulldog once more, who, having finally caught on, lumbered over to Brithelm for safety and consolation.

Alfric stopped laughing as it finally sunk in that no matter how preposterous the punishment sounded, Father was not joking. Sobering, my brother tried to say something—anything—that would express his own indignity. All that issued forth was some sort of nasal bleating, as though somewhere out near the stables the servants were shearing a sheep.

Father stared unwaveringly at his first-born, his heir. "If you only knew," he stated flatly, mournfully, "how grave a disappointment your actions have been to me, Alfric, that knowledge would be punishment enough."

"Whaaaa," my brother responded. The bulldog watched curiously from beneath Brithelm's chair.

"But you have no more knowledge of honor, of responsibility, of penance, than . . . than . . ." Father's eyes searched the room angrily, "than that bulldog crouched over there under Brithelm." He pointed at the bulldog, who cringed.

"Whaaaa," Alfric bellowed, and I couldn't help it. I began to snicker. The angry stare turned suddenly, forcefully, in my direction.

I could guess how the men of Neraka had felt when my father was young, guarding passes.

"And seeing as my youngest son, your brother Galen, has not accorded himself in a manner to be entirely above suspicion, he shall join you in this period of confinement, until the facts are before us and we can see where all the blame might lie."

"But, Father!" I began to plead. A panic-stricken sidelong glance at Alfric revealed a slow grin erasing his outrage and fear. We would be alone down in the dungeon, alone and out of earshot. And Alfric with yet another offense he could blame on me.

All I could do was stammer.

"But, Father! B-but, Father!"

Speechless for once. No better than Alfric.

* * * * *

The dungeon smelled of mold and oak and soured wine. I huddled in a corner in the dark. Then I moved toward the center of the far wall, still as far away from Alfric as possible without digging my way to freedom— which, of course, would be the first thing on the agenda if I survived the brotherly attentions that were sure to come.

Father stood in the doorway with Brithelm and Gileandos. Brithelm held a lamp that framed the party in flickering, dim light—Gileandos barely visible, for understandably, he shied away from flames, having last been ignited a month before in the last brotherly cooperation Alfric and I had enjoyed.

You could barely see the glint of light on his bandages.

"You'll be fed twice a day," Father proclaimed. "We intend to be stern, but not inhumane. Each morning you will be allowed a walk through the courtyard, for fresh air.

"There is a lesson in this," he continued. "A lesson for all of us. Though I shall be confounded if I can figure it."

He moved back out of the light. I could see only Brithelm now, holding the lamp, gazing at me sorrowfully, sympathetically, no doubt wishing he could take my place.

From the dark at a distance, I could hear Father say, "I trust you are aware of how disappointed I am in the both of you." Then the door closed, leaving us in total darkness.

And I heard Alfric growling, beginning to crawl my way across the dungeon floor.

CHAPTER 3

*Although I always hated poetry, I remember want-*ing to be a bard. For I had seen their overnight performances in the moat house, and the whole business looked like a good deal. You were fed, then you told a story which nobody dared to call a lie, so you could embroider as much as you liked. Then you were paid for lying. It was a life to which I could become accustomed.

I lost that illusion early. Indeed, eight years ago, on a night I remember clearly, the illusion, you might say, flew over the moat and vanished.

When Quivalen Sath, the most famous of elvish bards, sang before my father in the moat house two weeks after my ninth birthday, it was enough to put me off poetry forever.

The night of the bard was the night that the blackmail

began. Supervised by Gileandos, we boys cleaned the great hall of the moat house while Father prepared to receive the honored guest. Anxious that the hall look its best for the great artist, Gileandos was beside himself, even kicking a servant or two when he found the hearth still cluttered with ashes. I crouched, broom in hand, over the ashes, as the dusty boys ran from the room. I turned at the outcry of a stable groom, imported for the important job, who lay doubled up with pain beneath the table, awaiting another kick from Alfric, who stood above him smiling.

"A bit much, Alfric!" Gileandos exclaimed, as the old man swooned away beyond pain, clutching at the table-cloth as he lost consciousness.

"I got carried away," Alfric growled. Then he crouched, dusted his boot, and grabbed the servant by the hair. Dragging the man from the hall, he laughed and called over his shoulder, "A lover of poetry, that's me for sure!"

Even eight years ago Alfric would have set a table for a yokel with a cello if it meant a chance to kick the servants.

Quivalen Sath was no yokel, but in fact he looked like any other elf, no richer for his bardic experience, dressed in the green of a huntsman, his long hair slightly silvered. Still, he was solemn and eloquent, and, after all, he was a genuine celebrity, author of the same *Song of Huma* Gileandos had made me memorize last dreary winter in the same great hall, before my first retaliatory fire had singed his beard and half the face beneath it, cutting short our study of the classics.

Father and the elf exchanged pleasantries over dinner, and the inevitable pack of dogs crept into the room, drawn by the warmth of the fire and the smell of venison.

Alfric sneered at me from the far end of the table. I flashed him an obscene sign I had learned that morning from a stable boy. He bristled and stared at his wine cup, for this was the first banquet we had attended since he turned thirteen, and for the first time he had been allowed strong drink.

The elf stood to address all of us.

"I have chosen *Mantis of the Rose* for your evening's entertainment," murmured Quivalen Sath. There was probably some bardic grapevine to tell him Father's favorite poem, for the old man smiled, raised his glass, completely unaware he was getting what Gileandos had dismissed as Quivalen Sath's "earlier, second-rate efforts."

After the meal, the entertainment began. Bored at once by some abstract theological tale of free will and roses in the sky, I watched Alfric, who had slumped in his chair as low as his armor would let him, wiping the blade of his dagger upon the back of a snoring dog, whose leg twitched blissfully in imagining he was being petted and scratched. And Brithelm, my middle brother, often mistaken for being absent at public occasions, stood rigid in his garb like some inane red scarecrow, having mastered the art of listening without paying attention. He was probably meditating.

On the other hand, Father was the good host, listening even to the most ridiculous parts of the story.

Only Father, finally, offered the elf the respect his celebrity seemed to call for. It occurred to me afterwards, as the bard thanked my father for a dozen pieces of silver, tied his harp over his shoulder, and walked from the hall just as the red moon dipped into the west and the eastern sky began to redden, that if Quivalen Sath was so all-fired successful, why was he playing the backwater villages of Solamnia?

I was supposed to go straight to bed, but instead crept to the battlements, where I had left my toy soldiers when called to supervise the reception for the elf. The battlements were cold, even for an early morning in late summer. My legions were set in a convenient crenel overlooking the drawbridge and the low, swampy woods about a mile off to the west of the moat house. Some of the soldiers stood headless from extravagant use; others, quite intact, leaned against the battlements.

By this time Quivalen Sath had reached the other side of the moat, from where the well-tossed, iron-forged soldier must have stung considerably when it struck him on the back of his well-combed poetic head, and from where a nine-year-old would-be assassin could make himself virtually invisible, hidden among the clematis and ivy and the much more common weeds, undetected by even the sharpest of elvish eyes.

* * * * *

But by some stroke of ill luck, there were other eyes on the scene. Alfric had followed me to the battlements (remember I was only nine at the time, and not yet used to looking back over my shoulder constantly for suspicious brothers). Standing behind me, hidden by shadow and vines and crenelation, he witnessed the bombardment of Quivalen Sath.

The family heir seized me before the elf had rubbed his head, scanned the horizon, and returned to the path that led from our home toward the next way station in his endless poetic wanderings.

"I seen the whole thing, you little snit," Alfric hissed.

"You mean you *saw* the whole thing," I corrected, always delighted to remind my brother how I stood in greater favor with Gileandos than he ever had. It was not a wise thing to have said at the time, for Alfric was on me like a wild boar. My back to big brother, face pressed uncomfortably into the moss-covered stone of the battlement, head entangled with ivy and weeds like a wreath on the brow of a second-rate bard, I corrected my correction.

"Just what was it that you seen, Brother dear?"

"I seen you throw that soldier at the elf," he replied.

"But what you never *seen*, Brother, was what that elf was up to. There was something glittering—I saw it—he held up to the light and then slipped into the sleeve of that long bardic robe. Probably our silverware, a crystal goblet from Father's table."

"But there wasn't no crystal or silver at the table. We was entertaining poets, not merchants." He pushed my face farther into the stonework. I tasted mortar, moss.

"But you didn't see him mapping—mapping the terrain around the house. No doubt he's a Nerakan agent or a spy for some anti-Solamnic fanatics who plan to lay siege to Father."

Alfric's grip did not slacken, nor did the pressure of granite against my nose diminish. I tried the last tactic.

"Has it occurred to you, Alfric, that you have been made the victim of elvish enchantment? Of hypnotism? That what you have seen only appeared to take place?"

No change in his grip or my posture, for Alfric was balancing upon that edge in which stupidity becomes a kind of insight: he simply did not have the imagination to believe anything beyond what his eyes told him.

So I was forced to confess, to blubber and weep and beg, and to throw myself on his mercy, which, unfortunately, he had none of at the time.

* * * * *

But Alfric developed some imagination, to be sure, as the first faint glimmers of blackmail saw light in the months that followed. Hospitality was, as you already know, a big thing with Father, and my misdeed grew in my own imaginings, dangled constantly above my head by my brother's cruelty and greed.

It did not help matters that Quivalen Sath wrote one of his long-winded "epistles" to Father, in which he claimed to have been "granted a visionary moment" when a "godly missive" from the battlements of the moat house had struck him in the back of the head.

Was the object which plummeted from the heavens a gift from Branchala? As Sath never found the toy soldier (believe me, I took care of that by burying the entire army deep in the moat house midden), he took the evidence of a purple bump on his noggin as physical evidence that the artist must suffer to create.

Unfortunately, the visionary moments expanded into blackouts over the next several months, from which the elf recovered eventually, writing of his experience in the poem *Dark of Solinari*, which, though never published, passed through our part of Coastlund by word of mouth. Its reference to "a gray Knight's morning missive," though ambiguous, was enough to keep Father guessing whether one of his sons was at the bottom of the mystery, especially when he caught the servants doubled over, reciting the line.

No, Father would not forgive my insult to a famous bard. He would probably turn me loose to fend for myself in the swamp south of the moat house. 'Warden Swamp: from which, we knew, nobody returned.

Under Alfric's threats I took over his chores of cleaning the stables, of cleaning his private chambers. And when a

horse or servant showed up lame, it was Galen the youngest, not the responsible Alfric, who confessed and suffered
Father's anger. Indeed, as the months passed into years, I
began to wonder if owning up to the whole Sath business
would do me some good. Probably not.

*　*　*　*　*

This is the way things were, a time in which I found a
great delight in resentment, in plotting a revenge so sweet
and elaborate that the pieces only began to fall into place
eight years from that summer night, two weeks after my
seventeenth birthday, on a night I have told you of already.

From where I sat now, revenge had yet to become sweet.
For no sooner had the light faded from the corridor, had the
dungeon in which Alfric and I were confined resumed its
silence, than my brother, as I have said before, began to
crawl like a monstrous crab across the dark floor, stumbling
and cursing in the dark, muttering, "Where are you now,
you little felon?"

I leaped quickly behind the approaching voice, piped,
"Over here!" and leaped again. I heard the crab-brother
turn, curse, and again leaped behind the sound of that
movement. It was hide-and-seek for keeps, and I knew it.

"Over here!" I squealed again, and there was movement
at my feet. I leaped backwards, away from the sound, and
into the strong arms of my brother.

Now it was Alfric's turn. I felt a strong blow to the back of
my head, clumsy but certain fingers encircling my throat,
and I was falling somewhere, out of the dark into a greater
darkness.

*　*　*　*　*

I awoke to a lantern shone into my eyes, to Gileandos's
face. He crouched above me, holding the lantern at arm's
length, clutching in his other hand a plate of bread and
cheese. Two guards stood behind him, the amused keepers
of our cell. I knew them from the stables, knew they delighted in Alfric's imprisonment and were no doubt indifferent to
whatever befell me.

"My lad, you have been 'pummeled and cudgeled passing

well,' as the old poem says," Gileandos exclaimed.

It hurt me to sit up, to breathe, much less to remember any old poem. My left eye would barely open, and the light from the lantern hurt it terribly. Yes, *pummeled and cudgeled passing well* was a pretty good description.

But Gileandos was not satisfied, and continued.

"Such maladies are not unusual among the recently incarcerated. The combination of melancholy, darkness, and damp air is a painful one, but rarely deadly. There are stories of Santos Silverblade, Solamnic Knight and ancestor to Sir Bayard Brightblade, our visitor. They tell how Santos survived the Siege of Daltigoth, though imprisoned in the dungeons of that hateful city, how when Vinas Solamnus and his followers entered Daltigoth as conquerors, opening the prisons, Santos emerged, as the song says, 'battered and bruised but by no means beaten'. . ."

"Galen run into a wall," my brother interrupted from the corner of our cell. "It was a rat what scared him, caused him to jump untimely."

"Come, come, Alfric," Gileandos scoffed, turning the lantern to my brother's face, which appeared hungry but otherwise none the worse for wear. "It seems quite apparent that what we have is the aforementioned prisoner's malady, aggravated no doubt by the unseasonable coolness of the weather, which I have established conclusively to stem from the precipitous action of sunspots upon marsh vapors, all of which factors . . ."

"He run into a wall. That's the way it happened. Isn't it, brother dear?" Alfric never took his eyes from me.

I chose my words carefully.

"My brother is right, Gileandos. It was a wall, of that I am sure. And it was a rat that startled me, made me take the unfortunate leap that caused the wreckage you see here."

I lay back, trying to look even more beaten, even more pathetic.

"And what is more, I could have escaped injury had I only listened to Alfric, who had told me to stand still until he could light a small fire for us to see by—a remarkable talent of his, for he can start a fire in the most unusual places . . . from the most unlikely materials."

Clumsy, and maybe a little obvious.

"What's that?" Gileandos leaned forward, his attention mine at last. "What's that you say about fires?"

"Oh, never mind. As I was saying, I was startled," I whimpered, "and perhaps to a small degree prey to that very malady you have mentioned, but rest assured it was a rat—a large one, the largest of the litter, but a common rat nonetheless—that led me to this sorry state you see before you."

Gileandos leaned over me, squinted intently, set the plate beside me.

"There is more to a rat than the cheese he fancies," he proclaimed, a question in his voice. "Your breakfast. Before it gets cold."

He turned, closed the door behind him, and left us in darkness.

As his footsteps faded down the corridor, I heard movement in the far corner of the cell. I dodged, felt the wind of something large moving quickly past me, heard something hit the wall and my brother curse. I crept to the center—what I thought was the center—of the room.

"I got that part about the rat," Alfric growled from somewhere.

Good. Then Gileandos might, too. I stayed silent.

"And what was that about fire, anyway?"

Still I was silent.

And so I remained for what could have been hours, even a day, moving when I heard movement, standing completely still when there was nothing to hear.

I was trying to come to terms with the possibility that I would never sleep again when a key jostled in the lock. Light bathed the cell, and I discovered Alfric and I were standing back to back, scarcely a yard apart. He turned, grabbed for me, and before my brother could make purchase or I could even begin to dodge, Father was between us, clutching a torch in his left hand, the front of Alfric's shirt in his right, holding my rather abundant brother a good foot or so off the ground.

I marveled at the old man's quickness and strength, swore to myself I would be as devoted a son as was convenient.

At the door stood our two burly guardsmen, who stared at us, obviously trying to hide their smirks. At a nod from the old man, they busied themselves with fixing leg irons to the dungeon wall. Upon another nod from my father, Gileandos stepped into the room.

I counted only two chains in the hands of the servants.

Father, still dangling my eldest brother, nodded once more to Gileandos, who explained the new circumstances in his best lecturer's voice.

"Never lie to your elders, Galen. You haven't the subtlety nor the experience. For speech, my lad, is a text wherein the trained mind can discover wonders, and there was indeed no way that one of your age and . . . lack of sophistication . . . could have known that in lying, paradoxically, he was revealing the truth."

It didn't sound good for me. The old man continued in senile revery. I longed for coals, for phosfire, for Father's torch. He was asking for yet another enkindlement.

"For every text, verbal or spoken," he droned on, "has a subtext, and the subtext of your lie revealed quite clearly that *Alfric was the rat* of your little story, that your injury involved no rat in what we might call the literal sense, no wall beyond the simple—albeit violent—constraint of the aforementioned brother. Am I correct?"

"Yes, Gileandos." Why confuse him with the full truth? I tried to appear awed, shaking my head, smiling stupidly. He smiled back condescendingly.

"And what is more, you unraveled a mystery the heart of which I have sought to penetrate these six months passing, since the initial, unfortunate conflagration? Am I correct?"

"I don't know."

"Come, come, lad. Did you think I was content to burst unexplainably into flame every now and then without getting to the heart of the matter? In seeking to cloak your brother's bullying, you have indeed uncovered what we might call his . . . more dangerous tendencies. Now wouldn't the truth have been more wise from the start?"

"I suppose so, Gileandos."

As the servants placed a fuming, sputtering Alfric in the leg irons, Father glared at him, waving the torch like a mythical sword.

I knew better than to speak now. Gileandos continued.

"Your father and I have counseled over your punishment, Galen, and we have determined it would be most fitting for you to see your brother made an example for his misdeeds. You will continue your stay here in the dungeon until Sir Bayard recovers the armor. We trust you will be edified by the fate of your brother who, having grown to manhood, will be disciplined, no doubt, as befits a man."

My father expressed puzzlement at how he could have fathered an arsonist, a mystic, and a liar, with no promising Knight in the whole bunch. The two servants were probably wondering if all wealthy families were like this.

They left the dungeon in silence. Then, across the cell in the darkness, I heard the chains rattle like in a bad horror story. My brother begin to elaborate on what he would do if he could get his hands on me.

I sat, rested my back against the door. I took stock.

"As I see it, Alfric, these threats and dire promises aren't worth much while you're in the leg irons. And the way things look, you'll be in leg irons forever. The odds are you'll be stuck here for at least another decade until another Knight decides to comb up some renown for fairness by giving you a last try as a squire.

"How many times has it been, anyway, Alfric?

"'Too great a reptile to be a squire.' Wasn't that what Sir Gareth de Palantha said when you were fourteen? When he found you had rifled an alms box to buy those enchanted spectacles from the merchant, those spectacles that were supposed to let you see through Elspeth's clothing? Even I could have been a squire at fourteen, could become one tomorrow if I set my mind to it. That is, in any other family.

"But Father has to farm you out first, because you are the eldest. Can you imagine how embarrassing it is to him, when other Knights of the Order have sons in the lists of Knighthood, have grandsons as squires, and he must care for a twenty-one-year-old slug who lolls around the house eating his venison, drinking his wine, dreaming only of thrashing servants and riding horses to death?"

A cry arose out of the darkness. With relish I continued.

"And now it'll be another ten years for sure. By that time it'll be the last try, because even an idealist is going to be embarrassed by a thirty-year-old hulk lugging his armor around. The priesthood'll be all that's left for you by then, and perhaps you'll be even a little too old for that, as we both know Brithelm will be well on the way towards spiritual purity and you'll be some grizzled novitiate whose sum of life experience amounts . . ."

It was pat, like the old comedies when you mention someone's name and he walks in immediately. The key rattled in the door, and led by candlelight and a gust of warmer air from the sunlit rooms above, my brother Brithelm, the one true innocent in the family, entered the room of conspiracy behind the impatient guards.

It was getting busy down here, to be sure. And it was irritating, especially when I was in the midst of enraging Alfric, who was wrenching himself against the chains.

But after all, it was Brithelm. And being the one true innocent, he felt sorry for us.

"How are you, brothers? This damp, smothering cell—the rats, the darkness, the smell of decay. I hate it that we've kept you here this long. But I think it's nearly over."

"What's nearly over, Brithelm?" asked my oldest brother, his voice rising in pitch and volume as, after my speech, he no doubt imagined himself in boiling oil, at best a thick and dangling noose.

"You're to come with me at once," Brithelm continued, crouching beside me, holding the candle in front of him, the better to see the family heir dangling from the wall, "to an audience with Father in the great hall. Bayard returned not quite an hour ago, and he has the thief of his armor in tow."

The Scorpion! This was what Brithelm called good news.

"I expect the truth will out," he continued, "and the name of Pathwarden will be cleared by both of you."

Yes. Unto the fifth generation.

* * * * *

Torches smoldered in the sconces, lit hurriedly against the gathering dusk and the gathering crowds. For the great hall was alive and astir, and dog-infested: mastiffs, beagles, and bloodhounds clambered on the table, fought by the hearth, romanced behind tapestries. In his haste to render swift and merciless justice, Father had not bothered to clear the room.

The dog act preceded the main show, which involved us.

Father and Bayard sat in places of honor, ornate and official, dressed to question the prisoner in black. The servants had gathered, eager for gossip, and even the peasants had returned at the prospect of blood.

But it was the prisoner that concerned me at the moment. Thin, almost skeletal, his pipe stems scarcely resembling the strong, wiry legs of the visitor I recalled. He was decked in black all right, but sixty years old if he was a day. I awaited the voice to confirm my hopes.

I was sure that Bayard had brought in the wrong party.

Which was fine by me. Far better a scapegoat than the real item—the Scorpion who could implicate me in a web of wrongdoings that might entangle the family unto the fifth generation. I walked to the middle of the hall with the guardsmen and Alfric. Brithelm took his place at the arm of Father's chair.

Bayard was watching us closely, leg dangling over the arm of his chair, fingers steepled, gray eyes fastened to our faces and gestures. I expect the same idea had occurred to him: that the man in black was hardly the rugged type, no match for Alfric, let alone the rustic likes of Jaffa. This poor soul had probably dropped his weapon at first sight of Bayard. I was half-tempted to identify the rascal in front of us as the Scorpion if it would shake us loose of the cellars. But I kept my tongue, knowing that such an identification would raise ugly questions as to how close a view I had gotten of the assailant in the first place.

The rascal in front of us had no such restraints.

"That's him. That's the one who helped me," he said, in a voice as harsh and dry as old paper. He groveled in front of Father and with a bony finger pointed directly at me.

"You must mean Alfric," I claimed in desperation. "I have never seen you up until this moment."

Bayard rose from his chair, watching me even more intently. He cleared his throat, spoke calmly to the prisoner, his eyes, like Father's, fixed on me.

"Do you know at whom you are leveling charges, man? For theft is a grave charge . . ." Bayard paused, looked toward the fire, and then leveled his gray, stark eyes upon me again. "Theft is a capital charge, not a simple failing such as . . . such as dozing on the watch. Someone's life could hang in the balance, lad."

I had begun to dislike Sir Bayard Brightblade, who was making me uncomfortable. So I spoke up.

"Well, sir, never did I obtain clear view of the culprit, as I have said, and never would I conspire against your property or person. You can believe me, or you can believe this wayward sort you have captured red-handed with the evidence." I gestured dramatically toward the prisoner.

All eyes fixed on the man in black who quivered in handcuffs at the my father's feet. All eyes except those of my father, who was deferring in these circumstances to Bayard, whose eyes were focused on me, gray and ever intent.

"If that is my choice, I'll believe you, young master," Bayard replied, rising from his chair and turning his back to me. He stepped lightly over a retreating dog and walked toward the mantle of the fireplace, stopping to stand over his recovered armor, which lay in a glittering heap on the hearth.

"But that is the one who helped me, and I can prove it," the prisoner insisted.

Hardly an orator, but his words drew fire and attention. Now Father sprang to his feet, hearing what he had wanted to hear all along, I suppose—that his precious eldest son, poor Alfric, was really guilty of no more than being petty, dimwitted, and in the wrong place. Bayard did not move, but turned away, staring into the fire a long and suspenseful time before proclaiming:

"Once again, let us hear your version of what happened that night, Alfric."

Clumsily my brother began, his eyes darting back and forth—looking for approval first to Father, then to Bayard. I had seen the look before. He was trying to figure out if he needed to lie to stay out of trouble.

It was beyond him, so he barreled on into a cloudy version of the same old truth.

"That night I come up from the banquet, all set to police

the upstairs quarters, for as you have always told us, Father, the times is hard ones, and but a few honest men about."

"May it not be one less than you're claiming, boy," Father threatened, reddening under his red beard and eyebrows. Bayard sighed, returning to his chair as a cloud passed over the sun outside and the windows grew dark, the blue in the wings of the stained glass kingfishers fading to a flat gray until it looked as though someone was standing at the east window. For a moment, preposterous though it seemed, I thought that someone *was* standing at the window—a spy on the proceedings, perhaps. I looked at Bayard to see if he had noticed.

He was seated, listening to the words of my brother.

"I seen Galen at the door of Sir Bayard's chambers, and being as I intend to be a squire all protectful of my master's interests . . ."

"Yes, yes, Alfric," Bayard pressed. "You opened the door for your brother . . ."

"Who said there was a suspicious sort lurking on the grounds outside. Things become kind of hazy from that point on, sir. I don't reckon I saw what hit me. Could of been that felon there.

"Far as I know, could of been Galen."

He smiled blamelessly, his treacherous heart fulfilled at last.

There was muttering among the servants and peasants— this, in fact, was great entertainment for the likes of them. Father reddened to the brink of apoplexy and sat back in his chair, gripping its arms until I could hear them creaking and expected the wood to splinter. Brithelm leaned over Father's right shoulder, his sorrowful face so pale and compassionate that I began to wonder if he, too, was hiding mischief. Bayard sat back, squinted at me, and looked pained.

"Next thing I knowed," Alfric continued serenely, "I was being dragged out of the closet by yourself, regaining my wits at the tail end of that little weasel's alibis."

I began to blubber and whine.

"Father, this is absolutely unfair."

That was good. I choked, looked to the floor, then walked quickly toward one of the corners where a gutted torch smoked in a sconce.

". . . and you, Sir Bayard, whose trust I fear my brother's unkind words have taken and twisted and broken like so many snap beans . . ."

A bad comparison, but homespun, and sure to get the sympathy of the servants and the peasants, which I could use at the moment. I stared wide-eyed at the sputtering torch, allowing the smoke to pass over my face, make my eyes burn and water.

Nearest thing to weeping one can get. I turned back to my audience, tears streaming. The prisoner smiled faintly, reached into the folds of his cloak. Bayard noticed the movement and stepped quietly away from the fireplace, on his guard, staring intently at the disheveled man in black.

"Oh, you fine gentleman, my negligence has left me a disgrace to my Father and his glorious past . . ."

I bowed my head. Brithelm stepped forward and took my arm gently.

". . . a disgrace to the family Pathwarden five generations back. Five generations hence."

"Galen. Galen." My brother Brithelm rose to his consoling best. "Surely nothing you have done . . ." I tore my arm from his comforting grasp, buried my face in my hands, and continued.

"Would that it were so! But my negligence is shameful. I shirked and nodded as well as my older brother . . ."

"Did more than nod, Galen Pathwarden," the prisoner brayed triumphantly. "More than nod, for you embraced the business with greed."

To my astonishment, from his cloak the bony prisoner drew my naming ring, the token that he—or someone who had stolen the armor that fateful night—had taken from me, taken to assure my silence.

A torch in the far corner of the hall went out, but the servants were too enthralled by the drama to move and the light went untended. I stammered, fumbled for a story.

And came up empty. All I could manage were stammers and squeals, a feeble, "How did he get my naming ring? It can't be mine! It must be a forgery! Oh, to compound burglary with counterfeit goods . . ."

Father was on his feet, the huge chair rocking as he leaped from it. Dogs scattered, whimpering.

"Silence, Galen!" the old man thundered. "How did he know your name? How could he copy your naming ring, when only one exists in the world for the copying?"

"I don't know, sir. Perhaps he . . . wrested it from my unconscious hand the night he stole the armor?"

Father wasn't buying.

"Show me your hand!" Father commanded in a tone that brooked no quibbling.

I had no choice but to comply. My bare, quivering hand caused a ripple of murmurs and *I told you so*s among the attentive servants. Father's face turned a dark shade.

"But . . . but—"

"And why," asked Father in an ominously hushed voice, "have we not heard about the disappearance of your naming ring until this very moment?"

I was hard put to come up with a quick lie for that one. The silence was deadly.

"Galen, I am sorely wounded," Father said after an interminable lull, his voice low and dispirited. "When I consider this armor thief, when I consider you and your brother and what all of you have done, collectively and separately, I'm sore tempted to execute the thief and thrash the both of you until you long for execution. But I suppose that's against Solamnic code, no matter how it conforms with good sense. I'll leave all judgments, all sentencing to Sir Bayard Brightblade."

With that I was escorted from the room, as roughly as my brother but fortunately not back to the same cell. Alfric was allowed the run of the house, still under punishment for his oversight but I was temporarily confined to Gileandos's library. We saved the real cell, for we only had one, for the man in black.

There among lecterns and desks, books and scrolls, bones and specimens and alchemical alembics and tubings, I cast the Calantina once more, receiving the nine and eleven, tunnel on stone, the Sign of the Rat. I consulted the books, the commentary, and again was baffled by my fate.

I waited for hours, the only sounds the tolling of the bell

in the tower tolling three, four, then five. Some time in the late afternoon the faint shrill of a jay outside the library window, and twice the unmistakable sniffing and heavy breathing of my brother poking about outside in the corridor.

Once he tested the door. To his disappointment and my relief, it was locked, and after the events of a fortnight past, he was no longer keeper of the keys. Nonetheless, I hid the bag of opals deep in the pocket of my tunic, then passed time until evening.

I read a book on dwarf lore and another on explosives. I tried on several of Gileandos's robes, hung fastidiously in the alcove of the library, and played awhile with the elixirs and powders he kept by the alchemical machinery. Finally, I climbed upon a table and slept amid papers and manuscripts, until I awoke to a darkness outside and the disturbing feeling you have when you wake in a room and know you are not alone.

"Wh—who's there?"

No answer, but eventually the sound resolved itself into a brief, erratic fluttering noise over by the window. Evidently something else was trapped in here besides a youngest son.

I lit a candle, held my breath, moved toward the sound.

It was only a bird perched on the sill—a huge, ungainly raven who battered the dark panes of the window with its darker wings. I reached over the bird and opened the window, whispering, "How did you get in here, little bird?"

The creature stood on the sill, regarding me listlessly. For a moment it seemed like a stuffed bird sitting there, and I wondered had I dreamed the movement, the noise.

Then it cocked its head slowly, almost mechanically, and spoke in a dry voice out of nowhere.

"In much the same fashion as you, little boy. I meddled with those more powerful than I."

"What?" The candle slipped from my hand. I snatched at it by reflex, fumbling it and burning my hand on the hot tallow as the wick went out.

We were in darkness again, but a darkness broken by moonlight through the now-open window. The raven backed along the sill, bathed in the red light of Lunitari. He cocked his head again and leaped sluggishly into the air, landing atop the lectern with scarcely a flap of his wings.

"Did you think I would abandon those who . . . obeyed me? That I would throw you to the Solamnic wolves?"

The voice was flat and without music in the throat of the raven, but instantly I recognized its rhythm, its soothing phrases covering iron and poison. The air in the library grew colder.

"I . . . trusted you would come back, sir," I lied, shivering.

"You're lying." The bird hopped once nervously. "But nonetheless I am back.

"I have further need of you," the voice of the Scorpion said.

"It is an absolute delight to be of service to you, sir, and let me add that . . ."

"Silence!" The voice seemed too large for the bird, too large for the room itself. I backed into a chair, which tumbled over into an array of tubing and retorts and glassware containing the gods knew what elixirs.

"You still have much to do for me, Galen Pathwarden. Much to do to save that skin of yours."

All of this struck me as slightly less ominous coming from a bird.

"What now? Haven't I tangled myself in enough webbing for your satisfaction?" I scrambled to my feet, knocking over still another beaker in the process.

"Hardly." The raven regarded me with a brief, dull-eyed stare. "You see, I make friends for life, and, after all, you didn't expect a half dozen opals for what little you've done, did you?

I wrapped one of Gileandos's robes about me; it was genuinely cold in here by now.

"Do you think I am trapped in this shape? That I could not become an adder, a leopard, your coiled friend with the sting in his tail from a few nights back—you remember the night?"

I nodded stupidly, forgetting it was dark.

"A few nights back, you ran up your debt, little boy. And you have only begun to pay it."

"Would you like the opals back? We could call it even."

"But 'even' it is not, Galen. For I lose my valuable servant in the bargain—the man confined to your cellar dungeon, who can no longer serve me because I chose to play by the rules."

"I beg your pardon?"

"So I must be returned a servant, little Galen, to make up for the one I have lost. I suppose it is needless to add that you are that servant."

I was thunderstruck, gaping for words.

"So it is you who will do what I say. You will accompany this Sir Bayard on his trip into southern Solamnia, on the road to the tournament he desires so fiercely to win. You will attend to his weaponry, his wardrobe, his livery—all things a squire attends to.

"And during your journey with Sir Bayard, you will provide me with intelligence on occasion—little things as to his whereabouts, his state of mind, what he intends to do next.

"Above all, you will take your time getting to the tournament. You will see to it that Bayard Brightblade takes his."

What strange new twisting and turning was this? Why was I so unlucky to be the chosen one?

"You'll have to okay this with my father, sir," I replied in relief. "For I'm to be confined here for a while—awaiting punishment. Remember, you saw to it that Father saw my naming ring in the hands of the man in black, and connected me with this whole unsavory business. No, I'm sorry, sir, but I don't see how I can be of any help. You'll have to look elsewhere for a qualified cohort, although it grieves me to disappoint you in this fashion."

"Ah, but I cannot be disappointed, little man. Oh, no, for I carry your freedom in the crook of my claw."

"I beg your pardon?"

"The naming ring. Since we are in the business of returning things desired to one another." The bird took wing, sailing straight at me. I flinched, covered my face, then felt the soft prickling of claws on my shoulder. I lowered my hand and stared directly into its dull eyes.

"Look to my feet, idiot," the raven croaked.

"My naming ring! You have it around your ankle! How'd you—"

"Never left my possession," the bird declared smugly.

"You were sent up the river by spurious goods."

"And I suppose I just tell Father that and he releases me on the spot?" I walked to the window, raven perched on my shoulder.

"Of course not. But when he sees this ring and compares it with the one already in his possession, he will realize how close he came to losing a son to forgery."

The bird tucked its head under its wing as the light of the red moon passed over us once more.

"Which is why," it continued, lifting its head once more, "that it is Bayard who will show him the ring. Bayard will find the ring in his quarters this very night, and in addition to seeking your release will also seek to make amends."

"How will he make amends?"

The raven spread its wings and crouched. "Oh, you will see. And when he does, you will know what to do."

With that it lifted off into the night air, gliding over the courtyard until it turned sharply and was lost from sight somewhere in the back of the moat house.

*　*　*　*　*

I slept fitfully once more, my dreams filled with scorpions and the terrible sounds of beating wings. And I awoke to the same unsettling feeling—that once again I was not alone.

I looked about cautiously and saw a candle bobbing at the library entrance, behind it a tall figure.

I reached to my belt in a desperate search for my knife, which I now recalled had been taken from me at the outset of my stay in the dungeon.

"Who is it?" This time a little more steadiness in my voice. I tried for menace and failed.

The candle raised, and the one lamp in the library began to glow.

Sir Bayard Brightblade stood beneath it, outlined in the red and yellow and gold of the lamp flame, that now-familiar look of puzzlement and amusement on his face.

"This room is rather sparsely lit for a library," he observed, turning to face me across a wide vellum-littered table.

"Gileandos's doing . . ." I started to explain, but the

Knight was off and running.

"My business with you is brief or long, Galen, depending on your choice."

Sir Bayard paused, looked down at the table in front of him, thumbed the page of a manuscript, and read for a moment. His shadow was long, magnified by the slanting light, stretching the length of the table and losing itself in the dark.

"It seems that you are reprieved," he said softly, and opened his hand.

My naming ring glittered in his palm. I could recognize the engraving from where I stood.

It was sensible to be silent now, to hear what he had to say.

"I found it on the mantle in my chambers not an hour ago. Placed there perhaps by someone who knew the thief's ring to be a forgery and had pity on you, was my first guess. A servant, perhaps?

"Whoever it was did you a good turn. This ring is almost identical to the one in the thief's possession—I compared them in your father's chambers—almost identical except that the one in the thief's possession is now demonstrated to be a fake."

"Then someone returned the original to show . . . that I hadn't given it to the thief! I was innocent all along!"

"It appears thusly," Sir Bayard brooded. "Although it leaves the questions of how your ring was copied by the thief, or where it has been concealed all this time, unanswered. Troubling questions, I should say."

My heart sank. "Magical means? Or Alfric, perhaps?" I prompted innocently.

"Perhaps. Perhaps," Bayard replied distractedly, his face impassive. He coughed impressively. "Be that as it may, you are in the clear and I am no closer to filling the position of squire and keeping my appointment in the southlands. Which is why . . ." He paused here and cleared his throat again, nervously, it seemed to me. "I am offering that position to you."

"But Alfric . . ."

"Had a responsibility, and didn't do all that well with it.

Alfric is still under a cloud here and Sir Andrew will not hear of it. I've thought long and hard in the last hour, Galen. You could have lied your way out of the thief's accusations—made up some story about being intimidated into giving him the ring, or having it taken from you in a struggle. But you did not. You kept the silence, willing to suffer false accusation rather than lie to save yourself."

I liked his version of the facts.

"That's the kind of squire a Knight looks for."

"B-but . . ."

"And if I'm wrong, Galen, time and the road will show it. I'm in need of a squire now, and of all those available you seem most suitable."

CHAPTER 4

BEING a SQUIRE WAS NO GLAMOROUS THING, I DISCOV-
ered. There are only so many times a boy can see his face
reflected in a polished breastplate and pride himself in how
well that breastplate has been polished. My particular limit
was once.

I quickly grew to despise this Sir Bayard Brightblade
more than any brother or teacher or servant, especially
when he set me to buffing his armor.

They had moved me out of the library and into Brithelm's
quarters, chosen because the room had no windows by
which I could escape, no standing furniture from which I
could fashion weapons. It was barren and bleak in there.
The only comfort was a rug and a straw mattress on the
floor, the only conveniences a walk-in closet, a fireplace,

and a single lamp. I had little to distract me, and armor aplenty to buff and polish.

On a dark, chilly morning, several days hence, we made final preparations to set off on whatever harebrained quest Bayard had planned. The weather inclined toward rain—promising the kind of morning I would usually avoid altogether, sleeping in until afternoon. But I was readying to embark in the rain and the early cold, with only four hours of sleep, bound for the gods knew where.

"What's the difference?" I began, talking to myself, perhaps a little loudly. "I would like to know what's the difference, thank you, since my new employer is downstairs with Father and Brithelm, sitting at a farewell breakfast in the great hall while I am upstairs with the polish and the rags?

"For the life of me," I whined, setting my cloth to the intricate visor of the helmet, "I can't see much difference between this and cleaning Alfric's chambers. Who is this Bayard Brightblade, after all, but another taskmaster? Only this one is set to cart me off to southern Solamnia where he bashes the heads of other Knights and wins the heart of the damsel while I get to polish armor and tend to the horses and run little errands. I'm already tired of being some *damn southern hotshot's factotum!*"

I liked that last phrase, closed my eyes, repeated it.

I then surveyed my squirely work and realized that I had no idea how to put the armor back together. Greaves lay by the fireplace, the breastplate on the mattress where I had set it aside out of boredom, the gloves on the plain rug in front of the fire, and the helmet half-polished in my hands. Cords of leather lay strewn everywhere. There was elaborate lacing to this machinery, but I wasn't a party to its workings.

"The pieces never fit together," I whimpered. "None of the pieces fit, in Bayard's armor or in Bayard himself. What am I supposed to tell the Scorpion when I don't know what I'm spying for, can't figure out the man I'm spying on?"

I walked to the fireplace and held my hands to the warmth of the little blaze.

"First of all, he doesn't believe me when I identify his prisoner as the Scorpion. Of course, he *wasn't* the Scorpion, but Sir Bayard couldn't know that. Anyway, he doesn't say anything, but I figure he can't believe me because of the questions he asks. Now where was that wax?"

I reached into my pockets, took out the high-pitched dog whistle I had used to disrupt the great hall time and again, turning Father's formal reception room into a churning frenzy of hounds, terriers, and mastiffs. I tossed it onto Brithelm's mattress by the breastplate.

Then my even more prized possessions. First, the red Calantina dice, twelve-sided wooden curiosities from Estwilde. There were one hundred and forty-four numbers you could roll with them, and tradition had assigned to each number a symbolic animal and three lines of verses that were supposed to be prophetic, but usually turned out to be too obscure to be helpful. Only later, when you looked back on the reading, could you usually say, "Oh, that's what the reading meant."

It wasn't ever much help, but it made you think there were ways to see things coming, and the thought was strangely reassuring.

After the dice, my gloves. I had purchased them from a merchant who swore they had adorned the hands of a Solammic captain at the Battle of Chaktamir. I paid for them with the servants' money when they had heard that Sir Bayard was coming. He had quite a reputation for heroism, and before his arrival the younger servants had begged me in the scullery, in the broom closet, in the downstairs corridors, offering me their pennies for just one peek at the fabled armor.

Those pennies were gone now, spent on the pair of thick leather gloves I tossed on the bed by the dice. I had not dreamed of wearing them around the moat house, since their stitching was intricate and costly, down to the phases of the red moon dyed and stamped upon the knuckles. Sporting such attire in front of Father would raise uncomfortable questions.

But the servant children raised no such questions, being the innocent and trusting souls they were. The night before the theft I had gotten around to telling them that viewing the armor would be impossible and that it had cost me all of their pennies even to ask for such a viewing. They bought my explanation, too, thinking perhaps that such was the way one transacted business with a Solamnic Knight.

With the whistle, the dice, and the gloves on the bed, I continued to ferret through my pockets.

"There must be wax in here somewhere . . ."

I gave up on the one pocket and moved to the other, all the while pondering my change in circumstances. Pondering Bayard Brightblade, who *was* a mystery.

"First he strips Alfric of squirehood for nodding off and losing the armor, then he takes me on for the same job when he seems to suspect I did far worse. And it isn't softheartedness on his part, some bygones-be-bygones kind of gibberish. He slapped the poor man in black in the heart of the dungeon and is talking execution. Beheading! I didn't know the Knights of Solamnia let you do that kind of thing, much less that Bayard would take it on himself to do it! The joke on him is that the poor fellow is hardly the Scorpion, for the Scorpion, as I and only I well know, is cavorting in the body of a raven presently. Ha! Ha!" I glanced over my shoulder nervously, just in case someone was eavesdropping. No one.

Exploring the new pocket, my fingers brushed against something leather. I drew out the little purse and looked in it for wax, but it was empty except for the six opals that came in it that fateful night of the Scorpion's first visit. I remembered the scorpion standing in my hand and shuddered.

They looked like eggs, those stones, and I wished the raven had settled for them. I started to hide them in Brithelm's room, thought better of it, and set them lightly on the bed by my other possessions.

The wax was growing more necessary. For it seemed like a good plan: to melt bits of it over the pieces of armor, using it as a sort of makeshift glue or mortar. It wouldn't hold them together long, but it might work long enough so that I could ask an unwitting kitchen servant to move the suit to Bayard's quarters, blaming the poor boy loudly when the suit fell apart.

Such was my strategy, but you probably know what they say about the plans of mice and men.

That goes for weasels, too, evidently.

*   *   *   *   *

When I heard the rattle of a key in the lock, I thought of Alfric, who was even less fond of me now that I had become Bayard's squire in his stead. He was still condemned to fester in the moat house, while Father pondered his inadequacies, and though his hand was usually stayed by the presence of others, I did not doubt that he plotted outrage.

So it was deep into the closet for me, closing the door behind me and slipping under the hanging robes as though they were a curtain. I checked to see if they were a curtain indeed, testing the back wall for secret doors, for passageways, but with no results. I was backed into here, brought to ground.

Outside I heard the movement of metal on stone, the muffled ring of metal on metal.

Someone was doing something to the armor.

Sometimes curiosity outweighs prudence, and this was one of those times. I parted the curtain of robes and opened the closet door ever so slightly, admitting the light from the fireplace and from the one lamp in the room.

Needless to say, I thought first of illusion when I looked through the crack of the closet door and saw Bayard's breastplate floating above the bed, nothing supporting it but the dark air below it. Done by mirrors, no doubt. I mean, isn't that the first thing you think when the magical intrudes in your otherwise unmagical life? I did what almost all of us would do: I looked for trapdoors and fictions.

Which there were none of in view at the moment. Only Brithelm, standing motionless in the center of the room. He watched calmly, even playfully, as the armor glowed red, then yellow, then white. Slowly it collected itself. The greaves got up and walked from the fireplace to the pallet, as though strapped to the body of an ancient phantom. There, as an unearthly music began to tumble out of the walls of the room, the greaves joined the assembling suit.

And all of this having something to do with my middle brother, standing serenely, left hand in the air, singing along with the music from the walls. The armor, now entirely assembled, stood shakily in the air, as though suspended in water. The music faded, and Brithelm laughed softly and sat down upon his mattress.

I fell back into the closet, marveling. Sat there for a few minutes, marveling further. There was a soft rattle of metal in the room outside my door, then the sound of movement, of Brithelm walking across the room, then nothing but silence. Outside the window the song of a nightingale started up, much as it had on the night the intruder crept into Alfric's quarters and started all this mess. The last song before departure.

Beyond the sound of bird song rose the whicker of a horse. Bayard had sent the grooms to the stables and was readying things for our journey.

But I nearly forgot departure in the face of this revelation—this trick my middle brother could do with armor, which was probably not the only trick in his bag. Apparently, I had been duping the wrong sibling for years. If Brithelm could rearrange armor like that, imagine what he could have done with dice!

Which reminded me. The gloves, the Calantina dice, the dog whistle, and the purse lay out in the open, well within the view of even the most distracted of brothers.

I stepped into the room. The armor had settled, reassembled, in the corner by the door to the hallway, as though it had been donned by a ghost who, now tired of wearing it, had laid it carefully out of the way.

Brithelm was carefully out of the way himself, lost in thought or meditation or revery, seated on the thin and obviously uncomfortable pallet in the center of the room. I called to him softly, called again, and then a third time, but there was no answer. He sat cross-legged, palms upward, eyes closed blissfully, like an icon in an old temple, the kind that you still chanced across if you traveled far enough into the swamps or high enough into the mountains, abandoned hundreds of years back.

It gave me the willies, that was for sure. And it was worse when Brithelm began to rise from the pallet himself, not standing, mind you, but hovering in the air like a hummingbird, while he still sat blissfully, sat with his eyes closed and his palms raised. Once more I tried to rouse him, but it was no use.

Judging from the sound outside the window, Father was helping Bayard prepare the horses in the courtyard, giving him final advice as to how to care for me.

"I suppose, Sir Bayard," his voice boomed, "that the time will come when you have to teach him a better horsemanship than he's accustomed to, the teaching of which may involve beating some sense into the lad."

"That it might, Sir Andrew. Tighten that cinch there, if you'd be so kind."

"And he isn't a lancer. I spent my time with Alfric in the lists, and he's the best jouster of the three, but our best is none too good. The time will come when Wea—uh, Galen will have to sit the charger, the teaching of which may involve beating some sense into the lad."

"Indeed, Sir Andrew. Is Valorous's bit too tight?"

"I think not, Sir Bayard. And in swordsmanship . . ."

"I suppose I'll beat him there, too. Are the stirrups high enough?"

And so on. Father could think of many things I lacked the sense to do, so he could be trusted to keep talking for an hour or so, after which Bayard's politeness would be stretched to the absolute limit and he would ask where his squire and his armor had gotten to.

I glanced over at Brother Brithelm, who floated above his thin mattress of reeds. I reached under him, collected my belongings. Then I went to the door and started to hoist the armor, but turned suddenly.

I set the whistle in Brithelm's palm as a keepsake, as a mystery he might well ponder when he awakened to reality. This was no more than mischief, for I knew that addle-brained Brithelm would no doubt spend hours trying to decipher the meaning of the dog whistle that had materialized in his palm. I thought at first of giving him the opals, but considering the road and those upon it, I fancied I could use them more. How could I know that the dog whistle, in different hands and in different ways, would continue its history of disruption?

*   *   *   *   *

67

The horses resented their loss of sleep, too. The courtyard filled with their coughs, their snorts, their other, less polite sounds. About their legs scurried dogs, who barked hysterically at the cold and the surprisingly early movement of people and livestock. Steam rose from the horses' bodies, steam also from Bayard's breath and Father's breath, clouded by the mysterious winter which had come early to our part of the country.

With Bayard's help I managed to sling the armor over the back of a pack mare, who stared at me over her shoulder with pure and absolute hatred. I covered the armor with a light canvas blanket, strapped on my own sword—a pitiful little weapon it seemed now—and Bayard helping me once again, I managed to rise to the back of another horse. To my embarrassment I was riding old Molasses, a horse we kept about so that visiting small children might be entertained with brief rides around the courtyard.

Father still had no respect for my horsemanship.

My last minutes at the moat house were occupied in receiving advice.

"You are to be a good squire to Bayard, boy. That means you don't lie or steal, which I know is asking for profound change in your conduct, yet nonetheless, I ask—no, demand it.

"Do not let the armor get dirty. Keep the weapons in good condition—they may save your hide in some unforeseen circumstance."

Some unforeseen circumstance. I liked that. The old man was waxing chivalric. But the whole ritual of advice and farewell was tiresome. I peeked into my saddlebags.

"Pay attention when I am addressing you! Carry the messages word for word. Curry the horses when Bayard tells you, and nose at their shoes for stones and bruises. Moss grows on the north side of trees—that in case you find yourself lost. When you encounter evil, face it bravely—as the Order says, 'Without regard to personal suffering.'

"As life is a precious and most holy gift from Paladine, in whom we breathe, fight, and dream for the betterment of all, see that no life is ever taken or sacrificed in vain."

A cold gust of wind swept over the walls and into the

courtyard, and Molasses twitched and shivered.

"We should be on our way now, Sir Andrew," Sir Bayard announced, rising into the saddle atop Valorous.

"But a moment, Sir Bayard. Never enter the water until an hour after you have eaten, and never enter the water with a storm brewing, for rivers and streams and ponds draw lightning, as do the blue branches of the aeterna tree."

Bayard muttered something, flicked the reins of his horse. The big chestnut stallion began to move, the pack horse and Molasses following him by instinct. Father walked along-side me, not finished yet.

"Excess of drink before the age of twenty blinds a boy. As does gambling of any sort, or foul language.

"Most of the women you will meet carry knives."

Despite my fear of what lay ahead of me, of the road that stretched uncertainly beyond the moat house and into the farthest regions of Krynn, where Bayard had some adventure brewing for the both of us—despite all of this, with the clamor and the confusion of dogs and directions, whatever lay waiting at the end of that road seemed less forbidding now. Seemed, you might say, a kind of relief.

*   *   *   *   *

A relief, but only until the moat house sank quietly in the darkness behind us, into the morning mists as though it burned, slowly and without flames, on an ocean at mid-night. Just when the walls had almost become indistinguish-able from the darkness of morning, the tiny form of a man appeared at the battlements.

I watched for a moment, as he surely watched us dwindle away from him, from the moat house, from home.

Father, perhaps?

Then the shape burst into a sheet of orange fire—a candle in the windows of home.

"Gileandos," I chuckled, remembering.

A parting shot in return for lectures in a dungeon. All sorts of chemicals can find their way into the pocket of a robe, when one gives a weasel the run of the library.

*   *   *   *   *

Already the night birds had begun to hush, and what little sun there was washed the green tops of the vallenwoods with a lighter green, almost a yellow. Occasionally I heard the quarrels of jays above us, and the rising songs of birds I had heard before but never thought about until now. Still, the songs themselves were familiar, so it seemed pleasant in the upper branches, but below the light and noise, the way before us was quiet and dark. It was cold, a morning drizzle had begun, and the road looked dire and unfriendly.

The horses moved in single file now, Bayard leading on his stallion Valorous, followed by the pack mare. I brought up the rear on my excuse for a horse. The distance between us widened as the day went on and as Molasses tired. I wished for a mule, but more than that, I wished Bayard would talk, would say something, as my several attempts at conversation had been met with only casual reply.

No doubt his mind was south of here, preparing for the lists at this almighty tournament he was so set on winning.

It was as quiet as a dungeon on the road. As dull as a dungeon, too: the knocking of the horses' hooves against the rain-spattered ground as regular as the dripping of water in a cell, the air as cold and damp and uncomfortable, the company as listless and silent.

"So . . . ," I began, and my companion leaned forward in the saddle, looked straight at me, and spoke for the first time in almost an hour.

"Castle di Caela."

"What?"

"You were going to ask where the tournament will be held, weren't you?"

"It gives me confidence to know that kind of thing, Sir Bayard."

He looked back at the road, then once again at me.

"Castle di Caela. A fortnight's journey from here. In southwestern Solamnia, about halfway between Solanthus and the Vingaard Keep. If we make good time we still have three days before the tournament begins. You can set up our tent, carry my regards to Robert di Caela, and enter my name in the lists."

"Aren't you . . ."

"A little old for the lists?" Though he put it bluntly, he had guessed my thoughts. Slowly the drizzle built to an actual rain, and the path ahead of us grew even darker, even more uninviting. "I suppose. But that's what happens when you court a girl of eighteen. You grapple the eighteen-year-old boys to get her attention."

He hooded himself against the rising rain.

"Should be a lesson to you," I muttered unwisely.

Sir Bayard smiled, lowered his face so that the water tunneled down the front of the hood. No longer could I see his expression when he replied.

"And your first lesson should be respect."

* * * * *

The morning progressed into early afternoon, and the rain showed no intention of letting up. All about us the road was filled with sounds of wetness—the splash of horses' hooves in standing puddles, the tumble of rain through the leaves and branches of the surrounding trees. After a while these sounds blended into a constant murmur, became a continual rushing sound, as familiar as breathing, so that any unusual movement or noise was more sudden, more disturbing.

Twice something crackled in the underbrush beside the road. Twice I drew my sword and tried unsuccessfully to steer Molasses away from the sound. On the third time Bayard pushed back his dripping green hood and stared at me flatly, disgustedly.

"Badger."

"Pardon me?"

"Badger. You are drawing your sword in the presence of badgers."

"How in the world do you know? For sure, I mean."

"The wise man talks with his ear to the wind," Sir Bayard answered, drawing a tinderbox from beneath his cloak.

"I shall make a better knight for knowing that, sir."

"We'll stop here, rest and eat," he continued. "I'll try to wrestle a fire from this quagmire."

We nestled beneath a huge, spreading vallenwood, our backs to its hoary trunk. Nothing seemed cheerful in this cli-

71

mate; even the crickets and frogs were silent, too stunned by the cold to celebrate the rain they usually loved so dearly, so vocally. Bayard crouched above the tinderbox and removed his gloves. His large hands seemed ungainly in such a delicate task; it was as though he was tying a net for dolls.

"About the tournament . . ." I began. "Who is the lucky noblewoman?"

"Daughter of Sir Robert di Caela, Knight of the Sword. Surely your tutor touched on current politics. You have heard of the House of di Caela?"

"Old Solamnic family," I repeated from memory, watching a rabbit, soaked and sullen, poke its head out from under a large patch of creeping juniper. It looked as though it had been spat upon or worse. Well, we were birds of a drenched feather, that rabbit and I.

"Old Solamnic family," I began once more, thinking of my warm room and bed at home. "Founded by Duncan di Caela, cousin of Vinas Solamnus himself. In wartime— brilliant, inventive. In times of peace—brilliant and just. But in generations nearer our time the family di Caela has withdrawn unto itself, for reasons it has chosen never to make public."

The rabbit ducked back under the juniper. At least he had a burrow nearby, to which he could retreat when the rain grew heavier, the day colder.

"Robert di Caela is the last of the male line," Bayard added. "For the first time in the recorded history of the family, the di Caela heir is a girl. After Sir Robert, the House of di Caela falls into history and obscurity, if his daughter does not wed. Which is why he has called a tournament."

Bayard's new fire smoldered and showed a hint of flame.

"Which is why the younger Solamnic Knights will gather from all across Ansalon—There!"

A fire burned low and steady beside us. Bayard put away the tinderbox, continued.

"Which is why they will gather in tournament, each of them seeking the hand of the Lady Enid."

"Enid!" I exclaimed, with a little more bitter pleasure than I should have shown. Of all the names in Krynn, Robert di Caela had chosen "Enid" for his daughter? An Enid is almost always a big, square-jawed woman with her hair bound like a loaf of bread.

I mean, what could you expect from an Enid besides excellent pastries?

I began to chuckle. Here I was, practically drowning myself in the miserable midst of nowhere, and all in the service of a knight who had his mind set on winning a tournament where the first prize was a girl named Enid!

Bayard frowned, looked away from me.

"I mean nothing ill by the laughter, sir," I explained quickly. "Please don't take umbrage at idle merriment."

"There is no umbrage to be taken, Galen," Bayard said calmly, staring up at me with those cold gray eyes. "Nonetheless, I should appreciate a little more . . . esteem here. After all, I am supposed to marry Enid di Caela."

It was too much. I laughed the harsh laughter of the doomed, and suddenly Bayard drew his sword.

Well, I thought I was done for. I rolled into a ball, started to shout, to offer my birthright, Brithelm's and Alfric's birthrights as bribery, but Bayard's hand clasped quickly and forcefully over my mouth and hushed me. I tried to bite him, but he was holding my mouth shut.

"Quiet, boy!" he whispered, and paused, head raised in the air like a leopard sniffing the switching wind for signs of the quarry. And through the constant sound of the rain I heard movement, a scuffling noise in a stand of fir across the road, some thirty yards away from us.

"Not badger," Bayard hissed, and loosened his grip on my jaw. He nodded toward my sword, which was all the command I needed. I winked obediently, stole my hand to the grip, as if to pledge my loyalty.

But believe me, I had no intention of drawing that weapon as long as there was any avenue of escape, any place to hide. Father had judged my swordsmanship correctly: I was more likely to injure myself or Bayard than any enemy arrayed against us. At that moment, however, I must have looked fierce enough to convince my fool of a companion that I would stand behind him in whatever bloodshed was about to follow.

In fact, I was behind him but also considerably above

him, for when Bayard turned again toward the source of the sound, I scrambled up the vallenwood to safety, perching in its lower branches where I could see what was about to happen and where I hoped devoutly that nobody—not even Bayard—could see me.

"Who goes there?" arose from the stand of fir. Bayard had been right, unless this was a rather miraculous badger.

"Sir Bayard Brightblade of Vingaard, Knight of Solamnia. And who asks my name of me?"

I banged my head in disbelief against the thick vallenwood branch I was straddling. No telling who or what lay concealed across the road, but anyone betting hard-earned money on the situation would wager that it was peasants. Peasants who, if you recall, had never forgiven the Knights of Solamnia for a little thing called the Cataclysm that altered the face of the planet and killed a few million of them in the bargain.

More to the point, peasants who would carry more recent memory of the misdeeds done in the very armor that lay atop our pack mare. Yes, a Solamnic Knight would be the last person they'd be ready to step out and welcome.

But step out of the firs they did, one after another, until a full half dozen of them stood in front of Bayard—stern and muddy and rather rough-looking peasants. They were all frowning, all bristling, and each of them brandished a club or an axe or a hammer at least as long as I was tall.

Bayard could have taken any one of them easily. He had cast his cloak over a bush and stood before them, open to the rain and clad only in a leather tunic, his broadsword drawn and resting lightly in his right hand, a short but wicked-looking dagger balanced in his left.

He could have taken any two of them—maybe three— with a bit of a scuffle. But six seemed overwhelming, and they knew it, spreading out as they crossed the road, forming a large and ragged circle around him.

I felt sorry for Bayard. I also climbed to a higher branch.

"Knight of Solamnia?" asked one of them—not the largest but certainly the most fierce-looking, sporting a bald pate with a huge red scar down its middle, a trophy from the gods knew what roughhousing. "You did say 'Knight of

Solamnia' then, didn't you, sir?"

"And if I did?" Bayard asked, turning slowly, elegantly clockwise, fixing his gaze on each adversary in turn, then passing him by, facing him again as he changed directions, turning counterclockwise. This all happened slowly, like some old and revered ritual or dance. And meanwhile, Bayard and Scar Head talked quietly, cautiously, as the peasants drew nearer and nearer the turning knight.

"Well, if you did, sir," answered Scar Head, setting his axe upon his shoulder as lightly as he would a cane fishing pole. "If you did, perhaps you kindly misunderstood my question, seeing as Solamnic Knights are not altogether welcome in these parts. Perhaps you are another kind of knight entire, or perhaps you are of a different order that me and my men have not heard of yet, and who we wouldn't have any hard feelings against, you understand? Karrock?"

He nodded at the man to his left—Karrock, evidently. A big, brutal-looking man with hair as red as mine and a darker beard—that strange combination you often see in folk of our coloring. Karrock moved slowly, but this time definitely, toward the pack mare, stretched out his hand toward the saddlebags.

"I'd stop right there if I were you," Bayard snapped, striding instantly to within sword's length of the big man. The peasants tensed. Bayard turned and addressed Scar Head.

"Stop dancing like a philosopher around names, man. If there's a reason I should hide my service to the Solamnic Orders I'd like to know it now, so I can dispel your illusions."

"I think this one means it, Master Goad," Karrock whispered to Scar Head, taking a step back from the mare. "I just came for militia work, not to tangle with zealots."

"There's six of us to one of him," Goad replied, motioning with his club to the men on his right, who halved the distance between themselves and Bayard, slipping between Molasses and the pack mare. "And you saw what his kind done to the village."

"'Swhy I'm here, sir," Karrock nodded.

"I mean," Goad chuckled coldly, addressing Bayard, "I may not have my letters, but I can count. And even a

Solamnic Knight will tell you there's a certain philosophy in numbers."

"Militia?" Bayard relaxed a bit, though from the way his shoulders turned I could see he was keeping an eye on the men approaching from Goad's right. "Then you're guarding your village? Against what?"

"Against Solamnic Knights such as yourself, sir, who think a suit of armor and a rich family allow them certain . . . liberties that even the old King-Priest of Istar would of had no rights in taking. We had a visit from one of your order several weeks back . . ."

I hugged the branch I lay upon and breathed a silent prayer. But I made sure the prayer was completely silent—not even whispered or breathed. For Karrock had recovered his courage, stepping toward the mare once more, his inquiring hand about to pull the canvas blanket off her back.

* * * * *

Sometimes, as Gileandos taught me in the theology lessons I avoided as much as possible, the gods give unexpected answers to our prayers.

For you see, Molasses was old. Not just getting on in years like a man will say of himself when he turns sixty or even seventy. Molasses was over thirty years old—had been put out to pasture by Father by the time Alfric was born. Molasses was past venerable, past ancient, was pushing fossilized. Remember also that for the last ten years his adventures had been limited to carting small children in an ever-narrowing circle around the moat house courtyard, and that the closest to danger he had been in the last twenty years was within fifty yards of a dogfight broken up in an instant by a quick serving boy. All in all, you can understand why the situation may have seemed a little threatening to the poor horse.

Perhaps you can understand why he fell over dead.

It was just the law of averages catching up. But catching up at just the right time. The heavy thud as the poor old creature collapsed startled the men who were approaching steadily from Ando's right toward the pack mare standing just to the left of Bayard. The yokels spun about and raised their weapons, expecting that some reinforcements had come to Bayard's aid, leaping from a tree, perhaps, and landing behind them.

They had no idea how quick their opponent was. Bayard vaulted the pack mare, armor and all, and landed heavily, noisily between our baggage and the militiamen. They turned back to him quickly, but it was too late. With the broad side of the blade he slapped one of them heartily on the ribs—it sounded as though someone were beating a rug with the dull thumping sound and the *whoosh* of escaping air. As soon as he turned, the man was on his knees, gasping.

His comrades paused, stunned, as if something large and supernatural—a dragon or a pillar of fire, perhaps—had risen in their midst. Bayard spun, caught Karrock with a high kick to the chest. The big man grunted and staggered backwards, Bayard moving steadily toward him in a half-crouch. Meanwhile, the rest of the militiamen stood motionless, their hands vaguely about their weapons.

Except Goad. Smoothly, silently, he sidled to his right, moving slowly until he stood astride the sword-whipped man, directly behind Bayard who, intent on discharging Karrock from the local militia, hadn't noticed at all.

Certainly this was the time for me to do something—at the least to shout a warning to my noble employer, at the most (and I shuddered to think of the most!) to drop from the vallenwood onto the enemy in some kind of heroic plunge.

At the moment I felt that to do either would be too showy. Instead, I sat and watched events unfold.

Then a curious thing happened, as if somehow a truce had been arranged out of all of this bluster and threat. Instead of pouncing on Bayard as I was sure he would do, Goad stooped and hoisted his winded comrade to his shoulders. Meanwhile, Bayard had toppled Karrock with a strong punch to the ruddy jaw and was turning to guard his back. His eyes met Goad's, and it was hard to tell what passed between them besides the nod that seemed to end it, as Goad backed into the stand of firs, as Karrock scrambled to his feet and scurried after his commander, none the worse for combat were it not for a bruise noticeable through the dark beard on the left side of his hamlike face.

Now I leaped down from the vallenwood, rolled a bit in the dust so I would look somewhat the worse for wear, bit my lip—not hard, but hard enough to draw convenient blood—then scrambled to my feet.

"Let that be a lesson to you, affronting a brave Knight of Solamnia," I shouted.

Bayard turned again, this time slowly, and fixed me with a withering gaze. "See to your horse," he ordered coldly.

As you can guess, there wasn't much seeing to do on that account. We said our farewells to Molasses, then transferred my belongings to the pack mare, who could hardly be said to be grateful for the additions, and I dreaded receiving the news as to how we would travel the rest of the way to Castle di Caela. I decided to postpone asking, perhaps letting Sir Bayard's temper cool in the meantime.

The mood and our clothes had been dampened considerably. Bayard returned to the fire, silently insisting that if we were to have lunch, then by the gods, we would have that lunch at that very site.

We ate abruptly. Bayard drew dried beef and dried fruit from one of the countless pockets and packs on the mare. The fire, unfortunately, was for warmth, not cooking. It was a dry and dismal meal we had there beside the road and under the vallenwoods, with the horse and the mare shivering beside us and the rain steadily falling.

I cast the Calantina for comfort and received two and eight, the Sign of the Horse. As I mulled over this reading, tried to remember the verses that went with the sign, Bayard leaned over my shoulder and spoke.

"And what's this?"

"Sign of the Horse," I replied shortly. I wasn't in the mood to exchange pleasantries with my judge, jury, and executioner.

"I mean . . ."

"The Calantina. Fortune-telling dice from Estwilde." Maybe he would take that as an answer, go back to his side of the fire, and dry some perfectly edible food into something indistinguishable from the saddlebags you carry it in. After all, we might need our appetites killed once more before we reached the castle.

"Garbage is what it is," Bayard said softly, drawing his knife and walking toward Valorous.

"I suppose," I agreed absently.

"Then why do you do it?" he snapped, crouching beside Valorous and lifting the stallion's front leg.

"Do what?"

"The Calantina, of course. Parlor game in Estwilde. That is, wherever they have parlors. They invented it and don't take it seriously. Why should you?" He snorted.

"The Calantina provides me with insight on various occasions, Sir Bayard. As to my future, my place in the ever-changing relationship of things. As to my courses of action."

"Garbage," he spat again, beginning to clean mud from the hooves of his stallion.

"Garbage?"

"Garbage, Galen." He smiled. "You know. Offal. Refuse. Ordure."

Then he turned to me, no longer smiling.

"There are many kinds of magic in the world, boy. This is not one of them."

"How can you be so sure?" I asked, leaning back against the vallenwood, my hand still in my pocket, clutching the dice tightly.

"All right," Bayard said calmly as he reached under Valorous for the stallion's other front hoof. "All right. What sign did you say you cast?"

"Sign of the Horse," I muttered, glancing away from Bayard toward the stand of firs, still fancying that the militia might return for our heads at any moment.

"Just what does that mean?" my employer asked, beginning to clean the hoof.

"Could be the journey we're on. Could be what happened to poor Molasses."

"Not very definite, is it?" Bayard asked victoriously, moving to Valorous's hind hooves and chuckling.

"Could mean many things, combined in a way we haven't discovered yet." I knew it was weak, but I thought he couldn't argue with it. I was mistaken.

"Hindsight, Galen. I could litter this road with omens by

hindsight. Magic is as rare as a struggle between honest men on this road."

"But I've seen magic, Sir Bayard," I blurted out, thinking of Brithelm.

"And I've seen honest men struggle on this road," Sir Bayard conceded quietly, intent again on his work. "Goad and Karrock and the rest of that militia think we are criminals— honestly think so—and that man back in your father's dungeon hasn't helped matters on that account."

He paused, looked directly at me, then turned back to Valorous. He cleaned the fourth hoof, flung the dagger into the ground, where it stuck, then rose to his feet.

"All Goad was doing," he stated flatly, "was protecting his village against what he imagined was a raiding knight. He hates the Order, probably thinks we're all rogues and traitors. He has a lot to learn. You have a lot to learn, too, Galen," he concluded, walking toward the pack mare. "Provided I stay alive long enough to teach it to you."

I started to retort, to let Bayard know that, as I had it figured, he didn't have all that much to teach me, and that I was more than willing to learn my lessons elsewhere if he would only escort me to a place free of rain and bullying militia. I started to tell him this, but he stopped in his tracks midway between horses and stared once again at the stand of firs, now almost hidden behind a wall of rain.

"There's something moving over there again," he whispered, backing toward Valorous, where his sword lay tied to the saddle.

I followed his gaze out to the line of evergreens, blurred in the gray movement of water. Something was going on across there, but at that distance and in the rain-distorted light I could not tell.

"What is it, sir?"

Bayard remained quiet, eyes fixed on the distance.

"Goad said something about 'philosophy in numbers.' Do you suppose it's the militia, back with more philosophy?"

"If it is, Galen, you'd better take your position in the vallenwood. I expect I'll need a lookout as direly as I needed one the last time." Bayard reached out, calmed his horse with the touch of a gloved hand.

The calming didn't work for squires.

"You might try killing a couple of them this time, sir," I offered. "Just a little something to swing the philosophical advantage in our direction."

Now Bayard was reaching for his sword. I watched him, waited for him to turn for the weapon so I, in turn, could turn for the vallenwood.

But none of the turns came. For behind Bayard, behind Valorous, I could see four burly fellows, chest high in a small grove of dogwood. Over the rain I could hear the shuffle of hooves on the forest floor. They were no longer bothering with secrecy.

They were mounted, and we were not. Or so it seemed until they crashed through the dogwood branches toward us, when we could also see that they were horses from the waist down.

I thought of the Sign of the Horse as I toppled backwards and saw the trunk of the vallenwood. Then saw its branches only. Then saw not much of anything except grayness and faint light. Finally, I saw nothing at all.

CHAPTER 5

All of this commotion, and I had not yet traveled ten miles from home.

Scarcely ten miles east of the family moat house lay a swamp that extended forty or fifty miles north and south—I didn't know how far for sure—and circled back upon our property until the moat house and almost all our holdings were bordered by marshlands. 'Warden Swamp was a lucky accident in the recent Pathwarden past, rising up quickly and unexplainably about a century ago, named for us, though the country folk shortened the name, as country folk will. Though we looked on it with mistrust and with fear, daunted by the rumors that things grew too quickly there, that strange, half-rotten things lurked in its heart, the swamp conveniently surrounded the Pathwarden estate and protected us from the hostility toward Solamnic Knights that had arisen in Ansalon following the Cataclysm.

You all know the story regarding the Fall from Favor. The people of Solamnia, of course, decided that the Knights had known the Cataclysm was coming for years but had been unwilling or unable to warn everyone. This popular sentiment became the excuse to waylay every Knight who passed through their particular part of the countryside.

Nonetheless, it could have been worse for our family during all the noise and persecution. First of all, we never lived in Solamnia proper, where most of the trouble was; we were slightly to the west in Coastlund, protected by our remoteness and, as it turned out, ringed by 'Warden Swamp. Although many men were eager for Knight-bashing, few wanted to go out of their way or cross dangerous terrain to get their bashes in. So the swamp had been our good fortune—my family's and mine.

Which is not to say that you'd ever have caught me near the nasty place, with its snakes and crocodiles, and bandits only a little less cold-blooded and a little more human than the reptiles. Until now, I'd always done my best to avoid it.

*   *   *   *   *

I awoke on horseback, or so it seemed. For I was draped like a dirty blanket or a saddle, face-down over a broad, dappled back that smelled of sweat and horse. The ground rushed by below me, and the wet afternoon wind whipped across the side of my face.

I shifted my position and tried to sit up in the saddle. But there was no saddle to sit up in. Instead, a rope was bound tightly about my wrists and a strong hand pulled at my hair, restraining me. I twisted, tried to kick against restraints—against the hand, at least—but found no rider where I had every right to expect one.

Then I remembered the men-horses crashing toward us through the bushes and the undergrowth. I raised myself as far as I could and looked straight into the burly back and shoulders of one of the creatures.

I was draped across what appeared to be a centaur, headed for swamps and for torture most likely.

Where was Bayard?

Had they taken him prisoner? Or worse, had he simply backed away and given me over to them while I lay in a faint underneath the vallenwood? Draped across my captor, I sulked bitterly and awaited the trampling that surely would follow. I pictured the man-horses rising high upon their hind legs, brandishing weapons and pummeling me into fodder.

The one who carried me stepped lightly, smoothly for a creature of such size—more graceful, even, than a horse, perhaps because all of that muscle and speed and balance was guided by an intelligence at least equal to that of a human. It was a combination of that natural grace and evidently of knowing the territory, for we moved quickly and impressively toward our destination.

Whatever that destination was. It grows tiresome not knowing your whereabouts.

But maybe whereabouts was the least of my worries. Only minutes after I woke, my captor stopped on a rise in the swamp amidst cedar and juniper and aeterna and other evergreens I could not identify. He stood there, breathing only a little heavily, waiting for someone or something, while I tried to scramble into a more comfortable position.

I shuddered. The light in this clearing was shades of green. And menacing. With all those cedars surrounding us, it smelled like a good place to die. The smell of swamp, the faint smell of sweat, and the stronger smell of horse sank beneath the clean odor of evergreen, like when you put soiled clothes back in a cedar chest so the smell sinks into them, so the clothing doesn't smell like you have to wash it—a boy's trick that usually keeps you from having to bathe as well.

After a brief look around the clearing, my captor seated himself, sliding me down his back and onto the moss-covered ground. The moss was thick and soft; still, the tumble jarred me some, and I lay face-down for a moment, recovering my senses before I scrambled to my feet.

The centaur stood over me in a dodging green light, holding a scythe at least seven feet long and as big around as one of my legs. Escape was out of the question.

"We wait until thy master joins us, little one," the man-horse rumbled. He offered no leverage—no margins for disagreement.

"Are you a centaur?" I asked finally, breath recovered and mud and evergreen needles brushed from my face.

"It is the name used by thy people," the centaur replied distractedly, staring down a wide path of broken branches and underbrush, expecting arrivals, evidently. I followed his eyes briefly and watched the path cover itself. Watched the brush bend back, the standing water settle and calm on the path itself, watched—

The vines grow back? Reeds growing out of the water?

I marked it off to the tricky light in the clearing and the knock I received when I dismounted. Now the centaur was looking straight at me again. Escape was still out of the question.

His eyebrows bristled, dappled brown and white like his back. He was young—only a year or two older than I, if centaurs measured their years as we did. "I thought you were fables," I murmured, and glanced about the rise, looking for passages small and narrow into the swamp and . . . Safety? Among crocodiles and quicksand and diseases?

Maybe I should take my chances with the big spotted fellow before me. After all, anyone who said his *thee*s and *thou*s sounded a little less like a murderer to me. If he was young, he might be stupid and easy to manipulate.

It's a safe rule to go by, and Agion was no exception to it.

For that was his name, though at the time I couldn't have cared less. Once he was sure that we were alone for a while, my new companion became talkative, almost breezy. Quickly I received his life story: he was no celebrity within the centaur ranks, but was young and considered a little slow and awkward by his company. "Indeed, watching over you is the first real duty my elders have given me in this war we're in," he stated proudly.

"War? Wait a minute, Agion. What's this about a war?"

The big creature paused, blushed.

"I might have said too much. My companions will tell thee what thou needst to know, when the time is fitting and proper." He trotted to a corner of the clearing, peered back into the leaves and mud and darkness. Behind him the moss and grass crushed beneath his hooves grew back readily, unnaturally. I couldn't get used to it.

"Agion, you don't dangle statements such as that in front of whoever's listening, then drop the subject entirely. It's just not done outside of a swamp somewhere. Civilized people don't hint when it comes to disaster."

Agion frowned. "I'm sorry I let fall such news, young sir, but that is my nature, I fear. The others tell me that I squeeze things so hard I drop them." Suddenly he brightened. "Though they say I am good-hearted."

Were all centaurs such simpletons? I dearly wished for cards, for seed money. This was another Alfric, without the malice and with two extra legs. I lay back on the grass, which had grown about an inch since I was deposited there.

Despite what Brithelm had said on our seemingly long-ago walks through the courtyard, apparently some of the rumors about this place were true. Something was strange about the vegetation that altered and grew underfoot. I sincerely hoped it was harmless. Meanwhile, I tried the first of my strategies—a simple and direct one, but who could say there would be time for long explanations?

"If you are good-hearted, Agion—and you seem to be—then maybe you should think of this. I don't know anything about any war—where it's taking place or what the sides are, or how not to run into it, even—and here you've dropped this torch on the tinder, as they say. I have been separated from my honorable master—by the way, where is he?—and isn't it kind of your duty to put my troubled thoughts to rest—dismiss the suspense and all?"

Agion walked a few steps down a trail, ducking to avoid the low branches of a pine. He turned about, ducked the branches once more, and returned to the clearing, tracking mud and weeds across the dry ground. Though pulled from their roots, the weeds continued to grow.

"Well? I mean, you're the one who brought the war up, Agion."

"Nor should I have done so, little friend." He squinted down still another pathway into the swamp, as I marveled that he could call me "little friend" after such brief acquaintance, and especially when I would have gladly sold his organs to the goblins for the information he was bent on not giving me. "Now where are they?" he asked impatiently, fidgeting with the enormous, wicked-looking scythe.

"Relax, Agion," I offered. "You look like a painting of Equestrian Death wielding that thing. Sure you have the right clearing?"

"Passing sure," Agion replied. "They said to meet at the second outpost if it had not overgrown since we met here this morning and . . . by the gods, I've betrayed even more secrets to thee!" He slapped his forehead with a blow that would have left me simple-minded. I had to gain his confidence quickly, before the others arrived. I stood up, walked slowly towards him, talking all the way.

"I don't know where we are, what the second outpost is, or why they wanted to meet here in the first place. You've captured a real blank slate here: I know nothing about the war, what it's all about, or what damn side the damn centaurs are on, if you'll excuse my waxing profane and all, but it's dreadfully frustrating to hear all of this talk about a major world event and not have the foggiest idea as to . . ."

"Th'art rattling, little friend," Agion cautioned me, raising his scythe in a gesture I mistook for anger. "I think it might be of use for thee to rest thyself a moment, recover thy breath. I can tell thee nothing until suspicion is lifted from thy countenance." Casually, he sliced branches from the pine tree beside him, so that he could pass under. The branches grew back.

"And what is my countenance guilty of, Agion?"

"Spying, little friend. Had thou been in Solamnic armor, like your friend, we'd have held thee as a prisoner of war—no more. But concealing thy colors is like to spying in wartime.

* * * * *

I stared woefully up at Agion, who looked down on me with not a little sympathy. A lark sang briefly in the bushes to my left, whether "left" was south or north or whatever. Though the rain was lifting, the situation looked glum and soggy.

"Ah . . . pardon me, Agion, but what's the common punishment in these parts for spies?"

"My folk seldom wax dramatic, little friend," the centaur smiled. Then his big face darkened, the spotted eyebrows bunching into one thick line of hair above the bridge of his nose. "For the most part, we drown the poor souls. Take them by their poor little ankles and dangle their poor little faces in pools or in brooks. Facing upstream, of course.

"We suspend them there 'until they pay the full price for their intrigues,' as the elders say."

A pretty grim use of Coastlund's waterways, if you asked me.

"Does that apply to the young ones, too?"

Agion nodded. "As far as I know. Mind, I've never *seen* a spy put to death, young or old."

"Does it apply to those dragged unwillingly into espionage—say, those who really have nothing against centaurs, but become spies when it's a choice between that and death?"

"As I said, little friend, I've never seen the putting to death. Nor have I seen any trial where such things are brought to counsel. Truly, I cannot answer thee."

"Then perhaps you've heard things, Agion. Like what is done with someone who informs in a case such as this. Suppose someone were to reveal a network of spies—from mere lookouts and agents among the peasants who live nearby, on up to the ringleaders, some of whom you may already have taken prisoner? And suppose this very cooperative person does so for the promise that his head will not roll when heads roll, or drench when heads drench, if you understand me?"

"I am sure if thou hast such a promise from the elders, thou art safe from harm," Agion proclaimed seriously. "But if thou were to uncover a network of spies, thou wouldst betray some of thy friends, no doubt?"

He paused, cocked his head, looked at me curiously.

"That is, of course, if the other two are friends of thine."

The other two? Friends? I knelt, pretended to pick up something from the ground—a blade of grass, a rock perhaps. I was pretending not to care, though the curiosity was great and I was stringing out my nets blindly, hoping that somehow Agion would stumble in.

"So you caught us all, then? I mean, all *three* of us?"

The centaur's mouth was off and running before his brain awoke.

"Only the two for the time being. Thee and the Knight thou servest, though he was much more difficult to bring to ground, judging from the fact that my companions are late in joining us here.

"As for the third, he escaped us up the road. He was the one we saw first, but on open plains too near that Solamnic moat house and at such a distance that we could not hope to capture him. So we found the two of thee, hoping that perhaps all three would be together when we overtook the Knight himself—that the lookout thou settest so cunningly a mile at thy rear would betray thy whereabouts in the hurried attempt to warn thee."

Agion gave me a puzzled look. I nodded for him to continue. I was thunderstruck by the news of a third spy, but determined not to show it.

"Else the armor might well have been hidden," he said, "for we had intended to watch thee only, until we heard the Solamnic talk with the militia. Then we had to close with thee, to search thee for what we suspected we would find— and did."

For now I was sure someone was following us.

I remembered the dark recesses of the library, the movement of dark wings.

Who else could the third man of Agion's story have been?

So what if I escaped these four-legged kidnappers? Who knew what other forms of mayhem awaited me?

Had Bayard not entered the clearing at that moment, escorted by half a dozen centaurs, I might have tried to strike a bargain with Agion, offering him money, land, half the moat house to escort me safely back to Father's disfavor and a place of honor in his dungeon—damp and dark and infested with bullies, but safe from scorpions, at least.

Apparently Bayard had not come easily. One of the centaurs nursed an arm in a sling, another a bloodied nose. Nor did Bayard look much better himself—the right side of his face swollen and discolored, his left hand bleeding and clutched in his right, which had little else to do, the centaurs having tied his wrists together. His wrists were burned by the tightness of the ropes.

Without ceremony, the centaurs pitched him to the floor of the clearing, then encircled us both. Lying in a bruised heap on the ground, Bayard smiled ruefully up at me and staggered to his feet.

"It is here and now thou wilt answer for thy conduct, Solamnic," one of the centaurs proclaimed—a burly specimen whose skin was dark and weathered like a cypress tree. His hair was white, also, but unlike Agion's, white with age and if not with wisdom, at least with a certain badlands cleverness. Swamp-smart, you might call him.

Apparently the old fellow was the leader. He looked as though he were accustomed to being answered.

But Bayard had been jostled a little too much, it seemed. There were cracks showing in his courtesy as he rose to his full height and faced the old centaur.

"For my conduct it is easy to answer, sire. It is that of a Solamnic Knight when he and his squire are attacked without warning—and I might add, without reason—by seven folk who are supposed to be allies of the good and the just. That's my answer, sire—quite simple and direct, I grant you, but when your men ambushed me, I assumed we had passed beyond formal introduction."

I believe the old centaur smiled.

"So thou doest admit," the old fellow asked, "thy allegiance to the Solamnic Orders?"

Despite my gestures, my throat-clearing, my elbow in his ribs, Bayard answered as he had before—in all honesty.

"'Admit'? Nay, I proclaim it, sire! For despite what you have heard, the Order still stands for principles noble and true in a time unprincipled. Stop elbowing me, Galen!"

"And the armor?" the old centaur asked, staring me down with his wild green eyes, glittering like emeralds on leather.

"The armor is mine," Bayard maintained, "though stolen from me briefly days ago, and worn by one for whose crimes I cannot answer." He folded his arms across his chest and awaited the centaur's response.

Which was as I had feared.

"Sir Knight, if thy testimony stood against only what I have heard, by my troth I should be inclined to lenience. But there is the matter of the satyrs, and in that matter the testimony of mine eyes is witness against thee, and the eyes of my brothers have also looked upon thy misdeeds."

"Satyrs?"

Bayard looked at me in puzzlement. I shrugged. What did I know from satyrs?

"The satyrs!" the old centaur continued. "The goat-men!"

Several of his traveling companions nodded roughly in agreement, shaking their manes in a most menacing fashion. Bayard paused, then spoke frankly.

"I promise you, sire, that I know nothing of what you call 'satyrs.' Indeed, the very word is new to me. And I promise you that I had never raised my hand against you or your people, until you rode out from hiding a brief while ago upon the road."

The old centaur inclined his enormous, shaggy head, whispered to the bloody-nosed captain at his right, and the two of them galloped off to the far edge of the clearing. Two more joined them shortly—to my relief, neither was the one whose arm Bayard had disjoined in the recent struggle, for I was sure that whatever was to be done to us was soon to be put to a vote. A lively discussion began, but I could hear nothing from where I stood.

I could do nothing from where I stood, either. So I reached into my pocket, sat down, and cast the Calantina. The grass was ankle high by now, and I had to brush it aside to read the dice.

Six on twelve: Sign of the Goat. I consoled myself that the virtue of the goat was that he could survive just about anywhere under just about any circumstances. I hoped that applied to swamps and captivity, because I saw us staying here awhile.

"What do your tea leaves say, Galen?" Bayard whispered, seating himself painfully beside me.

"They say that sometimes the whole truth is a foolish thing to tell, sir," I lied. "But then, you've told me you don't believe the Calantina, anyway."

*   *   *   *   *

The centaurs who were left to guard us seemed more informed than we were. Two of them inspected us from a distance, brandished their clubs, and grinned maliciously. Only Agion remained friendly, and it was fairly obvious nobody was listening to him.

"Don't worry," he encouraged me, as he picked several of the small, glittering nuts from the blue-needled branch of an overhanging aeterna tree and dropped them into his mouth. "Archala never delivers punishment unjustly."

Of course, that did nothing to lighten my worries. Far better that this Archala not deliver punishment at all, for I did not care whether he disciplined justly or unjustly, as long as I escaped intact.

I considered telling Bayard about the third party—the man the centaurs had seen following us a mile or so back down the road. But what would I tell Bayard about who I thought was following us? What would I tell him about the honey-voiced man who scaled the moat house on a mission of burglary?

To be quite honest, I had no real desire to clear my conscience before the centaurs turned me up by my ankles and drowned me for espionage. Sometimes the whole truth *is* a foolish thing to tell. So we sat there in silence, Bayard rubbing his bruises and I thinking frantically of ways to dodge judgement. Any judgement.

But since nobody was moving or scuffling or breaking branches, the sounds of the swamp resumed—the weird songs of unfamiliar birds, now and again the bellow of a bullfrog or the whirring sound of an insect, for these animals had come from hiding when the rain had stopped and the sun had emerged. Around us the air was warmer, but still terribly heavy and humid. Though you could not see the plants growing—not really—you could look away from one and look back in a matter of minutes to find it larger . . . or what you thought was larger.

It gave me the jumps.

I thought of what Gileandos had said about 'Warden Swamp: *something that grows so rapidly grows like a boy;*

therefore it cannot be trusted, pointing to it on the map as it stretched for miles south of the moat house. Of course, stories had come to us through the peasants, stories of animals who had grown to unnatural size or changed unnaturally and roamed the recesses of the swamp. There was talk of legless crocodiles, and huge carnivorous birds, eyeless because they no longer needed eyes in the swamp's green darkness, moving clumsily but swiftly among cedars and among cypress trees by leaps and lunges, their wings useless in a country covered by branches and leaves

There was talk, of course, of the man-eating flying fish.

Now, there may not have been a great deal of truth to such stories, but other things were undoubtedly true. I knew them firsthand. For we had lost peasants, servants, and on occasion a visitor or two in the dark hollows of the swamp. Indeed, a band of visitors—a party of five dwarves from Garnet who came to visit Father the summer I was seven—had reached the far edge of the swamp when they decided to lie down and pass the evening in safety before continuing a journey they figured would be too dangerous in the dark. They awoke the next morning to find themselves surrounded by swamp, which had reached out to cover them in the night.

Two of their party were missing, and though Father combed the outskirts of the swamp that afternoon and again the following morning, combed it with servants and torches and dogs and shouting, we never heard what befell those dwarves, nor anyone else who strayed into the swamp and lost his way.

Such events brought about healthy respect, even a fear, for the green swath Gileandos had marked on the map in his study, the spot he enlarged every spring as the marsh swallowed the countryside.

That night we slept fitfully. Several times I woke to see Bayard pacing at the edge of the clearing and at the edge of the light from our small fire, his hands clasped behind him as though they were tied together. There were no stars visible beneath this canopy of leaves and vines, so the night was dark without and within.

After finally getting to sleep in the early morning, I awoke to see Bayard crouching over me, looking down upon me pensively.

"Sir?"

"Galen, if tomorrow brings some form of . . . severe punishment . . ."

For a second my spirit soared. I hoped devoutly that my companion's innate nobility would compel him to bear the weight of that punishment, no matter how severe, and find a sly loophole by which he might send me unscathed back to Father. However, his nobility compelled him toward other things.

"If that severe punishment does come, I shall rest easily knowing you did not misunderstand something I said."

"Yes, sir?"

"About the Lady Enid." He slowly began to stand.

"About your betrothed, sir?"

"Yes. And that's it. For you see, the Lady Enid isn't really my betrothed."

"No?"

"I mean, I'm not engaged to the Lady Enid or anything."

I had been wakened for this?

"But you said you were 'supposed to marry her.'"

"But not engaged," Bayard emphasized, then turned to face the opposite end of the clearing, where another small fire glowed and where the centaurs still deliberated.

"It's more like destined."

*   *   *   *   *

I was awakened by a rough jostling. I started to shout to the servant, to Alfric, to whoever it was to begone and leave me until a reasonable time—say, well after noon. But I looked up through the dusky green light into the stern and bearded face of a centaur, and remembered my bearings and my manners.

Bayard stood between Agion and the centaur whose arm had been injured in yesterday's struggle. My bearded companion fell in behind us as Agion took me by the shoulder, as the injured centaur took Bayard by the back of his tunic, and as we were half-carried, half-led to the opposite end of the long clearing, where judgement awaited.

Our escorts deposited us at the feet of Archala and the other centaurs with whom he had taken counsel.

The fellow whose nose Bayard had bloodied in the scuffle was a herald of some sort. He scowled at us, wiped the blood from his upper lip, and started to speak.

"All things stand against thee," he proclaimed, in a honking voice transformed, surely, by the sorry state of his nose. I would have found the honking funny, would have laughed, no doubt, had the message been other than that *all things stood against me*.

"The armor, we fear, is terrible, strong evidence," he stated. Then he paused, and you could tell by the look on his face that he was delighted that someone who had altered his nose was liable to search and seizure.

"And yet," the herald continued with what was obviously the bad news for him, "Archala persisteth in the old laws, according to tradition, according to his wisdom. For he saith that thy words arise from an honest heart and countenance unfeigned."

It galled the others to no end, I could tell, that the jury was still out. Except Agion, who watched the proceedings in admiration from a distance.

"Nonetheless," brayed the herald, clearly favoring his nose by now, "nonetheless, the question of the satyrs, of thine alliance with the satyrs, troubles us all."

"No more than it troubles us, Master Archala," Bayard interrupted, looking past the speaker and addressing the old centaur himself. "Especially since, as I said before, we know nothing of these satyrs or goat-men or whatever you call them. Nor why you suspect our alliance with someone we do not know."

"I need not be reminded that thou hast spoken to the issue already, Sir Knight," Archala replied, smiling patiently. "Of course, thou wilt understand why we remain . . . in doubt of such explanations when among the ranks of the satyrs— indeed, in a position of command as we saw it across lines of raised weapons—rode a knight dressed in the very armor thou carried upon thy pack mare when first we met thee on the road."

Bayard started to protest, but Archala raised his enormous hand, signaled for silence, and continued.

"But thine armor was stolen. As thou sayest. It was away from thee briefly. As thou sayest. Within which time, of course, the thief could have taken up with our enemies.

"As thy story would have us believe. Surely, Sir Knight, thou canst see why I refuse to hang the fate of my people on the breezes. Still, our verdict as to thy guilt or innocence awaits the test of seven days and seven nights, during which thou shalt stay with us, under our watchful eyes and guard. Perhaps by then we shall see how thy presence within our midst affects the satyrs."

Well, Archala's judgement pleased no one.

The centaurs stood behind Archala, obviously more than ready to grab us by the ankles and find the nearest source of water. I'd have bet a fortune that Agion would be our guard, as nobody else wanted the job.

Bayard was sure we would be found innocent, for the simple and foolish reason that we were innocent. Naturally, he was furious at the delay, for the tournament at Castle di Caela began in scarcely more than two weeks' time, and any suitor absent from opening ceremonies . . . well, one doesn't stand up a rich man's daughter.

Even so, I admit I was surprised—even though nobody else was—when Bayard offered to mediate between centaur and satyr.

* * * * *

"Mediate?"

Archala blustered at the offer, that wise and tolerant smile gone almost immediately, replaced by one I didn't like nearly as well. "I suppose thou wouldst want to negotiate a peace settlement with them?" he added ironically.

"In fact, sire," Bayard responded, "a peace settlement may not be possible without you. Perhaps I could set the groundwork—a temporary truce, for instance—and then you and your counsel, and the leader of the satyrs and his counsel, might meet in a neutral spot . . ."

"Archala, we have respected the old ways quite long and quite faithfully," the herald interrupted, his nasal voice suddenly brittle and cold. "If thou hast designs . . ."

But Archala raised his knotted hand, and the clearing was once again silent.

"Surely thou art not so foolish," the old centaur began, addressing Bayard, but then stopped, turned slowly away from us, muttering strangely to himself.

Bayard and I glanced at one another in puzzlement. Bayard started to speak, to ask what was troubling Archala, or so I suppose.

But it was at that time that Agion offered to guide us to the camp of the satyrs—as "an emissary of peace," he claimed, adding, too, that he believed Bayard's story.

Archala ceased muttering and stared at the big innocent.

"But that is just what the Solamnic wants, Archala," the herald bleated. "An escort to his own lines and to safety!"

"But what if I'm telling the truth, Archala?" Bayard implored. He had no intention of missing the tournament.

Archala thought about it.

"Leave the boy with us, Solamnic," urged the herald, "as surety of thy good intentions."

"Absolutely not!" Bayard exclaimed. "This is my squire, and as such he belongs with me, not with you as hostage to your fears and mistrust."

The herald snorted and bristled, but Bayard stood his ground. A half-smile spread over his face, and he regarded the huge and menacing creature with an indifference that danced on the edge of contempt.

For a long time nobody spoke. Something shrieked far back in the swamp—a small animal, a bird perhaps—and the pools around the clearing rippled as even smaller creatures sought safety in the waters and the deep mud.

Then, Archala raised his russet arms and nodded at Bayard. The herald sputtered, but an icy glance from the old centaur stilled his clamor.

But for the life of me, I could not find a way out of the proposition as they set me on Agion's back and the two of us rode beside Bayard and Valorous out of the clearing, in search of the satyrs, the light becoming greener and greener around us until even my hands looked like leaves.

Behind us the vines were reclaiming the trail.

CHAPTER 6

Passing through the swamp was like traveling in a glass bottle: the stillness, the closeness, the light filtered green by the leaves overhead. And the strange feeling that the leaves and even the stillness and closeness were somehow transparent—that we were watched from behind them.

For I was sure that we were being followed.

This feeling of uneasiness changed little as we traveled farther into the swamp. I caught myself no longer noticing the sudden hush of animals as we passed by, mainly because the marshes were quiet for miles around us now. It was the first of several bad signs. Wherever we went, it was as though the swamp had been startled by something minutes before we got there.

Early in the journey, the centaur took the lead. Bayard

followed on foot, leading our two remaining horses through the unsure footing of the swamp. That arrangement seemed reasonable to Bayard and to Agion himself, the only one of us who had any idea where we were going. Unfortunately, I was on Agion's back when the decision was made.

I didn't like the idea of being the trailblazer. But given the choice between riding at the front of the party and walking beside Bayard, I chose reluctantly to ride. After all, an ambush could strike any of us, from in front or from behind, but quicksand and crocodiles struck from below, and they would be so busy with the first thing they came to—centaur or horse—that the rider would have a chance to escape.

As we traveled, Agion labored us with stories.

"Some of the elders remember the times before there were marshes here," he began, "but I spent my earliest days gathering herb and root in these very mires. Many's the time I remember gathering figwort and purple medic with my Aunt Megaera, she who always told me, 'Agion, purple medic follows the dove, figwort the pigeon' . . ."

"This is all very fascinating, Agion," I interrupted, looking desperately back at Bayard, whose attention was on the trail in front of him solely.

"Yes, but there's more, Master Galen," the centaur continued. "Aunt Megaera and I once had to fight a nest of bees away from the purple medic when we were making winter poultices and the compresses the older centaurs use for the arthritis. Dozens of bees there were, with the nagging bite of the horsefly and what is always worse with bees, the swelling afterwards. And Aunt Megaera says . . ."

Agion began to chuckle.

"She says . . . Oh! but she was a caution!"

His loud laughter shook the environs. A pack of small marsupials leaped shrieking from a nearby dwarf vallenwood and scurried off into the recessed green darkness. Bayard looked at me uncomfortably, his hand on his sword.

"Agion," he interrupted, softly and urgently. "Remember we're traveling toward hostile ground."

"Right thou art, Sir Bayard," said Agion, not much more softly. "But listen to what Aunt Megaera said, when we

99

came out of the medic patch, our flanks swollen and knotted with bee stings."

Bayard raised his eyebrows, politely attentive. His hand was still on his sword.

"She says . . . Oh! such an oddity she was!" And he began to laugh again. "She says, 'It is a blessing tonight we sleep standing up!'"

By an unspoken agreement, Bayard and I steered him away from further stories about his life before he met us, which we had soon discovered to be not only boring but noisy. Instead, we asked more and more about the satyrs, and found out, to our dismay and irritation, that the centaurs—or at least this particular centaur, who didn't strike me as all that knowledgeable—in fact, knew little more than we did.

"You don't even know where they come from?" Bayard asked, for the first time showing a little impatience like a dent in that righteous spiritual armor. It was about the fifth question in a row to which Agion had no answer.

"It is simply as I told thee, Sir Bayard," the centaur insisted, brushing something small, buzzing, and irritating from the bridge of his nose. "The satyrs have been here awhile—a month or two, I suppose, though even that is difficult to tell for certain.

"When they first arrived, we thought they were legendary creatures. Those from stories of the way things were before the Cataclysm. Thou rememberest the little goat-footed pipers in the story of Paquille?"

Bayard and I looked at one another. Neither of us had any idea.

"Of course, we tried to befriend them," Agion went on. "We thought they were something from the old time, when it is said that the races of Krynn were bound more closely to the land and the animals who dwelt upon it. It made us yearn for things past."

Bayard and Agion traveled awhile in silence, until I grew tired of the suspense.

"Go on, Agion. What happened when you tried to befriend these creatures?"

"As thou canst see, little friend, it was ill-fated," Agion

continued sadly. "At first, the satyrs kept a distance. They snarled. They brandished weapons."

"I would have taken those as not very favorable signs, Agion," I interrupted dryly. Bayard hissed my name, then shot me a scolding look. I sneered at Bayard, then softly, almost sincerely, urged the centaur to continue.

Which he did, after a moment's pouting.

"But we thought they were only being cautious in a new country," he said apologetically. His big tail slapped his rump, swatting at some buzzing thing. Something screamed in the distance to our right, and I nearly jumped from Agion's back, but neither the centaur nor Bayard seemed alarmed. Instead, they seemed almost relieved that something had broken the increasingly heavy silence of the marsh.

For they, too, had noticed the silence.

"As I said, we thought them only cautious," Agion repeated. "At least until they killed two of our folk."

"This is the part of the story I have awaited eagerly," I said. "For I dearly love stories of murder set in the very surroundings I am passing through when those stories are told."

"Dost thou want me to cease the telling? It is passing sorrowful, I grant thee, but also passing strange, and worthy the regard of those who will hear it."

"Then tell the story, Agion," Bayard urged, as we approached a menacing pool of murky water lying in the middle of the road. The water bubbled as Agion and I stepped over it, then calmed to a few narrowing ripples, then bubbled and boiled again as Bayard reined Valorous around it. Then the pool calmed once more as the pack mare, bringing up the rear of our little group, stepped by sure-footedly.

"I was not there when the killings took place," the centaur said, reaching out cautiously with the end of his scythe to touch a vine dangling into the path ahead of us. Assured at last that it was a vine, he sliced it neatly from the branch where it hung, then ducked as he passed beneath the branch. "But I heard the story from Archala himself, who is always truthful of sight, truthful of telling. Here is what he told me.

"Six of us there were: Archala and Brachis and Elemon and Stagro the Younger and Pendraidos and Kallites. Six captains set off at high summer, to the middle of the marshes to deal for peace and friendship with the newcomers, the goat-men."

Though I can stand the occasional tale of murder or war or other arbitrary bloodletting, I hate stories of mysterious death, especially when told to me in a mysterious and desolate place. Agion, on the other hand, told the grisly yarn with delight and with relish. It turns out that a good number of the stories the centaurs choose to remember and tell again end in the mysterious death of most, if not all of the characters. I didn't know at the time, but casualties were light in this one.

"Six of us there were," Agion chanted, "and four stories only that returned to high ground out of the fenlands.

"The first was that of Archala, leader of soldiers, the eldest, who saw them fall, Kallites and Elemon, who saw nought else but the falling, heard nought but the cries. Then saw the Solamnic Knight riding away.

"The second was that of Pendraidos the surgeon, who saw them fall, Kallites and Elemon, who saw no wounds on their bodies, until we were like to believe there had been no wounding, that nought had come to pass but their great hearts giving. He, too, saw the Solamnic Knight riding away.

"The third was that of Stagro the Younger, the archer, who saw them fall, Kallites and Elemon, and yet who saw no enemy, hearing his friends cry out, hearing the cries of the satyrs answer mockingly, hearing one cry above all of them, that one cry raised in a rich and musical and honeyed laughter, while Kallites and Elemon thrashed in pain amid the leveled reeds of the swamp. Then heard he, Stagro the archer, his friends cry out a last time in pain and in mortal wounding. And saw the Solamnic Knight riding away."

Bayard frowned. He inclined his head forward to hear the details. Something about *honeyed laughter* gave me pause. I thought of the Scorpion.

"The fourth was that of Brachis the huntsman, who kept the dogs of Archala, who saw no falling, but . . ."

* * * * *

It happened quickly. Indeed, so quickly I barely had time to panic and take flight.

Valorous snorted, then shied from some bushes at our left, which suddenly began to churn and boil like the pools of water we had passed near the edge of the clearing. It looked as though the bushes were being chewed, shredded by something enormous and invisible.

Agion raised his scythe and turned quickly. Far too quickly, in fact, for his rapid movement threw me from his back, dropping me in weeds and in six inches of standing water.

Bayard had almost tumbled himself, Valorous's great tug at the reins pulling him off the ground. With an oath, he let go of the stallion, who leaped to the side of the trail and stopped, facing the movement in the underbrush. In the process, the rein by which Bayard had kept the pack mare following us snapped cleanly in two when the mare tugged upon it in panic. The pack mare shrieked wildly, kicked out at nothing I could see, then lumbered headlong into the swamp—probably gone for good.

Not that I had time to worry as to the whereabouts of the mare. For battle had been joined, or so it seemed. Bayard and Agion slashed their weapons through the air, through an air that shimmered and danced about their blades like they were trying to cut water. But that was all the enemy I saw, that eccentric shimmer of air. That is, until I scrambled to my feet and back onto the path.

There were four satyrs in the center of the road, locked in deadly combat with my two companions. I blinked rapidly and backed away, still at a loss as to how these things had arisen out of so much swirling air.

Husky fellows the satyrs were, and even uglier than the description "goat-men" would make you imagine. True, they were horned, their lower bodies covered in patchy, filthy hide. True, they had short, ratty tails and were hoofed. True, I could smell them from where I stood. But more than that, their faces were layered with bone and skin, their features resembling not so much those of a goat—who can be a noble-looking animal, even when he isn't all that

pretty—as they resembled the features of giants or hid-
eously deformed men. More to the point, all four of them
were clutching knives and short spears, bearing down on
our party.

It seemed to me we were overmatched.

If a strapping young creature like Agion and a skilled and
seasoned fighter such as Bayard had little chance to defeat
whatever it was that was attacking them, I certainly
couldn't see how they would suddenly triumph when joined
by a skinny, weasel-faced boy carrying a glorified long
knife.

So I crouched at the edge of the trail while my comrades
waded into the enemy. Bayard stepped around the spear-
thrust of the foremost satyr and gave the creature a solid
kick to the backside. The satyr tumbled over into the tall
grass at the side of the path, but not before Bayard's foot
sank—or *seemed* to sink—ankle-deep in its back.

Bayard cried out—not in pain and certainly not in fear,
but in surprise. As he did, a second satyr leaped onto his
back, dagger bared, groping for his throat.

Agion, seeing the mortal struggle, dropped the two satyrs
he was holding overhead, one in each hand. The goat-men
hit somewhere in the rushes, where they bleated, thrashed
about, and then lay still. Then the centaur lunged forward
and plucked the assailant from Bayard's back.

The satyr struggled, shrieking as Agion lifted him high in
the air, shook him like a terrier shakes a rat, then hurled him
a good five yards in the direction his comrades had fallen.
There was a crashing sound and a silence, followed by the
sound of reeds and rushes being trampled under as
something—maybe several somethings—staggered away.

Again the swamp was silent, except for the occasional call
of a bird. The whir of the crickets resumed.

So much for our mission of peace.

My companions relaxed and took stock of the first
assault. Agion dusted his hands dramatically and nodded at
Bayard, who sighed wearily, sheathing the sword he had not
used. He walked toward Valorous, stroked the big stallion's
mane, and whispered something in Old Solamnic.

Only then did he remember.

"The pack mare! She's gone, and she's carrying my armor!"

It was then that the swamp—so quiet for the last hour or so—burst into sound, and I wondered what it was I had despised so in the silence. On all sides of me arose terrible noises—bird calls fashioned in the throats of things that were certainly not birds, but were by no means human. Something in the calls was amused, was taunting, and I thought that I heard my name, though I was so afraid I might well have fashioned it out of nonsensical sound.

I remembered the darkened library, wondered if there were ravens in the chorus.

Bayard glanced around quickly, his thoughts turned to finding the source of the strange clamor. Silently, efficiently, he pointed to Agion, then toward the rushes to the left side of the trail.

The big centaur nodded again, and lumbered off in that direction, soon lost amid the dense greenery.

Now it was my turn. Bayard pointed at me, and motioned off to the right.

"I beg your pardon?" I whispered.

"Oh, Galen, just get off the trail about ten yards or so and take up a position! Guard our flank over there."

"Guard? I'm not sure I heard you correctly. You did say 'guard,' now, didn't you?"

Bayard rolled his eyes and, drawing his sword and hoisting his shield in front of him, started up the trail.

"By Huma's lance! Just . . . call out if you see anything."

Reluctantly I stepped off the trail to my right. Cattails and stray branches slapped across my face, and once or twice I stumbled, tangled by the vegetable kingdom underfoot. My last sight of the trail was that of Bayard rushing toward the noise, crouched low and moving swiftly like some spectacular panther.

I, on the other hand, cut a less predatory figure. Ten feet at most away from the trail, I pushed the reeds aside to stumble upon a tiny clearing, complete with a rotten log and two stagnant pools of water. Again the swamp fell into a curious silence, the calls and cries fading as quickly as they began into the more natural noises of the swamp: now midges whined around my ears, and overhead the deep and mysterious quiet of the sky was broken only by the cry of a raven.

I drew my little sword, figuring that noise or no noise, it might well come down to steel and close quarters, and that perhaps even I would have to join in the production. Better steel and close quarters than captivity.

Time passed—too much time. In the midst of my worrying came a noise nearby—a loud rustling of leaves and underbrush. Quickly I began to dig into the swampy ground, hoping I would have time to bury myself and escape detection. But the ground was too wet; the hole filled with water as rapidly as I dug it, and it was dawning on me that whether they found me guilty of spying or not, the centaurs were about to get me drowned.

Then Bayard came out of the leaves and branches, his right hand clutching a sword, his left urgently signaling for my silence. In a crouch he moved quickly toward me and knelt at my side.

"Where have you been!" I exploded, my whisper rising to full voice and almost to a shout before his gloved hand slapped over my mouth and muffled me.

"You are all right, aren't you?"

"Yes. Well, actually, no. It's this leg of mine, sir. I fear that it's broken or otherwise damaged. If you have a way to escape, I suppose I could brave the pain and follow. Otherwise, the leg's no good—completely useless for rushing a position or most any other kind of attack you have in mind."

"Then you're intact," Bayard whispered. "You must get over your romance with concealment, Galen."

"So I shall, sir, when our enemies get over theirs."

Something whistled, fairly near us but still from the other side of the trail.

"Agion," Bayard explained, nodding in the direction of the sound. "Galen, they're everywhere around us. They know the country here, know how to fight in the swamp. For the life of me, I scarcely saw what hit me when they ambushed us. What's more, we're surely outnumbered, and judging from the noise they're making, outnumbered at impossible odds."

"That lifts my spirits, sir. Perhaps we should regroup? I could ride Agion back to the centaur lines. My leg would bother me less upon horseback. The odds will not change in our favor if we stay here."

"Retreat is simply not an option," Bayard said doggedly, leaning his forehead against the oak, closing his eyes.

"Then what are we to do?"

Bayard opened his eyes, frowned at me, then rose to a crouch.

Again something whistled from the opposite side of the trail—this time more loudly, more urgently.

"Something's brewing over there," Bayard concluded. "No doubt Agion has spotted them."

He rose to leave, and I to follow, but he turned and motioned me back to the spot where he had found me.

"Things are about to be nasty."

He glanced briefly, humorously at my sword.

"I suspect you're not . . . accomplished with weaponry. But you can shout a warning if a warning is needed.

"So watch this ground in case they come in behind us."

With those encouraging words he was off, slipping quietly into the green tangle behind me, and I set myself to the job of staying put.

* * * * *

Which is not the easiest of jobs, considering you are tempted to do anything but wait. The day moved on into late afternoon, and for a while the sounds seemed close. Within the calls back and forth, within the braying, the bleats, the occasional whistles and shrieks, I could hear traces of words, but never enough to make out even a sentence, a statement. It was as though what the satyrs were saying was made of marsh fire, always a step or two beyond earshot.

I sat for what must have been an hour, swatting insects and dreading everything imaginable and some things beyond imagining. The noises rose and faded, rose and faded, until finally the swamp lay quiet. I began to wonder just where Bayard was—why I had heard nothing from him. I was tempted to stand and break cover, then thought better of it. I knew how a turtle must feel in his shell, playing the complex guessing game of when it was safe enough to expose your neck.

Then something shrieked, harsh and terrible, somewhere far off to my right. It was as if a raven's wing had brushed by my face, bringing the cold scent of night and death.

This was no place to be when the darkness came. I rose to my feet and began to walk, wandered in a nightmarish circle for what must have been the longest few minutes of my life, then crashed out of the undergrowth onto the path, which I knelt and kissed in an ecstasy of relief.

I began to walk in the direction Bayard had gone—or the direction I thought Bayard had gone. Slowly, more familiar sounds resumed as the green of the leaves darkened and blurred with approaching dusk. Somewhere behind me a brace of frogs called one to another; an owl awakened. Eventually, the swamp became loud, almost lively. I was tempted to seek cover, to leave the trail for good. To shelter myself while there was still enough light to take shelter by.

But as I deliberated, as I looked as far as I could into the swamp at my right, all the sound stopped off to my left. I picked up my sword again, watched as the reeds and ever-greens parted in that direction, and waited for them to bub-ble and spin and boil as they had right before the ambush. I was relieved when they did not.

Agion thought there were three of us. Someone else had crossed into this mire.

I thought of the Scorpion and of how this place was quiet and out of the way.

Or perhaps Archala had changed his mind. Perhaps we were confirmed spies now. Perhaps we were already sen-tenced.

Indeed, of all those I suspected or expected, the last was Brithelm.

But it was Brithelm, indeed, my elder brother who sat in the air above a mattress, eyes closed and dog whistle clutched tightly in his hand. His face lit up as he saw me and he shouted "Galen!" so it could be heard throughout the swamp, even back at the moat house, perhaps, reaching the ears of the satyrs who were not far away, no doubt seeking my whereabouts while slowly, lovingly sharpening their weapons.

Brithelm walked toward me, unaware of satyrs and of ambush, unaware of even darker dangers and of the sad fate that befell Kallites and Elemon. From across the pathway, from somewhere safe under cover, I heard Bayard (who was pathetically nearby, as it turned out) shout, "Stay down!" And hearing the shout, Brithelm brightened even more.

"My little brother. Happy in the service of Sir Bayard of Vingaard. Allow me first to greet the Knight, as is only proper and customary. Then we shall have a brotherly talk."

With that, Brithelm was past me, striding quickly across the path, Sir Bayard and Agion shouting at him from somewhere in front of him and I shouting from behind him. But he didn't listen to a thing we shouted, intent as he was on greeting the Knight "as is only proper and customary." I started to run after him and grab him but, hearing movement in the underbrush to my right, thought better of it and slid quickly off the path.

Thinking better of it and sliding probably saved my life.

Two satyrs, armed with small but wicked-looking hatchets, leaped out of the underbrush and bore down upon Brithelm.

Who had not seen them. Who was still walking casually down the path.

I was paralyzed, as though I were watching one of those huge, hypnotic snakes brimming with poison, which the men of Neraka mail in baskets to one another during times of political upheaval. I saw movement across from me; saw Bayard for a second as he began to rise, to go to my brother's rescue; saw a strong arm—probably Agion's—drag him back.

Saw Brithelm *pass through* the satyrs unharmed. Saw the weapons wave ineffectively through the air. Saw the satyrs blend back into hiding so quickly that it seemed they had vanished from the spot.

Brithelm had noticed nothing.

He continued walking casually down the path, then turned, parted the reeds with his arms, and shook hands with a thunderstruck Bayard, then with an equally thunderstruck

Agion. Then Bayard stepped into the clearing, the centaur behind him, neither of them taking his eyes off my brother.

Since the satyrs had temporarily dispersed, I came out, too.

We stood around Brithelm, agape. Brithelm looked from one of us to the next, smiling, nodding—you almost hated to break the news to him that he had been assaulted.

I finally broke the silence, addressing my commander, the supposed brains of this rapidly unraveling operation.

"You figure this one, sir."

"First, we should get back off the path," Bayard insisted. "The satyrs may return at any moment."

"If they do, we can always hide behind Brithelm," I offered.

Bayard shot me an annoyed glance as he led us back to where he and Agion had been hiding—a little clearing made larger because it is hard for tall grass and reed to stand up to the weight of a centaur. Already, though, the foliage was righting itself and even growing again, and we stood chest high in the rushes—well, flank high for Agion and waist high for the other two men. Agion cleared the place of reed and vine, swinging the scythe he had recovered where it lay in the road, untouched by satyr hand.

It reassured me, somehow, that Brithelm's account of how and why he was here was familiar, even soothing.

My brother was every bit as harebrained as ever.

It seems that Brithelm had wakened from a trance on the morning I left, and found me gone. That much, he admitted, he had expected—that his younger brother would be gone, off on his "knightly calling," as Brithelm put it so generously. Bayard was generous not to laugh.

"But I also awoke to the unexpected, little brother, more unexpected than you could even imagine or dream. For accustomed as I am to receiving signs and visions, never have I received one so . . . manifest, so tangible as this."

Brithelm fumbled in the pockets of his robe and brought out the dog whistle.

"It is a dog whistle, Galen," he explained serenely, "used for . . ."

"For calling dogs. Really, Brithelm, I know what the thing

is and how it got there."

"As do I, my brother, as do I," Brithelm exclaimed blissfully. "It is a sign from Huma. A sign from Huma that urged me to come to the hermitage."

Bayard smiled broadly and nodded encouragingly to my poor addled brother.

"For you see," Brithelm went on serenely, "I had been meditating on whether to return to this hermitage after the bees drove me out."

I remembered when that happened. My brother was all welts for weeks. Agion nodded in sympathy.

"Did you learn to sleep standing up?" he asked my mystical brother, who smiled and nodded, though I do not see how he could possibly understand what Agion had said to him.

"This whistle is the sign," Brithelm continued. "I shall call to the animals, to the things of Nature, and they shall answer, shall come to me. Shall commune."

There was a sound on the path, rising from the center of the swamp and coming slowly in our direction—the sound of reeds rustling, of splashing. I could guess that Brithelm had been bumbling delightedly in our direction for hours, blowing that whistle, alerting the entire swamp to the whereabouts of one fool at least. There was some chance that the oppressive silence we had been traveling through was the whistle's doing. There was an even greater chance that now, with Brithelm in our midst, we were much more likely to commune with satyrs.

Bayard signaled for quiet, so at the moment I had no chance to tell Brithelm that the whistle had come from my pocket instead of from Huma's Breast, somewhere beyond the stars.

Not that it would have made any difference.

* * * * *

But we were speaking of satyrs. There were four of them crouching on the trail, each clutching a toothed scimitar. I could not imagine a more nasty-looking weapon.

Agion, crouched painfully low for a thing his size, peered through the bushes at the creatures, then turned to Bayard and whispered—much too loudly, I thought—"I think we can take four of them, Sir Bayard, even if the holy man carries no weapon and does not fight."

"Fighting isn't the point, Agion," Bayard hissed. "At least not until we try to make the peace I promised Archala. The point is how to manage this so that the satyrs don't attack out of sheer preference when they see us, so that we don't have to fight them to get things calmed down enough to talk."

"Why don't you show them your armor, sir?" I whispered, tugging at Bayard's sleeve. "You can tell them you're just a knight and leave out the Solamnic part, and maybe they will escort us."

"That would be just fine except for two things, Galen. One, the armor is probably still galloping through the swamp somewhere, on the back of our pack mare."

I had forgotten that.

"Two, even if we do not have the armor beside us, I could not advance a lie, which is what you're suggesting. The armor is Solamnic, forged in Huma's name. I would dishonor it by resorting to falsehood, for every falsehood discredits the Order."

"But, Sir Bayard . . ." I began.

"Fighting is not the point at all," Brithelm interrupted. "Nor is imposture," he pronounced in a loud and joyous voice. "For you are mistaken. These are innocent creatures, full of trust and altogether harmless." He stood and walked toward the satyrs, his arms extended.

The rest of us hurried to our feet. Agion and Bayard followed my generous brother, scythe and sword at the ready. I started to follow, reluctantly drawing my own little sword.

It was then I felt it, that icy grip in my blood that held my feet in place, that sucked me down like the quagmires of the swamp will entrap the unwary traveler who steps into them.

Upon my shoulder I felt the prickling of talons. I felt the soft brush of feathers, smelled flesh and loam and the distant scent of decay and heard the voice again, unchanged from the night in the library.

"Follow me, little one," it whispered. "The first payment of your debt has come due." The wings fluttered at my ear, the weight on my shoulder was lifted.

All of a sudden, there seemed no choice. As I was bidden, I turned from the trail straight into knee-deep waters that slowed my retreat from the negotiations or impostures behind me, following the fitful path of the raven through the branches ahead of me.

* * * * *

Now there were only false trails and hidden places among the leaves. Those, and mud, and night approaching. And crocodiles, of course.

Now the bird had vanished. Diving through a tangle of broad-leafed plants, it had not emerged, evidently, and search though I might, I was left alone at this juncture. The light in the swamp was all but gone.

I sat down upon a cypress tree in yet another large clearing—a clearing that branched into a dozen trails like it was the hub of an enormous wheel. I had no idea how far I had traveled, but I was sure to be out of earshot of my companions.

And within earshot of other things.

I took stock.

Perhaps I should try to go back. Perhaps my companions would believe that I had been protecting them from possible ambush by scouting the rear. At great personal risk, I might add.

Brithelm would buy it. After all, he believed that Huma was in the business of dispensing dog whistles.

For my other two companions I could not speak, except to be sure that Agion would be easier to convince than Bayard, since the centaur was slow-witted to begin with.

But Bayard was another matter.

Perhaps I could cut myself. Only slightly, mind you, but enough to exhibit. Then perhaps I could invent a terrible knife fight with a satyr—no, two satyrs, I'd say—bent on circling around us for another ambush. Two small satyrs, since Bayard would be listening. Yes, it just might work.

Unless the satyrs had defeated them. Then I would be walking into the hands of the enemy. That would demand an altogether new set of lies.

Then, of course, there was the raven, which had conveniently dropped out of sight. Was I free to go, even if I could make up my mind? Would I be allowed to escape the summons of the Scorpion?

The cries of birds and reptiles around me seemed more hostile now, and branches and tree limbs leaned even farther over the dozens of paths that ended in nowhere or, even worse, ended in danger. What's more, I was steering only by moonlight now and could see scarcely ten feet in front of me.

I started down one trail, which narrowed into nothing scarcely a dozen yards from the clearing where I had picked it up. The next one I tried ended in a wide pool of bubbling and boiling mud like those we had seen only hours ago when we set off toward the satyr camp.

So I returned to the clearing, seated myself once more on the cypress tree, tried to calm myself and push down my rising voice of panic.

Lost. Lost. Spiralling down into the quicksand. Eaten by crocodiles. Snake bitten and poisoned, crawling down a trail to nowhere.

All of a sudden, the clearing grew quiet. To my left a covey of quail took wing, flying overhead in one of those brief, scrambling flights they make in the face of danger. I followed them with my eyes, watched them settle on the other side of the clearing.

When they were lost to sight, when I turned my eyes and thoughts back to the clearing in which I was sitting, he was only a few strides away.

It took a second more to make him out in the darkness. I was startled anyway. I gasped, fell backwards off the cypress tree, and managed only one word before I hit the ground, before I landed on my back, helpless as a capsized turtle. Before the familiar strong hands began to throttle me.

"Alfric!" I shouted, as he pounced.

CHAPTER 7

Alfric's grip tightened on my throat. He scrambled, trying to get footing on the wet ground, then suddenly was kneeling above me, pinning my arms beneath his knees, grinding them painfully into the mud. For a man whose highest ambition was Solamnic Knighthood, he was awfully skilled at dirty fighting.

Struggle as I did against my brother's strength and weight, the only thing I could raise from the ground was mud. My arms hurt under something edged and metal; Alfric was wearing Father's armor, of all things. It made you feel as though you were being assaulted by your entire family tree.

"This time we'll do things right, Weasel," my brother whispered hatefully. In the dark I couldn't see what he was about to do, but I was sure that it wouldn't seem all that *right* to me.

"None of your talking. None of your wheeling or dealing or bargaining. Not this time. You left me back in the moat house. Left me there so's you could go parading off in glory around the countryside as a squire—the squire I would of been, had politics and brothers not kept me from it."

I heard the sound of a knife being drawn from its sheath. Alfric was ready to clean what he had trapped, evidently.

"I beg you, Big Brother, to reconsider what you're doing here."

"I'm not listening to you. Remember, I said no talking."

I felt the edge of a blade at my throat.

"Look, while we are struggling here in this swamp . . ."

"Oh, I don't see us struggling all that much, Galen. The way I see it, you're pinned down, waiting for something you can't escape."

I could see him grin in the dark.

"You see, little brother, I been watching this swamp ever since I got here. It sure grows quickly, don't it? Why, it may well be years before anyone finds your bones, and by that time they won't know who you are. Even if they do, who's going to suspect me?

"I'll probably be head Pathwarden by the time your leavings surface up. I'll own the moat house and all lands pertaining. Nobody rich ever murders.

"I'll be just as sorry as I can about the remains of my long lost brother who disappeared many years past when he followed Sir Bayard Brightblade of Vingaard, trying to become the squire he really didn't have it in him to become.

"Do you like my story so far, Weasel?"

Hardly. At best, it promised to be a long gloat.

Still, I didn't want to rush him towards the conclusion he had in mind. So I stayed silent, yielding, but above all listening. Far more than whatever foolishness my brother had to say, I was interested in the sound of someone—anyone—approaching.

I had guessed by now that the man the centaurs had seen following us was not Brithelm, but Alfric. But it no longer made any difference.

After all those years of throttling me, of strangling me until I almost blacked out and he remembered that Father frowned on fratricide, Alfric was out of the moat house, far from the long arm of the old man's discipline. He seemed prepared to go through with it.

I saw his knife glint in the moonlight.

"Alfric."

"Shut up, Weasel. I will do whatever I please from this point on. And whatever I please is . . . to become squire to Sir Bayard Brightblade of Vingaard, Knight of Solamnia."

"Oh, that can be arranged, Brother," I exclaimed, bargaining frantically for anything that would stop the blade from menacing my throat, listening desperately for any approaching footsteps, any hoof beats, any reason to cry out. "You can take my place polishing his armor at the tournament."

"Tournament?" The pressure of the knife blade slackened. "What tournament?"

"Indeed. At Castle di Caela, over in southern Solamnia. All the bullies and thugs will be there, vying for the hand of Enid di Caela and the deed to her father's holdings. It's a place to make connections, I assure you. In fact, I'll help arrange your squirehood. I'd be more than delighted to . . ."

"You'll do nothing of the sort, Galen. You see, Sir Bayard's going to be short a squire when his pet weasel submerges somewhere in this swamp. That makes me an obvious candidate for the vacancy. I won't need introductions or letters of reference from you. I'll be all that's left.

"From there, it's but a little maneuvering and some tournament folderol and, who knows, in the end perhaps they will consider me for the hand of this Lady Enid di Caela. I can sit a horse as well as the next man. I can handle a lance."

"But, Brother," I improvised, the edge of the blade now tight once again on my gullet, as my brother followed phantasms of glory. "Let's start with your first obstacle before we make you head di Caela and all. Surely you realize that you're going to arouse some suspicion, crawling out from under some rock the instant the job of Bayard's squire is open."

"So we do it my way. And here is the way I have it figured," he proclaimed, lifting the knife. I took a deep breath, pretended to listen respectfully as Alfric gleefully, almost rapturously, explained his foolish plan.

He paused for a long time. I could almost hear him figuring the angles, hear those rusty wheels turning in the great gap of his head.

"Here it is," he began tentatively. "I shall tell Bayard that . . . Father . . . found some evidence that you, not me, was the negligent one."

"And that evidence was?" It was uncomfortable, lying here draped over the heavy arm of my brother.

Again a long pause.

"Well?"

"Shut up, Weasel. I'm contriving."

"Something about . . . " he drawled, then shook me with excitement until my head ached. "Something about your naming ring! That was what sprung you in the first place, Bayard finding it on his mantle, of all the dumb Weasel luck!"

"What about the ring?"

Another long pause, during which the knife withdrew. Then my brother lifted me, setting me down roughly on the cypress tree, and turned me to face him.

"Uh . . . what do *you* figure, Galen?"

I figured he was mine now.

"Oh, that's easy," I began, scrambling for a reasonable story. "How about . . . that Father looked more closely at the rings . . . and discovered that the man in black had the real naming ring, and that the one Bayard found was a forgery, planted to make him do precisely what he did do, which was pass over you and take on your 'wronged' younger brother as a squire. Then Father sent you with the news to Sir Bayard so he could set the whole squire business straight at once."

Alfric nodded joyously and eagerly. He was the only one stupid enough to believe a story so close to the actual truth.

"You know, I just think Sir Bayard will believe that one," he said, hopping up and down until he tottered in the heavy armor.

I nodded innocently in agreement.

"Oh, by the way, Galen. The man in black? Well, he's dead."

"Dead?" The news gave me a shudder.

"It was the strangest thing, Father says. An hour after you leave, he sends the guards down with food for the culprit and finds him dead. The door is still locked and the bars on the windows was intact—so nobody got in to do him in. He was wrapped in his black cloak, and the smell, the guards said, was just horrible.

"What's most peculiar about this, Galen, is Father says the body was all decrepit and mummified, as if the prisoner was a good year or more dead."

"But . . ." Double shudder.

Alfric nodded.

Suddenly I didn't want to be still in any spot, especially in this raven-infested swamp. I moved toward one of the trails that branched from the clearing—any trail. I was no longer particular. But Alfric stepped in front of me.

"Just where do you think you're going?" demanded Alfric, gripping his knife threateningly.

"Why, to find Sir Bayard," I said, as convincingly as I could, "and confess."

"How're we going to find Sir Bayard?" he asked suspiciously.

"Follow me. I know where he is," I lied.

I had not taken two steps when Alfric's hand came crashing down upon my shoulder, holding me in place.

"Don't try to go nowhere without me, Weasel," he muttered ominously. It was back to the old brotherly ties.

So we began to walk in a random direction, Alfric's left hand resting heavily on my shoulder, his right at his belt, on the handle of the sheathed knife. Or at least that's where I suppose his right hand was. By now, it was really too dark to tell.

We walked slowly, in silence at first, *away* from Bayard, of course, or so I hoped. Far ahead of us, the swamp was alive with insects, with the bellowing of bull frogs, with the sound of awakening owls. Around us it was constantly quiet, except for occasional splashing or cries of alarm or fluttering of wings—sounds that were always moving away from us. Yet if we were making enough noise to silence or scare off the smaller animals, we were making enough to draw the larger ones.

If a larger animal drew near, it wouldn't hurt for me to be more quiet—and for Alfric to be louder. All the better to focus the attention of that larger animal.

"How did you do it?" I began, not whispering but keeping my voice low.

"Do what?" my brother asked, his voice like a foghorn in the darkness of the swamp. Something directly ahead of me skittered away in panic, leaving behind it a trail of shrill noises.

Good. My brother was loud.

Bring on the carnivores.

"Why, how did you escape, Alfric? It's no mean trick to slip out of the moat house under Father's attentions. I'd like to know how you managed it."

"Only an hour or so after you left," Alfric began his story serenely, his large hand digging uncomfortably into my shoulder, "I take stock of the situation and realize that it is time to call in a few debts owed me. For you see, little brother, you are not the only one who has debts to collect."

He laughed, laughed with what the old stories call *a rising hysterical laughter*. Believe me, it is as disturbing as it sounds, especially when you are alone in a swamp with someone who is doing it. Again I was sure I was about to be portioned. I kept walking, carefully testing the ground in front of me.

Then Alfric's laughter faded, as suddenly and as disturbingly as it began. He said nothing more for a while. We walked farther, the only sounds around us the shrill winding noise of the crickets, which grew slower and slower as the damp night air grew colder.

"It was scarcely an hour after you left that I just walked over the drawbridge and out across the grounds. You see, Father was feeling a mite sorry for me on account of losing my squirehood and all, so he wasn't as watchful as he usually is. So I was off after you almost before you was out of sight, following the tracks of the horses until I noticed them tracks was crossed by the tracks of others . . ."

"Centaurs," I interrupted, and received a box on my ears for the information.

"I know that, Weasel! How come you think I stayed so far behind you when old Molasses dropped over? I could of caught up then, but I wanted to catch you alone and I couldn't be sure what was going to happen.

"So when they took you off to that clearing and judged you I was not that far behind, and when you was ambushed and my saintly middle brother came through to save the day and complicate things, I was where I could see that, too.

"Oh, yes, I been watching all along," he said ominously, and pushed me from behind.

But at the moment I wasn't moving.

"Alfric, there is something in front of us that might be dangerous."

I stopped completely. Alfric did not. The heavy breastplate jarred against the back of my head. The metal on the breastplate rang. So did my ears.

"What is it?"

"I hear something moving up there. Something bubbling, the gods help us!"

"Go on, Galen."

"No, it's true."

"I mean, go on!" And he pushed me in the direction of the noise. I paused uncertainly, took one step, then took it back.

My loving brother pushed again. Toward quicksand, lava, a pit of adders—it was all the same to him.

"You heard me. Go on. Don't worry. I'll protect you. At least until we find Bayard."

It was scarcely reassuring, like being one of those legendary sparrows the dwarves take down with them into the mines. When the bird drops dead in its cage, the dwarves know that the air in their tunnel is too thin, too unhealthy, and beat a quick exit.

I stood fast, resisting the push of the armor behind me, until the push of the breastplate was joined by the push of a knife blade.

"Very well, Alfric. I'm moving. I'm going forth into uncertainty and very possibly death. You are responsible for this, of course. For whatever happens to me."

My brother chuckled in the dark behind me.

"Well, Galen," he drawled, "I expect I can live with that."

*　*　*　*　*

I expect it was a quagmire—a pool very much like the ones we had passed over and around in the daylight, more dangerous in the darkness simply because you could not see where it began, where it left off. The first step into it was enough to confirm my fears: the bubbling sound, the feel of something sucking and dragging at the bottom of my boots. It was dangerous—could take you under to the ankles, to the waist, take you under entirely, depending on how deep it was.

Quickly I ducked, slipped my shoulder out from under Alfric's hand, and rushed across the mud, trusting that it was only a larger version of what I had seen before.

So it was. Only larger than I had figured. After a while of running, I felt myself sinking. Frantically I tried to recall what I knew about quagmires.

Do not move. Movement gets you in deeper trouble.

Hold still, completely still, and wait for help.

Help from a dim-witted oaf wearing a hundred pounds of armor?

My legs churned even more quickly. I windmilled my arms, hoping devoutly that I could outrun the present terrain.

Twice I sank to my knees, once to mid-thigh, but each time I managed to scramble out of where I had been mired. All the while Alfric called behind me—his voice not quite clear above the bubbling noises of the pool—shouting names, commands, threats.

It would make for a good story to say that my feet found dry and solid ground just as I was about to give up. But it was long after giving up, I suppose, that I discovered I was no longer sinking—that knee-deep in mud I had found a bottom to the quagmire. My body had kept moving out of reflex, out of sheer panic, even after my spirit had failed completely.

It had failed embarrassingly. By that time I was shouting for help from anyone—Bayard, Agion, Brithelm, the satyrs, the Scorpion, Alfric, and whoever else might be within earshot. I prayed to the gods, then bargained with them, promising to spend the rest of my life in an obscure priesthood, after having surrendered all my possessions to one of the temples of Paladine in Solamnia. My next thoughts had been scarcely as profound, as I peeled the bark from the nearby cedars, with language that would have made stable hands blush. I had tried weeping, blubbering, even *rising hysterical laughter.*

I am grateful for whatever prayers or promises or cries or curses got me to the other side of the quagmire. For I do not know how I covered the last few yards to safety except that it involved pulling myself out by a long, thin vine that lay atop the pool, a vine I had entangled around my waist, my shoulders and neck, until I had stood a great chance of being hanged by my own lifeline.

Whatever happened, I lay on solid ground at last, wrapped almost completely in leaves like some sort of elf dinner, gasping for air and listening, as the rest of my senses recovered from the strains and the shocks, to the sound of something behind me in the dark—a noise rising above the churning sounds of the pool I had just passed over and through.

The sound of cries for help. Which were pretty familiar by now. But this time they weren't mine.

Alfric's cries—pitiful, yes, but music to my ears.

"Galen, are you out there? Galen? Help me!"

I sat on the wonderfully dry earth and disentangled the wonderfully strong vine from around my elbow.

"Help me! I know you're there! Father's armor is heavy, and I'm going down!"

Quickly, I fashioned the vine into a lasso.

"Galen, for the sake of Paladine and Majere and Mishakal and Branchala . . ."

His voice trailed off. Alfric had always been poor at theology; he had run out of gods, evidently.

"What do you expect me to do?" I shouted out across the quagmire.

"Throw something out on this mud or quicksand or whatever it is, something I can grab onto and pull myself out."

"Alfric?"

"What, Galen? Hurry up! I've stopped sinking for now, but I'm up to my waist in soil!"

"What's in this for me, Big Brother?"

Silence across the quagmire.

"But, of course," I continued, "there is brotherly affection, which I so deeply cherish . . ."

"Stop toying with me, you damn Weasel, and cast out a life line!"

"A little more . . . respect out there, Alfric! All right. There's a vine set to come in your direction. Now, I don't know if I can throw vegetation that far, or if it's long enough to reach you, or even if you can see it in the dark, but I'd say that once I cast it out there, your odds will leap from nothing at all to just this side of slim."

I cast the vine in the direction of the voice.

"Be of good faith, Brother. Things grow quickly in this swamp, as you said yourself. If the vine doesn't reach you, maybe it will grow in your direction.

"And if that fails, surely you've found the bottom of the quagmire. Just stand there until someone comes along."

I turned, walked off into the darkness, unsure of my direction, but filled with a deep and satisfying sense of poetic justice.

* * * * *

The things Alfric called behind me I should not repeat. I suppose that I deserved the new names he was inventing. After all, I relied on trust—and on trust only—that he'd eventually be able to wade his way out of the fen in which I had left him. If it turned out that he was a little worse off than I had foreseen, that Father's armor was a little heavier than I had thought . . . well, it calmed me to realize that if the vine and the darkness failed Alfric, if it turned out I deserved worse than simple name calling, my punishment wasn't likely to arrive soon. At least not by his hands. I walked confidently off into the darkness, away from the sound of Brother's curses and shouts and, finally, his screams.

Darkness, though, does all kinds of terrible things to confidence. It was the kind of night with nothing to offer the traveler, the kind you should sleep through or wait out. Around me, Alfric's shouts and curses faded, to be replaced by other noises less certain, more threatening: the sounds of quick scuffling and quicker movement; of things I could not see splashing and swimming in waters I could not see; the sound of those waters themselves moving; and the occasional, threatening laughter of some marsh bird. I was good and lost.

After about an hour, the trail I had been following dwindled into nothing but a snakelike crease through the reeds. I stopped on the rapidly narrowing path, wondered at what kind of creature had made the trail in the first place, and then, faced with no other choice, continued in the same direction, though soon entirely without direction or even the sense that someone or something had been here before me.

Remembering a fragment of the advice Father had hurled at me when we left the moat house, I crouched and checked the bole of a cypress tree. Moss grew on all sides. North, it seemed, was everywhere.

A snorting sound brought me to my feet, clutching my sword and expecting mayhem. I gripped the trunk of the cypress, eager to get behind it if I could figure out where "behind" was—where the sound had come from in the first place.

A louder snort followed, and a strange stirring that seemed to come from somewhere off to my left and below me. Cautiously I moved to my left, prepared for centaurs or satyrs or the legendary carnivorous birds that were supposed to infest this swamp. Down on my hands and knees I went, crawling toward the source of the noise.

But not slowly enough, evidently. I had not crawled ten feet before the ground in front of me gave way under my hands. For a moment I stood over a yawning incline of mud and flattened reed, looking below me into a clearing darker still, where something large and indefinite glistened as it moved.

Just when it dawned on me that I did not want to go down there, I had no choice, sliding rapidly face first over the mud and the slick, leafy surface down into a puddled depression.

Where something monstrous splashed and snorted.

I lay still for a moment, having heard the old story that predators will not harm you if they think you're dead. I hoped devoutly that the predator would think that my fall had killed me.

For a long minute I lay still, hearing nothing but the breathing and slow movement of a large creature. Then I felt warm breathing on my neck, and a wet snuffling that was anything but predatory. It was like a dog or a calf . . .

Or a horse.

I turned onto my back quickly, and stared into the wide-eyed face of the pack mare.

* * * * *

We had been traveling for some time, wrestling and kicking at one another, as I tried to steer the stubborn pack mare through the dense undergrowth and she, burdened by my weight and that of the armor, struggled to leave one of us behind on the soggy ground of the swamp. I was clinging for dear life when the darkness finally began to break ahead of us. It was nothing like morning, which was still hours away. Nor was the green light in the trees anything like sunlight filtered through leaves and through the needles of evergreens—that fresh color I was to remember fondly in the darker times up the road. Instead, this green was a timid and unhealthy one, fading to a yellow or an off-white I had never seen in nature, unless it was the color of a snake's belly.

The color was that of phosfire. I can tell you that now, though at the time I had never seen the lights in the wilds.

Phosfire was what the elves call "midnight blaze," the burning gases that rise from the scraps and remains of the dead things a swamp consumes. Phosfire gives off heat only when it has been condensed, when it drips from the tubing of the still (like the one in Gileandos's library, which of course he seldom used to distill phosfire, but which could be used in any way an enterprising student cared to use it, as his incandescent farewell from the battlements had proven).

As a liquid, phosfire is highly flammable, burning within

minutes after contact with air. As a gas, it is only a harmless source of light, not unlike the luminescent powder found in a firefly's abdomen, though it does become more thick, does look more bright and fevered, the closer you travel to the center of a swamp and the center of all the death it has swallowed through the years.

At the time, I was encouraged by the light, as was the mare, and we both followed it eagerly. I urged my mount on, sure that the light had a source somewhere on drier, safer ground—a dwelling, perhaps, or the campfires of a surviving Bayard, Brithelm, and Agion.

Of course, I did not notice (or refused to notice) that the green light gave off no warmth, moved nervously ahead of me, and illuminated nothing but itself. It was only when the phosfire gave way to firelight, when the green faded into the friendlier glow of reds and of yellows, when the smell of woodsmoke greeted me, and finally the warmth of actual campfires, that I began to recognize that the light which had led me farther and farther into the swamp had been something unpleasant and lifeless.

I dismounted and led the mare into concealment behind a small cluster of laryx bushes. I surveyed.

Below me now, probably at the lowest point of the swamp, lay a small rise, as though having bottomed out, the swamp intended to take heart and return to sea level. Lowlands these were indeed, but surprisingly dry from the looks of it; dry enough to support what appeared to be a circle of smudges, small campfires designed to provide light and warmth and also drive away the last insects of the season. Piles of unlit kindling lay strewn from one fire to the next, completing the sense that whatever lay within the band of flames was protected and encircled.

But within that circle of fires stood only a rickety cabin on stilts, its near wall nursing a large hole near the back corner, its roof nearly ruinous, smoke rising through its many holes. Indeed, at first I assumed the cabin was on fire. Such was not the case; perhaps the chimney suffered from a damaged flue. Whoever lived there was most unfortunate, dwelling in misery beneath the constant layers of smoke.

About the house I saw a herd of goats—at most a dozen,

including the kids—trotting about within that circle of fire and wood, as though somehow the fire contained them, kept them from wandering off.

It looked as though the goats were right at home in those ramshackle surroundings. They were a long-haired breed, the kind you would expect in the highlands or the mountains, but here in the marshes their long hair was streaked and clotted with mud, with vines and lichen dripping from their beards and horns. They were almost frightening to look at.

There was fire nearby, and a promised warmth. The pack mare snorted with yearning. My boots were soaked through, my trousers muddy and wet well above the knees, and despite the cold discomfort I felt, the insects still seemed to relish me.

I stepped out from the undergrowth behind which I had been hiding, and moved down into the small bowl of the swamp toward the cabin, the fires, the goats, the whole show of lights, leading the mare behind me.

When I approached, the goats were as goatlike as I expected, watching me with those drowsy, stupid eyes and slowly chewing whatever nameless greenery they had grazed in the clearing. The smell was pretty much as I had figured, too, so I approached more rapidly, eager to get the strong woodsmoke between me and the only apparent residents. The pack mare snorted once and pulled back strongly against the reins, but I made a soothing sound with my tongue and led her on.

Once we stepped within the circle of fires I realized my mistake.

Suddenly the flames began to move and waver like phosfire. I turned, intent on beating a quick exit, but it was too late.

Now the kindling stood on end, began to grow and expand at a speed that was grotesque even for this swamp. Within seconds I was surrounded by a high palisade fence— a fence containing no opening, no exit I could see.

Now the goats were changing, too, their long hair growing back into their bodies as quickly as the palisades had grown from the ground. They rose to their hind legs, adopting human form—or at least a form approaching human. The changed creatures—no longer goats, but satyrs—eyed me sleepily, stupidly, as if they were waking up. They walked to the fires, drew burning branches from the midst, and held them aloft like torches. Slowly and menacingly, they encircled me.

My first idea was to drop the reins, leave the mare to her own devices, and scramble into that small, smoky cabin in the center of the clearing. There, above the pack of satyrs and the confusion, I would have time to think, to invent, to patch together an escape.

But I was losing the chance to act. For while the fences and goats had risen, the cabin had changed, too, rising and reassembling in that sickly green light until it was no longer a cabin at all, but an enormous and hideous throne, standing on stilts in the midst of a fortified stronghold.

Seated upon that throne was the Scorpion.

I must admit that the whole arrangement was pretty impressive. The throne was skeletal: thin and intricate and a nasty off-white color from base to crown. Over its surface, black on a background of bone and ivory, hundreds of scorpions danced, rose, or lifted their poisonous tails.

He sat on the throne, lean and menacing. Beneath that heavy black hood, he might have been anyone.

But there was, I am certain, only one with that voice.

The same voice I remembered from the moat house— musical and honeyed and laced with ice and metal and poison. The voice of the raven.

For as soon as I recovered my balance and brought my frantically rearing pack animal under control, as soon as I had taken in the entire scene—the throne, the vermin, the man cloaked and hooded in black—then came the voice from the man, confirming my fears.

"Little Galen, your worst nightmare has returned upon you. Oh, yes, you have dreamed this and wakened with a start, or in sweat and with your small heart racing, for in your sleep you behold me and are afraid past all assurance and comfort."

Actually, he had never been a part of my worst nightmare, which involved a huge faceless ogre wielding a huge and impossibly sharp axe. But he was nightmarish enough, and I was certainly not inclined to argue with him. I gaped and nodded my agreement. My knees began to give.

"I believe, little friend, that a part of your debt has come due?"

"It surely has, Your Grace, and I had every intention of paying it to you. Paying it to you with interest, for you were exceedingly kind to let me out of that prison of a library on such short acquaintance and in such highly unusual circumstances . . ."

He leaned from the throne, stared down on me like a predatory bird stares down upon the rodent of the day.

"But it's more complicated than that. Of course, as Your Grace is probably well aware, I haven't been allowed the chance to collect my thoughts, much less any good information regarding Bayard, over the last fortnight, being imprisoned and pressed into service and all."

The Scorpion sat back and steepled his long white fingers. The circle of satyrs around me narrowed, and with it my options. I began to bargain.

"I have, of course, access to the kind of thing you were bargaining for in the first place," I began, motioning to the back of the pack mare, where Bayard's armor lay bundled. "A fine suit of Solamnic armor, scarcely used of late, which if your followers don't mind a little clean-up detail— scraping off the mud and all . . ."

"Enough." My host rested his hands quickly, lightly on the arms of the throne, scattering the scorpions.

"And what do you think I want with armor, boy? Do I look like a dealer in breastplates, satisfied by merchandise alone?"

"No, sir. Your Grace looks like my worst nightmare."

"In that am I satisfied. And I take it that Bayard Brightblade remains somewhere in this swamp?"

"Yes, sir." Questioning was clearing my head. "That is, as far as I can tell.

"In fact, I'm sure he is somewhere in this swamp, but I am so misplaced, so spun around and squandered by circumstance, that I won't be able to tell you where east is until morning, much less point out for you where the Knight in question has mired himself."

I didn't feel so bad about betraying Bayard. After all, it wasn't my choice to be here. I couldn't call Bayard a friend—not really—and was I really his squire, when he had forced me into service? More like his prisoner, and the duty of a prisoner is to escape, isn't it?

I stopped stroking myself with logic when the man on the throne continued firing questions at me.

"Do you know what a will-o-the-wisp is, boy?" he asked.

"No, sir, but I expect that I soon shall."

"The floating light in the swamp—marsh gas, fox fire, call it what you will—that is always a step or two ahead of the traveler who follows it. Like the fire that brought you here."

I nodded in stupid agreement, doing my best to contain the wildly trembling mare I had in tow.

"It is a light that the traveler follows at his peril, for it leads him farther and farther toward the heart of the swamp— wherein perdition lies."

He chuckled, and the scorpions stirred beneath his hands.

"You, little weasel, are my will-o-the-wisp. For it is your job now to bring your companions here to me, to mire them in the center of this fen and keep them here through long and costly delays. A simple task, but one so worthy of my gratitude."

"I'd love to help, sir," I began tentatively, "but for the life of me, I've no idea where Sir Bayard is."

"Don't play the innocent with me, boy!" he spat, the scorpions rushing away from him, startled by the noise, the anger charging the air. It felt like that time in a storm before lightning begins. I stepped back and watched one of the satyrs—a small one, virtually beardless—turn and leap into the palisade wall, vanishing into the wood. A larger one followed him, and then another.

"Well, I do know that Bayard is somewhere here in the swamp . . ."

"Much better," he interrupted, "Much more . . . positive and optimistic." His voice had returned to a calm and honeyed instrument. Slowly the scorpions were gathering once again on the throne.

"You have such little trust in me, Galen. Did you think I

would leave you so . . . ill-provided? Have you already forgotten the good turn I did you in the moat house library? No, Galen. What I need is someone to lead Sir Bayard to this very spot."

One of the satyrs stepped back through the palisade, as easily as if he were walking out of a fog. Paying him no mind, the Scorpion continued.

"For you see, I know where Bayard is." A globe of light began to glow green in his hand. "And the light that led you to me will lead you to him, will lead the both of you back to this cabin, this encampment."

"And no harm will come to Bayard?" I asked, puzzled.

"My hand shall not shed blood in this undertaking. My word is always kept, through centuries of fire and flood and wrack. Unlike the word of others."

"That sounds pretty binding, sir. Given that assurance, I would be glad, by force or by farce, to bring Sir Bayard of Vingaard into your august presence, so that you might draw from him the information you need in whatever way you choose to draw. However, I should like to earn my freedom in the bargain, and a safe escort back to my father's house. After all, Sir Bayard may not want to trouble himself with my company if my treachery is suspected."

There was a long pause. The Scorpion deliberated, I awaited his decision, the pack mare tugged less urgently at the reins, and the satyrs did nothing much at all except walk in and out of the fortifications through the palisades.

"I shall allow you that chance," the Scorpion said finally. "I shall guide you back to your companions, and you, in turn, shall guide them to me. I shall allow you that chance, but I shall be oh so watchful. I shall be a hawk, a nest of owls to your passing, little Weasel, for I am not sure whether your eagerness to betray your comrades is a lie or is the truth."

At that time, neither was I.

CHAPTER 8

*That is how, by following the deathly glow of phos-*fire away from the clearing, I rode the mare back to Bayard's camp, where the master, the brother, and the means of transportation sat (or in Agion's case, stood) around a campfire, drinking roka.

Well, they welcomed me back with nothing short of joy—better than I expected or deserved. Bayard and Brithelm were on their feet immediately, Brithelm with his arms spread wide preparing a brotherly enfolding, Bayard more reserved, as befitting his station, but scarcely concealing his delight and relief. Agion was literally prancing like a colt, back and forth between Valorous and the pack mare.

And I would lead these innocents wherever the Scorpion commanded.

I had never liked this hidden arrangement with the hidden enemy. It had begun to bother me that my surveillances were part of a mysterious plan that might well end in outrage to some folk who didn't deserve it. But call it what you would, it was their skins or mine. Put bluntly and in those terms, it was easy to restrain those higher feelings.

Brithelm was all embraces and questions as he led me to the fireside and set a steaming mug of roka in my hands. I sniffed reluctantly at first, smelled the roka nuts and the cinnamon, then tasted it. To my relief, the roka was of someone's brewing other than my spiritual brother's.

I sat back, felt the warm sedative of the drink course through me, and thought of the end of an old fable: *And so they took the adder into their midst, and fed and sheltered it, nursing it back to health.*

Gave it roka to drink, no doubt. The world is not a kind place.

As I drank, I replied to the array of questions arising from my knightly protector.

"But I don't *know* where I have been, except through this swamp and in and out of a quagmire or two.

"And I don't know what I saw for sure, aside from the fact that it was pretty confusing.

"I was passing this way and noticed the light. If I hadn't seen the light, I probably never would have found you."

None of the answers were lies. At least not directly.

"No matter how you returned to us, Galen, I thank the gods for that return!" Brithelm exclaimed, embracing me yet again. Agion gamboled about and nodded vigorously in agreement.

Only Bayard stood back from the merrymaking, to the side of the brotherly chat, watching me closely—perhaps even a little distrustfully, though perhaps the distrust I saw in his face arose from my sense of my own misdeeds, from my fear of discovery. I was, after all, the Scorpion's agent in this matter, and a little bit of a skunk in the bargain, if you stopped to think about it.

Bayard spoke tersely.

"I can't imagine your being lost, Galen, without marking carefully some of the things you noticed, if only in passing.

If you hadn't gathered, I'm fairly tired of your appearances at times of calm and departures at times of need. I suppose you were 'on surveillance' again somewhere safe in the marsh country."

Bayard then crouched by the fire, warming his hands against the cold that was once more unseasonable.

"I know, sir, that I deserve that bit of mean-spirited viciousness from you, even if it is uncharacteristic of a Solamnic Knight. I know that I have been hiding when I should have been . . . participating more enthusiastically. But it so happens that by accident I did recover your armor, for which I would prefer a little acknowledgement."

Bayard looked into the fire and nodded reluctantly.

"And what is more, Sir Bayard, in the midst of this path-finding and retrieval, I managed to put in some genuine scouting, of which you should hasten to hear."

I told him about the encampment at the center of the swamp—the circle of campfires, the house on stilts, the occasional goats in the midst of the place. Of course I left out the Scorpion—not to mention Alfric—shaping my story quickly and naturally, drawing on the instincts I had developed in the moat house.

Whatever suspicions Bayard might have, though, were not shared by the others in our party. Agion continued to gambol, Brithelm to rejoice and to talk.

"Goats and houses and fires aside, little brother, what a relief it is to know you are safe, before I retreat into hermitage, before I return to my place of meditation. I suppose I could never have gone back with a light heart had I not known your fate."

"Brithelm?"

"Yes, little brother?"

But what could I say?

"Do watch yourself as you retreat into hermitage. The swamp has changed from your early days of wildlife communion."

"Watch myself? Why, Galen, nothing in this swamp poses any real danger. Even the satyrs are not satyrs."

I glanced quickly at Bayard, who shrugged.

"Well," I responded, "it has been my experience that

quicksand and crocodiles, not to mention satyrs, can bruise the faithful and the gallant as quick as the rest of us."

"That's just it, Galen," Bayard offered from his corner of the fire, never removing his gaze from me as he spoke. "Brithelm doesn't believe in the satyrs. Says they don't exist."

"Wait a minute. Don't exist?" I was not about to give away what I knew. "Well, you've seen them, haven't you?"

Bayard nodded.

"And you, Agion?"

The centaur stepped back into the firelight, said, "Yes, Galen. Indeed I have. But that is not the point."

"Not the point?"

The big centaur leaned forward to warm his hands by the fire. A puzzled look spread across his vacant face. "Not the point," he explained, "for Brithelm has told us that the satyrs do not exist, whether we see them or no. He is a holy man who is used to things unseen."

"I understand. Perhaps one of you can tell me what has happened in my absence, then. If something that climbs on Bayard with a knife, that kills two of Agion's friends, that I have seen with my own eyes doesn't exist, then I'd like to know . . ."

*　*　*　*　*

Theirs was a tale brief and bitter and mysterious. As the story came to light, it resembled more and more one of the legendary gemstones from far-off Kharolis, which is a different color depending upon the angle from which you look at it, or resembling even more closely those old prophetic poems from the Age of Dreams, in which each reader finds his own catastrophes foretold.

Bayard began the telling.

"I looked for you, Galen," he said calmly, "but found you nowhere."

"And when we could not find thee," Agion took up the story at once, "we broke cover and charged onto the road, where we engaged half a dozen satyrs."

"Four," corrected Bayard.

"None," corrected Brithelm.

"None?" I asked, moving closer to the fire.

"Our stories part company almost from the outset," Bayard explained, moving away from the fire. "I saw four of them, Agion six, and Brithelm saw four goats. The goats come later in my tale."

Bayard broke off an aeterna branch and stirred the fire with the blue, fragrant stick. He began to speak again.

"Whatever our version, the struggle was over quickly. What struggle there was. Agion claims that two of the satyrs escaped unharmed and headed toward the center of the swamp."

Toward the stockade, no doubt. It sounded reasonable.

"I, on the other hand, saw only four of them, as I told you," Bayard claimed. "And all of them put up a fierce fight, wielding clubs, short spears, those swords with the curved blades . . ."

"Scimitars?" I suggested.

"I suppose that's one name for them, Galen. You should know; you've read more of the old stories than I have. Whatever they're called, the goat-men knew how to use them and it took Agion and me a brief but hard fight to dispatch them. In which your brother had no part. But fighting seems to be a trait that none of you inherited from your brave father."

He glanced at Brithelm with exasperation. Brithelm smiled back serenely, nodding that he continue his story. Bayard smiled too, despite himself.

"Up until then, I could account for the differences in our stories as arising from the confusion of battle," Bayard explained. He leaned back on his heels, smiled dimly. "I recall my first engagement, a brief, nasty skirmish with the men of Neraka near the Throtyl Gap a dozen years back. There were seven of us there, all between the ages of seventeen and twenty."

He laughed, shook his head.

"There were seven versions of that skirmish, where the enemy ranged in numbers from ten to two hundred. Only a week later did we find that we had outnumbered them."

He paused, still smiling, then stared at each of us in turn, his gray eyes growing serious.

"But this was not a first battle," he stated quietly, fixing his stare on the changing light of the fire. "I have lived thirty years and been blooded in clash, in skirmish, in battle, from here to Caergoth. Yet I am puzzled at what came to pass in the aftermath of the fight with the satyrs, when things were calm and when a seasoned man is not apt to illusion.

"For neither Agion nor your brother saw what happened next, as I bent above one of the dead satyrs for a closer look at our enemy. Agion claims that nothing happened next."

"That nothing changed, Sir Bayard," the centaur interrupted, folding his arms across his chest. "Nothing, that is, save the look upon thy countenance, which liked to frighten me, thou wert so taken in thy disbelief and horror."

"Agion," Bayard explained, "did not see the satyr turn into a goat." The Knight sat, drew his knife, and ran his finger lightly over the blade.

"It was as if death had unmanned him," he said finally, staring once more into the fire. "As though the dying had taken all *humanness* from its body, leaving only goatish, inhuman remains."

"Which was all there was from the beginning, Sir Bayard," Brithelm said, patiently but much too loudly for this dangerous terrain. "It has the makings of a proverb," he added with a smile. "'If you fight goats, expect to kill goats.'"

"Whichever," said Bayard, his voice low and oddly troubled. "But of one thing there can be no doubt: things are passing strange in this forsaken swampland. I am anxious to leave, but first, I'll fulfill my pledge to confront the satyrs, be they real or imagined, and then hasten on the way to my appointment."

Bayard looked long and hard at the fire before rising. He stomped off to attend to Valorous and the pack mare. Something fluttered in the bushes to my left. I started, thought of ambush.

Then I recalled it would not happen here, that it was my job to lead these folk to ruin—back to the house at the center of the swamp, where, if ambush was coming, it would come.

Meanwhile, Agion had busied himself with gathering bundles of reeds and leaves, which he fashioned into a

makeshift mattress on the floor of the clearing. As the others
set about their business, he caught my eye and motioned
toward his handiwork with a big, ungainly hand.

"My lord Archala said seven days and seven nights
among us will find thee out," he observed, his face widening
into a smile as kind as it was ugly. "But he never ordered thee
to spend all that time in waking."

I crawled onto the mattress gratefully and, with my enormous companion and captor standing watch, slept heavily
through the morning and the afternoon.

*   *   *   *   *

I figured that Bayard had lost all patience with Pathwardens for the moment. Even the time I slept was time he had
to make up on the road to Castle di Caela.

But there was good in this impatience, for while I was
asleep, Sir Bayard seemed to have forgotten about pressing
me for further details about my adventures of the night
before. Or had let it pass on purpose.

As he attended to the horses and Brithelm moved away
from the fire to the far edge of the light, where he sat in what
seemed to be meditation, I stirred sleepily on my bed of
reeds, reached in my pockets, and drew out the Calantina.

One and ten. Sign of the Adder.

Well, then. Best do what adders do.

I roused myself and walked over to Bayard, who leaned
against the pack mare, his big hands on her saddle, intent on
tightening what the swamp had loosened. He looked over
his shoulder at my approach, then returned to his work.

"Bayard?" Again I called softly. "Bayard?"

He dragged his armor off the pack mare and began to put
it on. He looked up at me, smiled, motioned me over. I felt
more viperous by the minute.

"I hope you slept well, Galen, but we must be moving. I'm
sure we can find the satyrs near that place you spoke of.
How far would you say we are from that encampment?
Help me with this."

I stooped, tightened a greave, and answered.

"Not far, I expect, sir. It should be easy to find again."

"Think, boy," he urged. "You have no idea how serious

this delay is to me."

As I helped Bayard to his feet the phosfire began to shine above our heads, at first spangling the early evening air as though it had settled, like an army of fireflies, in the branches of a huge, mossy oak that overhung the clearing where we had camped. Shortly, the light arose from the branches and began to move, back in the direction from where I had come.

I pretended not to notice the phosfire at first, but soon I was aware that none of my companions had seen it. So I could follow the weaving light easily, stopping once in a while to pretend at pondering my whereabouts before pretending to recognize a tree, a standing pool of water, a bend in the path. Soon I had to pretend no longer, for my companions followed me unquestioningly, involved as they were with the swatting of midges, the breaking through underbrush, and the swearing at terrain and at each other.

All the while, the light hovered above us and a little ahead of us, my signpost through the treachery of the swamp. And the night dropped upon us with that terrifying quickness it can possess only within deep greenery.

At Bayard's orders I took the lead as the guide. Walking at my side, Brithelm carried one of the torches, and Agion brought up the rear carrying the other. Bayard led Valorous and walked between the lights, now wearing his full suit of armor, which creaked loudly and weighed him down in the soft ground of the swamp. He must have foreseen the possibility of a pitched battle taking place at the spot to which I was leading them, and he wanted to be dressed for the occasion.

What distressed me the most was that Brithelm was coming with us. What the Scorpion had in mind for our little party, I couldn't guess, but my innocent brother did not deserve my treachery. But he was intent on accompanying us. My brother was along for the duration.

Always, the green, unhealthy phosfire danced a few yards in front of me, guiding us all toward the encampment and who knew what destiny.

When, ahead of us, I smelled woodsmoke and heard the bleat of a goat, I stopped and took stock.

I searched my history there at the edge of the encampment, ankle-deep in wet mud.

Secretly, quickly, I drew the Calantina from my pocket and cast the red dice in my hand. Sign of the Adder again. I was being told something, but I could not figure it out.

Brithelm laid his hand on my shoulder. I started, then turned to find him staring at me, face filled with worry and concern.

"What ails you, little brother?"

"Ails me? Why, nothing, Brithelm." I looked behind me cautiously: Bayard was soothing an increasingly skittish Valorous.

Suddenly, the sound of shouts and shrill cries burst from the clearing ahead of us.

Bayard drew his sword, grabbed me as I tried to run back up the trail, and cast me to the ground.

"Draw your sword, Galen!" he ordered softly and urgently, his teeth clenched. "By the gods, you've enlisted for this one."

Yanking me to my feet, he carried me bodily under his left arm into the clearing, clutching his sword in his right. I heard Agion snort behind us, heard Brithelm say something and Bayard answer, "Just stay under cover and hold the horses, Brithelm." Then I was blinded by the strange, artificial daylight of flame and phosfire.

* * * * *

There were twelve of them I could count, and I counted quickly. After their initial outburst, the satyrs regrouped under the cloudy platform—whether it was the house or the Scorpion's throne hidden by the image of the house I could not tell. The goat-men moved in and out of the shadows, their cries and calls mingling one with another into a low but threatening murmur. Most of them had bows, some of them short, wicked-looking spears.

"I shall take the eight on the left, Sir Bayard," Agion shouted. "Thou and thy squire may have the four on the right." And he charged.

It was the kind of division of labor I liked. Now I could only hope Bayard was planning on taking the other four all by himself.

I hoped so even more devoutly when the clouds above the satyrs began to clear.

For above them sat the Scorpion on his throne. As the satyrs nocked bows, set themselves to hurl spears, their leader reached into the folds of his black cape and drew out something shiny, something flickering. It was a pendant of sorts, from this distance as clear and as shining as a crystal, which he dangled casually from his left hand, swinging it softly through the air.

While his troops prepared for battle, the commander's total attention was not on the conflict unfolding, but upon the bauble in his hand. For why shouldn't he sit there, playing casually with glittering trinkets? His satyrs outnumbered us three to one—six to one if you counted the fighting worth of the Pathwardens—and it was obvious that . . .

"Don't look at the pendulum," Brithelm urged beside me, having left Valorous and the pack mare to their own devices and joined us in the clearing.

"See to the horses, blast you!" Bayard cried, and I forgot the warning, the pendulum, and the Scorpion himself, as the volley of arrows and spears was upon us.

I was still lying under Bayard's feet when a big satyr drew his bow and sent an arrow flying in my direction.

I could see the yellow of the feathers on the fletching, but I could do nothing but try to scramble to my feet. But just before the arrow struck, as it certainly would have struck, as I was growing rapidly to believe it would strike, Bayard's large, well-armored sword arm moved into its path and deflected it into the ground in front of us.

Beside me, I heard Agion grunt, and a quick glance told me he carried a satyr's spear in the fleshy part of his arm. All of a sudden I feared for his largeness, which had seemed only an advantage before. Now, under fire, he was just a big, stupid target.

The biggest, but not the most stupid. Or so it seemed as Brithelm suddenly burst past us and headed at a trot for the throne and the satyrs. Arrows sailed around him, the closest tearing through his cloak on their way to lodge harmlessly in the ground. Bayard dropped me and started for my brother, but it was too late—Brithelm was well past him, nor was there any question of pursuit, since Bayard was having trouble staying on his feet under the weight of all that armor.

"If it's not one Pathwarden it's another!" he sputtered, then sank to his knees, watching along with the rest of us as my brother rushed cheerfully towards the Scorpion.

The lines of the satyrs parted weirdly in front of my brother, as though the nasty-looking armed creatures were reeds in the swamp he was pushing aside in search of a trail. Some of them not only moved, but vanished entirely at Brithelm's approach. Beside him, where satyrs had once bristled with menace and weapons, several goats grazed calmly, scarcely noticing any of us.

That was enough for Bayard. All of a sudden, he moved lightly, gracefully. He looked back at me, where I was sprawled in the swamp mud, beginning again to dig for cover, and spoke quietly but assuredly.

"Get up at once, Galen, and follow your brother. The army we stand against is peopled with illusion. There is nothing dangerous in this clearing. Do you understand? Nothing dangerous in this clearing."

The evidence was against him, I figured. But he gazed at me so unflinchingly, so sternly, that I feared going against his will far more than I feared any satyr.

What was more, illusory or not, the satyrs were having a rough time with my comrades. Agion grabbed two of them by their wooly napes and battered their heads together, as though he were playing hairy horned cymbals. The swamp resounded with a hollow, cracking sound, and the satyrs fell unconscious. Laughing, the centaur rushed at two more of them, who stood cowering beneath the Scorpion's throne.

With his sword drawn, Bayard walked calmly through the midst of the satyrs toward the platform where the Scorpion was seated. The satyrs encircled him, shrieking and hopping like carrion birds around something that is dying, but none of them got near him. One lunged at him with a sinister-looking long knife, but Bayard parried the weapon, sent it skittering across the floor of the clearing, kicked the satyr aside, and kept walking.

Indeed, mere looks from Bayard seemed to stop the rest of their attacks, as the satyrs snarled, brayed, and sidled away from him.

It was something out of a story.

I scrambled to my feet and ran after my brother, who was standing beneath the base of the platform. Satyrs had begun to surround him.

I looked toward Agion, who was occupied, juggling two more satyrs, and then to Bayard, who was still yards away from my brother. Neither of them would reach Brithelm in time. I started to call out, with no earthly idea what good that would do, except that it was *something* to do, and then stopped, gaping in my tracks.

For Brithelm had raised his arms and was now rising slowly through the air, borne on the wind, perhaps, except there was no rustle of leaves, no movement of branches. He rose head and shoulders, then waist and ankles above the milling satyrs, whose weapons slashed harmlessly about him.

His hands glowed with a silver light that seemed to cleanse the green and sickly light of the phosfire until the clearing glowed with a fresh white glow like that from a marvelous candle.

With rising courage and confidence I rushed through the midst of the enemy, calling for Brithelm over the sound of their shrieking, which was changing slowly to the bleating of goats. The satyrs turned to face me, but did nothing, and I passed among them easily and without harm.

I rushed to one of the posts that held up the platform and scrambled up it like a squirrel, until I stood on the rickety platform, puffing, sweating, and shouting in triumph.

That was when the Scorpion rose from his throne.

The dark hood still covered his face, but there was something about the bend of his shoulders, of his knees, that signaled defeat. It was a gesture someone would make in a bad painting.

But as Brithelm rose onto the platform, the Scorpion stood to his full height, threw back his shoulders, and stared into our faces.

His eyes whirled red, then yellow, then white, then blue,

like the burning of a thousand suns. He turned the shimmering crystal towards us in the shifting swamplight.

It flashed green and yellow and green. For a moment Brithelm lost his balance, plummeted into the empty air, then caught himself on the side of the platform. I staggered backward toward the edge, toward the long drop onto the floor of the clearing. In that moment the battle had turned. We were both defeated.

But not Bayard. As anyone could see in his gait, in the straight and dauntless arch of his back as he leaped for the base of the platform, armor and all, and grabbed it firmly and easily, pulling himself up onto the platform in one incredible movement. The Scorpion turned to face him, with only one satyr, although a big one, between the Knight and the sinister caped figure.

The satyr lunged at Bayard, and his spear passed through the Knight, who kept walking as though nothing had happened, straight through the wavering, translucent body of his adversary, as though the satyr were made of smoke or steam. The creature evaporated and in its stead a goat, looking confused and a little embarrassed, clattered into the smoke-filled cabin behind us.

Now Bayard stood beside the cowering Scorpion. He raised his sword, holding it in both hands like an executioner or a woodsman, and brought it crashing down.

Brought it down through hood, through cloak, through tunic, and into the rotten wood of the platform.

And through nothing else.

For there were only three of us on the platform, not counting the goat. Bayard and I stood around a dark robe spread like a pool over the platform, over a dark tunic and a pair of shiny black boots. We stood at the front of a ramshackle cabin I remembered from earlier that night, and behind the cabin the swamp was beginning to redden and glow—not with the fires that earlier encircled this place, but with genuine and entirely welcome sunlight.

Brithelm pulled himself painfully up from the edge of the platform where he had been clinging.

Below us, Agion rubbed his shoulder quietly, gaping amidst a herd of goats. His wound had closed as the sunlight first touched the clearing. When I saw that, I was gaping, too.

"That, I suppose, is that?" the centaur called up to us, gently nudging away a spotted kid that came up to nuzzle his leg.

I glanced at Brithelm, who rubbed his head quietly, staring up at the cabin with admiration and wonder.

He was silent, was lost in the strange thoughts of the blessed.

So I looked again at Bayard, who stood astraddle the heap of abandoned clothing, looking back at me.

"What do you think, sir? Is that, that?"

"No, Galen," Sir Bayard replied, sheathing his sword and casting a puzzled look off into the swamp. "Though I understand little else of what has just transpired, I can tell you this much. That is anything but that."

Part II

House of di Caela

Three on eight, light upon flood,
Sign of the Centaur in a lost season.
Generations of light that the flood has covered,
The old water singing of reverence.
And here on continuous banks of rivers,
The light is moving, is lost, is moving.

—*The Calantina* III:VIII

CHAPTER 9

"No matter what you say, little brother, this is the kind of place I have sought and awaited. The kind of place I have dreamed of, continually and in humility, I hope. I have prayed to the gods for such a place, in which to take hermitage, alone with thoughts and meditations and with the gentle creatures of the marshes."

So I kept hearing from Brithelm, who had found meaning and purpose in the struggle we had waged in the swamp, there in the very clearing where we still sat by midmorning, pondering several of many imponderables.

Bayard, too, was tired of listening to Brithelm's praise of "the gentle creatures of the marshes," especially since some of those gentle creatures—namely the satyrs—had been looking to waylay us since we arrived in the swamp.

"My dreams take me to other places, Brithelm," he said. "And I for one would arise and travel to Castle di Caela in quest of the hand of the Lady Enid, were it not for the restraining commands of our centaur companion." Bayard nodded curtly at Agion.

This had been going on for hours: a running argument between Sir Bayard and Agion as to whether obligations had been met, so to speak. Bayard claimed that the swamp was now free of satyrs and whatever evil had led them against the centaurs in the first place. He claimed that since there was no longer any enemy to fight, our job in these parts was done. And since we had cleared our names in this issue beyond any doubt, the centaurs should allow us to go on our way.

Agion, on the other hand, would have been much more comfortable if he could carry back to his centaur friends some satyrs' heads on pikes. According to him, a grisly trophy was better than peace or than any number of strong promises. And there would be no trophies nor peace offerings from mysteriously vanished satyrs.

I could understand Agion's point of view, and by this time I rather liked the big, stupid thing. But as long as he held out for evidence, we were stuck in the swamp—there were no satyr heads for the having simply because there were no satyrs any longer, if there ever were any to begin with.

Bayard, on the other hand, had not given up the tournament at Castle di Caela. He still had designs on being there in time to enter the lists in the match for the hand of Enid di Caela, for whose unseen smile or unseen approving glance our hero would gladly batter senseless all the unmarried men of Ansalon. That was still eleven days away, he said, and if we left at once we could be in Castle di Caela in plenty of time, and exhaust neither Valorous nor ourselves all that much. All this providing we left at once.

Leaving at once sounded pretty good to me, too. This was a miserable place, and I had not forgotten the other elder brother, no doubt entombed in my father's armor somewhere nearby, who could be more than embarrassing for me if, dead or alive, he somehow came unswamped.

"Agion," Bayard argued, "we have stood by one another, have fought side by side. If we were to go over the events of last night, I am sure each of us could find a moment, an occasion upon which he might argue that he saved the other's life. Given that closeness, the bond of trust that has arisen between us, could you still keep me from leaving?"

"Yes."

I had to step in. Things were going absolutely nowhere.

"Look, Agion," I began, leaning heavily against the wall of the cabin, then becoming aware of what I was doing and backing off gingerly in mistrust of rot and of bad architecture. "Look, Agion, what is it that keeps you from letting us simply walk out of here, when we've shown you our innocence through our actions? Or do you still think we were the ones who stirred up the satyrs?"

"Oh, thou art truly the most noble of souls, Master Bayard and Master Galen!" Agion exclaimed. "This I cannot— indeed, would not—deny. But by similar token, Archala and my elders are—well, they are Archala and my elders. It is to them that I owe my allegiance, my promises."

"Just what was your promise, Agion?"

The big centaur frowned at my question and scratched his head in a gesture that reminded me, disturbingly, of Alfric.

"As I recall, Master Galen, 'twas in these words exact. That I should 'Never let either—the Knight or his squire— stray from your sight until you have returned them to the custody of the elders.'"

Perfect.

"So you promised simply not to let us from your sight until you returned us?" I called down at the centaur, who had wandered away from the platform to a nearby vallenwood, from which he was stripping leaves.

"Yes, Master Galen," he called in reply, stuffing a handful of vallenwood leaves into his mouth.

"Then come with us."

Agion swallowed. "Come with thee?"

"Come with us?" Bayard clanked to a stop upon the platform.

"Why not? You've heard of leaving the letter intact, haven't you, Agion?"

"Yes," he said hesitantly.

"For you see," I continued, "if you come with us, Agion, you haven't broken your promise. There may well come a time—no, there *will* come a time, without a doubt—when our innocence is clear, even to the most mistrustful of judges. But until that time, we have business. Which includes a tournament in eleven days' time, at which," I nodded masterfully at Bayard, "our presence is expected."

It left Agion struggling for purchase. He folded his arms and, lost in meditation, pawed the wet ground of the clearing with his right foreleg. His was a dilemma I could only imagine, and my heart went out to him in his denseness and good intentions.

Agion bought my argument. He nodded his head vigorously, his dumb face breaking into a dumb grin. He kicked suddenly, startling several of the nearby goats.

"I see, Master Galen! If I do not return to the elders without thee, I have not broken my promise! So my best choice is to go with thee!"

*   *   *   *   *

Castle di Caela was still some way from us. We would travel south by southeast, cross the Vingaard mountains at a path Bayard remembered, then continue over the southwest shank of the Plains of Solamnia, fording the southernmost branch of the Vingaard River and stopping midway between the ford and Solanthas. It was a week's journey as the crow flies.

Unfortunately, none of us were crows, and we would be hard pressed to make up for the time we had lost while mired among centaurs and satyrs and Scorpions. Ten days, Bayard figured it, and that was with good weather and no distractions.

Astride Valorous, dressed only in a cloak and a muddy tunic for the long road, Bayard led us free of the marshes. Riding uphill into clearer and drier ground, we reached what I thought was a little knoll, but turned out to be a leveling off of land, a rolling countryside stretching east eventlessly except for a patch of woods here and there and except for the road upon which we were riding, still muddy from yesterday's bout with rain.

It was a pretty landscape, but dull.

Looking back upon the swamplands we had just left, I preferred what lay ahead to the tangled and entangling mystery behind us. I had never seen the countryside before me—never been this far from home. Looking back I noticed that the swamp was changing, but not with the rapid growth that had been a source of wonder and irritation during our stay in its midst. For now the swamp was browning, graying at its edges. I knew it had something to do with the Scorpion's disappearance, but I also felt as though our leaving was bringing autumn to the country.

Nor was the swamp all we were leaving. I thought of Brithelm standing on the platform, waving goodbye to us as we left the bare central clearing of the swamp. He had decided to stay in his hermitage—there among goats and mosquitoes—to settle in and think upon the grandeur of the gods.

I wished Brithelm no harm, though I was mightily glad to be rid of him. He was foolish and exasperating, but probably the pure best of a sorry bunch of Pathwardens, myself included. The problem was that the world couldn't take a pure best. Both my brothers were better off swamped, and in the way fate had swamped them.

Still, I recalled the farewells, as my visionary middle brother stood dangerously near the edge of the swampy platform, surrounded by goats, watching the three of us ride away.

"Don't look at things directly, little brother, for insight dwells in the corner of the eye," he shouted, a last piece of advice for the road.

"What does that mean, holy man?" Agion called back, but Brithelm had turned his back on us and entered that ruinous cabin.

At my last view of Brithelm, before he stepped through the ramshackle door into shadow, he had drawn something silver from his pocket and placed it to his lips.

Huma's dog whistle.

From the surrounding greenery, goats converged on the shack.

I turned, sentimental and a little sad, on Agion's back toward the front of my journeys—the east, the future.

"That's better, Galen," Bayard said, and I had no idea what an earbending lay ahead of me. "It's better to look ahead of you than behind you, for behind you are quagmires and quicksand that may swallow your very best intentions."

What was this? Did he know about Alfric? I kept quiet, prayed silently that the honor he so treasured would keep him from guessing—or even believing—that I had bogged my wretch of a brother.

But no, it was a little philosophy to begin his long and intricate story, filled with usurpers and violence and going without and man's inhumanity to man. There were times that it bordered on interesting, and times that I wished I had Agion's talent for shutting things out entirely.

This is how it went.

* * * * *

"The third chapter of the *Book of Vinas Solamnus*, the great text found in its entirety only in the Library of Palanthas, concerns itself with the fortunes of the di Caela family—a history from the time they came mysteriously from the North, through the gates of Paladine, from the time that the founder of the line, old Gerald di Caela, joined with Vinas Solamnus, adding his name to the earliest and proudest list of Knighthood."

Along with the Brightblades, who were also early and proud upon that list.

To which the Pathwardens were latecomers, I knew. Bayard was far too polite to mention that fact, but we had been instructed early and well as to how our not being one of the dozen or so Old Families would influence our lives.

"So the family thrived in honor and in prominence for a thousand years and more, until some four hundred years ago the title—the di Caela, if you will, the *paterfamilias*—fell to a Gabriel di Caela. It seems that old Gabriel had three sons. The eldest was named Duncan, if my memory serves, and the youngest son was a Gabriel also. But it is Benedict di Caela, the middle son, who stands at the center of this dark and troubling story— by accident of birth disinherited."

Agion leaned forward as he walked, rubbing his knotty hands together and smiling. "In most of the old tales," he offered, "there is a peculiar blessing that comes to the middle son. He stands to inherit little, and ends up with the best inheritance of all."

"But what we are hearing is history, Agion," I interrupted, "in which the middle son is most likely the passed over, the dumped upon, unless something untimely happens to the Duncan in Sir Bayard's story. What is more, it's usually the youngest who is most blessed in the stories, least blessed in the actual workaday world."

Bayard sat back in the saddle and raised his hood against the cool wind of the afternoon. "Both of you are wrong," he stated flatly. "Perhaps you should listen more carefully," he added, "instead of setting forth your harebrained theories of justice.

"The story of this Benedict," he resumed, shifting the reins casually from one hand to the other, "began in envy and, as far as I can tell, ends there. He kept at remove from his brothers, there in old Gabriel's castle—the Castle di Caela, it came to be called, for obvious reasons.

"There young Benedict plotted, 'mixing poison in his thoughts, dreaming of accidents,' as the old *Book of Vinas Solamnus* has it. But accidents can be traced, and in those times the clerics of Mishakal had ways of stopping, of entirely reversing the spread of poison. Even if they were too late, if the poisoned wretch lay dead and past their powers of reversal and healing, they could still trace a poison in the bloodstream, determine its ingredients, when it was administered, and who had mixed it.

"When that failed, they could make the dead talk, uncover the murderer. So for years young Benedict mixed the poison only in dreams, for he was far too timid to murder outright. Instead, he sat alone and brooded, and he thought vengeful thoughts.

"The greatest poison, of course, is that of envy," Bayard pronounced, and stared pointedly at me, demanding some sort of response.

"Well, sir, I should put hemlock above envy in your poisons, for I have seen envious men live for years. But I am no apothecary. I have no talent for chemistry."

"Or for metaphor," Bayard retorted, and picked up the story once more.

"So in a sense—a *metaphorical* sense—Benedict poisoned himself there in the castle as his thoughts wandered. And when someone is so envenomed, poisoned in thought and in deed, his every discovery is poisoned as well. His every touch is poison."

"Like the Scorpion?" I asked, and instantly wished I could take back those words. For I had given my nemesis a name in that moment, had revealed I knew more of the man in black who haunted the moat house and the swamp—knew more than an honest boy should know. I bowed my head, closed my eyes, and waited for trouble.

But I heard Agion add, "Or like the viper," and looking up, saw Bayard nod in agreement.

"Or like the poisonous creatures of legend and of history, Agion. Yes, you might say Benedict was one of those creatures, in a sense.

"For the poison had grown inside him until even the things he found, which might have been used to the benefit of all around him—might indeed have won him an inheritance passing that of his brothers—he turned instead to things monstrous and wicked. As he did with the pendulum."

Pendulum? There was something about . . .

"Found it he did," Bayard explained, "in the cellar of the very Castle di Caela he coveted, while he fumbled through the darkness searching for a place to practice at the illusions he was learning, fanciful and increasingly insane. He clutched the pendulum to himself, thinking nothing of it for a while. That is, until he brought it out into the light, taking it to his quarters in the upper chambers of the castle. There, drawing it from the folds of his robe, he saw it for the first time.

"Gold was its chain, and the ornament upon that chain was crystal."

Was crystal. Bayard's words struck me like the light of a hundred stars in the darkness. I remembered the swamp, the clearing, the goats, the scattered fires . . .

"And dangling that pendulum in front of his eyes, Benedict thought his poisonous thoughts, dreamed his dreams of accidents. As he looked through the crystal, a spider in the corner of his chamber grew to unnatural size, took on unnatural shape . . ."

Like the goats who changed suddenly, unnaturally, into satyrs.

"And would have crawled from the web of its own devising and poisoned him for sure . . . had he not looked once more and seen the creature for what it was all along—the simple spider he had watched in the room's corner those two days past."

Bayard paused and looked up at Agion.

"This tale of the spider explains the Curse of di Caela—or at least gives it birth in the histories we know."

I was taken aback.

Surely not. Surely this old chestnut from the *Book of Vinas Solamnus* had nothing to do with what I had witnessed two nights back in a clearing in a swamp. Surely books had nothing . . .

But Bayard was taking up the story again.

"Benedict knew, then, from this accident of vision, that the pendulum was a piece of power. But from whence had it come? Historians disagree.

"Some claim it had been dropped by a kender, who had found it the gods knew where and in what residence, for there were kender then even as there are kender now. Some claim the pendulum had become dislodged, by accident or by some large and evil design, from the cornerstone of the castle, where it had lain imbedded for generations, awaiting one so envious, so devious, as to use it in the ways that its use was intended. But of course, there are many such legends on the face of Krynn.

"Does it really matter? For the results were the same, whether Benedict acted on an evil that was born within himself by his own discontent and envy, his own early and dark studies, or whether he acted as the instrument of a larger evil that was reaching its hand into the fabric of the world.

"Smaller evil or larger, rest assured that the rats in the cellar adopted new and monstrous forms as Benedict dangled the gold and crystal pendulum in front of his eyes. Legend has it that they sought out Duncan's room as Benedict instructed, and that when old Gabriel heard the cries of his eldest son and rushed into those chambers intending to rescue the boy, he opened the door onto a scene most unspeakable, which the histories shrink from recording because of its horror.

"Yet the same historians affirm that Duncan's body was neither bruised nor scarred, that it lay serene, so unmarred by death that the embalmers paused in their grotesque, unhappy task, fearing coma, catatonia, or the mystic's sleep. But dead he was, and the clerics of Mishakal could find no wounds upon him, no poison within him."

Like the centaurs in Agion's story.

"Gabriel the Younger, however, smelled a rat, you might say." Bayard smiled, raised his gloved hand. "He had been hunting at the foot of the Garnet Mountains on the night Benedict discovered the pendulum—on the night henceforth known in Solanthas and surrounding parts of Solamnia as the Night of the Rats.

"Though the clerics found nothing in Duncan's chambers that suggested foul play, Gabriel the Younger knew that foul play it was, and sent word to his father that the clerics of Mishakal should make Duncan speak from beyond the darkness.

"Old Gabriel recoiled at first, as any father would. For there was something of violation, of a fierce and unnatural disturbance in this practice, even when it lay in the hands of the white-robed clerics with their holiest of intentions. But his youngest son urged him most passionately, saying, 'Far more unnatural it is, Father, that brother should arise and murder brother for his inheritance and holdings.' Old Gabriel was inclined to agree, ordering the clerics to grant speech unto Duncan that night in the sepulchre.

"Meanwhile, Gabriel the Younger hid in the mountains.

"His one surviving brother was there, at Castle di Caela, awaiting the ceremonies on the night of the equinox when the priests assembled. Whether his guilt was that of the murderer, or of a more subtle guilt that none could name, none could say. Nor will we ever know for sure.

"Whatever the case, the fire that broke out in the sepulchre the night before the sounding was a fierce one, and was set by hand. The robes found in Benedict's quarters had suffered burns at the hems, and smelled darkly of lamp oil and phosfire and ash.

"The body, needless to say, was ashes also, and beyond recall. Old Gabriel was now beside himself, sure that the middle son had plotted outrage. So on the night of the equinox, in the chapel of Castle di Caela, in the presence of sixty Solamnic Knights and twenty clerics of Mishakal, the funeral chants arose for Duncan di Caela. But the chants arose for Benedict di Caela, too."

"I don't understand," Agion interrupted. "Was Benedict dead?" The centaur scratched his head in puzzlement.

"Upon that night, Benedict's father pronounced him dead over strong protest of Knights and clergy, naming Gabriel the Younger sole surviving heir to Castle di Caela. All of this without ever a shred of proof as to the guilt of Benedict di Caela.

"Who, it must be admitted, did not conduct himself in the days that followed as though he were innocent. Benedict fled the castle to raise an army in the lands north of Solanthas—an army of thieves, of goblins, and of the very bounty hunters sent out for goblin heads by the Kingpriest of Istar. It was a disreputable crew, to be sure, and one that set about to tax, extort, and do Benedict's bidding in the southwest provinces of Solamnia."

"Did anyone support Benedict when he raised the army?" Agion asked, his face just a little obscured by the waning light and the onset of evening. "I mean, any of the Knights and priests?"

"Most of the priests—not every priest, mind you, but certainly most—saw through Benedict's illusions to the rats and spiders that peopled them, and what was more, saw that it was Benedict who was shaping those illusions. But there were many Knights who, seeing the legions he could muster, saw power for themselves as well, or what was even worse, feared dangers they dared not brave.

"His ranks, I am ashamed to say, were not free of our

own. Solamnic Knights rode at the head of his columns in defiance of their most profound oaths."

Bayard paused in the telling, stood up in the stirrups and looked about him, then flicked the reins lightly on Valorous's neck as we began to ascend into a region where the once-thick grass grew patchy and thin.

"So this family you seek to join is descended . . ." Agion began to say, after a brief silence.

"From Gabriel di Caela the Younger, of course. He deposed the brother who had deposed him. He destroyed the usurper, though not utterly. For north and west went Benedict, toward the Throtyl Gap and toward Estwilde beyond it—that very Estwilde from which your foolish dice game comes, squire."

I nodded in agreement, passing by our old argument to hear the end of Bayard's story.

"It was there that the Gabriels caught up with him— Gabriel di Caela the Younger at the head of thirty Knights and two hundred foot soldiers, and his father at the head of a force almost twice that size. When the two joined, there was no hope for Benedict.

"Outnumbered, misguided, Benedict tossed illusion after illusion, some of which worked at great cost: thirty foot soldiers died crossing a bridge through the Throtyl Gap when it turned out that the bridge was not there, had never been there. Thirty more were stung to death by scorpions in their sleep."

I sat back on Agion, breathed deeply and rapidly until the big centaur reached back and steadied me.

"What ails you, young master?" Agion asked, his big, stupid face narrowing with concern.

"Altitude, Agion. I'm not good with heights. But we're interrupting Bayard. Go on, sir."

Bayard frowned at me and continued.

"But all of these illusions were as naught when the battle was joined—when Gabriel di Caela the Younger waded through a barrier of renegade Knights, of goblins and goblin hunters and thieves and mercenaries until he stood facing his brother. In that moment, both of them no doubt knew that hundreds of years were hinging upon what happened next.

"Still, there was no choice, as there seldom is in the heat of battle. Gabriel the Younger raised his sword and slashed at his brother with a quickness and an accuracy born in the training of the Order. Those who were present said that the world seemed silent as Benedict di Caela's head tottered a moment, severed above his shoulders, as the face went entirely pale and the eyelids closed. And who knows what the head was thinking when it fell from the shoulders, seeking the ground and oblivion."

"But I gather that wasn't the end of Benedict di Caela," I said finally, when the silence between us had grown uncomfortable, almost oppressive.

"Something it was in pronouncing him dead," Bayard mused, "that indeed unraveled the fabric of things. When Gabriel the Younger struck Benedict down, it seemed as though that was the end of it, that the di Caelas could sit easily upon their wealth and holdings from that time forth. But in the old age of Gabriel the Younger it came—the first visitation of the curse on the family di Caela and the castle in which they lived—a plague of rats and the diseases the rats carry. Two of Gabriel the Younger's sons were lost—the eldest to disease and the middle son to madness.

"It was the youngest this time who survived, who was forced to the most radical of methods to lift the curse. Quickly young Rowland ordered Castle di Caela evacuated, carrying the old man Gabriel the Younger out through the iron gates on his shoulders, the old man screaming and cursing in protest with every step. It was then he fired the castle, and as flames licked through the stony parapets, over the crenelations and in the upper rooms of the towers, it was said that you could hear the rats screaming and a scream above those tiny fevered screams which was lost in smoke and in the sound of old dry beams collapsing. All that was left was the stony shell of the walls, and Rowland di Caela rebuilt the castle from the inside, ruling wisely and peacefully for thirty years, until again the curse returned.

"It is here that the story clouds, for Castle di Caela has been visited by the curse for nigh onto twenty generations, and each time it takes a different form. For the flood failed when Simeon di Caela introduced sluices in the moatwork, and Antonio di Caela stopped the plains fires by opening the right sluices at the right time. The ogre invasions were turned away by Cyprian di Caela, and Theodore di Caela turned back the bandit armies headed by a mysterious, black-robed captain.

"Even the Cataclysm had a hand in Benedict's foiling, for at the end of the fourth generation since the curse it was goblins and goblin miners and sappers who tunneled to within a hundred yards of Castle di Caela, filling the inhabitants with panic for the enemy was unseen, beneath them somewhere. When the Cataclysm came, shaking the very foundations of Krynn, the tunnels collapsed upon their makers, upon Benedict himself.

"So with each generation he has come, unwearying, relentless. In each generation he is turned back, by the eldest di Caela son, sometimes, and sometimes by the youngest or the middle son. Often by the sole surviving heir, for Benedict's assaults, though ill-fated, take their recurrent toll.

"Upon this generation a silence has fallen, as Robert di Caela repelled the last attempt some forty years back, when he was a lad of sixteen. Since that time, the House of di Caela has dwelt in peace, and those in the surrounding country have for the most part concluded that, since the sole surviving heir to the holdings is the Lady Enid di Caela, and whomever she marries, her heirs will take their father's name and the land will pass from the di Caela family forever.

"For the most part, they have concluded that. But the di Caela family is not so sure."

"And thou, Sir Bayard?" Agion asked as Bayard paused once more in the telling. "I have heard this four-hundred-year-old story of wrongs and vengeances and violence heaped on injustices, and I must confess I have many questions. The largest of these is thy part in an ancient story of woe."

"That, too, is a long story," Bayard began, waving as though he'd had enough of stories for the afternoon.

"Oh, but tell us please, Sir Bayard!" Agion insisted. "Galen and I love stories!"

"Agion, perhaps Sir Bayard is a little tired, and . . ."

"Never mind, Galen," Bayard said wearily. "For both of you deserve to know, since all of this concerns you."

And he began again, with another lurid tale, as his audience rode beside him.

*   *   *   *   *

"My childhood promised to be not unlike yours, Galen. I was the heir to a large castle in central Solamnia."

"Which is very like my childhood, sir," I agreed sarcastically. "For after all, I am about third down the line to inherit a rattrap of a moat house in northwest Coastlund."

Bayard ignored me, bent on continuing his story, determined to teach me something or kill us both in the process. Is there any story of any successful man's childhood that is not a hard luck tale?

"It was no soldiers of Neraka, no bandits from Estwilde, who were to rob me of my birthright, my castle and lands which took years to recover. No, none of our old enemies conspired to take my inheritance from me. Instead, it was our own people who rose against my father one summer night—around this time of year, it was, when I was fourteen. They killed my father and mother. Killed the house servants and retainers, too, for 'harboring sympathy for the oppressors,' it was. And when I was fourteen, they would have killed me, had not my good luck and their excitement conspired to save me."

"The villains!" I exclaimed, thinking that exclaiming something was what was expected of me.

I was wrong, evidently. Bayard turned to me, frowned, and shook his head.

"Not villains. Though I, too, thought so at fourteen, and swore to avenge myself upon them and all of their kind. I was too young to understand either their anger or my oath. Not villains, for the most vicious result of the Cataclysm— when the world collapsed and the landscape changed—was that the poor suffered first and most, Galen. I knew nothing of that at the time I swore my oath, knew nothing of the rage that arises when one sees someone not starving simply because he or she was born not to starve. I learned of that rage firsthand in Palanthas."

"Palanthas?" I interrupted. "Let me get this straight. You were orphaned down near the Vingaard Keep, left alone at fourteen, and you still found the courage and the where-withal for a week's journey alone, through the Vingaard Mountains, to the city of Palanthas?"

Agion, too, had become attentive, the name "Palanthas" having roused his thoughts from nowhere. He turned and addressed my protector.

"Palanthas, Sir Bayard? Thou hast visited Palanthas?"

"Yes, Agion. And dwelt there."

"Then perhaps thou canst tell me. Do they eat horses in Palanthas?"

I thought it was centaur superstition and prepared to laugh, but saw Bayard nodding in response.

"The poor do, Agion, when they can get them. But they get them rarely, and are forced to survive on other things. Indeed, I know this firsthand, as I was saying."

He continued, his eyes on the road ahead of him, while I looked at Valorous, at the pack mare, and tried to imagine them gracing a table.

". . . so the keep safely behind me, I rode half a mile away, to where I could no longer see the flames from the watch-tower, only the smoke. Then I picked up the westbound road and was out of my father's lands, into what we once called 'hostile country.' Now it seemed to me that the hostile country was what I was leaving behind, what I would have inherited had the times stayed the same."

He paused, drew Valorous to a halt.

"We'll stop here and eat. A flank of goat can spoil even in brisk autumn weather, if you aren't careful."

Whatever had come to pass in Palanthas, and whatever it had to do with di Caelas, Sir Bayard Brightblade had learned the lessons of survival.

* * * * *

The story paused at the fireside, the goat flank turning on a makeshift spit, Agion standing, watching around us for anything drawn to the smell of roasting meat.

"Enough story for now," Bayard insisted. "You should

rest."

I nodded, then cast a sideward glance at Agion, now idly nuzzling an apple and staring off behind us toward the west and the swamp he could probably barely remember.

I dozed awhile at that stopping place, as did Agion. Bayard picked up telling his tale to us where he had left off, when we were once again on the road southeast, passing through countryside flat and dreary—the landscape for which Coastlund is justly famous. As I watched a hawk wheeling in the deepest part of the eastern sky, he resumed.

"The journey to Palanthas was a perilous one, for the Vingaard Mountains are wretchedly cold at any season. Had it not been summer, the outcome of my story might well have been different.

"Palanthas, of course, is justly famous for its riches, for the library and the colleges and the splendid tower to which mages from all over Ansalon come to be tested and instructed. If that were all that pertained to the city, its love of learning and of wisdom," he stated, smiling ironically, "I would surely have found better welcome there."

I imagined the city of gold, a paradise seated on a hill overlooking drab countryside in all directions. I did not know then that, despite its riches and glimmer, Palanthas was a rough port town sloping into a deep water harbor, and that from that harbor came mariners who spoke in languages none of us had heard or would ever hear again, men who carried daggers with intricate handles and with poison lacing the toothed edges of the blades.

Bayard's story was the first I had heard that hinted at the poverty, the dice and the knives upon which the city's foundation lay. I listened, unbelieving at first, but the parts of Bayard's story "went from one to the other," as Alfric had said before he sank beneath a sea of swampy mud. Agion, however, needed less convincing. He nodded agreement throughout—not that he had been to Palanthas, of course, but that he was sure that the seamy side was the only side of human cities, where small, violent, two-legged creatures gathered in their places of stone and baked mud and dead wood.

"When I arrived in Palanthas," Bayard explained, leaning

forward and picking a burr from Valorous's mane as the horse slowed to a walk, "there was nothing for me in the southern part of the city. Shops there were, and merchants everywhere you looked, and most cared nothing for buyers, intent as they were on buying the wares of other merchants in their attempts to be, say, the only tea merchant, or the only furrier in the city. Those who indeed were looking for someone who might buy their goods looked only to the rich—to the mages in coaches, to the spice traders in their gowns, who rode through the streets on their thoroughbred horses. Can you imagine keeping high-strung horses such as those pent in a city?

"No, there was no employment for me there. I could not even buy food with what little money I had saved from my room at the keep—these merchants were not interested in paltry sums.

"So to the west of town I went, through the ruins of the old temples devoted to gods these people had set aside because such gods were 'inconvenient.' It was here I saw the fabled Tower of High Sorcery, from a distance only and for a short time only. I had no energy to admire architecture. . . ."

* * * * *

Well, it gives you an idea. As Bayard spoke, went on with his tale, a layer of bitterness began to cover every event he touched upon. And I began to understand, when I heard how he slept on the docks, dodging the rats and the cutthroats and the press gangs, why he had turned to burglary when the hunger and the cold began to weigh upon him. Sir Bayard told us of how, finally, the hunger and cold had overwhelmed him in the midst of rifling the chests in a wealthy East End house, how he had found nothing but blankets, had wrapped himself in one and fallen asleep, only to wake in the custody of a Solamnic Knight who was staying in the house on a visit to Palanthas and had, consequently, carried few riches with him for a burglar's taking. He told of how the Knight had known another Knight who had known another who had known Bayard's father, and how only then—through this knowing of someone who knew—could he escape the cold and the hunger and the poverty. How only then, many years hence, a Solamnic army at his back, could he set about to recover his lands and the castle at Vingaard Keep.

"Given the circumstances, sir, I would have called upon any family connections I had myself," I consoled, Agion nodding in agreement with me. "Your castle was yours, handed down through generations, and you simply used those friendships to drive out the rabble who had robbed you."

"But there was no driving out to do against that so-called rabble," Bayard explained. "For they had never taken up residence in the keep. They felt that if they lived in the luxury of those who had 'oppressed' them, as they called it, they might grow to be as ill-willed, as evil, as their oppressors."

"Do you mean they preferred their straw-covered huts to the halls of Vingaard Keep?"

Bayard nodded.

It seemed impossible to believe.

"Then they deserved the driving out and whatever else befell them later, on grounds of sheer stupidity alone," I pronounced.

This time Agion was not as quick to agree, the prospect of thatched housing no doubt appealing more to his appetite than the prospect of stone walls. Nor did Bayard agree, shaking his head slowly, frowning, and squinting as he looked off to the eastern distances.

"Galen, I cannot answer that. What passes sometimes for sheer stupidity is principles in disguise." He kept looking east, then nodded as though he had discovered something at the horizon's edge, which indeed he had. He turned to me, spoke seriously and directly.

"I have just enough trouble with my own principles that I can't pass judgement on someone else's." I sat back in the saddle, prepared for another pompous lecture, but instead Bayard nodded to the east and changed the subject.

"The Vingaard Mountains."

"Sir?"

"The Vingaard Mountains. You'll see them soon. You'd see them now if you knew how to look over distances." He smiled, tugged on the pack mare's reins and brought her abreast of Valorous. "We bear due east from here, and we should reach the mountains close to where the pass lies."

* * * * *

They were black, those mountains, as the evening sky darkened to a deep blue. That night we camped under their shadows, the foliage around us just beginning to grow more sparse as the ground slanted upward and the soil became more rocky.

We slept heavily, or at least I did, and the morning found me no more fresh than when I bedded down the night before. Bayard shook me to wake me, and when shaking did little good, he nudged me with his foot. The side of the boot atop fresh saddle sores did not sit well, in a manner of speaking.

"Another brisk ride today, Galen," he announced cheerfully—cheerfully and, indeed, energetically. "If we continue to ride briskly, and if the gods grant us a clear path and no obstacle upon the road, we can still be at the gates of Castle di Caela in five days, on the eve of the tournament."

CHAPTER 10

It is time for a story of my own.

This one takes place not long after Bayard told his story, and begins while we were clambering through the Vingaard Mountains on our way to Castle di Caela.

As Bayard had feared, the delays in the swamp had made us late, though not irretrievably late, for di Caela's tournament. Still, the tournament waited for no one. Over two hundred Knights had gathered from all over Solamnia, all over Ansalon. The story is told that one Knight came from as far away as Balifor, wearing blue armor and an exotic array of yellow plumes, but he was long gone by the time we reached the castle, having been bested at once in the jousting lists so that he carried no lady back to those eastern mountains at the edge of the world, but a great bruise and a crack in his collarbone.

Yet the Blue Knight from Balifor was not the most unusual contestant to vie for the hand of the Lady Enid di Caela. When you draw contestants from all over the continent, you can rely on a number of them being a trifle . . . outlandish.

There was Sir Orban of Kern, whose forked beard and eye patch made him look somewhat disreputable, almost piratical, though the story goes that no Knight carried within him a heart more innocent and noble. Perched on the shoulder of Sir Orban was a talking parrot, all orange and red and shifting in colors as the sunlight and the moonlight shifted. The parrot spoke constantly to Sir Orban, who answered him in kind, and indeed spoke little to anyone else.

There was Sir Prosper Inverno of Zeriak, the southernmost of the Solamnic Knights who had assembled there at Castle di Caela. His armor was thick and translucent like the Icewall Glacier that lay half a day's journey from his holdings. Thick and translucent, and glittering like sapphires, so that those assembled wondered if it were made of ice or of precious stone. He wore the white skin of a bear around his shoulders, and there were stories that the air at his encampment was colder than that surrounding it, that even wine left in a cup by his tent was crusted with ice in the morning. But no matter the rumors, he was known as a lancer of surpassing skill and surpassing power, and no Knight wanted to draw his lot when the tournament began.

Then there was Sir Ledyard of Southlund, who had spent, some said, too long on the seas. He had seen from a distance the Blood Sea of Istar and his eyes had turned red from the sight. Just as strange was the helmet he wore, with the swirl of conch shells fashioned in metal about the ears so that Sir Ledyard looked like something risen from the Blood Sea itself. Within that helmet, within the conch shells at the ears, it is rumored that the sea always sang, always called him back.

There was also Sir Ramiro of the Maw, a Knight more easterly than the Blue Knight of Balifor, and also more sizable: he must have weighed four hundred pounds, not counting his armor. He was constantly cheery, and fond of traveling songs—faintly obscene ones at that—and I am sure the Lady Enid breathed a sigh of relief when he fell to the Hooded Knight in the first day of the lists.

For the Hooded Knight was the one who set Castle di Caela most abuzz with rumor and speculation. He came on the last night before the tournament began, and he pitched camp a good two miles west of the castle walls, away from all other contestants. Many of the Knights, even the easygoing Sir Ramiro, shivered uneasily on the tournament eve when they looked westward unto the Hooded Knight's encampment, black and silhouetted against the blood red setting sun.

Sir Robert di Caela himself was troubled at the presence, though he did not know why, and found himself looking westward beyond that farthest encampment, looking to the feet of the Vingaard Mountains for some sign of movement, some glint of last light off of the fabled armor of the approaching Bayard Brightblade—some sign that we were there at last. Then Sir Robert could commence the events with confidence, knowing that destiny was in the wings, that the Brightblade he had awaited had come at last.

But when darkness fell, Sir Robert turned from the battlements in disappointment, for the Brightblade had not come, was surely delayed on the road. Meanwhile, more rumors began to spread through the camp.

The Hooded Knight was said to be the heir of a family outcast from Solamnic Orders, who had come to the tournament in the hopes that victory might reinstate his family and win back the honor they had lost generations back at the Cataclysm.

Or the Hooded Knight was an enchanter cursed to wander the earth until he could win a tournament such as this. Then, released from the curse and from his bondage to this sad earth, he would vanish, leaving nothing behind.

Or the Hooded Knight was Sir Bayard Brightblade in disguise, for he had come without attendants, and wasn't it so that Bayard had been wandering through Coastlund in search of a squire?

These stories and more Sir Robert took in that night in the

master bedroom of Castle di Caela. As he pondered all of these stories, there was a knocking at the gates and an outcry from the guards—brief and startled, but whether joyous or fearful Sir Robert could not tell.

It is too late to pay respects this night, Sir Robert thought, or so he told me. *Whoever it is can wait until morning, for the list will go nowhere overnight.*

But then he thought of Sir Bayard Brightblade, somewhere on the road to Castle di Caela. Who knew? He might be outside the gates, awaiting Solamnic courtesy—a warm room, a cup of wine, a polite and ceremonious entering of his name in tomorrow's lists.

Buoyed by his imaginings, Sir Robert rose from his bed, his joints no doubt creaking and cracking.

I can see him now—see him, and hear it all as though it is happening before me.

Sir Robert puts on his armor over his nightshirt, his helmet over his nightcap, and there before the looking glass in the bedroom—the mirror that is one of the last relics of a wife who died beautiful and far too young—the old man adjusts the breastplate and the shimmering visor, trying for a balance between comfort and dignity.

Not bad for a man of fifty, he is thinking. *The hair a little yellow-gray, no doubt, and the poundage straining a bit at the laces of the armor. But all in all, not a far cry from the days in active duty, and certainly good enough to receive the likes of these young combatants.*

Who, except for Sir Bayard Brightblade and perhaps a couple of others, are only pale copies of the Knights who manned the Orders in my youth.

Down the stairs he starts, coughing a little at the hour and the cold. Somewhere in the recesses of the castle, three mechanical cuckoos whir and call out. Sir Robert fumbles with a candle, which flickers briefly and fades, leaving him in the dark. He swears a mild oath and reaches above him, seeking to light the wick from the glowing remnants of a torch on the wall.

It is then that he hears the voice, rising from the foot of the stairs. Even though he has never met the man, he knows this is not Bayard Brightblade as he had hoped; that it is the

Hooded Knight who has pitched camp far to the west, who has waited for darkness before coming to the castle to pay respects and to sign for the lists.

"I assume you are Sir Robert di Caela?" the Knight asks out of the darkness. And di Caela thinks of a dozen things to say—of angry, brave words, of sharp retorts that would let this trespasser know that around this castle we conduct business in the daylight hours—but when he hears the cold, wasted words from the Knight at the bottom of the stairs, it is all he can do to answer with a feeble *yes*.

Sir Robert finds himself backing into the bedroom. Those legs that served him well in a hundred tournaments, that stood stalwart in the pass at Chaktamir where my father became a hero, are moving now before he has even noticed. He stops himself, wonders why he has to summon so much courage to do so.

At the bottom of the stairs there is movement.

"I have come, Sir Robert, to pay respects," the voice says icily. "Yours is a splendid castle, splendid and well-kept. Its restorations are scarcely noticeable, which shows the handiwork of a master craftsman."

"Thank you," begins Sir Robert, recovering from the ill ease, the unnameable fear of the moment past. "Thank you, Sir Knight, though a knowledge of restoration and of castle decorations is, I fear, beyond me. I am a rough man who drops crystal by accident, the kind of man who wipes his chin on the tablecloth when he should be polished, refined, a fitting heir for his old family forebears."

"If that is your greatest failing as a Knight, Sir Robert," soothes the dark voice, "you may hand over your holdings to your heirs, knowing . . . you have served in all ways well. It is my guess that the state of your holdings—your finances, your lands, the welfare of your servants and your tenants—is as healthy as the look of your castle."

"Well, well," di Caela blusters, leaning heavily against the door frame, no longer certain that he dislikes this visitor altogether—indeed, seeing within the young fellow a certain . . . discernment, a wisdom beyond his years, to know how hard an estate could be in the upkeep, how it could sap a man of energy and of needful sleep.

Indeed, were it not that he expects Bayard Brightblade to arrive at any moment . . .

"I assume you have come to put your name in the lists, young fellow," Sir Robert begins heartily, and the man steps into light on the stairwell.

He is dressed in black, as though in mourning for someone dear to him, Sir Robert notes. *And the hood over his face is not nearly as menacing as old Ramiro made it out to be.*

No doubt it is some kind of sorrow he is trying to live down, trying to live past.

"You must be the one they call the Hooded Knight," Sir Robert states—no question in his voice because he is unaccustomed to questions. Questions, indeed, are weakness.

"Gabriel Androctus," comes the voice from the folds of the black cloth, calmly and smoothly. "It will sound better in the lists. Less . . . theatrical."

"Step forward, lad!" Sir Robert exclaims, this time even more heartily. "Come into my quarters while I find a quill."

But Sir Gabriel stands on the lowest step and does not budge.

"Are you deaf, young fellow? Step forward!"

"Ah, but it's late, Sir Robert. Later no doubt than . . . either of us knows," soothes Sir Gabriel. "Now that I have paid respects, have entered the lists, I beg your dismissal, so that I might return to my encampment. The night is short, and I should be rested for tomorrow's contest."

"Indeed, indeed," Sir Robert calls over his shoulder, halfway back to his desk where the quill sits in the inkwell, where the rolled parchment list of tomorrow's contestants lies tied with a velvet ribbon.

He unrolls the list and hears the sound of a door closing distantly below him. He sets the pen to the page, pulls it back with an oath.

"I forgot to ask Sir Gabriel where he comes from, damn it!"

But the halls below are silent. Outside a horse whickers in the stable, and the night gives way to the call of owls and the slow whirring of crickets.

* * * * *

As the tournament lists are displayed the next morning, Sir Gabriel's name is listed without place or lineage at the bottom of the scroll. Of course, Sir Robert wishes he had gathered that information, had completed the lists in proper ceremony.

But the name is there, joining those of the rest of the Knights assembled. What more could a man ask, who prepares to give his daughter to the most resourceful, the most gifted of Solamnic manhood?

He could ask for Bayard Brightblade to be there.

Sir Robert stands at the window of the low tower and looks west across the pennants flapping from the tents in the encampment. There is Ramiro's great bear, the fish in its jaws, and beyond it Sir Prosper's silver mountain of ice. Beyond that still is the strange, flat black banner of Gabriel Androctus.

Beyond that, the mountains, with no rising dust on the paths leading east and downward.

Bayard is not coming. Not yet.

Sir Robert exhales heatedly. His squire begins the burdensome process of helping the old man into the ceremonial bronze armor and the chore over at last, hands him the shield bearing the standard of the House di Caela—red flower of light on a white cloud on a blue field.

Sir Robert descends the tower stairway. It is time to begin the three days' ceremony of giving away his daughter. Of giving away his last name, for in the generations that follow, this place will no longer be known as Castle di Caela— of that much, he is certain.

Castle Inverno, perhaps?

Or Castle Androctus?

Pausing on the landing in the long and winding stairway, he looks once more out the western window. Nothing at the foot of the mountains.

Well then, thinks Sir Robert di Caela resignedly, *let the tournament begin.*

* * * * *

As the morning warms toward noon and the Knights assemble, the elaborate preliminaries that mark a Solamnic tournament take place one by one: first, the prayers, led by the white-robed clerics, to the Great Dragon, to Kiri-Jolith, and to Mishakal—for honor and for skill in the lists and for no wounds mortal.

Then the blessings of the bards, with songs to Huma and to Vinas Solamnus and to Gerald di Caela who fathered the family in whose name this tournament is given.

By the time of the blessings, nearly all of the Knights are there—more than fifty assembled. Four of the most prominent are late.

Sir Prosper Inverno does not arrive until the white-robed clerics of Mishakal are singing the praises of Kiri-Jolith, lord of battle. The large man passes on foot through the ranks of the Knights, his mysterious translucent armor glittering. A murmur arises when the Knights are aware just who it is who walks among them. Sir Robert smiles at the entrance: he has heard southerners have a gift for the dramatic.

Easterners, on the other hand, are at the mercy of less premeditated impulses. Or at least one easterner, for Sir Ramiro of the Maw arrives as the prayers to Mishakal are ending, too late to receive the healthful benedictions of her priests. Apologetically he nods to Sir Robert, who can tell from his eyes that the wine was flowing freely in his encampment last night and has left him drained, aching, and tardy this morning. No doubt his indulgence has ruined his slim chance for victory, as Sir Robert knows it has done in other tournaments at other times.

Later still is Sir Gabriel Androctus, conspicuously absent through the prayers, through the bardic songs, through the arming of the contestants. He only appears at the last possible moment, when the trumpets sound and the Knights step forth as the herald reads their names from the scroll. It is then, as the reading begins, that Robert di Caela sees Sir Gabriel, already armed and mounted, already with lance in hand, riding his horse at a walk through the milling contestants.

It is no surprise that his armor is black. Again Sir Robert feels the uneasiness he did last night on the stairway and wonders why he signed on this man so amiably.

Must've still been half asleep, he thinks. *But surely Orban or Prosper . . .*

Surely their lances will do the work before it comes to . . .

He gazes, this time with dwindling patience and a rising anger, toward the foot of the mountains to the west.

So much for Brightblade and destiny, he thinks. *So much for prophecy.*

* * * * *

Though Sir Robert would never arrange the drawing of the lots so as to provide a disturbing Knight—say, Gabriel Androctus—with a formidable opponent—say, the Blue Knight of Balifor—he breathes more easily when those are the lots drawn. When their lots fall from the silver ceremonial helmet, the number "3" falls in kind from the gold, signaling that they would be the third joust of the day.

Good. It will be over with soon.

Sir Robert muses through the first two lists—contests which are over almost as quickly as they begin. Sir Ledyard and Sir Orban dispose of two young, ungainly Knights from Lemish. Ledyard's effortless victory, in fact, gives rise to a quip from Ramiro that "if Sir Ledyard is the flower of Southlund, is his opponent the blemish of Lemish?"

Sir Robert would usually laugh long and loudly at such foolishness, especially when phrased in Ramiro's peculiar eastern accent. So too would he usually laugh at the dancing bear and the jesters who clown in front of the viewing stands while all wait for the next contest. But now he is silent, attentive to the next contest on the day's card, as the tourney marshals set about the lengthy business of positioning the next two Knights—the Blue Knight of Balifor and the mysterious, black-garbed Gabriel Androctus.

Finally, the herald's trumpet sounds, and the jester act breaks off to a scattered applause from the servants and the less attentive Knights and ladies. Those who know the jousts have already turned their attention to the contestants, each at a far end of the grounds, half concealed by the rising, churning dust. The Knights hold the lances "in arrest," as they say—in upright position, so that they tower like flagpoles or obelisks nearly twenty feet into the warm afternoon air.

Androctus is lefthanded, Sir Robert notices with concern. *It will make it more confusing for the Blue Knight. But he has faced more daunting problems before, judging from the stories.*

At the trumpeted signal from the herald, both men are to close their visors and proffer lances—a sign of preparedness to each other, a sign that the contest should begin.

But here we have a problem. The visors of both Knights have been closed since they appeared this morning, each preferring the drama of his anonymity.

A drama Sir Robert rapidly resents.

"Gentlemen, raise your visors!" he calls out in his most official, most theatrical voice. As he expects and maliciously enjoys, there is hesitation from both parties.

Then, to his surprise, the black-armored Knight raises his visor. It is a pale face—one that women might call handsome, but men would certainly call dangerous. Sir Robert wishes his daughter Enid were beside him, keen judge of faces that she is. But she is not in attendance, having chosen to remain in her quarters and having dismissed the entire event as "so much well-dressed hooliganry." So he is left to his own resources.

But the face in the helmet is as inscrutable as that of an icon or a dead man. It is the face of a man who looks somewhere between twenty and sixty years old—Sir Robert can determine no more closely than that. The eyes are green—a pale, almost yellowish green, and the eyelids unnaturally red, as though painted clumsily or unaccustomed to light.

It is a terribly familiar face, for all its eeriness.

Sir Robert scarcely even looks at the Blue Knight. He is never sure whether Sir Gabriel's opponent raises and lowers his visor. For the Hooded Knight closes his helmet with an echoing snap, leans back in the saddle, and proffers his heavy lance in his right hand—taking no unseemly advantage.

It takes horses of this size—the huge bay destriers of Abanasinia—a few moments to get moving. The large legs and thighs, the barrel chest of the horse are heavy weights, not to mention the armored knight on its back, and to attain anything close to jousting speed takes time, takes muscle. But once such a horse is moving, it is virtually unstoppable, like an avalanche or the cascading flow of a river out of the mountains.

Straight on at the approaching black Knight, the Blue Knight of Balifor spurs his horse, and for a moment the big animal under him shies and whickers, sensing perhaps some unexpected turn in the contest. But soon both men, mounted and armed and lances at the ready, rush toward the center of the grounds, where two pennants—one solid sky-blue, the other black as the eye of the raven—flutter from lofty flagstaffs.

In an instant they collide and their lances splinter. In an instant the Blue Knight topples from his horse to a clatter of armor, leaving one iron-blue boot in the stirrup as the frightened animal gallops off dustily, pursued by the marshal on horseback and by grooms on foot. At the site of the collision, the Blue Knight lies virtually still. For a moment his helmeted head rises slowly, as though he is trying to get to his feet. Then the head sinks down, and the body writhes in pain.

Sir Robert is to his feet at once, thinking of fraud, of some tricky and marginally legal pass with the lance. But everything had seemed clean—scrupulously so—and as the Blue Knight's squire and other attendants rush to the side of their master, Sir Robert looks once more at the victor.

Sir Gabriel seems indifferent to the suffering of his opponent, having made no gesture to ask chivalrously after the well-being of a fallen adversary, as did Orban and even the eccentric, sea-changed Sir Ledyard. Instead, the black Knight sits his horse at the edge of the grounds, broken lance in arrest. Slowly he walks the big destrier toward the viewing stands, and when he is directly in front of Sir Robert, he raises the visor once more.

The look is ironic, the smile as cold as the mountain wastes. It is a smile that stays with Sir Robert through the long first afternoon of the tournament, the sounds of lances breaking and of cheering fading in his ears until they become trivial background noise to his troubled musings, noises like those the mechanical cuckoos make that night in the halls of Castle di Caela, as Sir Robert, having dismissed his servants for the evening, paces hectically in his unkempt chambers.

Surely tomorrow. This Sir Gabriel Androctus will find his match in Sir Orban of Kern. There was a time when Orban's lance was known from here to Tarsis.

Sir Robert sleeps fitfully, hoping that the time of Orban's lance is not over.

* * * * *

It is the fifth contest of the next day, according to the lots drawn from the golden helmet. Sir Robert is surly in impatience, this morning having scolded the Lady Enid virtually to tears (his own tears, mind you, for when scolded, the Lady Enid scolds back!). It is even rumored that on his way to the lists he slapped a dawdling servant.

It is as though a cloud has spread over the fields of contest, as Sir Robert di Caela sits sullenly, anxiously in the viewing stands through four lists he does not care about, waiting for the moment in which Sir Orban and the dark Gabriel Androctus break lances.

It comes at last, in the middle of the afternoon. The champions mount their destriers at opposite ends of the grounds, and their squires walk to the front of the viewing stands to present the champions' regards to the host of the tournament. Sir Orban's squire is a handsome, dark-haired lad inclining to heftiness, the nephew of Sir Ramiro of the Maw, who was defeated by his own wine and by Sir Prosper Inverno on the first day of the tournament. Ramiro, escorted by some unidentified young woman, now sits in the audience next to Sir Robert. They all are applauding the manners of this portly nephew.

Sir Gabriel's squire, on the other hand, is as great a mystery as his protector. A slight figure hooded in black, he had not attended the first day's contest; indeed, everyone thought that Sir Gabriel had arrived alone. No matter who he is or where he comes from, the squire is proficient: he recites the ceremonial words flawlessly and without warmth, returning at once to the side of his protector. Now slowly the squires lead the horses to the spots where visors close, where lances are proffered.

Again, Sir Gabriel Androctus makes a point of switching his lance from the left hand to the right. Sir Robert di Caela swears a most unSolamnic oath under his breath.

The villain is saying he can beat him with the off hand, Sir Robert thinks. And wonders if Sir Gabriel Androctus will make good his boast.

The first pass goes better than yesterday's, Sir Robert thinks, as the Knights cross paths, each splintering his lance against the other's bulky shield. Both Knights rise in the stirrups at collision, and Sir Robert's teeth grind, his shoulder wrenches with the remembered pain of tournaments long past.

Each of the Knights turns his destrier about and reaches out his hand for another lance. The charge begins again at a signal from the marshal. The horses lurch forward like huge, ungainly wagons, and the Knights lean forward in the saddles, lances proffered and menacing.

On the second pass things change, profoundly and terribly. With a crash and the shrieking sound of metal scraped and twisted, Sir Gabriel's lance strikes Sir Orban's shield full on, and the sheer impact drives the weapon through the layers of metal and leather, then again into metal as the lancehead dives into Orban's breastplate.

At once Sir Robert and Sir Ramiro are on their feet, calling foul. For no doubt the Hooded Knight's weapons had been sharpened beforehand, *arms extreme* instead of *arms courteous*—not blunted and padded, as the tournament rules had demanded.

All of this makes no difference to the downed Sir Orban. Twice he tries to rise, and the second time, with a great and painful groan, manages to climb to his knees. There, covered in dust and earth, blood beginning to trickle from the tattered dent in the breastplate, blood trickling also between the vents in the visor as he coughs and coughs again, Sir Orban reels on his knees and falls face first just before the attendants reach him.

His hefty squire, drawing strength from his outrage and panic, turns the armored body onto its back with a quick, smooth movement.

He opens the visor and bursts into tears.

"Receive his soul to Huma's breast," whispers Sir Ramiro.

Sir Orban's parrot shrieks as though it is on fire.

Strong arms seize Gabriel Androctus, who opens his visor and stares with bloodless anger at the sorrow and commotion on the tournament grounds. He smiles faintly once: that is when the head of the lance is drawn from the breastplate still bearing, to the astonishment of everyone, the padding wrapped tightly about it.

"*Arms courteous*," he says. "By your rules, di Caela."

By sheer force, unaided by blade or point or sharpened edge, he has driven his wooden lance into an armored opponent.

The marshals loosen their hold, out of astonishment. Androctus, not bothering to dismount, rides his destrier from the tournament grounds to his tent beyond the western edge of the encampments.

His opponent for the next morning withdraws from the lists. It is a Knight from Ergoth, Sir Lyndon of Rocklin. The Knight and his host stand in the great hall of Castle di Caela. A chair lies in fragments in front of Sir Robert, where he has dashed it to the ground in his fury.

To his outraged host, Lyndon explains:

"I know how this looks, Sir Robert, and how it reflects ill on me. But despite the hooded gentleman's assertions, despite the padding found upon the broken lance, something is surpassingly wrong here, surpassingly unfair in the doings of that black-garbed man."

"I know, Lyndon, and by Huma we've done our damnedest to find him out. We have given that lance the once-over . . . the twice-over! Unless my eyes are bad, unless the marshals themselves are blind, Sir Gabriel has done nothing visibly unlawful. Terrifying, yes, in its clean and blind . . . brutality. But not unlawful."

"Nonetheless," maintains Sir Lyndon, "not the Lady Enid nor her considerable inheritance is enough to compromise my honor. And compromised it would be, were I to tilt against one who had advanced unfairly through the ranks of the tournament, killing a most admirable Knight in his treachery."

"Do not confuse honor with fear, Sir Lyndon," booms a voice from the entrance to the hall.

It is Prosper Inverno of Zeriak, come to the great hall of Castle di Caela after his victory in the lists against Sir Ledyard.

"Impressive show of arms today, Inverno," Sir Robert manages to say, drawing his anger under control at the arrival of his honored guest.

"I thank you, Sir Robert," Sir Prosper replies cheerily. "Had I not unhorsed Sir Ledyard, he would have stood here instead of me. Indeed, I bear more bruises than he does, but he bears a large bruise, I am sure, where it will make it most uncomfortable for him to sit horse tomorrow. The fall was comical, and like a true Knight, he took it with laughter."

Laughing softly and wearily, Sir Prosper walks to the center of the room. His dark green tunic is torn at the right shoulder, where Ledyard's lance has battered against the incomparable translucent armor. Prosper seats himself gingerly, slowly. His legs ache from grasping the huge sides of the destrier.

"So, Lyndon. You're about to withdraw and leave this . . . Grim Reaper to me?" He smiles, leans back in the chair, and crosses his legs painfully.

"The least you could do is bruise him a little this morning—soften him up for the afternoon's joust against me."

"B-but, Sir Prosper!"

"Never mind, Lyndon. Many's the time I've broken lances with five opponents in a day. One more upstart with a self-important sense of his own mystery should be easy enough to handle."

"But your honor, Sir Prosper. Up against one who has fought unfairly? If it were battle, where it is kill or be killed, and no questions, that would be one thing. But a tournament is, after all, sport, and I do not believe that Sir Gabriel Androctus has fought altogether . . . "

"Enough, Lyndon!" storms Sir Prosper. "You think this is still sport, while Orban is lying dead in a wagon at his tents, his attendants and squire weeping and assembling his belongings? How would you like to be that squire and have to tell old Alban of Kern that his son died in a tournament run under *arms courteous* and the killer went on to win the prize?

"No, Sir Lyndon," Prosper concludes. "Sir Gabriel Androctus fights once more this afternoon, and by the Order, I mean to see that he loses."

*   *   *   *   *

Now is the time of emissaries to the tent. For Sir Robert sends a messenger in secret to Gabriel Androctus, asking that the final joust be postponed until the following morning. Then, he maintains, a brief period of mourning for Sir Orban may be observed before his entourage leaves with the body for Kern.

Though this is certainly in Sir Robert's mind when he asks for the postponement, there is also the hope that a night's rest will help Sir Prosper set aside fatigue and stiffness—that morning will find him battle fit and ready to consign this Gabriel Androctus back to whatever pit of snakes he had crawled out of to attend this tournament. It is not to be.

The answer returns, scrawled on a note in a bold and flashing script—the writing of an artist, no doubt, or of a man assured in his resources and afraid of nothing.

> *Nonsense. Why should we change procedure at the whim of a corpse?*
>
> *The tournament must continue. Sir Prosper drew a worthy adversary this morning; I, an unworthy one. Such are the lots in tournament. As I recall, he picked his first from the helmet.*
>
> *Such are the rules you established. Follow them.*

Seated at the desk in his chambers, Sir Robert reads the note he has been handed. He dismisses the messenger, and when the boy leaves, reads it again.

He sighs deeply and in resignation. He holds the note above a guttering candle and watches it catch fire in the last breath of the wick. He holds the burning note as long as he can before casting the withering paper onto the hearth.

*　*　*　*　*

So the last tilt of the tournament begins, and still there is time left to see the hopes of Sir Robert di Caela rise and fall and rise, only to fall again.

For as always, in the long, tedious preparation of Knights that precedes the announcements and the proffering of lances, Sir Robert scans the horizon—almost by reflex now, for he has given up hope of seeing Sir Bayard Brightblade approach from the foot of the Vingaard Mountains.

And yet . . .

What is that, stirring the dust some several miles to the west, there where the plains fade into purple at the edge of the foothills?

The stirring of dust nears and resolves itself into a figure on horseback, riding full tilt for the castle. As the figure draws nearer, out of the shadow of the mountains to where it catches the sunlight, Sir Robert sees the unmistakable glint of distant armor.

Brightblade?

By Huma's blood, would that it were so! For if it is, he is Gabriel Androctus's next opponent. It will be hours of argument with that rule-bound precisian Androctus, hours of searching for precedent in the Solamnic Measure of Knighthood. I would not be surprised if the Hooded Knight insists that the castle scribes and priests and scholars search all thirty-seven volumes of the Measure, Sir Robert thinks. *But even if I lose the appeal to the Measure, I will buy valuable time for Prosper.*

That is, of course, if the figure on the road is Brightblade.

Sir Robert raises his hand, calls a halt to the preparations. A rider approaches, he announces. Approaches rapidly from the west. These are troubled times, when a rapidly approaching rider may signal uprising, invasion, or the gods know what. In light of the times and the situation, then, he requests that "the two remaining contestants stay the first pass for but a little while, until the rider arrives and we know if there is pressing business at hand or" . . . and Robert di Caela laughs . . . "or if it's simply a young man late for a good seat at the final tilt."

Prosper of Zeriak nods politely.

Androctus, on the other hand, is not pleased. He sends message by his hooded squire that the final tilt was scheduled for this hour, and that if Sir Robert is a man of his word, the tilt will begin as scheduled.

This is too much. Sir Robert leans forward in his chair and shouts at the squire.

"Tell your Knight, Gabriel Androctus, that I called this tournament together on my lands. At my expense. For the hand of my daughter. And given that arrangement, tell Gabriel Androctus . . ."

With that, Sir Robert turns from the squire to the Knight, sitting atop his black destrier at the edge of the grounds, and raising his voice even further, until Sir Ramiro flinches beside him and the unknown but beautiful companion of Sir Ramiro stops up her ears, he shouts so loudly that even the thick-necked destriers startle:

"That on this matter, I shall do as I damn well please!"

* * * * *

It is high drama—Sir Robert's finest moment in the last three sorry days. Unfortunately, all of this shouting has a sorry outcome.

For the rider is not Bayard Brightblade at all, but a slow-witted, red-haired boy from Coastlund, dressed in armor that shines from only the shoulders up, since the breastplate and everything below it is caked with a dark, sandy mud, with dried algae and pigcress, and with other, even more foul-smelling things.

A Pathwarden, the boy is. Sir Robert remembers his father, and wonders how a fine old Knight such as Andrew could have sired this sniveling wreckage.

The boy announces his desire to enter the tournament for the hand of the Lady Enid di Caela. The viewing stands erupt with laughter, and Sir Prosper, conscious of the boy's hurt dignity, sweeps his lance mightily through the air. Out of respect for Prosper, the laughter dies.

All except for one man's. From across the tournament grounds, Gabriel Androctus's laughter rises—melodious and deep and almost beautiful. Enid di Caela hears this laughter through the open window of her chambers, wonders whose it is, and walks to the window.

Where she views for the first time any of this tournament, sees Sir Prosper of Zeriak, whom she recognizes from his cloudy, translucent armor, squared off against the man who laughed—a handsome Knight in black armor, whom despite his handsomeness, she dislikes instantly.

She notices that he is lefthanded. Though she has seldom watched a tournament, she knows that lefthanders spread confusion in the lists.

Enid di Caela finds herself fearing for Prosper of Zeriak. Though she would not delight in being Sir Prosper's much younger, much brighter wife, she knows him for a good man.

On the other hand, she knows nothing of the black-armored Knight except that he killed Orban of Kern and that his very looks, though handsome and refined, make her flesh crawl.

Below the Lady Enid's vantage point, the two destriers paw the earth impatiently. They are purebred warhorses, and eager to match strength and speed.

Such is also the case with Sir Prosper of Zeriak. He nods graciously, Solamnically, to his opponent. He shuts his visor and proffers his lance.

The Hooded Knight, Gabriel Androctus, stands immobile like a huge onyx statue at the end of the tournament grounds. Finally, as the herald glances to Sir Robert then raises the trumpet to his lips, Sir Gabriel's lance drops to the ready. The destriers lurch forward, churning the ground behind them, and the final joust for the hand of Enid di Caela begins.

* * * * *

For two such skilled and accomplished Knights, the first pass is tentative, even awkward. Androctus, no doubt daunted by his opponent's reputation, gives Sir Prosper and his huge cream-colored destrier a wide berth in the lists, and Sir Prosper feints clumsily with the big lance, clearly adjusting to the shield attached to his opponent's right arm.

Lesser men would have undone themselves in the first

pass, scrambling to topple their opponents at once in a flashy, obvious stroke. But poised and patient—what the older Knights called *scientific*—Sir Gabriel and Sir Prosper pass each other again, then once more. Only at the fourth pass does lance strike shield. The older, more experienced Knights, Sir Robert and Sir Ramiro included, settle back, expecting a long afternoon.

Even the oldest, most veteran of Knights is surprised at the next pass. For it is as though each man discovers a weakness in the other's defenses, and exploits it immediately. At the fifth pass the lances splinter, Sir Prosper's striking Sir Gabriel's shield head on, sending the Hooded Knight tumbling off the right flank of his destrier, where he catches his foot in the stirrup, is dragged a few paces, then tumbles free of the horse and scrambles unsteadily to his feet.

Sir Gabriel's lance in turn has hit Sir Prosper's shield head on, and as in the fateful tilt with Sir Orban, explodes through toward the breastplate of the charging Knight. But Prosper, though older, is quicker than his late comrade in arms: a lightening twist to his left avoids the padded end of the lance, which shoots by him at the speed of a meteor. Still, Sir Prosper's turn in the saddle costs him his balance. He falls over the central railing of the lists and lands on his side, rising painfully by pulling himself up along the side of the railing.

For a moment, surely each man thinks he has lost. Then, seeing his opponent dismounted, each draws his sword with renewed confidence and wades toward the other.

Ten feet from each other they stop. Sir Prosper reaches to the blade of his sword, blunted carefully in tournament fashion.

"*Arms extreme*, Sir Gabriel?" he asks, ceremoniously, politely, and coldly.

"If our host permits," Sir Gabriel agrees. "After all," he pronounces loudly, "Sir Robert has reminded us that it is his tournament."

"*Arms extreme*," Sir Robert declares, without hesitation.

"Then so be it," declares Sir Gabriel, and holds out his hand, into which the hooded squire slips a wickedly sharp sword. The squire of Sir Prosper follows suit.

Slowly and warily, the two Knights circle one another. Then, with snakelike quickness, they close. They lock blades.

"I can't even follow the swordplay," Sir Ramiro whispers to Sir Robert, then starts to say something else.

But in that moment a flickering movement from Gabriel's wrist strikes home. Sir Prosper wobbles, a deep and draining cut on the back of his right leg. It is all but over: tendons severed in the back of his knee.

"N-now, see here, Sir Gabriel!" Sir Robert cries out into the sudden silence of the tournament grounds. "Don't you think this is enough?"

"Enough?" Sir Gabriel calls back calmly. "Oh, hardly enough." Another abrupt move of the dodging left hand, and Sir Prosper falls to his knees, then over face first, completely hamstrung.

Still, never an outcry from Prosper. He is completely silent in the pain and in the prospect of pain—and worse— to come.

"You've won the tournament, my holdings, Enid's hand," pleads Sir Robert. "Now stay your sword."

"Who was it agreed to *arms extreme*?" asks Sir Gabriel. "For once, Sir Robert, for once in the history of your family, abide by your word."

For the last time, lightning-quick, the sword hand flashes down upon the defenseless head of Sir Prosper of Zeriak, who looks southward impassively in that moment before the blade strikes home.

*   *   *   *   *

So on the Sunday next, four days from now, Sir Robert di Caela will give the hand of his daughter Enid to her betrothed, Sir Gabriel Androctus. With his daughter's hand he will give, in time to come, the lands and holdings of the di Caela family. He will give Castle di Caela itself.

CHAPTER 11

While all of this happened, we were still in the Vin-gaard Mountains.

In the steep foothills, our progress had slowed considerably as a heavy rain washed down over the trails. Agion and Bayard had been forced to stop on two occasions, fell some nearby trees, and lay logs across the mired trail—because, mired or not, off-road was so steep it was impassable for horses, and the road was our only way through the mountains without going back and around and missing the tournament entirely.

After two days of mire and sludge and misery, we had begun to climb even more steeply, into a landscape of solid rock that formed the mountains themselves. That morning was gray but surprisingly cheery, for the sun rose veiled behind the clouds, and the promise of rain or worse weighed less heavily on all of us. Bayard rode at the lead of our party, flamboyant on Valorous.

The horse was obedient and danced gracefully on the pathway ahead of Agion, who was lost in the delight of an armful of apples he had gathered, and who carried me, sulking, on his back. I in turn was leading by the rein a pack mare whose sullenness had no doubt passed into smoldering rage back at the swamp, when Bayard returned the showy, burdensome Solamnic armor to her load.

The road began to level off at midmorning, and it was like passing through to the other side of the season. The grasslands of Coastlund, not yet lost entirely to autumn, faded to brown once we climbed into the foothills of the mountains, the rich soil that was the source of so much boring greenery and scenery giving way to a stingier, rockier ground beneath us.

* * * * *

It was getting on toward evening, and we had yet to reach Bayard's remembered pass when we first saw the ogre. He was a hefty creature, dressed in full battle armor, his powerful thick legs rising to a chest as huge around as a vallenwood trunk, and broad shoulders atop that, upon which sat a helmet surprisingly small. His fangs were yellowed and as twisted as cypress trees. His knobbed feet seemed to sprout from the metal legs of the armor as though he was sending out deep, grotesque roots into the rocks. He carried a trident and net, as though he had come from the sea. His horse looked freighted and unhappy.

About him the air seemed to shimmer gray, shimmer black. It was as though something within the armor was on fire. The bare branches of the scrawny mountain trees that lined the trail bent away from him as though he were poison or an intense and unforgiving cold.

Ahead of me Bayard nodded, made as if to pass, but the monster reined his horse into Valorous's path and stood there. Bayard saluted and tried to pass on the other side, but again found the ogre in his way.

From beneath me Agion called out, "The thing hath little

courtesy, Sir Bayard. Don thine armor and civilize it."

Bayard tried to pass the creature once more and was again obstructed. Now Agion's suggestion sounded better to him. He wheeled Valorous about and trotted back to the pack mare, where he dismounted, dragged the armor to the ground, and began to dress.

"Well, squire?" he asked, looking up at me from the disarray of metal he had scattered across the ground.

"Well, sir?"

"Isn't it your squirely duty to help me on with this?"

We sat there assembling in front of the monstrosity. I worked frantically, guessing which buckle went where, which strap tied over which, even which direction the visor faced as I slipped the iron helmet over Bayard's head. Finally, Bayard stood pieced together before me, and I boosted him back atop Valorous. Agion stepped aside, too chivalrous to join the fight that was about to take place, and too dense to see the great advantage there would be if he only cast chivalry aside.

Of course I thought about turning and running. But I knew I would not get far on foot, and that the big savage would kill Bayard first, then Agion, then ride me down over the rocky foothills, tying my severed ears to his bridle as some sort of barbarian trophy. As Gileandos said, my imagination was "prone to frolic at disaster's edge," and it was frolicking now, through fields of murder and torture and every kind of mutilation for which there was a body part to be disfigured.

Bayard mounted, drew his sword, and spurred Valorous off in a canter toward Sir Enormity, who stood waiting calmly, clutching his trident with both hands.

Disaster drew closer when Valorous broke to a full gallop and Bayard raised his sword. Instead of lunging with the trident, our huge enemy backed away from Sir Bayard's charge and, as casually as if he were beating a rug, swung the trident at the passing figure, catching Bayard with the flat side of the tines and sending him over backwards onto the rocky ground, where he lay as still as the stones around him.

It was a long time before Bayard stirred from that place.

Meanwhile, his opponent rode up the trail some distance, stopping where it narrowed and cut through a granite escarpment, where the stone that bordered the trail rose well above his shoulders. It was impossible to travel around the ogre as he sat on horseback, wedged into the pass like a boulder.

Agion had moved to Bayard's side at once, had knelt by him—not an easy thing to do for a centaur—and was treating him, trying to revive him with various strong-smelling herbs.

I, on the other hand, stood there. I watched the enormous creature sit on his horse like so much inert baggage. He did not move. He did not menace.

But I felt as though he was regarding me. And I had been regarded in that manner before.

I heard Bayard sputter behind me, heard the armor rattle as he rose to his feet.

"What is that you waved under my nose, centaur?"

"Goldwort, designed to . . ."

"I know, I know, to steal the breath and kill the patient. Now if you're done trying to poison me, perhaps you'd . . ."

It took Bayard a moment to remember where he was. He stopped suddenly and looked up the path, to where the ogre sat astride his horse, waiting like a huge metal barricade. I stood where I was, in no hurry to rejoin my companions. But as I watched Bayard stagger a little on the rocky incline, raise his sword in the Solamnic salute, motion to Agion to help him back onto Valorous, I felt something a little like shame.

Shame for not lending a hand.

Not that I let that bother me for long. After all, a fellow could get killed up here among the ogres and centaurs. I crouched by a stump downhill from the conflict and awaited the outcome, all set to run if the conflict turned against my protector.

Mounted now, Bayard wheeled Valorous about, and shouted out a challenge to the monster who loomed over the path ahead of him.

"Who are you who so rudely stands between us and our peaceful way across these mountains?"

No answer.

Bayard continued. "If you have aught of peace or justice in your spirit, stand aside and let us pass without quarrel or conflict. But if it is quarrel and conflict you desire, rest assured you will receive it at the hand of Bayard Brightblade of the Vingaard Keep, Knight of the Sword and defender of the three Solamnic Orders."

It sounded pretty, indeed, but the guardian of the pass stood where he stood, a darker form against the dark eastern sky.

Sword raised, Bayard charged at the ogre again.

This time it was over almost as quickly as it began. The creature flicked his net casually, entangling Bayard's sword and sending it clattering into some rocks south of the pathway. Then, he brought the flat side of his trident thundering down on Bayard's helmet, and again our champion toppled to the ground, where he lay still. The victor sat on his horse and watched as Agion galloped forward, lifted Sir Bayard in his arms, and carried him awkwardly back down the trail and out of immediate danger.

It was a brave move and a foolish one for the centaur, for who could say when that trident would descend with stabbing quickness?

Out of trident-reach, Agion passed me at a trot, and I turned to follow him, dragging a reluctant pack mare behind me.

A hundred yards or so from the waiting ogre, we settled in a small clearing of stones just off the road. Agion knelt again and passed the goldwort under Bayard's nose once more.

This time it did not work.

"Is he . . ."

"Just battered senseless," Agion assured me. "Sir Bayard is liable to be past recall for some time." He looked up the trail ahead of us. "And it seems our adversary has vanished."

I followed his glance. Indeed, the narrow pass was now clear of behemoths.

"Can you carry him, Agion? Maybe we can slip through there while Sir Largeness is away. Or maybe we can go back west, into Coastlund."

The centaur shook his head.

"We are here, my little friend, for the duration. The Knight is injured. He cannot be moved safely. So until he wakes . . . we keep a fire, keep a vigil, keep a watch for ogres."

I looked around us. It was scarcely a promising landscape. Bayard had· led us higher and higher into the Vingaard Mountains, past the tree line and into a forbidding, rocky country of gravel and ice and solid rock. Around us the world had fallen into a pensive, uncomfortable silence.

* * * * *

The next day was possibly the worst so far. Bayard did not respond to goldwort, to mimseng, or to switchweed. I know because Agion had me scouring the rocks for those herbs and for any others I could find. Once I had rooted around the clearing as far up the trail as my courage would take me, I returned to our campsite, where Agion knelt above a still unconscious Bayard.

"Did I ever tell thee what Megaera had to say about switchweed?" Agion asked.

"Look, Agion, I don't think this is the time—"

"'Good for what ails thee, Agion,' she would say, 'as long as thou'rt willing to wait a year for it to work.'" He tossed the switchweed aside indifferently.

"Agion—"

"Thou must keep watch for the return of the mysterious ogre. Between the weather's sudden turnings and the hidden properties of these foul-smelling plants, I have enough to worry about. As for me, I plan to make us comfortable for the night, for today the odds do not look good for Bayard's waking and our departure."

* * * * *

It looked even worse as the night approached. The air thinned and the temperature dropped even further. It was as though the season had suddenly changed to winter. The landscape around us was bathed in the bloody orange light of the setting sun, and our shadows grew taller and taller as the darkness rose out of the east in front of us. Soon our only light, our only heat, came from the meager flame Agion had managed to kindle from the sparse dried branches and leaves.

I drew my tooled leather gloves from my pocket—the expensive ones I had bought with the servants' money and hidden all of our long, swamp-infested journey in order to avoid suspicion. It was too cold for me to care what anyone thought of my accessories.

"Don't you think Sir Bayard is taking these games down in Solamnia too seriously?" I whispered to Agion. "After all, it isn't his life alone he's risking on this harebrained jaunt through the mountains, though he has done a good job at risking that."

"I know not," Agion replied. "Is it not written so in his Code somewhere—that the tournament is life and death?"

"I grew up among Solamnics, Agion, and I trust I would have heard such foolishness had such foolishness been around. What's life and death is this depth of winter we're about to plumb. Look at him there."

Bayard lay on a blanket beside us, bundled against the cold, descending wind. He showed no signs of waking, and it was twelve hours since he had moved.

"What wouldst thou have me do?" Agion snapped. "It is not the onset of death by cold, nor even the onset of frostbite. What thou sufferest is mere discomfort, Master Galen—the aches of a nobleman's son who finds the fireplace ready when the frost first touches the ground. Th'art soft, Master Galen, and though 'tis not my place to tell thee such things, th'art in need of the telling."

He turned to face me with a look of distaste he no doubt believed would make me repent on the spot.

"First and foremost, it is the cowardice that is most unseemly, most unbecoming for one in the service of a Knight such as Sir Bayard. But it is also the lesser things—the whines and the whimpers and the concerns with long odds and stormy weather. Th'art often a pain not worth the having, for if there's a burr in thy saddle, thou'lt find it, and a pebble in thy pallet, so that thou hast me marveling at what thou wouldst say in the teeth of real danger, real discomfort. I have said too much."

"At least in that you are right, centaur. You have said too much. Maybe I do whine and whimper about the weather, but look around you, Agion. It's getting colder the higher we travel, and a big thick-witted centaur is going to be the last one to feel any real emergency in the temperature.

"But emergencies happen. We could run out of food in the highest reaches of this pass. You've heard the stories—how the travelers go through provisions, then through the horses, then through each other? Well, after the traveling food is gone, it'll be the pack mare first, then Valorous—I'm sure we'll go in order of familiarity. Guess who'll be third, Agion? Folks wait until the last moment to eat something in their species—it's just human nature, everything's nature except maybe goblins.

"Remember who's the odd one out here," I whispered, closing my argument as menacingly as possible. "Species loyalty is a powerful thing."

So we sulked and refused to speak to one another. We traded off watches for the rest of the night, each sleeping fitfully when it wasn't his turn.

Agion surely did, snoring so heavily that at times I woke suddenly at my post on watch, filled with the fear that I was about to be covered by an avalanche or a rockslide tumbling down upon us from some peak we hadn't noticed.

All of this was silliness, was dream. But sleep was fitful because of the dreaming, as old fears rose from memory and imaginings to share my fireside and blanket. I dreamed of the Scorpion finding me, of Bayard finding out about the Scorpion, of Alfric rising from the mud of the swamp, knife in hand, and of Father on the road to meet us, clutching the order for my hanging tightly in his gloved hand.

Some time very early in the morning—the night was at its absolute darkest—I started awake from my watch again.

Good luck was with me. I had nodded off, and still no dire thing had happened. I sighed and looked overhead, where the Book of Gilean wheeled faintly in the sky above me, covered fitfully by the clouds that passed rapidly by from east to west. It was hard to see beyond the light of the fire, hard to hear beyond the crackle of the blaze, the breathing of the horses, Agion's snoring, and the dim cry of the wind.

But somewhere off in the darkness to the south—in the direction of the pass—the wind lifted a sound toward me, making me sit up and listen again, this time to a distant silence, as the sound did not repeat itself.

For an hour or so I sat there alert and silent, still listening. But from that point onward I heard only the snap of the pine branches in the fire and the rumble of the centaur, who slept untroubled by thought, I was sure, because he was so untroubled by any thought while he was awake.

What I had heard was the sound of voices passing. And for the life of me, they sounded like my brothers' voices calling my brothers' names.

When Agion replaced me on watch, for a moment I thought about following those voices.

But where had they gone?

Who was to say that I had heard brothers on the wind and not some monstrosity?

*   *   *   *   *

Bayard awakened the next morning, babbling to someone about securing the keep, that "Vingaard is once more ours, Launfal." He was a hundred miles away and a dozen years back, evidently, and it took us a while to explain to him where he was.

It took him awhile yet to recover. Sullenly he resolved to wait until the next day for us to travel, knowing that his wounds would not bear the journey on horseback.

When evening came, Bayard had recovered some. He relaxed and became almost pleasant. There was still no sign of the ogre, so he and I climbed an enormous, sloping array of rocks that peaked above the trail, leaving Valorous and the pack mare behind in the care of Agion. Bayard gestured toward the horizon.

"Perhaps they watched for dragons here back in the Age of Dreams, when there were dragons," Bayard murmured.

"Who watched, Sir Bayard?"

"Dwarves. Maybe men. Maybe a race older than both, or one born from both and since forgotten. We know so little of the time in which these rocks were placed here."

He looked at me reflectively.

"Indeed," he concluded, "we know just enough of our past to get us in trouble."

He was silent for some time. Below us and to the east, the faces of the mountains declined rapidly into foothills, then rolling hills, then plains I could see even from where we were standing—from great distance and in the growing dark.

This must have been the way this country looked at the time of which Bayard was speaking—back in the Age of Dreams, when men fought elves, when dwarves trusted nobody, when everyone looked out for dragons. Back then, perhaps, the trees grew more thickly in the altitudes, unhewn and unfired. Back then, even in autumn, there might have been more bird song.

As I reflected, a pinpoint of light flickered at the farthest east my eyesight could reach. It was followed by another, then another, and soon a whole patch of dark downward and eastward lay speckled and spangled with dim light. It looked as though you were looking down a well where someone—some mischievous boy, perhaps—had hidden vials of phosfire.

"Solamnia," Bayard said softly behind me.

I turned to see him looking beyond me, smiling.

"What you see lighting the eastern horizon is a village in Solamnia. A pleasant little place, halfway between the end of this pass and the south fork of the Vingaard River. We should be there by tomorrow night, the gods willing. And from there the Castle di Caela is but two days away—a day and a night of hard riding if we travel with spirit and the horses are able.

"As for now," he said and looked at me more directly, his gray eyes drooping with fatigue, "as for now, a rest well deserved. No matter my hopes of arriving on time to the tournament, I shall not risk the lives of my companions on rocky terrain in the blackness of night."

"Master Bayard? Master Galen?" Agion called from below, for the first time a note of fear in his voice.

He was afraid of the slippery rocks and sliding gravel beneath his large and clumsy hooves.

Bayard walked to an overlook behind us, to where he was in sight of the centaur.

"Agion, make a fire. We shall be down shortly, and then all of us will sit and talk, and sleep when the need for sleep comes."

The great pile of rocks stretched over the plateau for almost a hundred yards. Bayard knew the pass well, knew the plateau, too. If he had decided not to travel by night, we were crossing deceptive ground indeed.

On the leeward side of the rock pile the air was calm and dried branches lay bundled and stacked in an orderly fashion, as though the travelers before us had looked out for our comfort, never knowing who we might be or how much time would pass before we followed their footsteps.

Agion scraped together the fire, using one bundle of the kindling. The horses saw the spark from the flint, smelled the pine smoke, and moved closer to us as the light began to rise from the dried branches. We sat, our backs to the warmth of the horses, our faces and our outstretched hands to the warmth of the fire. It was there that I heard the rest of Bayard's story.

And understood that history was something like this notch in the road filled with abandoned bundles of kindling—that things are left within it to be picked up and used later, in ways that those who had left those things might never have dreamed.

Bayard was right about our past, that often it showed us only enough to get us in trouble.

"So there were Brightblades at the outset of this story of di Caelas," I began when the warmth had settled on my skin and the hardtack—almost the last of the traveling food we had brought with us from the moat house—had settled in my stomach. "But what are the Brightblades doing in the story now?"

Bayard stirred the fire.

"What is *the* Brightblade doing. You see, Galen, I am the last of the line, and therein lies the end of the story.

"For the history of the Brightblades touches that of the di Caelas twice—at the beginning of the family and at its end. Indeed, it is a Brightblade who is supposed to lift the di Caela curse.

"Don't tell me I've forgotten to mention the prophecy that ties our stories together."

He gave me a look of innocent concern.

"Yes, Bayard, I am afraid you 'forgot to mention' it. After dragging me through some swamp that nearly swallowed me whole, then past some behemoth of an ogre that nearly chopped up all of us, then into the coldest weather I've ever seen, where even my extremities give up on me, I can understand why you might 'forget to mention' that there is a genuine reason for all of this, and that we are supposed to do something about this curse."

"Calm yourself, Galen," Bayard urged, rising from the fire and moving slowly toward me. "Hear the rest of my story.

"It is the beginning of the end for the line of Benedict di Caela, or for Benedict di Caela himself, if he is, as some legends claim, four hundred years old and forever returning. It is the beginning of the end for him, or he wins and wins finally.

"For I remembered the prophecy, word for word, the first time I saw it in the Great Library of Palanthas, when there was little to do except read and wait and hope to gain wisdom. I found the book by accident, as such things are often found. I turned to the third chapter at random and read it only idly at first, my interest maintained when the Brightblade name occurred in the text, and I skimmed hundreds of pages to find that name again. It was there at the end of the chapter, in a scrawl in the margin that obviously had bearing on me.

> For generations down, the curse
> Arises in di Caela's hall
> And things descend from bad to worse,
> Until a girl succeeds to all.
> When things have reached their darkest pass
> The Bright Blade joins unto the bride,
> And generations from the grass
> Arise and lay the curse aside."

"Lots of verbal hocus pocus if you ask me," I commented. We had listened in silence to the night wind outside our shelter as it whipped across the plateau. "The first part is pretty clear, and di Caela's inheritance descends to a woman for the . . . first time?"

Bayard nodded. "In four hundred years."

"What's more, I must allow that 'Bright Blade' is doubtless no coincidence. But the last part is too gnarled and obscure and badly rhymed. Have you figured out any other way to read it?"

"Not for the life of me, Galen. Each time I read it, the meaning comes out the same. Which is, I allow, unusual for prophecy."

The wind raised its voice, and Bayard moved closer to the fire, regarding me calmly over the wavering flame.

"It also seems to me that when one finds himself written into the chronicles to come, whether in Sath's prophetic poems, or the History of Astinus of Palanthas, or a more humble work such as the one I found in the Great Library, when one knows he has a part to play in the unfolding of that history, one plays that part and trusts that his role, because he intends only good, will be for the good."

"But, Master Bayard, what if, despite the goodness of heart and goodness of intention, your role is a disastrous one?" Agion asked, draping a cloak about my shoulders.

The centaur was turning into quite the philosopher.

"Or what if, sir, your role is a good one, yet you destroy two equally well-intentioned companions in the process of finding your place in history?"

Bayard rested his head against stacks of granite and limestone. He closed his eyes, and the wind sang its desolate song all around our campsite. Outside this circle of fire and stone, the night was fit for nothing. It was much like I pictured the landscape of the white moon Solinari, claimed by the myths to shed good influence over the planet, but cold and extreme and forbidding on its surface.

"Don't you think I have considered these things?" Bayard asked finally, and like the wind over the plateau, a terrible, desolate look passed over his face. He seemed twice his thirty years for a moment, and it alarmed me.

"But after all," he continued, and the pained look softened, "it does no good considering these things so long before they happen and," he gestured about him, "in such a mournful place.

"Rest assured," he said softly, urgently, "that I put you at risk for no personal gain, for no ambition of my own."

Agion nodded and drew nearer the fire.

I was less convinced.

"What does Sir Robert di Caela make of all this business?"

"Sir Robert di Caela," Bayard answered hesitantly, "may not know of this *business*, as you call it."

"May not know of some prophecy affecting his family?"

"Some *obscure* prophecy, Galen," Bayard corrected. "Made not even by a historian, but by someone writing in the margin of an old history—in a different hand and a different ink."

"Whatever. You mean to tell me that you're the only one familiar with this . . . this oracle, sir?"

"That may be. It was shelved deep in the Great Library. I came upon it by accident—or rather, not by accident, but by curious design, as I like to think. The manuscript was in a wavering, disordered hand that even the young sharp eyes I was blessed with at the time had trouble reading—I suspect it was the original, and that it had never been copied by the scribes. And yet the hand that wrote the prophecy was bold, flowing."

"But I could write a book of prophecies, sir, and spin the future out of my most prized imaginings, or use these dice I wrestle with to predict a future you would say was a bogus one. Who's to say your sage is a genuine seer? That he isn't some mountebank selling trinkets, peddling at outrageous prices those oils he claims will restore eyesight if you place them on the ailing brow? But in fact the trinkets are glass, the oil is watered patchouli. And what's in that book may belong on the same shelf of shabby wonders."

Bayard nodded gravely.

"I've thought of that, Galen," he maintained, knitting his eyebrows.

"All I have to say," he continued, drawing his hands away from the fire, cupping them, and blowing into them, "is there is a coincidence that is not coincidence, that underlies everything we do that goes into making up history. It was chance that I should find the *Book of Vinas Solamnus*, but it was not blind chance. It was a chance that took place in a larger order I failed to recognize at the time."

"Like the roll of two red dice," I maintained flatly, and Bayard stared at me a long time, started to speak, then grew silent once again. The pack mare pawed the hard earth behind us and Valorous whickered, as though someone was laughing and dancing beyond the warmth of our fire.

"As for now," Bayard concluded, wrapping himself in the blanket, his breath steaming though he stood only ten feet or so from the heart of the fire, "as for now, it's best not to worry about such things. Best to sleep."

* * * * *

The ogre returned as it neared midnight, as Bayard had predicted he would. The brute was no worse for the previous scuffle and, as far as I could see, was spoiling again for contact.

Bayard, on the other hand, was still in terrible shape. Nevertheless, he raised himself slowly—wearily, I thought—and gave his enormous opponent the time-honored Solamnic salute. Holding his sword in the right hand, his dagger in the left, he stood by the campfire, faced the dark hulk on the horse and folded his arms ceremoniously.

Well, the dark hulk moved not a whit in response. I doubted that was because the big fool had any reverence for Solamnic ceremony, or any reverence at all, for that matter. Instead, he was probably sitting there looking forward to the little armored fellow's riding within the operating reach of his trident.

Agion and I were after Bayard before he rode to meet the ogre, both trying to stop him from tangling with the whirlwind.

"You're not obliged to fight this fellow, Sir Bayard," I urged. "Let's get him to chase us back up the trail and set a snare for him."

It seemed reasonable, or so I thought. Bayard, on the other hand, tightened a cinch on his greaves, his back to me.

"But if thou contendest," Agion added, "that our way

must lie through this monster in our path, then remember it is our road—mine and Galen's—too, not simply thine alone." He stared at the ogre, sizing up the opposition. "And that the fight ahead is our fight as well as thine."

"But I suppose that if we must go through with this," I swiftly interjected, shooting Agion a look of pure and blistering hatred, "that I must urge you to remember your own words, that 'this is a conflict between Knight and opponent.' As much as Agion and I would like to help, we really can't unless we kind of undo your principles altogether and as a result, make you kind of unworthy of Solamnic Knighthood."

"Which is also why I cannot resort to trickery, Galen."

"I understand, sir," I equivocated.

This time things began differently. Valorous, remembering no doubt the encounter two nights ago, had passed beyond skittish to lathered and twitchy, evidently having his fill of unequal contests. Weary and sore though he seemed, Bayard calmed the big stallion with one pat of his gloved hand, then turned to us.

The look I saw on his face was not that of a doomed man. Tired, yes, and no doubt a little afraid, but beneath the fatigue and the fear was a confidence I had not seen before, had not imagined.

"If I can hold him off a while, hold him off only this night, Galen, I shall defeat him," Bayard whispered. "Of that I am certain.

"For surely there is a reason that he fights by night alone. I wager that it's as simple a reason as those that run through the old legends: because he can't fight by day, because the sunlight weakens him and vexes him. Things of darkness are often like this. Think of the ogre's cousins, the goblins and the trolls, how they recoil at healthy sunlight."

Bayard turned Valorous toward the battle, glanced back over his shoulder, and smiled as he shut the visor of the helmet.

"Playing the fox, boy! Playing the fox!" he shouted, as Valorous broke into a canter and, once again under a confident and sure hand, into a gallop, straight toward the dark, imposing figure of the ogre amidst the rocks, off on a dangerous gamble.

I scrambled to a small plateau by the roadside, where I had a vantage point from which to view the evening's action.

As Bayard approached the mounted ogre, I glanced up at the clear and chilly autumn sky. The spiraling, infinite stars in the constellation of Mishakal, goddess of healing and knowledge, wheeled over me, and if I were a stargazer, such a sign would have given me courage.

Instead I cast the Calantina, there in the light of two moons, in the faintest glow from Agion's fire a hundred feet away.

Sign of the Mongoose.

I knew of the Snake Dances in farthest Estwilde, where the mongoose is brought in to the last movement of the dance, where with nothing but quickness and brains and sharp teeth it goes up against the deadly *ophidian* to the music of pipe and drums. And I became a little more hopeful that Bayard's version of events would somehow come to pass, that we were in a story where the sun would rise, the ogre would scream a withering, bloodcurdling scream, and vanish into smoke or melt away before our eyes.

By the time I had settled in to watch, Bayard had stopped some forty feet from the ogre—twenty feet or so out of the range of the net and the trident, where the rocks drew back from the side of the trail.

Where there was room to maneuver.

Bayard stayed where he was on the trail—unmoving, staring down his enemy. The ogre responded in kind, a dark cloud rising as though out of the ground, covering his horse until it seemed that he was borne on the back of a thunderhead. So still were the two combatants that a rabbit hopped silently out of the rocks by the side of the road, stood poised on her haunches between them, and then hopped unhurriedly away, never aware that she had passed through a region that might at any time explode in swordplay and metal and blood. It was that still.

When the rabbit had passed, when the trail lay in stillness awhile longer, there was suddenly the slightest of movements. But not from Bayard.

The ogre's hand moved slowly on the trident. He shifted his gaze to regard Bayard more directly, and as he did, Bayard's cloak fluttered out like a banner in an icy wind tearing itself from his shoulders and flapping off like a huge, ungainly bird down the trail behind him.

Still Bayard did not move. I thought he had become part of the landscape, that he had seen into the terrible eyes of the ogre and been turned to stone.

Slowly the trident raised, "proffered," as the old Solamnic term went, pointed like a lance, its three nasty teeth aimed directly at Bayard's heart.

Still Bayard did not move. Valorous twitched nervously, snorted, but the steadiness of Bayard's hand calmed him.

Motionless they remained another long while. Agion joined me on the plateau and placed his hand on my shoulder. His strong grip kept me almost as stationary as the combatants we were watching.

A raven lit on the ogre's shoulder. For a minute he looked comical, like a huge, ungainly wizard in a painting. Then the raven ducked beneath its wing, raised its head alertly, and fluttered off.

I had dark forebodings.

Then the fury was unleashed. Valorous broke into a charge, and ten feet at most from his waiting enemy, Bayard reined the big beast into a skidding, noisy turn toward the left side of the ogre.

Who hadn't been figuring on that. Who had raised his trident as he had before, like a club or a cudgel, ready to batter senseless whoever or whatever rode past him on his right side.

Before the big fellow could adjust, Bayard was on him, sword descending in a flashing blow that would have severed any limb short of a monster's. But as Bayard moved to the attack, the ogre dropped the trident and tossed the net into his face, entangling the sword in its downward arc so that even though it sliced readily through the strands of the net, all that slicing slowed it some, until, by the time the blow reached the enemy, it was one he could deflect with his heavily plated forearm.

The sound of metal on metal was a new one, unlike the

clang and clatter heard on tournament fields. Instead the ogre's armor rang clearly, resonantly, like a huge tower bell, startling the birds overhead, making me wonder where I had heard that sound before.

The cloud beneath the ogre took on substance, once more resolving itself into horse and movement. The eyes of the horse glowed red. It shook its tangled black mane, and shivered.

At once the advantage swung once again to the enemy, for Bayard was tottering atop Valorous, half-netted and off balance, while the monster tried to reel him in, and at the same time reached for a dagger.

It wasn't good policy, what I did next, but I had to do it. As the two of them tugged back and forth with the net, as Bayard leaned farther and farther forward in the saddle, moving inevitably toward the point where he would lose his balance and, soon afterward, his life, I sprang free of Agion, dislodged a hand-sized stone and winged it quickly at the ogre, who, his back to me, didn't see me, the stone, or anything coming.

There was a time—and not too far back—when I'd been a pretty fair arm with a stone. I had held my own against rodent and dog, servant and brother. In short, a stone in my hand had summoned a healthy fear in each major species at the moat house.

Such times were over, evidently, for the rock flew harmlessly over the heads of the two struggling figures on horseback to clatter and bounce into the darkness behind them.

I picked up another stone. After all, I had nothing better to do, and by now Bayard was clinging to the saddle by horn and stirrup only.

Of course, I missed again. Rock throwing is largely a question of confidence, which now I had none of. And Bayard, struggling against a strength that it was easy to see would overwhelm him eventually, still managed to hold his own, to cling to the same spot on the saddle as the ogre backed his horse and tugged at the net. And growled.

The noise sounded as though it came echoing out of a depth of water somewhere, or as though a strange and terrible creature had taken a throat wound at the bottom of some well and was lying there, drowning in its own blood. The cry was distant, deep, and boiling.

Sheer terror does nothing for rock throwing. My third and fourth tosses both went wide, and I watched with growing dread as Bayard lost the little balance he had maintained, as gradually he leaned back toward the enemy, who was now poised, knife in hand, reeling my protector into stabbing range.

Which would have happened shortly, had it not been for an accident. I connected with a stone's throw at last.

My seventh toss tumbled end over end like a dagger through the air, and found a resting place firmly on the rump of the ogre's horse.

The outcome nearly killed both of them. Actually, the horses, too, because for a moment the ogre's steed skipped backwards, whinnied, and reared, drawing the ropes of the net taut between its rider and Bayard.

Luckily, Bayard was not too battered to think quickly and clearly. The taut ropes meant better cutting purchase, and he began at once, his broadsword slicing through four, five, six strands of net, giving him finally just enough elbow room and leverage to break free of the tangle. He reined in Valorous, who had slipped and staggered and nearly plunged headlong into the wall of granite that came up to the road.

As though they were following an unspoken order, both combatants dismounted. Our enemy lumbered over to where he had discarded his trident, and picking up the weapon, turned to face Bayard with one of those alarming growls.

Meanwhile, Bayard had recovered balance and equal footing and room in which to maneuver. The first thrust of the trident he met skillfully, easily, deflecting it with a smooth downward stroke and a sideways step.

The trident skidded harmlessly by him, striking granite and imbedding itself a good six inches in the solid stone before the ogre changed directions, removing the trident as casually as though it were a pitchfork in hay. Bayard danced about the enemy, who turned quickly and fiercely to follow his movement, like a badger at bay.

I sat down on a rise of rocks above them. From this point on, I could hurl only insults, not stones. For they drew to close quarters, and given my aim and luck, I stood a great chance of hitting Bayard.

So I sat down. In the moonlight I could see Agion bending watchfully nearby, the fire behind him. Overhead the two moons were rising, bathing the sheer rocks, the pine and ash and juniper, and the two adversaries in silver light and in red. The fighters circled one another. Occasionally one stumbled or backed into a rock wall, but they circled nonetheless, eyes intent and weapons at the ready.

It was setting up to be a long night indeed.

I must admit that even with Bayard's life hanging in the balance, and mine most likely balanced there by his, after an hour of dancing and weaving and near-misses, the fight no longer held my interest. Twice Bayard had been cast to the ground; once he had lost his weapon. Under all circumstances he had managed to recover footing and arms, and once he managed to put the big fellow through some paces for, say, a minute or two.

Finally, I reclined and resumed my watching of the sky. The night was quiet except for the sound of metal on metal, the cries and shouts and growls of the two in mortal combat. All in all, it was pretty clear how this one was going to end. Barring a sudden flash of luck on Bayard's part, or barring the ogre's doing something so overwhelmingly stupid that it would be talked about for generations hence, the fight would be over when the bigger one finally wore down the smaller.

Unless, of course, Bayard was right about the sunlight.

Nonetheless, it would be a night of fending, of delay.

Until the morning, I could do nothing but wait.

* * * * *

Now, maybe the ogre had every good reason to be absent the night before. Maybe he was elsewhere bullying something; perhaps he had to hunt for food or had other passes to guard, which he did in the daytime; perhaps he had been answering the call of nature, which, in a full suit of plate armor, is a procedure that can take almost forever.

At any rate, it turned out his absence had nothing to do with sunlight, or so we found when the sun rose and he cheerfully tossed Bayard several times against the granite cliffs by the side of the trail.

So much for the prophecies of Knights, for stars and dice.

"B-but . . ." Bayard started to argue, to tell the big fellow that he was supposed to burst into flames or fall into dust. Another hoist and toss cut short the argument. Bayard rattled down the side of the cliffs, the ogre after him, trident raised.

It was now that Agion stepped into the battle. The big centaur had been restraining himself with some difficulty since the sun had risen and it had become increasingly clear that Bayard's fairy tale solution to this problem was a fairy tale indeed. The ogre's strength was, if anything, greater, and Bayard was faltering.

Now, with my protector rolling helplessly in his armor like a capsized turtle and the ogre poised above him, Agion charged toward the two of them, his large hooves skittering dangerously on the loose rocks underfoot. He waved his club overhead, and his ragged hair fluttered like scarves in the wind.

The ogre started, as if he had been aroused from sleep. Quickly he turned to face the centaur, who was closing the gap rapidly between the two of them with a strange and dreamlike speed. Bayard scrambled to his feet, tottered a moment in the heavy armor, and reached to the ground for his sword.

Now the ogre turned on Bayard with a swift and powerful swipe of the trident. My protector ducked, and it was a good thing. The tines of the trident whistled a deadly music as they slashed through the air over his head.

Agion stormed into the ogre. The collision shook the rocks around us, and the two enormous creatures slid over the graveled trail in a chaos of arms and legs and weaponry. Bayard rushed toward them, sword raised.

The ogre pushed Agion away and scrambled on hands and knees toward the trident, reaching it just as Bayard bent to help Agion to his feet. With a deep dry shout, the monster hurled the weapon at the Knight.

Who was not watching.

I shouted a warning, but it was too late. Bayard looked up from the rising centaur and saw the weapon hurtling at him. There was no time to think, to dodge. The Knight stood dumbstruck.

To this day I wonder how Agion moved so quickly, so gracefully, in that terrible and slow quiet that seems to descend when something awful is about to happen. Faster than my eye could follow, the centaur stood, standing between Bayard and the flying weapon.

By the gods, the tines went deep. All three of them pierced that large and foolish chest, sank quickly.

Stilling that large and simple heart.

Agion struck the ground with the sound of gravel tumbling, of breath surrendered.

It was the ogre's turn to be taken aback. Even from a distance I could see his eyes glaze over again. Now the beast looked around stupidly, as though he had forgotten where he was, and he was still looking about when a furious Bayard closed with him. One swift slash of the sword brought silence, the crackle of the ogre's head falling among branches and the snap of more branches as Bayard knelt by Agion in silence. I rushed to my protector's side.

Then, tangled by its matted hair amid the branches, the ogre's head began to speak.

Speaking with a deep mellifluous voice that by this time I should have expected, for was it not the Scorpion?

I could not look at the severed head, but not for fear and disgust. I could not take my eyes from Agion.

But I could hear the thing speaking. Oh, yes, I could hear it, as it raced through past and present and things to come with a coldness and menace and lifelessness that hurtled to the heart of me like a trident. I remember what it said, to the very word.

"I shall take leave of you now, Bayard Brightblade. And may you find the road . . . as clear as you would like into the heartland of Solamnia. May there be safe traveling and bird song to accompany you.

"For I have done my part. The deeds on this day have assured that you will not attend the tournament at Castle di

Caela."

"We still have time!" Bayard protested, taking one uncertain step toward the speaking head.

"Perhaps. If you leave your big friend to the raptori. To the vultures and the kites. But the tournament will soon be over. Sir Robert di Caela will have an heir, the Lady Enid a husband. And it is all my doing, for my power ranges far. Blame not the satyrs in the swamp, though their trivial menace slowed you for a night or so; not your traitorous squire, who is no real master of delay . . ."

I could not look up.

"Nor, Sir Bayard, this very ogre, from whose long-dead lips I prophesy and bode. Indeed, if there is a villain, call it your lack of resolution, your passion for delay. Call it what you will. But remember: I am that delay."

Bayard lunged at the gloating thing in the branches. With a deft swipe of his foot, he sent the head tumbling into the undergrowth off of the trail.

I looked back at Agion. Who seemed even younger than he had before. Why, in the way centaurs reckon things, he was no older than I.

I looked up into Bayard's eyes.

Where indeed there was nothing but pain. A pain past anger, past tears.

"'Your traitorous squire'?" he asked. Then he knelt by Agion.

For an hour he knelt in silence, oblivious to my summons. Once, when I tried to grab his arm, to shake him out of whatever stupor he had fallen into, he shrugged my hand away as though I had set a scorpion on his shoulder.

Not twenty feet from us, the head of the ogre steamed and stained the ground on which it lay.

* * * * *

After his hour of silence, Bayard arose and turned to Agion.

"I am sorry, Agion. I am dreadfully sorry. Tomorrow I shall continue to Castle di Caela, and when we get there I shall do what I have to do. Then I shall return to the Coastlund Swamp, there to answer Archala and the elders as best

I can. But I am going to sleep now for a while. Keep watch while I do, good centaur, if you will. Keep watch this last time."

Then turning to me, he stared above my head as though he were watching for stars (even though it was not yet midday), as though I sat huddled on the cold steps of some building far from this time and far from this country.

"Do what you will, Weasel," he said. "I have nothing to say to you. No need of you."

CHAPTER 12

The next day, we broke camp and, taking the ogre's horse along, joined the narrow trail of the pass once more, beginning our descent of the mountains through a steep, embanked region where the plants had frozen the night before. The dead branches glittered with ice and with the ascending sunlight. Bayard rode ahead, lost in thought.

No matter how beautiful the branches, they were still dead. And images of death and of loss were quick to the eye this morning, for all the previous day and night had been taken up with the long sad rite of Agion's makeshift funeral.

It was an awkward time after Bayard had rested. For tearfully we cleaned the centaur's body, and tearfully we searched for a place of burial. But we were in the mountains, and the ground was rocky—too hard for digging.

We were forced to let Agion lie in the spot where he had fallen —where he had taken the sharp blade intended for Sir Bayard. We stacked stones upon the still form of our companion, forming by sundown a rough cairn of sorts above the body.

Bayard stood above our handiwork, his tunic and long hair dusty. My hands and shoulders ached from the carrying and the lifting. An owl piped from somewhere amid the concealing thick branches of a nearby cedar.

"This, too, is awkward," Bayard said reflectively.

"Sir?"

"I know nothing of the centaur way in this matter," he continued, speaking softly as though I were not there.

"There is, however, the way of the Order. And though he was no Solamnic, I do not see why these words cannot apply, cannot . . . enlarge to contain him."

Strangely the night birds grew still as Bayard stood beside the mound of stones, chanting the ancient prayer:

Return this one to Huma's breast
Beyond the wild, impartial skies;
Grant to him a warrior's rest
And set the last spark of his eyes
Free from the smothering clouds of wars
Upon the torches of the stars.

Let the last surge of his breath
Take refuge in the cradling air
Above the dreams of ravens, where
Only the hawk remembers death.
Then let his shade to Huma rise
Beyond the wild, impartial skies.

* * * * *

As we descended into the foothills, the weather grew warmer and warmer, the temperature rising from numbing cold to what you might call "crisp." Eventually we found ourselves in country that resembled nothing so much as early autumn. The glazed branches gave way to living things, as the trail wound itself through vallenwoods, pear trees, and maples, the leaves of which were turning reds and yellows and oranges against the bright blue of the Solamnic sky.

We were in Solamnia proper, home of the legends. Almost every story I had heard at my father's knee had its beginning and usually its ending in this historic country.

But it seemed that on this side of the mountains, Bayard's mood was even more restless. You could see that Castle di Caela could not be near enough for his liking. He hastened. For the first time he took the spurs to Valorous, and the big stallion kicked, snorted, then did what his rider wished.

It was a pace I found uncomfortable, but after four hours or so it had really started to tell on the horses, who, don't forget, were doing the running. It wasn't but an hour or two until the pack mare began to sweat and lather and snort and smell bad, and by the time we had reached land that was altogether level, I was having visions of the mare falling over in midstride, her heart having given out. Bayard would go on alone.

Bayard showed no signs of mercy or of exhaustion. In fact, he no longer seemed affected by any of the hardships of the journey. That morning and that afternoon he urged on a flagging Valorous, moving through ragged countryside as though we were cavalry—or worse, scouts for a band of nomadic raiders. The occasional farmer or traveler we saw shied away from us, no doubt thinking, *True, there are only two of them, but judging from their faces, they're the advance party for a terrible bunch of freebooters.*

We went on like this into the night, when our relentless passage ceased, and Bayard, alighting from Valorous as though he were rushing also to rest, said simply, "Here."

Then he tied the reins to the low fork of an apple tree and, leaning against the trunk, fell into a sudden and deep sleep.

*   *   *   *   *

I sat up on my blanket. For a moment I thought I was back at the moat house, subject to some punishment, but my thoughts cleared and the surroundings tumbled back into place—the rolling Solamnic countryside, the stars of Gilean the Book glittering directly overhead, a huge armed man standing beside my blanket, saying something unclear at first, but then . . .

". . . until we get to Castle di Caela. From there you may find a dozen paths home, Galen. If not Knights returning from the tournament, then certainly merchants or bards or pilgrims will pass by on their way to the West—to Coast-lund or to Ergoth through the Westgate Pass—and they'll not mind an extra hand with the horses until you're back to your father's house.

"But as for me, I owe your father the courtesy of seeing to it that you're not lost or waylaid in Solamnia. Nonetheless, be ready and mounted at once, or I leave without you."

Bayard was always threatening, but after the events in the mountains, I had no confidence that he was bluffing any more. Gasping in the chill night air—the air that feels all the colder when you first awaken—I wrapped my blanket about myself, then grabbed onto the mare's mane for dear and desperate life as we galloped off after the galloping Sir Bayard, who was just underway in the dark ahead of us.

It was three days more to Castle di Caela.

In the early hours of the morning, we galloped like appa-ritions through the small town we had seen from the over-look in the Vingaard mountains—the town in which Bayard had promised we would rest. Side by side, we rushed between dark thatched houses, only a banked lamp or two in the windows to guide us through the sleeping streets, those lights the only signs at this hour that the town was not abandoned entirely.

Aside from the brusque awakenings, a shouted command or two, Bayard refused to speak to me, ignoring every ques-tion or statement I made, looking beyond me or even through me as though I were invisible. I felt like the puppe-teers of Goodlund, designers and performers of the kender puppet shows, who stand on the stage with their wooden creations, move them, and supply their voices. By tradi-tion, the audience has ignored these artists for so long, pay-ing attention only to their puppets, that many outsiders wonder if the kender see the puppeteers at all.

Yes, things had changed between us. As the sky clouded and the rains began once more, Bayard mired himself in silence. He looked at the road ahead of him only. And no doubt he brooded over the comments the ogre let drop.

The sameness of things those days on the road—the rolling hills, the silence, the gloominess of weather and of spirits—was so maddening that I was relieved and grateful, finally, to see a change in the landscape when we reached a rise in the road. Looking down into a valley sloping gently eastward, we saw Castle di Caela in front of us, the bright tents and pavilions of two dozen Knights pitched around it.

"Castle di Caela," Bayard said offhandedly, and pointed down to the stronghold below us. "We are late, without a doubt."

He should have been more impressed. Castle di Caela was no huge, imposing structure like, say, the High Clerist's Tower scarcely a week to our north; yet it made the moat house of my boyhood look like a cottage.

I pulled on the mare's mane, urging her to stop for a moment, even though Bayard was well on his way into the valley.

Castle di Caela faced west. We could see the main entrance and the drawbridge from where we stood. Four small towers rose perfectly from the corners of a huge square bailey, and these towers varied in height. The farthest one from us was the tallest by far, a square structure looming high above the two conical towers in front of it.

The upkeep was remarkable. Merlons and crenels altered on the curtain walls like gapped but otherwise perfect teeth. The westward faces of the towers, lit as they were by the sun setting behind us, glistened with a reddening light that made the castle seem brown or rusty, but flawless nevertheless.

I had never seen its like. I know I was a poor boy from the provinces, unaccustomed to solid architecture, but even though this place had stood for over a thousand years, it shone with the glint of newness as though, like the swamp we had left far behind us, it was constantly growing, constantly recovering from the damage of time and of weather.

"Something, isn't it?" I whispered to nobody in particular. The pack mare twitched anxiously, shaking me in the saddle.

I thought of Agion and of how he would have recoiled at the architectural foolishness of the castle below us, then remembered the few cottages and farmhouses we had passed between the swamp and the western foothills of the mountains, and how our centaur friend would recoil at the little buildings, as though they were somehow a mistake the earth had made.

The castle seemed to blur in front of me. There was no time to think of Agion. Sir Bayard was getting too far ahead of me. With a sharp clicking of my tongue and a slap on her haunch, I prodded the mare into movement. She galloped down the rise with her rider clinging on desperately, and sooner than I could have imagined, we reached the plain in front of Castle di Caela and started to pass by some of the pavilions.

Where Knights were striking camp.

The tournament was over, evidently.

Bayard was past the tents and the noisy encampments, almost to the gates of the castle before I caught up with him. He had stopped at the edge of the moat, shouted his name up to the sentinel on the battlements, and was waiting for the message to travel to the keep—no doubt to Sir Robert di Caela—and the huge gate to open and the drawbridge to descend. Rigid in the saddle, eyes fixed on the entrance to the castle, Bayard paid me no mind, even when I spoke to him.

"There is no chance, of course, that we will be offered a warm bath and a feather bed for the night, is there, Sir Bayard?"

From the moat's edge, the castle was even more impressive, the walls rising thirty feet or more to the merlons overlooking the gate. Half a dozen archers, perhaps more, stood up there on the battlements and gazed idly down at us. They were not curious at all—*Just another outlander Knight*, they probably thought.

Only this one is late.

Behind the archers, if you leaned back in the saddle and craned your neck almost to the point of snapping, you could see over the gate wall to the top of the tallest tower, there in the southeastern corner of the castle. Atop that tower fluttered a wide blue banner, clearly visible because it was held aloft by the north wind—the flag of the House of di

219

Caela, red flower of light on a white cloud on a blue field. It was all very rich, very blue-blooded and forbidding.

Nervously I looked to Bayard, who paid me no attention. Instead, he dismounted and rummaged through the blankets on Valorous's back until he drew out a thing wrapped in linen, large enough that it surprised me I had not noticed it before.

Indeed, had I been half a squire, I not only would have noticed it but have taken pretty good care of it.

It was a shield, naturally, that Bayard unwrapped there at the entrance to Castle di Caela. Not the one he had been using to absorb the battery of vanishing satyrs or mysterious ogres, but a shiny one, unscratched and unscathed, bearing the imprint of a red sword against the background of a burning yellow sun.

The Shield of the Brightblades.

As blue bloods met blue bloods.

The gates were thrown open for us, and Robert di Caela himself came down from the keep to greet us, all polite smiles and elegance. He was one of those men whose hair turns gray or even white in his twenties, who retains those youthful features under plumage that should belong to a man twice his age, and as a result looks even younger than he actually is. And within the young face hung a white moustache neatly trimmed over a highbred nose, as handsome and as curved as a hawk's bill.

His eyes were green as the ocean offshore. This was no man to wrestle hunting dogs in his great hall.

It was good blood, good breeding, a bone structure to be envied. I began to hold out hopes for Enid. Indeed, I began to hold out hopes for Bayard—that something had happened in the lists or in the musings of this important, elegant man that had left Bayard the swain of the moment, Enid di Caela's suitor of choice. That Bayard, according to his prophecy, would tie his family name to that of the di Caelas.

Or so I was hoping.

Until Robert di Caela spoke.

"Brightblade, you say? Ah, there was a time I feared that name had died out—in your youth it would have been, when the peasantry seized Vingaard Keep. Yes, the name figures mightily in our past history. Perhaps it might have figured mightily in our present . . . had you come in time."

"The tournament . . ." Bayard began, questioningly.

"Is over," Sir Robert stated flatly. "And my daughter is betrothed."

Bayard's face reddened.

"Betrothed . . ." Sir Robert continued, with a hint of coldness and of trepidation in his voice, "to Gabriel Androctus, Solamnic Knight of the Sword."

I could not tell if that coldness and trepidation had been saved for Sir Bayard, or whether they now belonged exclusively to this Androctus fellow. But I could tell that Sir Robert di Caela, despite his courtesy, was not reveling in the choice of son-in-law.

"No, Sir Bayard Brightblade of Vingaard," Sir Robert continued, this time even more coldly, "there were stories afoot that you would be here—indeed, that you might even have been favored to win in the lists. My old companion Sir Ramiro of the Maw was prepared to wager a substantial amount of money on your lance."

"I know Ramiro well," Bayard replied modestly. "He has a penchant for the long odds."

"Made even longer when the party in question fails to show!" Sir Robert snapped. Then he governed himself, smiled, gestured toward one of the doors to the keep. "The young man chosen by lance, though a bit rough around the edges, seems of impeccable breeding and singularly gifted with the lance."

Sir Robert looked pointedly at Bayard, who dwindled on each step across the courtyard. When we reached the door to the keep, Bayard seized the chance to leave Sir Robert and Castle di Caela gracefully.

"It is far from me to belittle hospitality, especially that of such a noble and gracious house," he began, gaining his confidence and balance as he spoke, "but my horses are tired. So also must be my squire."

That he added almost as an afterthought.

"With these duties in mind, I must beg leave of you until tomorrow. With your permission, I shall travel outside the walls and set up my pavilion among the other Knights."

The first problem with all this courteous withdrawal was that we had no pavilion to set up—not even a tent to pitch. But Bayard wasn't thinking of lodging; instead, he was all fired up to get beyond these walls, where, I could tell, we would shiver about a campfire until the early hours of the morning, when we would leave quietly, in the company of some of the other departing Knights. In only a moment's conversation with Robert di Caela, it had become evident that the great doubt in Bayard's thoughts had come to blossom: that the handwritten prophecy in the margin of the *Book of Vinas Solamnus* was at best a fanciful scrawling, at worst a cruel joke.

Bayard was beaten. Instead of embarrassing himself and the name of Brightblade any further, he intended to beat a quick retreat to the swamp in Coastlund, bearing the news of our comrade's death and fulfilling his promise to Agion by undergoing centaur trial.

"I respect the decision of my liege lord and protector, Sir Robert, but if it please Your Grace, I should like to stay in the Castle di Caela this evening."

Bayard and Sir Robert gaped at me.

We stood at the big mahogany doorway to the keep—as tall as two men and five times as heavy—and it was as though that door had fallen suddenly onto the four of us.

"Certainly, young man, you are welcome to the hospitality of this castle . . ." Sir Robert began. I could sense the big "however" approaching in that sentence, so I leaped in quickly.

"Then I shall accept your kind offer, sire." I turned to walk to the horses and retrieve my belongings from atop the pack mare, knowing that both Knights were far too much the gentlemen to make a decision in my absence as to where I would stay.

That's the best thing about good old-fashioned Solamnic courtesy: you can rely on the people you're taking advantage of to be basically more decent than you. Walking back toward the horses at the main gate in the curtain wall, I could relax, could take my first chance to look around me, knowing that no plots were hatching while Galen was away.

* * * * *

Castle di Caela was less a castle than a city within walls, or at least it seemed so to my eyes at the time. Thatched huts and lean-tos lined the inside of the gate wall. They seemed to be either homes or places of business for peasants and farmers who were there to peddle wares, to argue among themselves, to offer me chickens.

Once inside the castle gates, our horses had seemed more at ease, their only anxiousness that of hunger. While one of the farmers had turned to curse another, I dipped several radishes out of the basket at the front of his stall and offered them to the pack mare. She ate serenely, snorting briefly at the first spicy taste of the plant but then chewing loudly and delightedly, her big brown eyes half-closed in bliss.

I watched the pack mare chew, carefully drawing my bag of belongings out of the clutter piled atop her saddle. It was times like this that you wanted to be a horse or mule, free of memories of the past and worries about the future and most of all the politics of the present. Let my only concern be where the next radish was coming from, and I'd carry a hundred pounds of armor gladly.

I looked over my shoulder, careful to put my hands behind my back in case the pack mare were to confuse my fingers with further radishes.

At the keep door Sir Robert and Bayard continued to talk—calmly for all I could tell, although I could see, even from this distance, that Bayard was still red from his squire's disobedience. Be that as it might, I figured I was his squire no longer.

Which did not mean I had left his service.

For there is nothing that turns a boy's thoughts inward more completely than a long ride in silent company. Especially when he knows the thoughts of his companion, and knows that they are not friendly ones. Had all the rolling lands of Solamnia lay between the foot of the Vingaard Mountains and the gates of Castle di Caela, it would not have been enough traveling, enough time, to outrun the thoughts of that narrow pass, of the gloating head of the ogre.

Of our fallen friend and his humble cairn of stones.

What I had cost Agion I didn't see how I could return.

But I owed Bayard some serious penance. I intended to get to work on that, and far better to work from somewhere in this castle, where his hopes for power and matrimony lay shaken, than out of some solemn campsite. Far better to tunnel than to sulk.

After all, they did call me Weasel.

If all else failed, I could burrow into Robert di Caela's affections. In the days to come I would flatter the old man, cast admiration on his every word and action. I would even marvel at his gestures. Enid I would treat as my dear older sister, regardless of how stern and blocky she might be, and I would learn at Sir Robert's hand the management of the estate while this newfound sister was off in the barrens of wherever becoming disenchanted with Gabriel Androctus. I would fill Sir Robert's empty nest, and by the time a question of inheritance arose (which would be years, judging from the strength and apparent health of the di Caelas), I might well have flattered and groveled enough before him that I might be heard in the halls where wills are drawn up. I liked the size and shape and luxury of Castle di Caela. I hoped devoutly to stay awhile.

But first things first. In all this many-windowed splendor there had to be a prospect for Bayard.

As Bayard went to the gate and out into the countryside surrounding the castle, where he would spend the night on the ground surrounded by horses while I pitched camp in fresh bedding surrounded by silk, by a fireplace I prayed, he glared at me with such a look of disbelief and defeat and betrayal that for a moment I was angry, outraged that despite the Scorpion and his thefts and lies and misdeeds, Bayard thought I was the real weasel in the henhouse.

Then the smell of roast beef reached me from somewhere in the warm recesses of the castle keep. I followed Sir Robert through the huge mahogany door, into a well lit room of polished marble, filled with buffed armor and dark paintings.

It was the kind of lodging I was born for, I decided.

"I heard the name 'Galen' in my exchange with Sir Bayard," Sir Robert began, draping his magnificent blue cloak over a nearby chair. "Is the family name one I would recognize, or are you . . ." and he smiled without any irony I could see, ". . . from a faraway place where I might not know the names?"

"I'm a Pathwarden myself, sir," I said.

"I see," Sir Robert replied, and said nothing else, as he lit a candle resting on a mahogany table in the hall and beckoned to me to follow him.

We passed through the anteroom of the family di Caela. I knew the Brightblades had some sort of historical importance—and I was hoping devoutly that Sir Robert wasn't going to ask me to refresh his memory on my family history—but somehow both names paled in the glamor and traditions housed by this building. I was walking in a shrine of sorts—I knew Father and Gileandos would both be impressed.

For this was the seat of a great family, one who fought side by side with Vinas Solamnus. Who could trace their ancestry back a millennium. And the man who walked in front of me, holding a candle, was the heir to all this—not only the wealth, mind you, but the history and the heroism and the nobility. It was enough to impress the hardest head in Solamnia.

Sir Robert guided me past several paintings—ancient oils of his di Caela ancestors. I looked out of the corner of my eye for a portrait that might be Benedict's. The eyes of one portrait—that of a handsome old man with a livid scar on his left cheek—seemed to follow me as I moved down the hall. I thought of the childhood stories of haunted galleries, of things behind the walls who watched passers-by through holes in the portraits.

With my eyes on the painting, my thoughts on the likelihood of spooks in the woodwork, I didn't notice that Sir Robert had stopped until I walked into him.

"A Pathwarden, you say?"

"Yes, sir."

"Son of Sir Andrew Pathwarden?"

"Yes, sir."

"But I had been told . . ."

"Sir?"

". . . that Sir Andrew has but two sons," Sir Robert mused, tilting his head and, taking me by the shoulder, moving me beneath a sconce on the wall—no doubt so he could get a better look.

"I am often forgotten when sons are tallied at our moat house," I replied quickly, desperately, staring wide-eyed at the sconce above me, filling my eyes with the tear-jerking heat and smoke of the torch.

For some reason, my throat burned without aid of torch or smoke. And easily I burst into false sobs after the fire had stirred up the tears.

"My brothers keep me in the mews, Sir Robert. With the hunting birds!" I sniffed.

His grip on my shoulder softened.

"If that's so, they'll answer for it soon, lad," he declared— a puzzling statement, to be sure.

I looked at him curiously. He turned away, addressed me awkwardly.

"Now compose yourself, Galen. You're too big for tears."

As we passed beneath an arch into another room and approached a wide staircase, my eyes followed up the steps to a landing surrounded by a marble railing and statues of hawks and of unicorns. Intricate metal cuckoos perched upon swings that hung from the ceiling of the keep, their moorings lost in darkness and in height.

Suddenly a cuckoo whistled behind us. I turned to the source of the sound.

And saw a vision there on the landing, winding a metal bird.

Actually, it was a girl about my age, dressed in a simple white gown that a girl of almost any station—from princess to servant—might wear in comfort. It was obvious, however, that this one was unaccustomed to following orders of any kind. She walked the landing as if she owned it.

She had blond hair and fair skin, but even from where I stood I could tell that her eyes were dark, her cheekbones high like those of a Plainswoman. It made me wonder about her ancestry from the first, and I instantly believed she had gotten the best from both sides of her family.

The girl paid little attention to us, intent on fixing one of the cuckoos whose *cuckoo* had, evidently, ceased to function. With some tiny, glittering instrument, she inspected the head of the toy and made adjustments too small for me to see at the distance from which I stood.

"Tell the servants to set another place at the dinner table, my dear," Sir Robert called up to the girl on the landing. "We have a guest."

"You tell them," the girl called down, attention still fixed on her business. "You're heading in that direction."

Sir Robert reddened for a moment, clenching his fists. Then he laughed, shook his head, and continued walking. I doubled my steps, walked alongside him.

"Your wife, sire?"

"My obedient daughter, Enid di Caela," Sir Robert chuckled, as we walked up a small flight of stairs toward another mahogany doorway.

Enid? The pastry-baking, hefty Enid of my imaginings? Bayard had good reason to be downcast!

"Enid di Caela," Sir Robert repeated, this time more quietly, less merrily. "Soon to be Enid Androctus.

"Ah, and here is one of your brothers!"

*   *   *   *   *

It took a moment for Sir Robert's last statement to sink in. I was still wrestling with the idea that the Enid of fact far surpassed the Enid of my imaginings, still entangled in the blond hair, drowned in the dark eyes, as the poets might say. But when Alfric appeared from an archway ahead of us, it was all I could do to keep from turning and taking flight through the paneled and cuckooing hallways.

CHAPTER 13

My brother was disturbingly untroubled, almost serene, when he met me in the long corridor of Castle di Caela, though I expect it puzzled Sir Robert that two long-lost brothers did not rush into a warm, fraternal embrace.

While Sir Robert escorted us back to our assigned quarters, I began to entertain the hope that something on the road had transformed my brother, had left him a wiser and more forgiving man than when I had left him waist-deep in 'Warden Swamp. As Alfric kept conversation polite, even friendly, I decided there could be worse things than sharing his rooms for the evening.

When he sprang upon me as the door closed, fully intent on throttling me, it was all I could do to utter feeble protest.

"Please, Brother! P-please! You're killing me!"

This loud enough, I hoped devoutly, to call Sir Robert back. But no footsteps returned to the door. And all the while Alfric's death grip tightened.

"This is it, little brother. This time all the bluster and promises and crying wolf is over on account of I am going to kill you. Going to strangle you dead for leaving me back there mired in 'Warden Swamp.'"

"But what will Sir Robert s—" My voice was pinched into hisses and whistles.

Alfric's grip slackened.

"You're right, Weasel. If I was to do you in it could cause great harm to my prospects here.

"Even though you are not the favorite folks around here at the moment—you and your high and mighty Sir Bayard Brightblade, that is—it would not do me to fall into something as unSolamnic as killing a brother, now would it? Specially since you are no more a danger to me, and you no longer have got what I want."

He told me what he had learned about the tournament—of the lists and the sorrows and the cold power of Sir Gabriel Androctus, and Sir Robert di Caela's rising impatience as the days wore on and no Bayard Brightblade showed. He straddled me and reveled in our delays.

"I would expect that it's only Solamnic courtesy what keeps him from tarring and feathering the both of you and rolling you back to the Vingaard Mountains in a barrel."

"H-how did you ever manage to . . ."

"Beat you to the castle? Seems like everyone beat you and Bayard to the castle, don't it?"

He placed his hands on his hips and laughed. Laughed until he was red-faced and the veins stood out in his neck, and I began to wonder if my brother did not have a few cats in his bell tower, as they say. I used the opportunity to slip out from under him and crawl under a table in the far corner of the room.

"Brithelm," he declared, his laughter subsiding and his breath recovered. "Brithelm it was what pulled me out of the mire. And I explained to him that I needed to get to Castle di Caela. Told him about the tournament, I did, and that we'd have to rush to get there.

"So he's off in a flash back to the moat house, and he returns in a few hours with two of Father's best horses and a week's provisions and we're off for Castle di Caela. I didn't think I'd have much of a chance in that tournament, but I thought I might get a chance to skin you in the bargain, or at least take your place as Bayard's squire, seeing as nobody wants a squire who bogs down his own brother.

"Anyway, Brithelm not only knows to get the horses and provisions, but he knows this pass through the Vingaard Mountains way south of the Westgate. A pass he says is going to cut three days off our trip at least.

"You can imagine our surprise, Galen, when we seen you and Bayard and that horse-man . . ."

"Agion."

"Whoever . . . run up against that ogre in the high reach of the pass. I watched it from a distance. Brithelm couldn't see that far—part of his bumping into things is just bad eyesight, did you know? So I tell him Bayard was winning, and he believes me. Otherwise he'd of wanted to hike down and pitch in.

"So when I seen you folks had settled for the night, Brithelm and I passed by and made our way over the mountains."

"Then it *was* your voice I heard that night at the campsite!"

"Seems to me it's better to leave your brother on a mountain pass with two able companions than waist-deep and alone in the mire," Alfric philosophized. "Think about that if you get too pious."

I shrank back behind the table.

"You may have a chance for that squirehood now, Alfric. Because of some things that happened in the swamp and in the mountains, Bayard has no further use of me. Odds are he'll be looking for a squire at once. You can find him at his encampment tonight."

"It comes around, does it not, brother?" Alfric gloated, seating himself on the bed. "For I am no longer studying Bayard Brightblade. He was late. He is no longer the champion."

"Meaning?"

"Gabriel Androctus is," Alfric pronounced exultantly. "He won this tournament and the hand of the Lady Enid. He is about to become the most important Knight in this part of Solamnia.

"He that may be needing a new squire, and if he is, I plan to be that squire."

* * * * *

Outside the door of my chambers, the halls of Castle di Caela trilled with mechanical cuckoos.

I awoke from my nap. Alfric was still gone, no doubt preparing for the Feast of the Wedding Eve, the big dinner that precedes the nuptial ceremonies.

No doubt he was overdressing. No doubt trying for an audience with Gabriel Androctus—a chance to grovel and bootlick his way into squirehood.

Brithelm was somewhere in Castle di Caela, too, though no one was quite sure where. He had arrived shortly after the fateful meeting of Gabriel Androctus and Sir Prosper of Zeriak, and almost immediately wandered off—no doubt looking for some quiet spot in the castle where he could meditate.

Which was all very well. I needed some time to regroup.

A good healthy sleep was unlikely in these chambers, what with the chirping and song and questioning calls of the little metal birds outside my door. Had it been only one bird and a less wealthy house, I could have marked the time until dinner by its calls, for cuckoos were just becoming fashionable then as a sort of mechanical timepiece.

Fashionable, but not reliable. As most of the birds were of gnomish make, most did not call out at the regular intervals the craftsmen promised. Instead, they would not call at all, call once and continuously until they wore out, or call at irregular times with the sound of metal scraping across metal so that the listener wished either time would stand still or he had never purchased the damn thing in the first place.

The di Caelas, of course, were too old and wealthy a family to bother with keeping track of time. They lived in a mansion where past stood beside present, and nobody ever stated a preference for one or the other. What was more, they were so rich that if they had to be at any particular place at any particular time, the main event was held up until they got there. The birds were for decoration only, and for the pleasing sounds some di Caela thought they made, evidently.

Such sounds were not pleasing to this guest, however. The songs of the cuckoos disrupted my thoughts, which were disrupted to begin with by the questions I knew would sooner or later arise.

Why had I abandoned Sir Bayard Brightblade, who less than a fortnight back had generously consented to take me on as his squire, despite profound misgivings on my father's part?

Why was Sir Bayard late to the tournament in the first place, and what had I to do with any delays he might have encountered?

The longer I considered my situation, the more a return to Bayard seemed in order. I drew out the dice, cast the Calantina.

Sign of the Hart. Which had nothing to do with anything, as far as I could tell.

Well, I was losing faith in the Calantina, anyway. I tried it again, hoping for a sign more to my understanding, more to my liking.

Sign of the Rat. Again. I remembered the last time I cast that, which was at the moat house.

Well, so be it. I was leaving once more. Once again the Weasel was a Rat.

I stood, picked up my cloak from the bed, and walked to the entrance of the chamber. I set my ear to the door and listened. Outside, the hallway was fairly quiet, the cuckoos on this floor having apparently wound down or broken or made their noises for a while, gears grinding toward a time anywhere from ten minutes to three days from now, when like clockwork in a clock gone completely mad, they would sing once more.

I opened the door slowly and stepped into the hallway. On tiptoe I passed the still sentinels of metal birds and headed down the hall toward the stairway, still clutching my cloak in my hands.

The bird-lined hallway ended in an arch, which opened into a landing above the large room where Sir Robert had first mentioned his daughter's impending marriage. I stood at the arch, looking down the stairway.

It was on this landing that the Lady Enid had stood, had adjusted the birds. I bade the lady a silent farewell, hoping that someday in the great hall of the moat house, when the news came to Alfric that his younger brother had met an untimely death in a far-flung land, that the di Caelas— both the lovely Enid and her elegant father—would shed a sympathetic tear, perhaps wish they could have known this youngest Pathwarden, the irrepressible Galen, the mischievous but good-hearted Weasel.

I sniffled, having almost brought myself to tears with the pity of the scene I had imagined. I started down the stairs.

It was then that the bird to my right began to screech— loudly, painfully, as though someone were tearing it apart. Surprised, I spun about and tossed my cloak over the wailing mechanical thing, which continued to dance beneath the gray folds, its cry muffled but certainly not silenced. I looked behind me down the corridor toward my quarters, then once again down the stairs in front of me.

At the foot of which stood Enid, small hand on the banister, brown eyes regarding me with curiosity and amusement.

"Don't pick at the devices, boy," she said calmly. "You'll make them sound worse.

"Though in the case of that one you just cloaked," she continued, ascending the stairs, "it is very hard to imagine you doing anything that would damage the sound any more."

She smelled of lilacs and lost time.

I found my voice, which had no doubt scurried halfway back up the hall. "That one does seem a little . . . harsh, Lady Enid. But the rest of them, if I might be so bold . . ."

"Are hideous," she laughed, her merriment as musical as the sound of the covered cuckoo was discordant. "I do believe that had Mother lived, we would be happily free of these little tin outrages, no matter how much a part of di Caela family tradition they are. You cannot trust a man's taste in sound or in color—for in both, loudness pleases them far too well."

She passed by me on the steps and lifted my coat from the cuckoo in question, who continued with its grating, hysterical call. Reaching under the base of its perch, she tinkered with something, turned some toggle or switch, and the bird at last grew silent and still.

"Of course, you know all about family traditions, being of Solamnic stock and all," the Lady Enid said, linking her arm in mine and escorting me past the stairwell in a wave of lilac and light. "Don't you ever find this obsession with bloodline and ceremony just a little . . . tedious?"

I was speechless, this bright thing on my arm.

"I mean, every little gesture is part of some somber Solamnic tradition, the punishment for breaking which is really nothing more definite than losing face, which can be a dreadful thing, but certainly not as lethal as the Knights make it."

She laughed that laugh of music once again, and I felt my face go warm.

"I beg your pardon, sir. Here I am forgetting that you're in training for Knighthood, and probably all too concerned with such serious things."

"Knighthood?" I stopped on the steps.

"Are you not Sir Bayard Brightblade's squire?"

"Of-of course. Forgive me, Lady Enid. I was distracted by the beauties of this castle."

And of the lady of the castle. So much so that I was forgetting myself, forgetting to ask where I was going, among other things. Where was she leading me?

"Attractive man, this Brightblade. I saw him approach from the windows of my chamber. A good swordsman, I'd wager."

"One of the best," I agreed. "If you fancy that kind of thing in a man."

"Makes me wish I still had decisions, choices to make," Enid said desolately, then brightened suddenly and overwhelmingly, nodding at one of the portraits hanging on the wall.

"Mariel di Caela. My great-great-aunt."

"Lovely," I responded automatically.

"It's charming that the Order teaches boys politeness, Galen, but there is no need to parade it in these halls. Look at that face: an owl. A countenance only a troll could love."

"Did you know her?"

"Dead when I was an infant. Six months before I was born she locked herself in the top of the southeast tower—the tallest one, windowless except for the rooms overlooking the curtain wall. Locked herself in with her pets—a dozen cats. Can you imagine the loose fur in the air? Grandfather was *the* di Caela then—the lord of this castle. He let her have her way. It's a tradition that di Caela men make all decisions for their women— until they get old . . ."

She said that with some bitterness. I became more attentive.

"Then, of course, the men let them do whatever they want. Which by that time usually involves making life impossible for the men who have limited their options for years.

"At any rate, around the time I was born, Aunt Mariel began to refuse food. Being the domineering sort she was— remember, she was making up for half a century without being allowed a decision, half a century of following without question di Caela family tradition—she refused food for her animals as well. Of course, she was devoured by her cats.

"After a week of this fasting, the guards complained of Aunt Mariel's silence. Complained that she no longer shouted instructions and commands underneath the huge door of the tower room.

"Led by Father, the guards tried the door. Led by Uncle Roderick—who died not long after this, but that's another story entirely—they tried to pick the lock. Eventually, of course, they were forced to break down the door. The rest . . ." she smiled bleakly, "you can guess."

"Was that part of the curse, too?"

Instantly, of course, I regretted what I had said. But Enid showed no surprise.

"Perhaps indirectly. I never thought of it. Of course, indirectly the curse gets blamed for just about everything that goes on here, Galen."

She tilted her head and smiled curiously at me.

"You seem to know quite a bit about the di Caela curse. Especially considering you aren't a di Caela."

I was too struck by the smile to respond.

"Oh, never mind," she said dismissively. "I suppose all the Solamnics get wind when old Benedict returns."

"So it's the same person every generation?"

"None of us has the foggiest idea. It sounds like a better curse if it is. But whether it's old Benedict every time, or one of his descendants, or someone else entirely, this generation is supposed to be an important one. That's why Father called the tournament. He wanted me married to a redoubtable Knight before the curse returned again."

I nodded knowingly, having absolutely no clue as to how the curse really worked. Or how Sir Robert imagined it working.

We turned left down a hall running off the landing. The keep seemed larger and larger, almost a world in itself, the longer we walked.

As we walked, my thoughts cascaded.

"So it was this Gabriel Androctus who triumphed. Sir Gabriel Androctus, Knight of the Sword. A high-sounding title, but if you ask me, a Knight I find just a little bit wanting," Enid continued. She pointed down another hallway to our right, lined with windows on one side, with full-sized marble statues on the other.

"The first six fathers of the family di Caela," she announced.

"Which one is Benedict?"

"Benedict di Caela tried to destroy this family. He may still be trying. Why would we raise him a statue, silly boy?"

A door opened at the end of the hall, and another girl— about Enid's age, I guessed—emerged and came up the hall towards us.

"Cousin Dannelle," Enid called. "Come here and meet Galen Pathwarden, eminent squire." The girl slowed her steps and squinted down the hall to catch a glimpse of me.

"He's awfully small for an eminent squire," Dannelle called out.

"But charming nonetheless," Enid responded. "Come and look."

I must admit I squirmed a little. I hate being fussed over, and I could see a fuss approaching. Dannelle glided down the hall—she had the di Caela family grace.

But not its looks.

Which is not to say she wasn't beautiful, too. But instead of the blond hair, the brown eyes, the high cheekbones, her hair was red, her eyes green, her stature short and birdlike. She stared at me, and it felt as though I was looking into a mirror, only to see myself reflected as a lovely girl.

In short, it was really disturbing.

"There is a crack in old Gerald's pedestal, Enid," Dannelle stated quietly, eyeing me. "This boy looks more Pathwarden than human."

"Oh, Dannelle, stop it!" scolded Enid. "He can't be held accountable for . . ."

Then both the girls laughed, and Enid put a hand on my shoulder, raising the heat and the blush I had felt on the stairs only a short while back.

"Dannelle isn't all that fond of your eldest brother, though for the life of me I can't figure why, seeing as he has her coloring and all," Enid explained. Dannelle hooted in mock outrage, turned and made as though she were leaving us, walking back up the hall.

Enid called her back, and the two of them stared sullenly at one another for a moment or so before bursting into peals of laughter.

It was then I noticed the strongest family resemblance. Both laughs filled the long halls of the keep with warm and appealing music.

* * * * *

The three of us walked to the end of the hall of statues, lit by the afternoon sunlight. We turned right at Dannelle's door, moving back toward the landing, I guessed. Along the way, each of the girls pointed out various relics of di Caela family history.

I learned about Denis di Caela, who had declared war against the rats in the cellar of the castle—an uphill work at

its easiest in any castle, but in one this size (and at the time of
the curse) impossible. I heard how, after ten years of losing
battles, he had trapped a huge rat, then spent a year holding
the animal hostage, thinking that the rats would surrender
to regain the "freedom of their leader."

Also of Simon di Caela, who thought he was an iguana,
and spent his time basking in the sun on the roof of the low
northeast tower, waiting for flies to alight. It was a sudden
frost, the girls claimed merrily, that killed him.

Somehow, men such as these had held off the assaults of
Benedict di Caela for over four hundred years.

It was enough to give you courage, to give you confidence.

"What, if I might ask, Lady Enid, dampens your . . .
enthusiasm for the bridegroom in question?"

"The prophecy, silly boy. The scrawled prophecy in the
Book of Vinas Solamnus," Enid said flatly.

"Then you do know of the prophecy?"

"Of course," she replied. "Uncle Roderick made a special
trip to Palanthas when a librarian found it in the margin of
the text. It's foolishness, no doubt, but when each generation suffers some mishap, the family looks into all possibili-
ties.

"This one says something about a 'Bright Blade,' you
know," she continued, directing us left up another hall, then
right down another, one wall of which was covered with a
mural depicting the fall of Ergoth, the other blank except for
a door the girls claimed led to a balcony that overlooked the
dining hall. "And Father pounced upon that prophecy, taking it as a sign that we should marry into the Brightblades."

"Of course, the text of the prophecy doesn't really say
that," Dannelle added. "You could read it several ways—
something about 'the Bright Blade lifting the curse', or some
such obscurity Uncle Robert took to mean Enid had to marry one of them.

"That was the reason for the tournament. Uncle Robert
figured that if there was a tournament to be had, Bayard
Brightblade would figure into the arrangements. It was a
way to draw him here, among other things."

"Which did not work, of course," Enid sighed, picking up

the story. "Where was Sir Bayard—lost in the woods?"

If possible, I blushed even more deeply. Enid went on carelessly.

"Though I've seen him only once, he stands up well in comparison to this . . . Androctus."

"Whom I am obliged to marry."

"But—" I began, and Dannelle interrupted.

"Uncle Robert claims that it's nothing for Enid to worry over, that marriage to this Androctus—to any Knight, for that matter—will not change her life in any measurable way. He claims that anyone who marries a di Cacla becomes a di Caela, actually, and that she can stay here in the castle and live pretty much as before."

"Isn't there some kind of gnome proverb," I asked, "that goes 'if you want to find out about someone, marry him into your family'?"

Both the girls laughed sadly and nodded.

"Whatever Gabriel Androctus is like," Enid declared, "marrying him will be the last time I do anything which is not absolutely what I want to do."

Which did not bode well for the champion's marital bliss.

But I drew no joy from that.

There had to be a way that Bayard was right! Enid's husband was supposed to be a Brightblade, not some outlander tricked up like a jackleg executioner.

The di Caela cousins continued to charm me and lead me around the second floor of the keep. Fattening me with beauty and attention until, inevitably, they would have to bring me to the slaughter in the dining room, where Sir Robert would start asking the questions I dreaded and uncover the details of my recent criminal fortnight as Bayard's squire.

I slowed my steps, stifled a phony yawn.

"Please don't take that yawn as a lack of interest, ladies. I find this business of di Caelas and Brightblades fascinating, but I fear that . . ."

I paused, relying on politeness and good breeding. In which I was not disappointed.

"Cousin Dannelle, here we are transporting the boy about the premises when he'd much rather rest before dinner!"

Enid exclaimed.

"It's most rude of us, Cousin Enid! What must he think of the hospitality in Castle di Caela now?"

Dannelle reached out and straightened my hair. Again I warmed, reddened.

"Oh, I think no less of your hospitality, Lady Dannelle. But I *am* tired. If you would be so kind as to escort me back to my chambers where I might enjoy an hour's nap before dining, I should be terribly grateful."

Which they did without delay, fussing and apologizing as they went. With all the attention lavished upon me, it was all I could do to mark our path from hall to hall, past mural and statue and painting and stairway until, when we reached the doorway that was indeed my own, I still wasn't quite sure if I had mastered the maze of the keep or not.

I sat alone in my room for a while, casting the red dice once and receiving the Sign of the Sea Horse. I cursed myself for having read only three of Gileandos's commentaries on the Calantina, having left the volume on water signs "for later" because I didn't recognize the animals it contained. Dice or no dice, once the footsteps had faded into the sound of cuckoos outside my door, once I had stepped into the hall again and looked first left, then right, seeing no beautiful Enid, no beautiful cousin, my curiosity led me back along my path of the last hour.

For I wanted to steal a look at Sir Gabriel Androctus.

* * * * *

It was an easy path to retrace. Past the paintings, past the enormous marble stairwell, left down the first hall off the landing, then turning right, down the hall lined with statuary. I heard someone calling for me in the recesses of the building behind me. I stopped and looked out the windows over the courtyard and the castle walls, into the western fields. There, at a distance, I recognized the yellow sun of Bayard's pennant waving among those of several other Knights.

Where at least he had found shelter for the night.

I tiptoed past the marble di Caelas, who stared at me blankly, disapprovingly. Sure enough, old Gerald's foundation was cracked.

Judging from Denis and Simon, and lately Mariel, it ran in the family.

Then I crept past Dannelle's door.

I moved down the hall to the right, then left, then right again until I faced the hallway where, to my right, the siege of Ergoth raged silently and motionlessly, forever in paint upon the wall.

The door opposite the mural opened into a rich and warm darkness, into the smell of expensive cloth underscored with the slightest odor of decay. Somewhere beyond the darkness I could hear noise—conversation, laughter, the clatter of metal and crockery. Cautiously I stepped toward the noise until my extended hand touched velvet.

I was behind a curtain. I fumbled up and down the cloth like a bad actor, looking for the opening.

And found it after some difficulty, found that I was on a balcony that bellied out above a dining room that dwarfed the great hall of the moat house—as I had expected it would—but dwarfed it to a degree I never had imagined. For the dining hall of Castle di Caela was by itself the size of the moat house, and the cost to decorate that one great room alone would have drained entirely the Pathwarden treasuries.

Torches and candles bathed the room in a steady light, white and yellow and amber and red, and those preparing the room for the feast looked almost toylike below me— musicians tuning the guitar and the elvish cello, in the center of the room a brace of tumblers practicing, and around the entertainers what must have been forty servants bustling about upon specific duties— spreading cloth over the tables, setting plates and crockery and glasses in front of each chair.

I seated myself in the upper darkness and watched the banquet begin.

Not long after I parted the curtains, the musicians struck up an air, something basso and Solamnic and serious. I sneezed once into the thick velvet, then settled back to watch as, gradually, the residents of Castle di Caela and their guests filed into the dining room in stately order.

Ladies came first. Enid—all blond hair and flowers and

incredible blue linen—led the procession. Doubtless she would look even more beautiful come Sunday, when she led the procession in a full-dress Solamnic wedding, but from my seat I could see a worried look on her face tonight. Something was troubling those beautiful brown eyes.

Dannelle followed her, hands folded in front of her like a bridesmaid's, still indignant at the situation and her cousin's impending marriage, I could tell. She leaned forward and whispered something to Enid, and despite the ceremony, the cousins' shoulders began to shake with silent laughter.

After these two came several other ladies of the court, dim in comparison to di Caelas, followed by Knights, some of whom had attended the tournament, evidently. Most prominent among them were a tall man with a whorled sea-shell of a helmet and a four hundred pound enormity in gaudy ceremonial armor.

Sir Ledyard and Sir Ramiro, I was later to find out.

Sir Robert di Caela brought up the rear of the procession and sat at the head of a huge mahogany table in the center of the room. I watched the rest of the Knights stand by their chairs until the old man was seated, the high-backed chair at his right still empty—reserved for the groom, obviously.

Had these Knights been rivals to the groom, jousting and paying court to the Lady Enid? They seemed a little old for such foolishness.

Younger men followed, many of them carrying their first "tournament badge," as Father used to call it—a bruise or a sprain or even a break that marked the bearer's first entry into the lists. The arms of several sported slings and splints, and one of the men, his ankle obviously broken and set, came in on the shoulders of two others.

Alfric and Brithelm walked in among these fellows, both looking a little out of place amidst all this Solamnic style and glitter. Alfric looked like a buffoon, as usual, but it was reassuring to see Brithelm—all red-robed and unkempt, but healthy and intact and not about to put on airs regardless of the company. I suddenly found myself surprisingly glad that he had come, and that he had hauled my eldest brother out of the mire.

Despite all these young blades gathered together, despite

the usual good spirits that arose on the night before a wedding, especially at a banquet where the music and wine promised to flow freely, the feel of the place was somber, even cheerless.

Cheerless it remained until the Knights had almost all been seated. Then the music softened, and at the orders of Sir Robert, who was apparently an old sentimentalist himself, servants scurried throughout the room, extinguishing nearly half of the candles, half the lamps, and a few of the lights in the chandelier that hung from the ceiling in the center of the room. Now the light subsided to a deep amber. Illumined by the wavering light of the candles as it glittered on his polished breastplate, the bridegroom entered the room to a stirring military song played by the cellos and a little silver cornet that also glittered in the hands of the musician on the far side of the room.

In the height and darkness I couldn't see him clearly. His stride was purposeful and long, and I noticed that even some of the more formidable-looking Knights stepped aside timidly at his approach.

At a gesture from Sir Robert, those who were already seated stood up respectfully, each Knight lifting his wine glass to the approaching, dark-robed figure. The torchlight shimmered on the crystal, on the tilted red of the wine.

Before Sir Robert's table, Sir Gabriel stopped and stood at attention, his gloved hands clenched behind his back. I caught a glimpse of his face in the elusive light of the great hall of di Caela: his was a pale countenance, with a dark brow, and he was certainly handsome enough. Nor did he seem too old for a nuptial tournament, unlike some of the others in the hall who, if they had fought in the lists over the last several days, should have been ashamed at acting half their age.

Sir Gabriel also seemed to know what he was doing, gliding through the ceremonial movements of the banquet as though he were a dancing master born to pomp and ritual.

He was handsome, young, and stylish. Able to take care of himself, too, if winning this tournament proved anything.

Sir Robert stood before him, glass raised.

"Good health and long life to Gabriel Androctus, Solamnic Knight of the Sword," he began. "To whom, on the afternoon that follows this gaudy, ceremonious night, we shall give the greatest of our jewels."

"Good health and long life to Sir Robert di Caela, Lord of the House of di Caela," began the response of Sir Gabriel Androctus, but I confess I heard no more of it, stunned as I was by the familiar mellifluous poison of that voice. The voice I recognized immediately, that I had heard in moat house and swamp.

The bridegroom was the Scorpion.

CHAPTER 14

I was back in my bed before Sir Robert sent for me.
There under the covers I feigned fever, moaned a little
pathetically to the guards who had come to get me, then
sent them back to Sir Robert with my regrets.

Now came the hard part. Though the halls were mapped
in the back of my mind, I had no earthly notion as to what
lay behind most of the doors. Behind one of them was the
Scorpion's room, of course, wherein might lie some clue as
to who he was and what he really wanted.

The curse was overdue at Castle di Caela, and from Bayard's story back in the mountains, I was sure that old
Benedict—the Scorpion himself—was at it again.

* * * * *

I waited and fiddled inconclusively with the Calantina. I ran through my options. Outside the window, the darkness began to settle on the courtyard, the walls and towers, and the far-flung holdings of Castle di Caela. Somewhere above me—perhaps at the very top of this tower, where the di Caela banner fluttered red and blue and white in the last hour before some steeplejack of a servant clambered up to lower it for the evening—a nightingale began its dark serenade of stars and moons.

There were only three candles in the room, and I lit them all against the approaching night. Then I walked to the chamber window and looked down.

Already the bailey below me was in shadows, and within it the shadowy servants moved, each with a horse prepared for a departing Knight. Soon the banquet would be over: indeed, I heard uproarious singing from somewhere toward the great hall, a sure sign that the celebration had passed from venison to brandy.

Still no strategy. The weasel stuck in his tunnel. I stewed, tried the dice again.

Sign of the Dragon? Something I recalled from the verses—something about "destruction a mask for innocence." I could remember no more of it, so I let it go for the time being, walked back to the bed and sat down, looking toward the hearth and the glowing fire one of my brothers must have started before I arrived at the castle.

It was low, now, the fire was, and as it guttered even further it let the dark into the room.

I was reaching for a candle when I heard the noises at the window—the scratching and the heartbeat sound of wing and beak against the thick glass.

I walked to the window and opened it wide, full knowing—as you know something by insight or by instinct—what awaited me outside.

I still ask myself why I let the raven into the room. I knew where it had come from, and I knew about the one who sent it—had sent it or had transformed himself into it or had entered it like water into a pitcher. I never figured out the mechanics. Though all I knew of the Scorpion was brutal and often bloody, I opened the window.

Every possible fear arose in front of me as I walked to the window. I thought of the threats at the moat house and in 'Warden Swamp, of the goats mysteriously transformed and Agion dead in the Vingaard Mountains, the sharp tines of a trident mournfully deep in his chest. In fact, I had thought about it so much on that short walk from bedpost to shutter that when the living, breathing raven flew into the room, for a second I was relieved and even a little disappointed, having worked myself up for a monster.

It stared at me straight on, like a man or a horse would stare, instead of turning its head to the side and catching me with one glittering eye, like a natural bird would do. And the voice was not natural at all, yet frighteningly familiar.

"It is the Weasel again. Your foolish brothers were gossiping your arrival throughout the great hall tonight, and you've certainly aroused the curiosity of old di Caela. He has many questions for you."

"Me? I'm just a lowly squire. Ex-squire actually," I said, my mind racing.

"Well," the raven hissed, "he can't help feeling a little . . . sad for Bayard—coming all that way with a prophecy in hand only to be cast aside by plain bad luck and delay." The raven chuckled here, I swear. "Only you and I know *you* were the luck, my little friend. You caused the delay. Sir Robert suspects as much, but only you and I know."

"And yet . . ." I was trying to put together a strategy. "I do feel sorry for Bayard," I replied, trying my best to sound casual, light-hearted. "Just because he could not win the hand of Enid di Caela shouldn't mean that he goes away entirely bereft. Surely you, in all your good fortune, have a glimmer of compassion for him."

"My good fortune?" the voice began in outrage and in anger, rising to a shriek in the frail throat of the bird as the raven fluttered from mantle to bedpost in an increasingly frantic circle around the room. "You call four hundred years of fruitless striving, of fruitless planning 'good fortune'?"

The raven fluttered to the windowsill, motioning with its yellowed claw toward the heavens above the high tower of the castle. Beyond the conical roof, the flagpole now bare, above the thin strands of cloud, I could see where the warring constellations met, where the jaw of Paladine snapped at the tail of Takhisis there in the easternmost notch of the sky. Around that immortal, perpetual conflict, the lesser stars glimmered like thousands of inlaid jewels.

"No, my little friend," the voice continued, the raven raising a yellowed and bony claw from the folds of his feathers, his eyes glittering red, then orange, then yellow.

"Bayard rushes to fulfill prophecies written centuries ago. Prophecies assuring the downfall of Benedict di Caela and of his descendants."

I nodded stupidly, like a boy agreeing with the schoolmaster even when the lesson has lost him entirely.

"Prophecies recorded by men who received . . . a vision, perhaps. A vision received in a blinding moment of light and of insight. But afterwards, when the vision had passed and they were asked to make sense of it—of its chaos of words and names and reported events that had not happened but were to come—who is to say that they understood what they recorded?

"Who is to say Bayard has understood? For let me tell you, there is more than one way to read that prophecy of his."

The bird perched on the windowsill, regarded me brightly, cruelly. It was then I first noticed that its feathers were matted and dull, the down on its head thinning, as though the creature were in the grip of some strange and lingering disease.

I heard a soft spattering against the glass of the window. I turned to this new sound, keeping my eyes cautiously on the bird.

Snow was falling in the courtyard. A snow of early autumn—unnatural and weird, and as the snow fell, the raven spoke.

"You know the story of Enric Stormhold?"

I did not know the tale and mutely shook my head.

"Enric Stormhold—once a Knight of the Sword such as Bayard Brightblade, then a Knight of the Crown. Seeking to be a Knight of the Rose he was, and seeking that Knighthood not as much for the good he might perform through the offices of that order, oh, no, but for the trappings of honor and of glory that order might bring.

"Oh, yes, I know that a Knight can strive for both, can desire equally and richly the glory of Knighthood and the common good. I know that nothing is wrong with such a balance of desires.

"Nothing . . . necessarily.

"It was Enric Stormhold who led the Knights against the men of Neraka, down in the passes where your ancestor"—he gestured at me—"distinguished himself for bravery, if you can imagine, won the family name that you have rubbed into the dirt and stomped upon in the last few miserable months . . ."

"At your insistence!" I cried, and the raven laughed.

"That's neither here nor there, little Weasel. But back to Enric Stormhold. The story goes that he consulted a Calantine. Perhaps you have heard of them. They are the priests of the false god Gilean, or at least the false version of that false worship as found in Estwilde. They read the red dice and recite verses about animals. And call it prophecy."

His little black eyes glittered with malice. They were alert, the cold eyes of a viper.

"I know of the Calantina. But what of Enric?"

"Well, upon Enric's shoulders was the defense of Solamnia itself. Though he was a brave and worthy Knight, the burden was a heavy one. He was none too sure of the wisdom of his strategies or the strength of his heart, so he asked the Calantine the fate of the campaign. Had he not asked, had he relied on the prompting of his large spirit and trusted in the ways and will of the gods, would we not trust him and believe in him more?"

"The Calantine, sir. The prophecy."

"The Calantine cast the two and the ten," the bird proclaimed, then threw back its head and laughed harshly.

Two and Ten. Sign of the Raven.

"The oracle itself was right, of course. The Sign of the Raven is that of illusion, of false assurance in a dangerous country. Is that not right, Galen Pathwarden?"

I stammered for a moment.

"That's one interpretation, sir."

"Spoken like a Calantine," the Raven chuckled dreadfully.

"Of course the Calantines who read the dice for Enric nodded and nodded and said, 'The oracle tells us, sir, that your defense of Solamnia against the forces of Neraka will be the last defense you will make, that afterward peace will come to you and to Solamnia again.'

"And Enric rejoiced at the oracle, at its promise of success to him and to his armies. In one interpretation.

"But other things came to pass—things unimagined by Enric and unspoken by the Calantines who may or may not have foreseen them—what, after all, does it matter? The peace that came to Solamnia was indeed the peace that comes from a victorious campaign, engineered by Enric Stormhold, who left a handful of men in the pass at Chaktamir, where they held off the Nerakan army from sunrise to sundown, buying valuable time for the Solamnics at a staggering cost.

"Two hundred Knights, it is said, defended that pass. Fifteen lived to tell of that heroism.

"Your father was among them, Galen."

"Nor does he talk of it all that much. But what of Enric?"

"Enric. Peace came to him, too, just as the Calantine said it would. While the brave men held Chaktamir, Enric led his host to another passage, little known and not surprisingly open. They circled south around the Nerakans and came in behind them, bringing death from the east. Of the thousand Nerakans who filled the pass, not a man was left.

"But the peace that came to Enric was the sleep of death, brought about by a Nerakan arrow in the last hour of the battle. As he raised the victorious flag of the Solamnic armies, a wounded archer, lying as though dead in the center of the pass, scrambled quickly to his feet and fired a black arrow into Enric Stormhold's throat."

"A black arrow?"

"Raven feathers, Galen Pathwarden. So the Calantines were right, and the Sign of the Raven flourished in a manner that no man—not even the Calantines themselves—had foreseen."

"This is all very interesting, sir, but I confess that I'm at a loss as to the meaning of this whole Enric Stormhold business. How does it tie in with your being here in Castle di

Caela? Is it just that prophecies may mean something entirely different than we think they mean? If that's the case, I assure you I'll take the advice to heart. There's no need to haunt and bode."

"Oh . . . prophecies may mean different things to different eyes. Even places do that," the raven croaked.

"What does Chaktamir mean to you?"

The bird cocked its head curiously, wickedly.

"Why . . . it's history, sir. Where the Solamnics held off the Nerakans. Where Father fought."

"Oh, but it's so much more," the raven croaked dryly. "Places mean different things to different eyes. And so does history, little man."

"History?"

"The history, for example, of Benedict di Caela."

When the name was mentioned, the three thin candles sputtered and went out, plunging the room into a deeper darkness. Then I felt a pricking at my shoulders, the skittering of little claws, like a rat had boarded me. I struggled to shrug off the creature, but I found that I could not move.

Then the brush of a feather at my chest, and a smell of cologne, underlying it another smell of something old and beginning to rot.

And then the voice resumed.

"You have heard the story of Benedict di Caela? Hear it again, little Galen, this time the way it really happened. For history is a web, a labyrinth, and those who remember it remember only their own paths out."

"I knew it," I muttered, and the bird at my shoulder chuckled dryly, viciously.

"Knew . . . what?" it asked with a cruel playfulness.

"That you were Benedict di Caela! That the Scorpion and Sir Gabriel Androctus, that both of them— both of you— were Benedict di Caela!"

"*Are* Benedict di Caela," the raven hissed. "It's no great deduction, Weasel. I come back here rather often, you know. But I do that because this castle is mine. And the holdings. And the title itself.

"Four centuries ago I died twice. Once to the east here, at Chaktamir, which is more than a monument to Solamnic

251

saber-rattling. More than a pass where Enric Stormhold fell."

"I thought you were defeated at the Throtyl Gap near Estwilde."

"Yes, and the family version has it that I fell there. That I had traveled only that far to the East, gathering an army of rebels as I went. But the truth, little Weasel, is that I was hunted down like the common criminal they had decided I was. As I retreated eastward to Neraka, alone and disconsolate but bound for what I imagined was safety at last, a party of seven closed upon me. My brother Gabriel murdered me there, and my head tumbled from my shoulders.

"But I was dead by then, anyhow. That is, in a matter of speaking. For my father Gabriel had pronounced me dead in the great hall where I dined only this evening, pronounced me dead so he could smuggle his title and lands to my younger brother, my murderer. Whom Father always favored."

"Sir, I hate to keep being a . . . precisionist, but there is the small matter of your elder brother Duncan's mysterious death, how it seemed to be wedded to your mixing potions in the tower of the castle. After all, fathers don't usually pronounce sons dead for no reason."

"But it was for no reason, Galen. You know the Gabriels of this story by now, know that they are merciless against all adversaries, all rivals.

"That is all I was to them. Adversary. Rival. My poisons were for rats, no matter what monstrosities they imagined."

"I find it hard to give that credence, sir."

The claws dug sharply into my shoulder. I flinched and stifled a cry, as the warm, unhealthy smell coursed by me again.

"What you find hard to believe is no concern to me," the raven rasped. "Brother Duncan died of something. Who knows what it was? But whatever it was, it was not my doing."

"And the fire?"

"Was mine, admittedly. I burned my brother's body, yes, and in one of the tower rooms you can see from this window. It was a pyre most . . . Solamnic, for Duncan burned with his weaponry about him, his hands folded upon his chest, clutching a volume of the Measure.

"Of course they do not tell you how I sent him off heroically, content as they are in breathing the air of conspiracy and plot. Di Caelas are bad for that, I know—too intricate for their own good."

"But why burn Duncan's body? The clerics of Mishakal, who studied the dead for signs of poison—"

"Would have found what father told them to find. And he would have had his proof then—the testimonies of those sanctimonious men of the goddess would say, 'Yes, Sir Gabriel, your youngest son—the one named for you—is now your most capable heir, while the middle son is an abject villain, as you have always dreamed and imagined.'

"But I never harmed my brother. Indeed, I followed all the rules, the respectable second son unto the time that Father pronounced me dead.

"Then, over four centuries, I've tried to take by force what was rightfully mine, what was seized from me by inveiglement and ambush. You have heard, no doubt, of the rats, the floods, the fires, and the ogres. Each generation I would launch another natural disaster, and each generation some capable di Caela would find a way to steal my inheritance from my grasp once more."

"What's it like, sir? This being dead? And why wait a generation between attempts?"

A long pause, as the dark about me was awash in silence, with the too-sweet attar of flowers, with the flutter of wings.

The bird began to whisper.

"I can remember . . . or think I can remember . . . burning in the tower along with the rats I had unleashed on this castle. I remember drowning in the flood, remember all kinds of undoings in all kinds of disastrous circumstances. And when I remember clearly again, it is twenty years later, or thirty.

"Between those times is a hot, red darkness. I sleep through most of it. Sometimes I recall something of lights—scarlet lights, as though smoke itself were burning. And voices, though I can never quite discover words in the swirl of sounds around me.

253

"Once, the darkness resolved into a cavernous room, its floor a mirror of polished onyx. And about that mirror sat a score of Knights, their weapons broken, their heads bent as they stared into the mirror, which reflected nothing but stars.

"I do not know but that I dreamed those men, that mirror.

"Once the darkness became a landscape bare and cratered, and the moon that rose above it was as black as the onyx mirror, yet radiant somehow. Nothing lived in that forsaken country, but somewhere in the shadow of the rocks a creature was gibbering and whining—whether wounded or lying in wait, I could not tell.

"That was early on. Nor am I sure whether I dreamed that country, either."

He paused. A faint light crept to the edge of the window. Solinari was on the rise, and some things—larger things—in the room took on line and form. I could see the outline of the bed, the dresser.

"But regardless of the dream," the raven continued, "regardless of the cries and the torment and the long sleep, I have always awakened in sunlight, dazed but afoot upon Krynn once more. And once more I would set myself to the task of recovering what should be mine.

"This time, however, is different. For the first time in these four hundred years—for the very first time, mind you—the inheritance of the di Caela family descends to a woman. Descends to Lady Enid. And this time I have chosen to follow the rules once again. This time no rats, no goblins, no . . . scorpions. I shall murder nobody, steal from no one.

"Perhaps you wondered why I didn't descend on Bayard, on you, and kill you outright?"

"It occured to me long ago, sir, but I had no objections to your oversight, if oversight it was."

"I followed the rules. I murdered no one."

"Most people follow that rule, sir. In Coastlund it's considered a matter of course to pass the day without murdering someone. But what about the Knights at the tournament?"

"Slain under the fair and mutually accepted rules of

Solamnic combat. Which is not to say I didn't enjoy seeing Orban of Kern fall shattered or the blade of my sword find its home in Sir Prosper Inverno."

"And Jaffa? What of the peasant?"

"He came at me with a sword, Weasel. What would you have me do? And yet I loved watching him fall, knowing that Bayard Brightblade would suffer the blame."

I paused and took a breath before I asked:

"What about Agion?"

"Agion?" The bird stirred on my shoulder. Again I caught the smell of rottenness beneath the cologne.

"The centaur, damn it! Your marks were all over that ogre business in the Vingaard Mountains, and you can't tell me that—"

"That the fight between Bayard and the ogre was not fair? Of course I *can* tell you that. The battle was Knight against foe, and was not this . . . Agion warned that to intrude in a conflict of Knight versus foe would somehow be . . . dishonorable? The death of the centaur is regrettable, but you cannot deny that he received due payment for his little transgression."

I said nothing.

But in silence I made a vow to myself and to Agion that I would do whatever it took to undo this monster at my shoulder.

"But why? What earthly use do you have for the di Caela inheritance?"

"None." The wing of the bird brushed against me, and the smell of old decay passed over me once more.

"None anymore. On this side of the darkness the lands pale, the gems and gold shine like rotten wood, no longer with their accustomed light. Even the daughters . . . pale as I cease to remember them.

"No, I do this because the di Caelas would have these things, would pass them on into the warm, living hands of descendants.

"I do this for ruin, Weasel. Simple and straightfoward ruin. And for me, ruin has become enough.

"So I follow the rules and marry the Lady Enid di Caela. Then, beautiful bright thing though she may be, and as much as I may regret the loss of such beauty and brightness, I shall have to kill her. With a 'bright blade' of my own devising. For the rules are over then, little Galen. My inheritance is mine once more. I am *the* di Caela, and my word is law."

I tried to move, to throw the loathsome thing from my shoulder, but I felt stunned, paralyzed. It was as though I were one of those creatures that the scorpion stings before dragging it into a remote and dark place where it skitters over the helpless, dying prey and feasts.

"Do not breathe a word of this, Weasel," whispered the raven. "Oh, no, not a word. For Sir Bayard is already poisoned against you and Sir Robert is heavy with grievance. Of course, I am . . . eternally grateful for your assistance. But that would not stop me from gouging out your eyes and feasting upon them, from—what was it I said back at your moat house?—*dancing in your skin*? Or something worse, oh, so much worse, I assure you, if you ever betray my confidence.

"Apart from which, young mister Galen, we are bound together in sworn partnership, are we not? And I may yet have further call for your services."

There was no telling what the Scorpion had planned for me at that moment, in what dark recess he saw my role in the days that followed. Certainly he had told me more than it was wise to tell, if he intended only to marry the girl and leave me alone.

Brithelm came into the room then, carrying a tray of food on his head, and the bird took wing, battering itself against the thick glass of the chamber window and dropping to the sill, where it lay motionless and dark in the slanting light of the red moon.

For once I was glad Brithelm never bothered to knock.

"Supper, Galen!" my spritual brother sang out merrily, craning his neck to balance the laden tray. "The guardsmen say you're under the weather, that your feathers are drooping!"

I felt movement rush through my arms. I felt my legs weaken, knock together with relief and remembered fright.

"Why, what are you doing standing up? Bed rest for what

ails you, Galen, and soup. And wine, though I think you're under age. Why, once you're fortified, I'll bet that—"

"Brithelm!"

My brother fell silent and stopped in the middle of the room, tray rocking on the thicket of his red hair.

"Brithelm, I am not well."

As my brother wrapped me in blankets and fed me hot soup and mulled wine, he told his story.

* * * * *

"Alfric, too, faced the satyrs we faced in the depths of the swamp," Brithelm explained innocently. "He told me so. Nor did he know at the time that they were illusions only. He killed several of the satyrs, discovered—as we discovered—that they were goats, and filled with a noble rage . . ."

"'A noble rage,' Brithelm? Were those Alfric's words?"

"Yes, but I think they are fitting, don't you? For filled with a noble rage at the fact that innocent animals were being used for the most wicked of designs, he sought the encampment of the illusionist, and finding the villain not far from the site where he found the satyrs, put the entire group to flight.

"Perhaps that's why we had so little trouble in driving the villain from the swamp when we confronted him later."

"I suppose that is Alfric's theory, at any rate."

"Indeed. He suggested to me that it was his strategy that cleared the way for the heroics of Sir Bayrd Brightblade. Although Alfric quite humbly denies that credit for driving the evil from the swamp should fall to him alone."

"Quite humbly," I agreed.

I felt even worse. The sickness I had invented for the guards seemed real now, rushing over me in dizzying waves. I coughed, sneezed once. I wrapped the blankets more tightly about me, protruding my hand only so that I could pick up the bowl of mulled wine and drink from it. I looked to the window, where the small dark form lay still.

Brithelm babbled on about Alfric's bravery, about how he had rescued Alfric from the quagmire, and about how they had left together the morning after we had parted. How they had passed over the plains of Coastlund eventlessly,

riding horses Alfric had received as gifts of gratitude from
the centaur chief Archala for having helped drive the satyrs
from the swamp.

It seemed that even the centaurs had bought Alfric's harebrained story.

Brithelm went on and on. He spoke of how the time had
passed quickly on the road, and pleasantly except for the
rising fear in both of them that they would not find Bayard's
pass, would have to turn north and go nearly to Palanthas
in order to negotiate the mountains, and that the delay
would cause Alfric to miss the tournament. And Brithelm
went on, as to how "something" told him to follow a flight
of the ravens, that soon in their journey the ravens began to
perch in the branches around them, croaking forebodingly,
and when Alfric screamed or turned to flee, the birds took
wing toward the east and Solamnia.

I sipped more wine, looked again to the window, and
shivered.

Brithelm said that, by following the ravens, he and Alfric
found the pass. They crossed the mountains in the dead of
night.

I remembered the voices that had awakened me.

Discovering the pass, the quick, unimpeded journey
through it: it was all amazing to Brithelm, the ease a sure
sign that Fate's hand was guiding the fortunes of his elder
brother. And yet, when they arrived at Castle di Caela, to
his great surprise—and apparently Alfric's, too—the tournament was over. Sir Robert di Caela was polite, but distraught and abstracted, installing them in quarters at the
keep and praising both of them mightily for their persever-
ance over rough and dangerous roads.

"For some reason, though, Sir Robert is less than pleased
with Bayard Brightblade," Brithelm concluded, and stared
at me curiously. It was as though his eyes bored through me.

He rose from his seat on the bed and walked to the window. Tenderly he picked up the lifeless body of the bird, and
cupped it in his hands.

"The poor thing must have flown in here and battered
itself to death against the window. It's odd, Galen," he said,
turning to face me. "Odd that the servants hadn't disposed

of it before they moved you in here. It's been dead several days now. How sad." Unceremoniously, he dropped the bird out the window.

"Nevertheless, it's not the kind of thing a sick boy should have in his room."

Dead several days. Like the prisoner in the moat house.

Whether from the wine or the fever or from being tired of lying, I felt tears rush into my eyes. I had trouble keeping them down as I spoke.

"Brithelm, I have done some terribly wrong things."

He looked at me evenly and nodded. And I told my story, or, at least as much as I dared tell.

* * * * *

"So that bird was Benedict di Caela?" Brithelm asked between mouthfuls of boiled egg, balancing the empty tray on his head.

"No, damn it! That bird was a stopping off place for Benedict di Caela, for Gabriel Androctus, for the Scorpion, for what have you. Whoever or whatever he is, he's still about the premises, and plotting villainy."

Brithelm was to his feet at once, headed for the door.

"You and I will simply have to go to Sir Robert di Caela and tell him that this . . . Gabriel Androctus he fancies his future son-in-law is in fact the family curse come to roost."

"I think not, Brithelm. No telling the tricks that old Benedict has up his scaly sleeve."

"Then it's also time to tell Sir Bayard the whole story, Galen. So you won't be unprotected."

"Oh, I think not, Brithelm! The world may be as trusting a place as you seem to imagine, but one thing I can rely on is that Bayard Brightblade will dismantle me if this story is told to him."

"Then," Brithelm concluded, "it is time for dismantlement. Do you want your soup?"

"No . . . I'm far from hungry. Far from sober, too, with the mulled wine you've plied me with. I'm not drunk enough to confess everything in my dark past, though. I'm afraid that would take dwarf spirits or something stronger."

Brithelm nodded, his wide face buried in the soup bowl.

When he rose up for air, he had little to say.

"We'll go to Bayard as soon as you've weathered this fever. But we have to go there. After all, think of Sir Robert. Think of Enid—if half of what that raven boded is true, she's in dreadful danger.

"Think of Agion."

Something beyond wine and fever impelled me. This time I was sure.

"Brithelm, I have to go tonight. Bayard will be gone by noon tomorrow—you can count on it. He's too depressed to stay for the wedding.

"The wedding!"

"I had forgotten it, too," Brithelm declared calmly. "Are these potatoes in the bottom of the bowl? I had been avoiding them, thinking they were turnips."

"We must get to Bayard, and get to him tonight!"

"Very well," Brithelm agreed, bent curiously over the soup bowl.

He glanced up at me, once more staring me through.

"And no lies this time, Galen. Not like Alfric."

He must have seen the look of surprise on my face, for he laughed, looked down, and stirred in the soup bowl with his finger.

"Surely you didn't think I believed our brother's tales of heroism."

"Then why . . ."

He looked up again, smiled at me.

"Simply because it made him feel better. He was dreadfully embarrassed—passed over for squirehood again and again, and then, when he tried to do something about it, he gets mired by his baby brother waist deep in the 'Warden Swamp, squealing until rescued by his middle brother. He needed a little . . . ornamental passage in his story, a part where he was the hero."

"But then, what about me and having to tell Sir Bayard all about—"

"Same reason."

Again he looked down into the bowl and stirred some more.

"Potatoes get so confoundedly transparent when you boil

them too long. Are these turnips, Galen?"

He held up the bowl to me, smiling that vacant grin once more.

* * * * *

As you might imagine, Bayard was not overjoyed to see me. Shivering in the night air, which was burrowing into my cloak and tunic more ferociously than it ever did in the mountains, I approached the pavilion where his standard had been raised that afternoon and saw him sitting alone, away from the other Knights. Wrapped in the blanket from which he had drawn the ceremonial Brightblade shield, he also shivered in the brisk autumn night. He had left the shield face-down in the dirt beside him.

The night was still overcast and chill. Not far from Bayard, the other Knights drank roca and played music and told stories, enjoying the company before most of them struck camp and returned to Palanthas, to Caergoth, to Solanthus, to those few places in which the Order was still permitted and still welcome. Brithelm walked among them, slackjawed with amazement at the tales the Knights were telling.

"Do you suppose these are true, Galen—all these tales about sea monsters and abductions by eagles? Do you suppose Sir Ramiro over there really has a talking sword?"

"I suppose that it makes him feel good to tell the others about it, Brithelm," I responded vacantly, looking across the dappling of firelight and darkness into the campsite of my former protector.

Who sulked at the twilit edge of things, his attention evidently on the stars. It was almost a pitiful sight, and I suspect I felt almost sorry for Bayard.

I tried to slip by the revelry, and could have done so with ease, what with the citterns and the clatter of cups and the boasts.

But the smoke of the campfires or the dust in the rising wind—or just plain fatigue, if that is possible—brought on a fit of sneezing as though I had rolled the length of a country in goldenrod. The fit over, I sniffed, walked on as if I belonged at the encampment, or as if I had a message for my protector that would not bear obstructing.

Sir Ramiro of the Maw, all four hundred pounds of him, stopped me before I could get to Bayard.

"I would not approach him if I were you, boy. He doesn't seem all that pleased with any of the business that plagued this tournament, and I understand you had a little hand in delaying him."

"So he's talking about that, is he?" I began. But Ramiro waved his fat hands quickly, so quickly that his forearms quivered.

"No, no, boy, you'd never hear such talk from Bayard Brightblade. Your brother was quite vocal at the banquet earlier, and seemed altogether pleased that you'd played merry hell with Sir Bayard's intentions. Seeing as that's the case, if you've come for forgiveness, I'd advise you to wait on it until morning."

The big Knight stepped in front of me and folded his arms across his expanse of chest. It was like having a gate closed in your face, and I stepped back, almost into the cheery campfire of two Knights from Caergoth, and adopted my best official voice, lowered at least one strenuous octave.

"So Bayard isn't pleased with me, Sir Ramiro? Perhaps he'll be pleased when the family di Caela, the beautiful Enid included, is finally consumed by the curse it's been carrying for four hundred years."

"The curse again? I thought the di Caelas had put that yarn to rest."

"Please let me through, sir. The ill tidings are for Sir Bayard's ears first."

I coughed again, and began the long, circular route around Sir Ramiro. He started to stand in front of me once more, but Brithelm distracted him with some questions about the talking sword, and I was allowed to pass freely through the encampment to where Bayard sat, stargazing, huddled under blankets and gloom.

I paused and took stock as Bayard pondered the moon.

"Things at Castle di Caela, sir. They're in bad shape, I fear."

"So Robert decided he didn't want you, either?" Bayard asked icily, still staring above me at whatever pattern he saw in the stars. I followed his gaze to the zenith of the sky, where the two dragons danced around the Book of Gilean. Black clouds scudded rapidly past the stars. There was the promise of rain in the smell of the air.

Things were strange and forbidding, and I had a reluctant Knight on my hands.

"It's more complicated than that, Bayard," I began.

"Yes, it's a complicated situation, Galen," he snapped, eyes breaking from contemplation of the heavens to fix totally, bleakly on my face. "But I've solved the puzzle. The solution is that, despite all their father's good intention, the sons of Andrew Pathwarden are like crabs in a jar: one scrambles over another until he reaches the lip of the vessel, then the one below him reaches and claws him down. Except for the middle son, who clings to some kind of basic goodness."

He nodded at Brithelm as he said this. Then he stood and wrapped the blanket tightly around him against the rising wind and the smell of approaching rain. He stalked away from me, the silence and the long strides daring me to try to catch up, until we stood about a hundred feet apart.

Huge drops of rain spattered on the ground around us. Thunder rolled out of the south. I had to shout above the natural noise and drama.

"Benedict di Caela has returned."

Lightning turned the sky white over the field. For a moment Bayard was clearly outlined, clearly visible. In the thunder that followed, I could not hear him, but I clearly saw him mouth the word *What*.

As the lightning flashed and the thunder followed again, the rain began to sweep over the ground between us. I sprinted to join my protector, splashing through the new and sudden mud on the road as I ran toward him. Water soaked into my blankets. I felt cold and wet and aching all the way into my bones.

I must have passed out. It was Bayard's shout that dragged me back onto the rainy road to the Castle di Caela. He was standing beside me. He had me by the shoulders and was shaking me like a schoolmaster shakes a troublesome student.

"What's wrong with you? Galen? What's . . ." Then paus-

then shaking me again, but more gently this time. "Let's get you out of the rain."

Lifting his blanket above the both of us, he ushered me toward a grove up the road toward the castle. It was ever-green mostly, so the leaves remained on many of the trees, and the branches of those vallenwoods scattered among the cedars and junipers were thick enough to shelter a party much larger than ours from the downpour.

There we sat, Bayard draping the blanket over two low hanging branches above us, forming a crude lean-to that kept out the weather.

I lay down beneath the blanket, breathing in the old smells of wool and dust and faint rain and sweat and horses. Bayard crouched over me.

"What is it, Bayard?"

"'Sir Bayard.' Like it or not, you're back in my employ. There's not a dry stick or twig in the whole damn grove. Looks like we'll sit this one out without a fire."

A look of concern crossed Bayard's face. He leaned over, placed his hand on my forehead.

"You're burning up, boy."

Come to think of it, I was a little stifled, but I had fancied it was only being under blankets and all wrapped against the cold in the first place. I started to beg Bayard to take me back toward the fires of the encampment, where I could warm my feet and where I could mend, but then that didn't make any sense because my problem was being too hot in the first place and . . .

I remember Bayard asking, "Now what's this about Bene-dict di Caela?"

Then I remember nothing else.

CHAPTER 15

Light washed over my face, and for a moment I thought I was being blinded. I willed myself not to see the light, to suffer the brightness, but then in a blur I saw clouds above me darting in and out of my vision. At first I thought they were moving, those clouds, until I felt hard wood tilting and rocking below me, and I heard the clatter of hooves and the breathing of horses.

I was traveling somewhere under a daylit sky, shadowed by clouds and by birds flying overhead.

Brithelm's face was above me, too. I heard him speak, and heard Bayard's voice behind him somewhere, almost indistinguishable from the creaking of wheels and the song of a lark.

I tried to speak, to ask the obvious questions: *Where am*

I?, What happened to me?, and *Why all the hushed concern and the fuss?*. But Brithelm was saying something to me about resting, relaxing, and his hand on my forehead was as cool and soothing as the night air. Behind him I heard the voices of women, one of which sounded like Enid—that sweet, high music of birds.

I hoped devoutly it was Enid, for the voice brought back the sight of her in my memory and imagining. But the cart passed again into shadow, which in turn passed into great and abiding darkness.

* * * * *

I was in a room somewhere, remotely familiar. A tapestry hung on the far wall, blurred in my adjusting eyes and in candlelight. A face appeared over me, another blur of shadow and color.

Strands of wild hair, disheveled and as red as the red robe.

"He's waking, Dannelle. Go get the Knights."

The sound of a door closing softly. I tried to sit up. It was too tiring, and when I tried, the light in the room spun like stars.

"Rest, little brother," said Brithelm's voice, cool and soothing. "If you wrestle the fever, it will throw you.

"And besides, it's a hard task you have coming. I've tried to soften it some, explained the whole thing and how sorry you are, to Sir Bayard Brightblade. Argued with Sir Robert and that gentleman in black—"

Gentleman in black!

"—to postpone this . . . talk, but they would hear none of it. They insisted that we settle the matter now, and the three of them are on their way to these chambers, where they will hear your story.

"Rest now," Brithelm continued. "You are among friends."

I closed my eyes and resolved to appear as pathetic as I felt.

* * * * *

I must have dozed, as several voices mingled in the room, changing in pitch and tone and in the shapes of words every time I rose far enough out of sleep to hear them. At last there was movement by my bed and I opened my eyes slowly, pathetically, as though I were being called then and there from the borders of the afterlife.

Bayard stood at my bedside.

"Brithelm says you're better."

I nodded as weakly as I could, tried to appear brave but on the wane.

"You have other guests. I have urged them to wait for your recovery, as has your brother Brithelm, but Sir Gabriel insists that the wedding go on as planned. Nonetheless, Sir Robert di Caela wants to talk to you. And he's brought with him Sir Gabriel, who insists that he's never seen you before in his life. Much less transacted with you.

"You know, Galen, that I haven't the faintest idea whether you know something, or you're lying, or you've dreamed all of this up out of fever and wine and guilt.

"Let's just say I have to trust you now."

He laid his hand on his sword.

"And you can trust me, Galen Pathwarden. If what you speak is the truth, and what you say angers this Gabriel Androctus or Benedict di Caela or whatever infernal name he goes by or chooses next, rest assured that while Bayard Brightblade breathes, the man will not harm you."

"That's reassuring, sir. As long as you breathe."

Bayard laughed softly, then called over his shoulder.

"Let the guests in, Brithelm."

*   *   *   *   *

They stood around me as though they were on vigil. Somber, silent, they heard the story from its inception in the moat house through the swamp and the mountains and my surprising discovery here at Castle di Caela.

Androctus was disturbingly calm, hearing my accusations as though they were imagined out of delirium or had to do with someone else. He even looked touched when I talked about what happened to Agion in the mountains and couldn't go on for a minute. So I wondered until Gabriel Androctus spoke. For it was that nightmare voice that had haunted me since the moat house—all sweet and smooth and ruinous.

"This young man has been through terrible things," he said warmly. "No wonder that such hardships have . . . clouded his reason, made him see enemies where no enemies are. If there is anything I can do to make him more comfortable, I should be more than happy to do so *after* the ceremony."

Sir Robert glanced sidelong at his future son-in-law—a look that held no approval.

"But of course, Sir Gabriel," he sighed, "the question becomes that ceremony. For if there is an ounce of truth in what the boy says—"

"That I am Benedict di Caela?" Sir Gabriel interrupted incredulously, then burst into loud and terrible laughter. "There's too much malice in you, Sir Robert. You've been wounded too long by the curse your forefathers inflicted."

He smiled wickedly and leaned against the tapestry.

"But let us be fair. Does the boy have an ounce of evidence beyond his fevered testimony?"

Bayard and Sir Robert looked at me.

My thoughts raced.

Evidence? From the mountains? The swamp?

Nothing.

From . . .

"Bayard, please bring me my cloak. It's over there by the fire."

Bayard did as I asked, never taking his eyes from Gabriel Androctus.

Who looked puzzled now, and maybe a little worried.

Bayard handed me the cloak, warmed and partially dried on the hearth, but still wet in its folds from last night's drenching downpour. I coughed at the smell of wet wool, then fumbled through the pockets, past the Calantina dice, past the tooled gloves . . .

"Here they are!"

Sir Bayard and Sir Robert leaned forward eagerly. Sir Gabriel took a short, tentative step toward the door.

"These stones!" I proclaimed, opening the soggy drawstring of the bag, letting the half dozen opals tumble onto the bed, where they stood out soft and white and lovely against the rough bedclothes.

"So?" Sir Gabriel shot back quickly. "This is some sort of incriminating evidence?"

"I should say it is! These are the very opals you bribed me with when this whole unsavory business began. When you wanted Sir Bayard's armor back in my father's moat house, when you took it and performed the gods know what outrage with it—"

"Enough, Galen," Bayard cautioned. "You've made your point. Does this persuade you, Sir Robert?"

"Not unless he's a bigger fool than I think he is," snapped Sir Gabriel, as Sir Robert leaned over the bed, picked up one of the opals, and held it to the light. "How many places, I ask, could a boy of Galen Pathwarden's . . . proclivities have 'discovered' a purse filled with semiprecious stones?"

"What's this about being a 'bigger fool than you think I am,' Androctus?" Sir Robert snapped back, reddening. "Just how big a damn fool do you think I am, you sable-robed *prima donna*!" he roared, and Bayard leaped between the two men, parting them.

Androctus stepped once more toward the door. "You misunderstand me, sir," he soothed. "I was only saying that the lad might have found these anywhere, and the fact that they were on his person should not lead us to the conclusion that I bribed him with stones."

Sir Robert recovered his calm and his dignity. He spoke coldly, directly.

"But these are glain opals, Sir Gabriel. From Estwilde. Found only in Estwilde, mined only near the Throtyl Gap."

"Where Benedict di Caela fell!" Bayard exclaimed.

"Well, not exactly," I interrupted. "Benedict di Caela fell in the pass at Chaktamir . . ."

"How do you know that?" exclaimed Sir Robert eagerly, spinning to face me so rapidly that he lost his balance and toppled over the bed, scattering the opals. "That's the part of the story . . ."

"That the di Caelas hide?" interrupted Androctus, his dark eyes bright with fury, but his voice surprisingly level all of a sudden, even quiet. "And why do they hide that part of the story, Sir Robert? Why, because the whole sorry tale is brimming with villains, is it not? And not only the oft-maligned Benedict."

He turned slowly, fingered the edge of the tapestry. It was a charming picture of a hunt, five Knights on horseback, each bearing the recognizable di Caela profile.

With a quick step, Androctus stood by the center of the tapestry, pointing at the foremost mounted figure. "Gabriel di Caela the Elder disinherited a son who, by all rights, should have been the di Caela in the generation that followed."

The figure on the tapestry smoldered, burning slowly and smokelessly. We all gaped, dumbfounded, then considered our options. Sir Robert stepped toward Gabriel, then thought better of it. Bayard's hand went to his sword, waiting for Gabriel to make the first move.

As though the tapestry were a map and he was giving a history lecture, Gabriel's hand moved to the hindmost rider. "Then Gabriel di Caela the Younger amassed an army against his disinherited brother, defeating that brother in a battle at the Throtyl Gap, then hounding him westward over the plains of Neraka until they both reached Chaktamir, the high pass, and there . . ."

The figure of Gabriel the Younger caught fire in the same slow flame.

"Enough!" shouted Robert di Caela, and then more calmly. "And how do you know this history, Sir Gabriel?"

"Oh, common knowledge," Sir Gabriel smiled. "And common gems, too, even if they are the glain opals of Estwilde. I mean, the boy's dice are from Estwilde, too, and no burglar—"

"What dice are those, Sir Gabriel?" Bayard shot back. "How is it that you've never met Galen before, and yet you're familiar with the contents of his pockets?"

Androctus paused, stared at me.

Within the black pupils of those eyes glimmered a red fire, banked but unmistakably there in all its evil and evil intent. The fire smoldered, went black, and the dark Knight turned calmly to Bayard.

"His brother," Androctus explained. "Who is it . . . Alfric Pathwarden? He told me of Galen's superstition last night as he gloated at the banquet. Despicable little chap."

"Pretty thin, Sir Gabriel," Sir Robert stated dryly. "It does not satisfy our uncertainty. It seems we have no choice but to postpone the wedding another week. I regret the inconvenience to all the guests planning to attend, but the delay is unavoidable as we seek for the truth in this murky matter."

"The truth?" Sir Gabriel asked in outrage. "What do you know of the truth?" He turned from the tapestry, folded his arms in front of him, and glared at Sir Robert.

"The truth, quite frankly, is that I do not like you, Sir Gabriel Androctus," spat Sir Robert, his face gloriously red beneath the silver of his moustache and hair. "And I am still alive and lord of this castle, which I shall pass on to whomever I damn well please. I may lose a little face in the matter, but it'll be worth it if you are Benedict di Caela. Even if you are not, it would almost be worth going back on my word just to see the look on your face!"

A cold wind swept through the room. Mist rose out of the floor, and the tapestry flapped on the wall. Sir Gabriel stood taller, until he seemed to tower over Bayard and Sir Robert, who both were startled, stepping back from the strange, transforming figure in front of them.

Who spoke in loud tones that shattered the glass in the window, sending me burrowing into my blankets.

There in the darkness I heard a scuffling, the sound of fabric tearing, the shivering music of more glass breaking. And over it all, the resonant voice of the Scorpion.

"The truth, Sir Robert, is that once again you are wresting my birthright from me! And this after I played by the rules! After I fought fairly and danced in the lists with all your princes and popinjays, raising my visor and proffering lances at the beck and call of a brassy Solamnic trumpet!

"Oh, your Knights are in love with the sound of honor, the mouthings and motions of the old school, but with all of this posturing you seize what is rightfully mine.

"You have done me great injury, Robert di Caela!" he screamed, and I heard the sound of something else shattering.

"But nothing . . ."

His voice descended into quiet, into a cheerful, commonplace tone that was more frightening by far than the screaming of a moment before.

"Nothing compared to the injury I shall do you."

Sir Robert cried out in rage. I heard the sound of furniture falling. I burrowed out toward the light and peeked through the blankets just in time to see the Scorpion wheel away from a charging Sir Robert and sprint for the door my brother Brithelm blocked. Halfway to the door he paused, wheeled once more in his tracks, and quickly, with a strange, awkward gait like a grounded raptor, leaped toward the broken window and out, his cloak catching and tearing on a jagged claw of glass near the base of the sill.

Bayard sprang to the window and looked out and down. He turned back to us and shrugged.

"Disappeared from the face of the earth," he declared flatly.

Sir Robert drew his sword and split the back of the one chair standing upright in the room.

* * * * *

Brithelm sat on the edge of the bed and chattered as I stood by the fireplace and tuned the lute he had brought me.

"What a wonderful stroke of fortune, was it not, that the one most capable of taking care of you in your illness was your long-lost brother, with whom you you had reunited only an hour or so before you needed him direly?"

"Yes, Brithelm," I responded tactfully, politely. "I'd have to say there was tremendous good fortune all around in this matter. Is this"—referring to the lute—"in tune?"

"I am sure it's in tune with something, little brother. I do not believe it's in tune with itself."

I sighed and returned to tuning, following the old gnomish philosophy: "When in doubt about the pitch, tighten the string."

"What's keeping you here, anyway, Brithelm?" I asked. "I thought you were secluded for good, intent on becoming some kind of swamp saint."

He shifted on the bed, stood, and walked toward the fireplace, where he stood by me, warming his hands at the red coals.

"Seclusion it was, little brother, but I had to return to the world in order to answer a brother in need.

"I am here as a character reference for Alfric in his suit for the hand of the Lady Enid di Caela," Brithelm announced serenely, and a string broke as I tuned it far too tightly, whined and ricocheted and whipped against my hand. Brithelm started at the noise.

"Character reference? For Huma's sake, Brithelm, it's nearly impossible to find any character in our brother, much less to vouch for it. How in the world did he wrangle you into such a business?"

I stared hard at Brithelm.

"Well, I could tell that all his talk of heroics was only talk, but after all, Father had sent him. Alfric told me that the prospect of being wed to the Lady Enid dwelt with him night and day. He appealed to Father to perform the emergency Knighthood ceremony, which, of course, allowed him to enter the tournament—"

"Wait a moment, Brithelm. 'The emergency Knighthood ceremony'?"

"You know more about it than I do, Galen. You studied the Solamnic codes while I turned to theology.

"But isn't the ceremony a dispensation that the Order grants on the eve of a tournament in which the husband of a daughter of an Early Family is to be chosen? Young lads not yet squires but intending to be are allowed to forego squirehood altogether, moving straight to the ceremony which Father performed in our absence at the moat house, making Alfric a Knight and thereby eligible to marry Enid di Caela."

"Is that what Alfric told you about the ceremony, Brithelm?"

It was simply the worst lie I had ever heard—not the most cruel, the most base, the most foul, but surely the most stupid. There were a dozen places within this castle—as many as there were Knights—where Brithelm could turn and discover there was no such thing as an "emergency Knighthood ceremony." Something was approaching shore in Alfric's brain. Swimming in loneliness, that half-drowned idea had sight of land.

* * * * *

With all my enemies on the loose, it might have been foolish to travel abroad that night, but travel I did. It was no problem skirting the keep of the castle, asking a servant the whereabouts of a private place to sit and ponder.

Of course, when the Scorpion leaped through the window and vanished, none of us thought we were out of the woods, especially after Bayard and I recounted our history of encounters with the Scorpion—how each time he had vanished mysteriously, only to return in a new and equally deadly form.

When I told Sir Robert of the Scorpion's threats to the life of the Lady Enid, the old man flooded the courtyard of Castle di Caela with armed guards.

You couldn't walk, sit, or stand in the moonlight without being accosted by overly concerned protectors—by a "who goes there?" followed with a barrage of questions that dissected your business at the castle and your further business walking around at night, questions that traced your family tree back five generations with the genuine possibility that any ancestor remotely unSolamnic might get you a night in the guardhouse.

Which is why the orchard was a pleasant change. I had set up camp there, amidst the peach and pear trees beneath the Lady Enid's window.

Guards surrounded the orchard from a distance, and now and again I heard one of them call to another. But the Lady Enid's orchard was her own private preserve, evidently, and after a thorough search in the early evening, the guards had left it alone. Only an hour after nightfall, it was filled with nightingales and owls, singing their old quarrel from the trees.

Not only were there singing birds, but birds wrought of evergreen, too. The floor of the orchard was a topiary garden, filled with carefully tended shrubbery sculpted into the forms of various small animals and birds. Owls there were, and nightingales, and squirrels and rabbits and short-eared lutra, all cut from juniper, aeterna, and other greenery.

For a while I stood there, staring up at the dim and flickering light in Enid's window and breathing in the strong, fresh smells of the fruit and the shrubbery. It was a romantic's dream, this landscape, spoiled only by the occasional distant calling of a guard.

I backed against a juniper owl, pausing to relish the smells, the sound of birdsong, the soft light.

Suddenly there were hands about my throat and a coarse, familiar voice hissing in my ear.

"I have a lot of paying back to do, little brother. And it starts here."

It seems Alfric had followed me out of the entrance and around the keep, staying hidden under the branches of the trees and in the shadows of the walls. My face was half-buried in the back of the topiary owl.

"Please let me up," I muttered, my mouth pressed against needles and hard wood.

"Like you let me up back in the swamp? Oh . . . I have a mind to throttle you, Weasel, to make you burrow face down in the greenery. How do the needles taste, little brother? Where is the wisdom hiding now?"

Nonetheless, his grip loosened and I gained room to speak.

Letting me speak had always been Alfric's mistake.

"I said, better let me up, Alfric. If you mash or otherwise alter this familiar face, Sir Bayard won't have you as a squire. Nor will any of these other gentlemen gathered here, if anything deflects the splendor of my nose."

"Which don't seem bad to me, Galen, seeing as I plan to be suiting for the hand of the Lady Enid," Alfric announced proudly, pressing me even farther into the evergreen.

"It's 'suing,' and I'm afraid you're out of luck. Tournament's over, remember?"

After one more shove into the thick needles of the bush, Alfric let me up.

"My luck may be out, but there's something about that weasel's luck of yours that keeps you landing upright."

"Meaning?"

"Meaning you're here to press *my* suit. That's your story," Alfric growled. He put his hand over my mouth, muffling my cries for help. Then he grabbed my right arm, twisting it behind me until my elbow touched the base of my spine, my thumb the back of my neck. I tried for a witty response, but could think of none through the pain that tore into my shoulder and blotted out wit, blotted out everything but the sense of that pain. I was having trouble breathing.

"What is my motivation, dear brother?" I gasped, and prepared to black out.

"The swamp," said Alfric. "Remember the swamp?"

"Oh."

"I have heard tales of your confession, Weasel, but omitted by chance—by oversight, I'm sure—is the part where you stranded your older brother in deadly muck and mire. A most convenient oversight, no doubt, for we all know that violence against one's blood relatives is the worst transgression of Solamnic code. I do not think Sir Bayard and Sir Robert could overlook such a, shall we say, naughty piece of business? What do you think, dear brother?"

An excruciating pause. "At—your—service," I stammered, gasping for breath.

Alfric loosened his grip. Air and sense rushed back into me as my brother leaned above me and whispered.

"Good. I brung the lute. Now what're we going to do, Galen? You're good at these things."

He spun me about, pulled me up to his face, and drew his dagger, and I remembered the smell of my brother that was the smell of wine and of old food and of something that tunneled to the edge of insanity always beneath those other smells.

Alfric pressed the point of the knife against my chin, inflicting slight but menacing pain. Then he lowered me and took cover, drawing me roughly after him into the breast of the shrubbery owl.

"Everything is close to perfect," Alfric crowed. "I was late to the tournament, so I did not have to join the lists against anyone who would of mangled me in the first place. Then it turns out that the Knight who wins and I'm planning to be the squire for is a crook and did not win at all, and for a while I'm even madder at you because you kept me from being a squire again. But then I think it's even better on account of now the tournament don't matter and the Lady Enid and her inheritance are fair game."

"*Fair game*? What a . . . romantic way to put it, Alfric."

"That's up to you," my brother hissed. "You're better at putting things than I am. You tell me what to say underneath the Lady Enid's window. You play the lute and sing like you was me.

"If you don't," Alfric said, flatly and casually, "I am going to kill you."

As we had grown up in the tunnels and chambers of the moat house, each of us had dreamed of killing the other, I am sure. I can speak with authority that I often went wool-gathering over Alfric's untimely death. I would fancy it at night as I lay in my chambers, or in the daytime in my secret place behind the hearth of the great hall.

It usually involved large, hungry animals with fangs.

But we were too old for the old threats, the bluster of "I'll kill you, I'll kill you" that underscored our militant child-hoods. This time, Alfric might mean it.

"You better do good, Weasel," Alfric whispered.

He loosened his grip and pushed me completely into the belly of the owl. He dusted himself off, then licked his fingers and ran them through his hair like a grotesque, make-shift comb. He stepped into a clearing in the topiary, lit dimly by the stars and the firelight from Enid's window and other windows on this side of the keep.

I was allowed to woo, but from the wings only.

"Hello, Lady Enid," Alfric called up to the window. He looked back to me at once for advice or approval.

"Wonderful!" I whispered from the belly of the owl.

Alfric smiled stupidly and turned back to his courtship.

A small sound rose from the window—a muffled sound that I took as laughter, but Alfric, buoyed by what he thought was his own silver tongue, no doubt took as a sigh of adoration.

But he had no idea what to say next. He stepped away from the window, looked at me, panic-stricken.

I scrambled out from under the owl's wing, hoping to put shadows between me and my brother—shadows through which I could escape and return to my quarters. That way I could be at peace, and Alfric—well, Alfric could pursue the courtship of his lifetime with what talents he had. Left to his own charm and resources, my brother might make a four-hundred-year-old curse seem attractive.

Overhead, slate gray clouds scudded over the moons and shaded and shifted the light around us.

Alfric followed me, losing me only a moment behind the light blue needles of an enormous aeterna jay. He found me again soon enough, catching sight of me as I turned to run and finally cornering me against a larick nest of sparrows, who rustled and dropped their berries when Alfric grabbed me by the shoulders and began to shake me pleadingly.

"You don't know how hard it is to be the eldest, Weasel, to have so many responsibilities fall into your lap simply because you're the first one out. You have to put up with everything from your younger brothers—mysticism, theft, bad opinions—and you have to do so with a smile because you are the oldest and it has fallen into your lap to put up with those things."

"Stop shaking me, Alfric."

"Shut up. I listened to you long and often. But did anyone ever look out for Alfric? Did anyone ever ask what would please Alfric?"

"Well, I . . ."

"Shut up." His voice was a little too loud. He paused, looked around. "I'm tired of always seeing to the needs of others, of being the concerned big brother. What I would rather do is to win some attention on my own, for once to do something for myself and only for myself."

A look of pain and fear passed over his face. The scene would have been pathetic had I not known that Alfric's every waking moment since childhood had been devoted to doing things for himself and only for himself.

"And you are going to help me, little brother. You and your words and mischief and petty larceny," Alfric gloated, breaking a branch from the larick and waving it irritatingly under my nose. The sharp, minty smell of the red needles almost made me sneeze.

"You see," Alfric continued, "I am going to step back into that clearing, back by the wall of the keep, where I will be in full view of the Lady Enid. From there I can pay court to her. Make me up a poem to say to her, Weasel."

Suddenly he dragged me by my collar back beneath Enid's

window, where he held me at arm's length, dangling in the midst of a juniper nightingale, a rather woolly overgrown thing crouched beneath one of the taller pear trees.

I took refuge while Alfric stood in the clearing, in partial view, romanced by moonlight and shadows. He stood there—and I dangled there—for a good minute of silence, until I realized he was waiting for Enid to come to the window.

"She's not going to show, Alfric, unless you let her know that you're out here."

I choked and coughed as my collar tightened. Still he suspended me among the evergreens.

"Return to the window, my lady," I whispered.

"What?"

"'Return to the window, my lady.' That's your first line." I grabbed a branch in the midst of the shrub and, settling part of my weight upon it, took some of the pressure off my neck.

"I don't understand," Alfric muttered. One hand held me even more tightly among the needles and the branches while the other scratched his head.

"You wanted a poem, Alfric. I am obliging you with the first line."

"I forgot what it was."

"'Return to the window, my lady,' damn it!"

"'Return to the window, my lady, damn it!'" he called aloud beneath Enid's window. There was silence. A faint light shook deep in the chambers, glancing off the uppermost branches of the tree. Alfric looked toward me, awaiting the next line. I dangled and composed rapidly.

"While the garden dances with light."

"What?"

"Your second line," I explained. "'While the garden dances with light.'"

"You sure she will want to hear about a garden?" Alfric whispered. "Don't girls want to hear about themselves?"

"In a minute, brother," I replied, sliding away from his hand, crawling into the branches of the nightingale. "Meanwhile, you want to set the mood. It's what the poets call 'creating atmosphere.'"

Alfric stared into the shrubbery bird, looking long and mistrustfully for me. Finally he gave up, turned back to the window, spoke aloud.

"'While the garden dances with light.'"

A stifled sound descended from the chamber window.

Laughter? Who could tell?

I composed for a moment in silence, then prompted my brother.

"While the moon glides low in the evening sky, borne aloft in the hands of the night."

"What?"

"For Huma's sake, Alfric, open your ears and listen to what you're saying! It's not Quivalen Sath, but it does for topiary romance!"

He turned, faced the window, and spoke loudly.

"While the moon gets low in the evening, and something happens at night."

I didn't think the line was that bad, but it turned poisonous in Alfric's translation.

"Great, Alfric," I spat. "That's just magnificent. You couldn't win Lexine the cook's daughter with a display of oratory like that!"

All of a sudden, from the recesses of Enid's room above us came a scream, loud and frightful and filled with desperation. After the scream died, the keep and the orchard about it were terribly silent.

In astonishment Alfric pulled me from the nightingale. He and I stared at one another—that stupid, childhood stare that comes when you have broken something, when you stand there in the aftermath, trying to figure each other: "Is he trustworthy enough that we can conspire in silence?" or "Is he stupid enough that I can blame him entirely for this?"

As we stared, a long silence settled in the shrubbery and shadows around us. The orchard birds that had not grown quiet at Alfric's poetry grew quiet now at the sound of screaming above them.

For above us came the sounds of movement, commotion, and through it all continual screams.

I started for the keep wall, somehow intending to scale it, to vault in Enid's window . . .

But Alfric's hand restrained me. My brother crashed back into the shrubbery nightingale, drawing me with him.

It was this bird that swallowed us—my brother and me—just as Enid's window filled with shadows. Concealed beneath the shrubbery's overgrown wings, we watched as if paralyzed as a core of darkness rose out of the large keep window, and as that darkness moved rapidly down the wall.

Across the courtyard it moved, quick in the light of the moons. But neither the red nor the white light could enter its thickness, its opaqueness. Its surface was pocked and dappled like molten wax doused with cold water.

From within it I thought I heard screams.

I struggled with the green, fragrant branches around me. Once again I tried to break free of my brother, to storm the keep and rescue the damsel in distress as any good Knight in any old story would be bound to do. But Alfric only clutched me tighter, drawing his knife again and pressing it uncomfortably against my ribs. It was refreshing not to be the most cowardly Pathwarden.

In the shifting light of the moons I saw the shadow rush rapidly toward the gate, and two shouting guardsmen move almost as quickly in a desperate effort to cut it off.

The shadow gathered speed, as though something within it were guiding it, propelling it with an increasing sense of will and of urgency. It struck them with a sharp wet sound, and they fell over.

Their screams were unspeakable.

It was then I heard the screams once more, cascading from the window above me. They were no longer stifled, but muffled somehow, as if whoever was screaming was a great distance away and the sound was reaching me from afar and far too late.

Gradually the shadow grew smaller and smaller as it passed through the gate in the outer walls of the castle and from there moved toward the plains, in what direction I had no idea.

"Alfric!" I called aloud. There was no sound behind me but that of branches breaking, of sobbing, of something large and clumsy crashing away into the darkness.

"Damn it!" I muttered, and turned to follow my brother. I was stopped by the screams from above me.

When I remember it, it seems the most foolish thing I had done, at least until then. Why, helping the Scorpion steal the armor seemed like an act of genius next to this.

I grabbed the trellised vines against the wall of the tower and climbed up to the Lady Enid's window, where I heaved myself over the sill and toppled inside.

Dannelle di Caela lay screaming, bound on the bed, a vacancy beyond terror on her face. It was clear to me now that the Lady Enid was being carried from Castle di Caela in shadows, toward what murky destination and for what reason only the gods knew.

But I knew that somewhere in the days ahead the Scorpion would make good his most deadly threat.

It was all I could do to get to the base of the southeast tower, more than I could do to climb the stairs that encircled it from the outside. Nonetheless, I climbed the stairs, stopping to gain my breath twice, three times, wondering how Mariel di Caela ever got all those cats to this altitude, and filled with a rising sense of despair that despite climbing a topless tower, I would not see what I hoped so devoutly to see.

I was nearly to the top of the southeast tower when the spiraling stairwell gave me a view of the plains to the east of the castle. I stood on tiptoe, squinted, and cast my gaze to the limits of the horizon.

Where the red light of Lunitari shone on a dark shadow moving quickly toward the Throtyl Gap. And beyond to the gods knew where.

PART III

To the Scorpion's Nest

Nine after two the Sign of the Owl,
the old watcher, facing all ways,
Sailor in the perplexing night,
where countries burn and vanish, never were,
Seeing ahead of him, seeing behind him
where the possible ranges in firelight.

—*The Calantina* II:IX

CHAPTER 16

We learned what had occurred only after the di
Caela castle guard burst into the chambers of the Lady Enid
to find the very lovely and very unconscious Dannelle di
Caela, who on awakening told of the mysterious abduction.

The two of them, she and Enid, had been seated by the
Lady Enid's antique dresser, ridiculing the failed suit of
Gabriel Androctus, whom Enid had described as having "all
the glamor of an undertaker." It was then that a cloud—a
darkness of some sort—settled on the hearthstones and
blotted out the light of the fire.

"At first we thought there was damage in the fireplace,"
Dannelle explained weakly, propped up by maids and pil-
lows. "Something perhaps to do with the flue, I suggested,
since the flue is the only part of the fireplace I can name for

you. And Cousin Enid approached the hearth, drawing up her skirts and listening absolutely not at all to my warnings that she should stop there—that she would soon find herself in smoke and ash that would ruin her dress, not to mention her complexion. But you know Cousin Enid.

"She stepped toward the hearth and, all of a sudden, vanished entirely. I could hear her scuffling and shouting from somewhere within the darkness, and immediately I rushed to her aid . . . but found myself here, bound and gagged in this bed. I had no idea how much time had passed, but then I heard the scuffling and shouting just outside the window. It could not have been long.

"I struggled to break free of the ropes, to loosen the gag so I could shout for help. But for the life of me I could not move and . . . I don't want to talk about it any more."

Standing by the antique dresser, as far away as possible from where Dannelle lay, I listened to the distraught story. I felt ashamed at the point where Dannelle rushed to her cousin's aid, remembering how I had drawn back into the shrubbery when the shadow descended the wall.

As Dannelle told what had happened, Robert di Caela and Bayard sat attentive—and worried, obviously—in straight-backed chairs by the bedside. Brithelm stood at the notorious window with Sir Ramiro of the Maw and Sir Ledyard.

Alfric was somewhere slinking.

When the story was over, the men stared at one another—stared long and hard. Emotions rushed to Robert di Caela's face. Fears and angers raced over that noble countenance like scorpions over a white throne, or like a dark cloud over the moonlit wall of a keep. But the time for flocking emotions passed quickly. He was the first to speak.

"So my daughter has been taken Huma knows where. Then the problem that lies before us is a simple one· how do we recover her?"

Brithelm turned from the window. Bayard leaned back in his chair and folded his arms. Neither of them spoke at first, both a little nervous in the presence of the di Caela patriarch. I was no better, watching them from my position of safety behind the mantle.

"Would that it had not come to this," Sir Robert began, "especially in a time when we are so uncertain.

"Scarcely a month ago I received the news that Bayard Brightblade would attend this tournament. I received that news with joy, certain he was the prophecy's choice for my heir, and glad of it.

"And now the claims of that heir have been challenged by one whose claim to these holdings has . . . authority. One who wins the tournament, whose prize is my daughter Enid and all the di Caela holdings, and yet who turns out to bear a name that also figures in the fate of my family, though in ways more dark and terrible than I would wish or even imagine."

Bayard sat back, sighed, and waited for Sir Robert to finish.

"At least this poor girl has not been harmed," I interrupted weakly, gesturing at Dannelle.

She smiled, though wanly.

"Thank you, Galen Pathwarden," she breathed. "You're very . . . chivalrous. I shall not forget," the Lady Danelle went on disarmingly, "that you were the first to my side in my distress."

I'd surprised myself on that one, too.

"My pleasure," I muttered, and Sir Ramiro snickered by the window. I shot him a glance of white-hot hatred. Sensing my discomfort, Bayard spoke.

"Still, gentlemen, there is so much to piece together in this story. Perhaps we could convene elsewhere, where time and quiet are our allies and where we can think clearly about the situation in front of us, having left in the capable hands of maids and surgeons the welfare of those dear to us. Let us convene and reason together, gentlemen. We have tactics to ponder."

*   *   *   *   *

And ponder they did, in the main hall of the keep, where we had arrived after wandering down half a dozen corridors; across a huge stone bridge that spanned an indoor garden where Sir Robert kept exotic plants that smelled much too sweet for my liking; through familiar territory, where the di Caela statues and the sound of mechanical birds lay ahead of us; and eventually down the stairs to the main floor and the great hall itself.

It was here we debated where the Scorpion could have taken Enid. We stood there among the tables which had glittered with candlelight and polished armor only a few nights ago, and it seemed as though every place imaginable on the wide surface of Krynn was mentioned in the hour we talked. No suggestion was encouraging, and I found it hard to be attentive to what the Knights were saying.

Because all the while, something kept telling me that I should remember something about the raven in my quarters the night before . . .

Sir Ledyard suggested we might well find the Scorpion and his captive somewhere upon the Sirrion Sea to the southwest. Nobody paid any attention to him; everyone had known his answer would have something to do with the sea, and besides, the Sirrion was much too far away.

Sir Robert was all for looking in Estwilde because of the glain opals he had seen earlier that afternoon. After he made this pronouncement, he considered the matter settled.

Sir Ramiro thought that solution was too obvious, that someone as subtle as the Scorpion would not betray his hand so readily. He suggested we search first in the Garnet Mountains south of the castle, if for no other reason than it was cold and high and thin-aired—the most unpleasant place around and therefore, according to Sir Ramiro's reasoning, the ideal haunt for the Scorpion. The two old men began to bicker, and I wouldn't doubt they'd have come to blows had not Bayard stepped between them.

Bayard argued for the Vingaard Mountains. He felt he had seen the Scorpion's power at its strongest there, and wasn't there something about magic's being stronger the closer one got to its source?

None of the Knights were experts on the subject of magic. All eyes turned to Brithelm, who smiled inanely and shrugged.

"I don't know enough about the Scorpion's kind of magic, gentlemen," he explained apologetically. "After all, clouds and talking birds are beyond my powers."

"So what do we do?" Sir Ramiro asked impatiently. "Spread out and comb the whole continent? It would take years."

"And the Scorpion, as you call him, doesn't strike me as all that patient," Sir Ledyard agreed, his broad eastern accent ringing in the great hall.

Had things continued in that fashion, we might never have stumbled across the answer. The Knights would have blustered and pronounced until all hours, and I would have sat there trying to remember what it was I should remember—what the Scorpion had disclosed the night before, in the darkness before Brithelm had walked into the room.

But immediately after Sir Ledyard had spoken, we heard a tearing sound and a cry above us. The Knights turned, drawing their swords, and I, sure it was the Scorpion come back, was under the chair like a whippet in Father's great hall.

Alfric was dangling by a curtain from the balcony, cursing loudly and windmilling his stubby Pathwarden legs.

Evidently I had not been the only one to discover that particular hiding place and its advantages. Alfric, it turned out, had been up there while routes were suggested and questions were asked, and while leaning forward to hear just what was being said and how it might pertain to him, he stepped onto what he thought was a narrow extension of the balcony, a catwalk beyond its carved railing, but which was in fact nothing at all but thin air, a catwalk not even a cat could walk.

So there he was, suspended by a curtain he had managed to grasp when his fall began, beneath him several formidable Knights who were not overly concerned with his plight at the moment, and a brother who was whispering "drop him on his neck, please, Paladine!" Not an enviable place to be. As the curtain gave way and slowly lowered my brother to the floor of the hall, you could see him frantically scan the room for exits.

Sir Robert had Alfric by the arm and had thrown him into a table before my eldest brother's churning feet had touched the ground or Bayard could intervene.

"A fine array of guests I've entertained these last several days! One steals my daughter and another spies on me from my own balcony! I shall trust old Benedict before I offer hospitality again!"

Alfric cowered among the shattered plates, tangled in a fine linen tablecloth. Bayard stepped between Sir Robert and my cornered brother, who turned to me accusingly.

"Once again there is a council of the valiant, and everyone invited but old Alfric. You told them to leave me out, Weasel, so's I wouldn't have no chance to rescue Enid and win her hand in marriage."

"For Huma's sake, lad," Sir Robert began, "shelve your courtship for a while!"

It was just like Alfric to throw a fit of persecution and blame me for somehow organizing a conclave of Knights whose specific purpose on this planet was to exclude him from any adventure.

I thought back to his strange, almost psychotic version of what had gone on in the moat house as we were growing up—of the kind older brother he imagined himself, continually beleaguered by intolerable younger brothers.

It was incredible how someone could misread the past.

A banner in the hall swayed with a draft of wind. A single metallic cuckoo squawked above, from somewhere near the now-uncovered entrance to the balcony.

Misread the past.

I felt the memory of the dark, the brush of a wing. I smelled perfume and decay. For a moment the room around me blurred. Then it returned. The lights were even brighter, the colors more intense.

It had fallen into place, that memory.

"Bayard, quickly! What was that prophecy of yours?"

"This is no time for mysticism!" Sir Robert stormed. "By the horns of Kiri-Jolith, I shall hang myself before I let another Pathwarden clear the threshold of my house!" Sir Ramiro grabbed his old friend and wrestled him away from me.

"Please, Bayard! I'm sure it's important!"

Bayard spoke after a silence in which the big, torch-lit room seemed even more vast, even more desolate.

"As I have learned it from my young days of exploring the library at Palanthas, the prophecy went so:

> For generations down, the curse
> Arises in di Caela's hall
> And things descend from bad to worse,
> Until a girl succeeds to all.
> When things have reached their darkest pass
> The Bright Blade joins unto the bride,
> And generations from the grass
> Arise and lay the curse aside."

With that, he paused, having aired the future and found it confusing. We all faced each other, standing at the sides of one of Sir Robert's long and elegant tables. Somewhere in the depths of the keep a mechanical whir and a whistle burst forth, then silence.

A strange look of puzzlement took residence in the face of each Knight.

Then, of course, they looked at me, as if I were a disinterested observer, or someone capable of telling true prophecy from false.

"Honestly, sirs. It's in there somewhere. I'm sure."

"Listen again, Galen." Bayard insisted. "Maybe there's something I've missed all along, something so obvious it would take a child to notice."

Not a very flattering reason to ask my opinion, but I listened nonetheless, as the same tired old verses rushed over me, filled with their puzzles and wooden rhymes. I sat in Sir Robert's enormous ceremonial chair, dangled my feet over the edge, jostled the dice in the pouch of my tunic.

The Knights stood attentively after the recital, waiting for my judgment, my answer. I squirmed and huddled at the back of the chair.

"For Huma's sake, boy," Sir Robert began testily, "your protector is not in a bardic contest here! We're trying to recover my daughter, and we're looking for clues, not reveling in bad rhymes!"

"If you please, sir, I am just over a near-fatal fever," I began, but Bayard interrupted.

"Begging your pardon, Sir Robert, but I don't think the

boy is playing literary games."

He turned to me and continued, kindly but urgently.

"Go on, Galen."

"It's what the Scorpion said. Or didn't say. I don't think he ever said that the prophecy was wrong, just that you were wrong about it, Bayard. Indeed, now that I think on it, I believe . . . no, I am absolutely certain, he said that there was more than one way to read it!

"So the question becomes not how *you've* been reading it all these years, Bayard, but how *the Scorpion's* been reading it."

I had always wondered if anything Gileandos had taught me would come in handy. Taking a deep breath and rising from the chair, I launched myself onto the dreadful paths of conjecture, pacing back and forth in front of the assembled Knights.

"Look, it all comes from something he said to me about his 'own bright blade.' Apparently, he thinks that if Bayard isn't the bright blade of the prophecy, then it's a real blade indeed."

I turned again to Sir Robert.

"As I told you, sir, he said that before he threatened to kill your daughter."

"So?"

"So he's trying to lift a curse, too. Look, he certainly doesn't like returning from the dead to gnaw at your family tree once every generation. I don't think he has much of a choice."

"I don't follow," said Sir Robert, walking toward his chair and sitting down. "We don't invite him back. He is, after all, *our* curse."

"And *you* are *his!*" Brithelm exclaimed, and I could see from his expression that he was catching on to what I was after. "After all, the two Gabriels deep in the di Caela past didn't play fairly with old Benedict. One disinherited him, the other—regardless of what the di Caelas say about slaying him in battle and all—defeated him at the Throtyl Gap, then pursued him east to the pass at Chaktamir and killed him."

Sir Robert nodded.

"Very well. The Pathwardens are right about the family . . . mishap four centuries back. It's embarrassing—indeed, almost dishonorable—what Gabriel the Elder and Gabriel the Younger did, but I don't see why we need to haul that skeleton from the family closet."

"Because the skeleton has hauled itself out and is visiting the family once every generation, Robert!" Sir Ramiro replied with a low chuckle.

"Very well! Very well! What does it have to do with the prophecy, damn it!" Sir Robert snapped.

"The di Caelas are Benedict's curse just as much as he is theirs," Brithelm responded. "And he thinks that what he's doing will free him and destroy the family who has wounded him."

Sir Robert leaned back in the chair and fell silent. Again a cuckoo whirred somewhere on the ground floor of the castle. Outside, thunder rolled, and I could feel a closeness, a prospect of rain, gather in the air.

"Could the Scorpion be right?" Sir Robert asked evenly, locking his hands behind his head and staring up at the balcony. "Are we, not the Scorpion, the curse?"

"We'll have to go to Chaktamir to find out, sir," I replied.

"Chaktamir?"

"Remember what the prophecy says?" I asked. "'When things have reached their darkest pass'?"

Sir Robert nodded distantly, his mind still on the prospect of prophecy turned around, of the foretold end of the di Caelas. Wearily he shook himself from his musings, rose to his full patrician height, and paced across the room.

"I can't imagine things any darker than this," he declared.

"But maybe it doesn't just mean 'things have reached their worst state,' Sir Robert. Maybe whoever wrote the prophecy had in mind a real pass through real mountains."

Sir Robert paused and took that in. Distant thunder rumbled once again.

"Perhaps. But how do you know it's Chaktamir, Galen? Why not somewhere in the Garnet Mountains, or the Throtyl Gap?"

"I don't know, sir. At least not for sure. But it adds up, doesn't it? The pass at Chaktamir is dark to begin with because folks seldom use it any more, after Enric's battle with the men of Neraka. It's dark with Solamnic and Nerakan blood.

"Dark with Benedict's blood, for that matter. After all, Gabriel the Younger caught up with him in the pass at Chaktamir.

"Finally, it's dark because your history has made it dark. If the story is spread that Benedict died in the Throtyl Gap, then it's easy to believe he died in battle, rather than in some shabby and questionable di Caela hunt.

"I'd say the darkest pass by any reading is Chaktamir, Sir Robert. And I believe that's where you'll find the Scorpion. And find your daughter."

I looked about me. Brithelm was smiling, seated in a hard, high-backed chair, feet propped up on a table. Sir Ledyard and Sir Ramiro stood at either side of Sir Robert di Caela. Both these strange new Knights were nodding— agreeing with me. Bayard stared at me, his face impassive.

Alfric toyed with a tablecloth folded on a nearby chair, his mind scarcely on anything.

Sir Robert folded his arms and looked at me curiously.

"What about the 'generations from the grass,' Galen?" he asked.

"I don't have any idea, sir. Clever will only get you so far in a prophecy, I imagine.

"Most of all, I don't know whom the prophecy's for— Bayard or you or the Scorpion—but it's at Chaktamir where the whole thing is resolved, for good or ill or both.

"Of that, I'm certain. I guess."

Bayard smiled faintly and steepled his fingers. I remembered the pose—one I had seen back at the moat house on a morning that seemed like years ago.

Then his smile broadened. He stood, hand on the hilt of his sword.

"Then it's to Chaktamir."

* * * * *

"So comes to pass the most harebrained decision I have ever made," Sir Robert di Caela concluded, sitting even more heavily in the same chair into which he had fallen an hour ago. The candles burned low, and the shadows rose in the hall of the banquet room until even the backs of chairs stretched long and ominous shadows over the floors.

"My most harebrained decision," he repeated.

"We are to set off in a direction suggested by a seventeen-year-old boy of questionable honesty, who admits to trying his own fortune with the red dice of Estwilde, never quite understanding their meanings.

"We follow the shadow that this boy saw, knowing only that it went eastward—not how far it has traveled or even if it changed directions when it was out of sight. We go on the evidence of a prophecy we no longer know we are reading correctly."

He turned to me and addressed me frankly.

"You do not have the best reputation for accuracy, boy."

Bayard sighed and looked despairingly into the flickering candles.

"Nonetheless, Sir Robert," Bayard claimed hoarsely, "your daughter is missing, and Galen's is the best guess as to her whereabouts."

The old man nodded firmly.

Finally, Sir Robert turned from me, though something told me that he would like very much to dismiss me—to send me back to Coastlund in a wagon or a sack. I withdrew the Calantina dice from my tunic and held them palm up.

Nine and . . .

The light was bad, and Sir Robert began speaking again. I looked up and lost the reading.

Nine and something. Something large.

Sign of the Weasel? Sign of the Rat?

Or of something entirely unexpected?

"If I am to find my daughter, it seems that this . . . oracular boy is forced upon me."

He looked at all of us standing in front of him, shook his head in wonderment, then reddened and stood up wearily. His shadow darkened the entire south end of the hall, where the candles had guttered and burned out. He raised his sword in the ancient Solamnic salute, and his voice resonated in the high rafters of the great hall.

"Gather the Knights remaining at Castle di Caela. Gather

those encamped in the fields surrounding, and call back those within the sound of the clarion trumpet. This very night we are off to Chaktamir. And woe betide the Scorpion when we find him there!"

* * * * *

While the gentlemen rummaged through armor, I made my final preparations for leaving Castle di Caela. Prospects of escape now seemed impossible.

Nor did I want to escape, especially.

Alone in my chambers for a "time of contemplation" before we set out, I tried to recover the reading of the Calantina—the one I had cast in the shadowy hall scarcely an hour ago. Down on my knees like an unlucky gambler, I rolled them again and again in hopes of seeing the same sign, but as is the way with history and with dice, the reading was gone forever. I cast in vain, receiving the Adder, the Centaur, the Hawk, the Mongoose, the Wyvern—not a nine among them. With each roll, the dice became more confusing.

As is the way with prophecy.

So I gathered my things together, taking care to put on my best tunic and the tooled gloves I had kept hidden so often throughout our journey from Coastlund.

Enjoying my renewed appearance, my red hair watered and slicked and combed into place with my fingers, I waited for the water in the basin to settle, then looked at my reflection.

Perfect. You never could tell who would be watching.

Prepared, adorned, and even a little resplendent if you counted the gloves, I scurried from my quarters down to the courtyard of Castle di Caela, where perhaps a dozen more squires were saddling horses, gathering provisions, and putting all in readiness for the journey east.

Together we busied ourselves with the final preparations, saddling and bridling Valorous, Sir Robert's black mare Estrella, and more everyday horses for the other Knights and for my brothers. Three mules were brought from the surrounding farmlands, and that very night they were loaded with provisions and clothing and arms. Burdened and rained upon, they looked the sullenmost of all the beasts I had seen on this twisting, weather-plagued journey.

The pack mare also went with us, although reluctantly, straightening her legs and leaning backwards against the reins, snapping at a large stable boy until he turned and, to my great satisfaction, caught her a blow across the jaw that wobbled her knees and silenced her until she could be rigged and saddled and boarded.

For, yes, my place was on her back again. Bayard believed that she would keep me mounted despite terrain and weather and my own incompetence.

If the poor pack mare's load was made heavier by the addition of me to the freight on her back, then I wonder if it felt any lighter as we passed through the gates of Castle di Caela. For I felt a little lighter myself at that moment, when I turned to look back at the keep through the half light of morning and the rain that was now quite heavy.

I could swear that I saw, through the shifting grayness, a light at Lady Enid's window.

I could swear that I saw Dannelle di Caela standing there, graceful and pale and framed by the light of the window. And graceful and pale, she lifted her graceful, pale arm, and waved at me departing.

My ears were hot. Instinctively, my hand went to my hair.

Which was wet and plastered to my head like the pelt of some repulsive drowned animal. I raised my hood, pretended not to notice her, and faced eastward.

At the last moment before the gates closed I looked back over my shoulder as heroically, as romantically as I could manage from atop a beast of burden. But with the angle of the road and the morning shadows and the rising rain, the window was a blur of light rapidly fading, and Dannelle was obscured entirely.

CHAPTER 17

The road south from the castle was washed with rain already. The downpour had stripped whatever browned or reddened leaves had remained clinging to the trees, and now the countryside was bare and gray and gloomy, at last making good on the winter the skies had promised for a while.

There were twenty of us, only six of us Knights. Sir Robert could have brought his palace guards, but the practical man within him recoiled at leaving Castle di Caela undefended. He could have brought part of his escort, but the Solamnic Knight in him recoiled at "sending an army to do a Knight's work," as he put it. So they were left behind.

Though it seemed to me that this was the time for armies, for catapults and ballistae and engines of war—anything to take the Scorpion's attention from yours truly—the task ahead of us began with twenty of us, and twenty of us only.

Bayard rode in the lead atop Valorous. Sir Robert brought up the rear on Estrella—I believe he was back there to round up any Pathwardens trying to escape. I rode in the middle, sandwiched between brothers and soaked in the dismal morning showers.

Alfric's gloom was contagious. He sat atop his horse, wrapped in a bulky blue robe, the hood pulled so far over his face that he looked like a huge, animate bag of wet laundry. Even his horse, no monument to spirit to begin with, bowed its head sullenly against the cold morning rain.

He felt swindled, he had claimed back at the gates of Castle di Caela.

"For why," he asked, "is everyone so sure that Enid is going to marry Bayard if we rescue her? Seems to me that it's been decided a little too soon."

He fell into a sulking silence.

But if Alfric's gloom was contagious, Brithelm was thoroughly immune, his musings somewhere far from this road, this part of the country, as he sat benignly and unhooded to the worst the rain had to offer. Lost in thought, he was lost to the rest of us. His horse was his sole guide, as it followed my pack mare unquestioningly.

We rode without rest until mid-morning. It was some Solamnic notion, I suppose, that you traveled farther and more efficiently when you were so miserably uncomfortable that the prospect of ambush or a monster in the roadway would seem like a welcome break from the routine.

To make things worse, neither of my brothers was speaking— to me, to each other, to anyone, as far as I could figure. Brithelm remained lost in thought behind me, his eyes on the rain and on the eastern horizon, and Alfric was ahead of me, suspicious and sulking, no doubt trying to guess what goods I had on him and what I had told the Knights.

So I drifted in and out of slumber that morning, jogged awake by a sudden rise in the road or a dip when the pack mare slipped or sank a bit into the mud. On occasion a distant roll of autumn thunder would disturb my sleep, or the rain would drip inside my cloak and across my face, sprinkling and startling me.

One time I was jostled awake by Bayard, who had slowed Valorous and let most of the party pass him. Reining his horse in abreast of mine, he offered me a large, coarse cotton handkerchief.

"Whatever these vapors were that saddled you back at the castle, you haven't shed them yet. I can hear your sniffling all the way up the column."

"Who'd have thought it, Sir Bayard?"

"I beg your pardon?"

"All along you've made fun of these dice I carry with me. And now all of us are armed and appointed and drenched by the rain, following a prophecy that's every bit as many-sided and cloudy as any of the Calantina readings. What's the difference?"

"You explained the prophecy quite well for a skeptic."

"But you haven't answered my question. What is the difference?"

Bayard smiled and flicked Valorous across the withers with the wet leather reins. The big horse snorted and lurched toward the head of the column, and Bayard called back to me.

"Maybe no difference."

* * * * *

By mid-morning of the next day, we reached the swollen eastern fork of the Vingaard River.

There was no longer time for musing, for pondering mysteries. As I looked ahead of me into the gray rush of waters, I could see that the Vingaard had overflowed its banks. Fording would be dangerous, perhaps even deadly.

"Flood time nearly, boys," Sir Ramiro shouted, championing the obvious above the sound of the rain and the river. "Autumn is the flood season here anyway, and we have come at the wrong time . . ."

He looked up at Bayard sullenly, thick brows cascading water.

". . . Perhaps even to the wrong place?"

Things about us grew even more ominous, even more

gloomy as the rain fell and the river rose and the overcast day permitted no sun. Here at the banks of the Vingaard, it seemed as though everything was fixed against us: the clever enemy, the night's head start, the terrible weather. Even the land itself had betrayed us.

I sat atop the pack mare. Things could be worse. We could be out there in mid-current.

"Across the ford, then, young fellow?" an elegant voice boomed in my ear, and I started at the presence of Sir Robert di Caela beside me. There was the sound of more horses approaching, and soon Sir Ledyard and Brithelm had joined us.

"Well, Galen?" Sir Robert insisted, wrapping his cloak more tightly against the mounting rain.

"Galen?" Bayard chorused, leaning forward and stroking Valorous's mane as the big horse shouldered its way between Ledyard's big mare, Balena, and Sir Robert's smaller, more graceful Estrella.

"I don't know," I murmured into my hood. I crouched, curled up, and tried to look like a piece of baggage on the pack mare's back.

"Speak up, boy! These are old ears and clamorous raindrops!"

"It's just . . . just that I don't think this mare of mine is going to breast that current out there. You didn't see her in the swamp and on the mountain paths, Sir Robert. She's far more . . . anxious and roundabout than she seems on level ground and a wide road."

"We're all a little more jumpy at an impasse," declared Sir Ramiro, who had approached astride his big, forgiving percheron. Water cascaded off his gray wool robe like springs coursing down from a mountain lake.

"Get to what we need to do," he said, smiling wickedly. "And leave me . . . to encourage the mare."

Bayard pointed toward a stretch on the river bank, almost submerged in the rising water. Sir Robert nodded, and galloped over to inform the rest of our companions.

I could have mulled over this crossing for hours, stacked thought upon thought until I had confused myself completely and entirely, as Gileandos said I was inclined to do.

But there was no time for thinking. Immediately my companions began tying together the pack mare and the mules. The Knights hitched their cloaks tightly about their legs so as not to tangle in the rushing water.

And Sir Ramiro slapped the rump of the pack mare sharply with his enormous hand. She started and leaped toward the water.

We were fording the Vingaard.

The water was icy cold about my ankles. I drew my feet from the stirrups of the saddle, thought twice about it, and braved the water for the purchase on the back of my steed.

The mare grunted, then breasted the current. To the right of all of us squires, Brithelm's horse began to navigate the waters, and to the right of him was Sir Robert on Estrella. Beyond them was Alfric, then two other Knights, then Ledyard and Ramiro, and then Bayard, of course, active and secure atop Valorous.

Alfric, who had been challenging Bayard's authority at every turn of the road, was more than willing to let my protector take the rightmost path.

The boy to the immediate right of me, a blond-haired gap-toothed monstrosity from Caergoth, grinned hatefully at me.

"Got that mare in line?" he taunted nasally. "Or is it the rider that's got to be pushed through the water?"

"Those teeth will look good tangled in seaweed," I replied, and slapped the pack mare on the rump again. We slid farther out into the current, then sagged in the water a moment as the riverbed gave way beneath the mare and she began to swim.

I pressed my knees against her sides, I held to her mane so tightly that she snorted and shook her head at first; then I loosened my grip, but not too much, thinking of the current that could carry a drowned body almost all the way to Thelgaard Keep.

In midstream the waters were indeed tricky, plunging into an undertow deep and powerful along the spine of the river. When we reached that point in the crossing, we were pulled more insistently, more heavily.

One of the mules brayed behind us, and through the rain I

saw a bundle slip from its back into the driving current. The gap-toothed boy reached for it in vain.

"I'm losing hold!" he cried, and toppled into the water.

"Brithelm!" I screamed frantically as the boy slipped downstream behind my brother.

It sounded thin and shrill and cowardly above the roar of the river. I was almost embarrassed to have cried out, for certainly someone would haul the oaf from the water. But then a swell in the current rushed over us, knocking me from the back of the mare.

I was dangling from the saddle by my right ankle, which had lodged in the stirrup and had twisted in all directions. But the ankle held, and the stirrup held, and my head was above the surface, gasping and coughing out the water that rushed by me and into me.

I windmilled my arms frantically, recalling the times I had seen people swim and hoping that going through the actions would somehow give me control over the current that was dragging me southward to death. Several times I went under, and thinking too fast, I recalled the legends about going under for the third time.

How many times had it been? Six?

Another swell of water rolled over me.

Seven?

Through the glaze of river water and sunlight I saw a hand over me, large and extended somewhere up in the air I was longing to get to. My head surfaced for a moment, long enough to hear Ledyard cry out, "Here, boy!"

Then came the dark and marbled green of the water, and the sense of coming unmoored, of being carried by the current.

*   *   *   *   *

It was not too bad, really, this floating. It was for a moment like emerging from a deep and immensely satisfying dream, or returning there. I could not figure which, and soon I ceased to bother with figuring altogether.

Was this what the fish saw, looking up?

The light, green and then gold where the sunlight broke upon it?

Was this the last vision of the drowned, before the weeds entangled them and made them cold?

I did not care, relaxing, enjoying the movement and light, preparing to forget all of them: Enid and Dannelle, my brothers and Sir Robert and . . .

Bayard.

Who pulled me by the hair from the current, up into the cold and into the painfully bright light where it hurt so much to breathe that I felt dizzy and sick.

He draped me over the saddle, pounding on my back as he did so, and I coughed water for what must have been an hour.

Above the water, in the dry land of harsh air and duty and of thinking too much, I forgot the current and the dangerous dreams of the river. Bayard set me gently on the southern bank of the Vingaard: I wondered about Sir Robert, the Ladies di Caela, my brothers, remembered Bayard who had drawn me from the water and from certain drowning.

Remembered the rest of our party.

Who had been halved by the river.

* * * * *

There is, in the easternmost fork of the Vingaard River, a sudden surge in the midstream current even more powerful than the steady undertow which is the constant bane of the rivermen and of those who foolishly try to cross.

"The Vingaard Drift," the rivermen call it, and when they can, they defend against it by poling the boats across as you would a barge, by dropping anchor when the Drift is at its worst.

There is no prophecy that accounts for it, no way to predict its rise and its fall. Indeed, few know of it beyond those who make the river their living.

It so happened that the Drift had chosen to rise at the moment we crossed, sweeping many of us from our saddles into the merciless current. In the moment after Bayard caught me up from the tide that rushed around him, the huge, struggling form of Sir Ledyard followed in my wake.

"When I reached for him," Bayard concluded, his voice

shaking from loss of breath, from struggle and something more deep and disturbing and sorrowful, "he drew his arm away. Drew his arm away, Galen, shouting that we should save ourselves, that he would right himself downstream."

From somewhere around Bayard I heard the sound of weeping. Brithelm, no doubt, though I could not see through the water and the memories of the water now covering my face.

"Sir Robert? Sir Ramiro?" I asked.

"They have gone to follow the path of the river, hoping for a sand bar, a downed tree, anything to which our friends might cling.

"We have no hope, Galen. By now they are deep into the plains of Solamnia. In the country of the brave and the innocent. May Sir Ledyard find the seas at last."

"Receive them all to Huma's breast," rose a familiar voice behind Bayard. Alfric stood beside my protector.

"This blanket stayed dry, Weasel," he muttered, tossing a rough wool coverlet over me.

I do not mind saying that I wept a little while after Sir Robert came heavily back from downstream and from a luckless search. The Drift had swelled, had knocked a full dozen of us, mounts and armor and weapons and all, tumbling into its dark and rushing midst. It was a tangle of limbs and blankets and outcry, Sir Ramiro told me, when he returned from the search covered with mud and river weed. Squires and Knights had tumbled southward until they were lost from sight in the strong tow of the river.

Bayard was right. We had no hope of finding them.

I wept for Ledyard, whom I would never really know, for the dozen or so drowned with him, and for the gap-toothed blond squire upon whom I had wished outrage too easily and too unluckily.

I began to wonder if this, too, was the Scorpion's doing, if his hand was at the reins of the river, guiding the rise of the Drift at the worst possible of times.

The way ahead of us was cloudy, what awaited us at Chaktamir, dark and obscure.

Sir Robert sat wearily beside me, armor tolling metal on metal, the hour of sadness.

"It's terribly early, I know," he began. "All of us mourn, all of us are still . . . taken aback at the events of this morning.

"But another life depends on our quickness, our determination, our knowledge of the roads. Remember that Enid may be somewhere ahead of us. We must take up pursuit before something terrible happens to her in the eastlands.

"So take courage. Where do we go from here?"

His eyes were intent upon the east, the rushing sound of the river behind us and ahead of us the plains of eastern Solamnia as they rose and roughened into the tough little country of Throt—a thicket of roads and not-roads, paths and waterways, any of which the Scorpion might have taken with his priceless spoils.

We chose one path among all of these—straight to the pass of Chaktamir. Bayard rose in the saddle, shielded his eyes, and made out a copse of vallenwood on the eastern horizon that seemed to be a landmark of sorts.

Heavily and wearily we traveled east.

With the copse directly ahead of us, Bayard turned in the saddle and called back to the rest of the party.

"We go southwest from here, crossing two roads and a wheat field. Then we come to another road, which we take due east, keeping the Throtyl road to our left, the mountains to our right."

"And soon we will reach Chaktamir?" Sir Robert called back.

It seemed that Sir Robert knew little of the lands east of his holdings. Bayard rode back to us frowning, shaking his head.

He explained, politely but briskly, leaning across Valorous's neck.

"I'm afraid that the pass is still five days' hard ride from here, Sir Robert. On the day after tomorrow we should pass through the Throtyl Gap into Estwilde, then two days more until the road forks, the southerly branch leading to Godshome and Neraka beyond, the easterly toward the pass itself.

"Eventually we will reach the foothills of the Khalkist Mountains, and following this same road, we will climb steadily, almost a day's journey, until we come to Chaktamir, seated high in the land that once belonged to the men of Neraka and now is no creature's.

"It is there, Sir Robert, that the Scorpion will wait for us. And there your daughter will rest—unharmed, I pray—awaiting us also."

Their heads moved closer together, and the two men exchanged words in private.

Alfric leaned far over his saddle to try and catch what was being said. He heard nothing, evidently, and tried to right himself in the saddle.

But midway back to the upright position the weight of his armor took over, and he dropped from the saddle, face first onto the rocky ground. Brithelm helped my red-faced brother to his feet, while Alfric fired questions at Bayard.

"How do you know this?"

"I've been to Chaktamir before. Ten years ago . . ."

"So he has been to Chaktamir before!" Alfric exclaimed triumphantly. "You heard him say that, Sir Robert! Now I ask you: why in the name of Paladine should we let ourselves be guided by somebody who is suspiciously familiar with the places that the Scorpion goes to?"

Ramiro leaned his ampleness back on his long-suffering horse and laughed.

"Young Pathwarden, I've been to Chaktamir twice myself. Perhaps there's a conspiracy afoot you haven't noticed!"

"What's your problem, Alfric?" Bayard asked calmly, idly stroking Valorous's mane, clearing it of mud and stray brambles.

"Ever since we left the castle," Alfric whined, "it's been 'Bayard, do this,' and 'Bayard, lead us here'! When we get to Enid, of course she's going to want to marry you, on account of you're the only one Sir Robert lets do anything!"

"Is that what is bothering you, Alfric?" Bayard asked slowly, dangerously, and I huddled deeply into the wool blanket I had been given, for I could tell by the flatness in his gray eyes that Alfric had just passed into the eye of a great and powerful storm.

"That is what bothers you, when we have lost fourteen to

the current behind us?

"There will be plenty for you to do, Alfric," Bayard declared coldly. "And sooner than you'd like, I'd wager.

"For our enemy is already watching."

Bayard pointed to a spot not far ahead of us, where a bare-branched, dying vallenwood drooped heavily on the gray and rain-soaked plains.

In its topmost branches a raven perched.

*　*　*　*　*

Two days later, we passed through the Throtyl Gap. It is a country as rocky and forbidding as eastern Coastlund—plains, to be sure, but plains steeply rolling, rising gradually out of the fertile river lands to the west until the country around the traveler is parched and cracked, like the face of a moon through astronomer's glasses, or like a landscape ravaged by fire.

Through this desolate region of dark, volcanic rock we were led by Bayard, at a slower pace than before because of the terrain and also because the accident at the river had left many of our horses and mules bruised and skittish. They balked, bit, kicked, and brayed through the lengthened hours of the journey.

They were not alone in their weariness, their discontent. Each of us had suffered a pounding fording the Vingaard.

Bayard and I led the way, Bayard following a worn path through the glittering rocks, occasionally calling back something to Sir Robert, who followed us. Ramiro and Alfric followed Sir Robert. Alfric crouched uncomfortably in the saddle as though he expected a hail of arrows at any time, and Sir Ramiro grew less and less amused with my brother's cowardice and bluster as the miles wore on. Brithelm brought up the rear, and several times, to Sir Robert's great impatience, we had to stop and send Ramiro back for him. Once the big Knight found Brithelm bird-watching, once lifting a rock to inspect more closely the hardy insect life of Throtyl Gap.

A third time Ramiro found Brithelm dazed and sitting in the middle of the trail, felled by a low-hanging branch he had not noticed while riding along rapt in meditation.

Bayard occasionally lent a hand at guiding the pack mare, but more often he was examining the rocks for the trail, mounting and dismounting as our path was lost and recovered in the hard, volcanic terrain.

Ahead of us and above us, the only birds were predators and scavengers, the only trees were pine, spruce, and a ragged strain of vallenwood which could not sink its roots deep in the rocky soil and, as a result, grew stunted and bent in the dreary landscape.

"The country of hawks," Bayard muttered once, skillfully reining Valorous around me in order to herd the pack mare back onto the road. "The hardiest animals venture up here, and kill one another simply because there's nothing else to prey on."

"Sounds like growing up in the Pathwarden moat house," I ventured, and he laughed harshly, drawing beside me as the road widened and a cold wind struck our faces from out of the south.

"Or on the streets of Palanthas," he countered, smiling. Then he grew serious.

"Something's come over you, Galen, and in ways I could not have foreseen back in the moat house when you first pleaded your case in front of me. You're . . ."

"Less of a vermin?"

Bayard flushed.

"I'd have said 'more cooperative,'" he ventured, eyes on the road ahead of him. "Were it not for your size, and . . ."

He looked at me, smiled, and turned away.

". . . and for the absolute refusal to cooperate of that moustache you're trying to grow, I'd take you for the oldest Pathwarden among us.

"What I'm trying to say, Galen, is that there's Knighthood peeking out through your seams."

I had no time to bask in the compliment. For the road was rockier, and steeply ascending, and ahead of us the hawks were turning.

*　*　*　*　*

By noon of the next day, it was more than hawks ahead of us. On occasion the eastern horizon shimmered with that brilliant, metallic mist that is the hand of mirage, that makes you think you are looking through water at the country ahead of you.

The mirage itself was inhabited. Strange things walked upright through the blurred landscape. Nor could we make out their form all that clearly—it was, after all, a mirage into which we looked. But dark red and brown they were, and hairless, and ever running from one fading, dissolving rock to the next one.

Sometimes the mirage would vanish, only to appear again several winding miles east of where we last saw it. Each time it was peopled by dark, scurrying forms.

The horses grew skittish at something in the air.

"W-what are they, Bayard?" I asked uneasily.

"I am not sure. I do know we have crossed into Estwilde, and if the Scorpion knows we are coming, they may be his scouts. Or his first wave of illusions."

Sir Robert reached into his robe, drew something out, and cast it by the roadside. Sir Ramiro followed suit, and when he did I heard the faint tinkle of breaking glass.

"What's going on, Bayard?" I asked, but my protector had not been watching. His horse had moved slightly ahead of mine, and he rode with his eyes fixed to the road ahead of us.

"Beg your pardon?"

"Sir Robert and Sir Ramiro each reached into his robe, drew something out, and threw it away. I haven't the least idea what Robert discarded, but Ramiro's was glass, I am sure."

Bayard chuckled softly, murmured, "The old school."

"I don't understand."

"An old Solamnic custom. When a Knight rides into battle, there is always the possibility he'll be killed."

"Of course."

"If something were to happen to you, chances are there's something on your person—something small, perhaps, but there nonetheless—that you'd rather your people not find when your body returns to them."

"I see. And then what I saw . . ."

"Was our two older Knights discarding their vexations. I

have no idea what Sir Robert cast aside, but Sir Ramiro's was dwarf spirits.

"It always is."

Deftly, quickly, Bayard's hand flashed out from under his robe. Something small and glittering sailed through the air and into the rocks above the trail. I heard a metallic ring as something fell from rock to rock and finally settled and became still.

To this day I do not know what it was.

* * * * *

As we rode farther, the purple of the Khalkist Mountains rose gradually, mistily out of the eastern margins. Somewhere within those mountains lay Chaktamir, lay the pass, and when I first made them out on the horizon I thought again on the custom, of the prospect of my returning on a shield.

Yes, I had thought of it before, but always as some grand, dramatic scene out of the romances, in which everyone tore hair and wailed and apologized to my lifeless form for the injuries done me. My final return would be high theater, suitable punishment to Father for the lack of attention I received or perceived from my days in the moat house.

Now I thought of what I should discard—what it would be best if he never saw. It was between the gloves and the Calantina dice: the gloves ill-gotten, the dice smacking of eastern superstition, incantation, incense, and the sacrifice of birds.

It was a close call. For a moment I thought of discarding both, but I figured that would be excessive. Especially since I had absolutely no intention of returning to Coastlund, alive or dead.

I wondered what Enric Stormhold had cast away.

My aim had improved since the nightmarish time in the Vingaard Mountains. The dice skittered between the rocks, tumbling to rest somewhere in the high weeds that lined the path we followed.

It's anyone's guess what that final cast read.

CHAPTER 18

As we approacheð the Khalkist Mountains the grim signs of the Scorpion were everywhere. The rising ground was burned ahead of us—deliberately, not as if by wildfire or something natural and blind. Wide swaths of blackened earth lay in front of us, then land relatively untouched where the only sign of violation was the occasional dark, unrecognizable symbol freshly burned into the rocks rising from the borders of our trail.

It began to snow as we ascended the western inclines of the Khalkists. But even the snow would not settle on the scars of the foothill fires, as though the spots were still warm. As we reached the mountains proper, the mists descended and the snow receded behind us.

It was there that we saw the first of the pikes. They leaned on the eastern horizon like dark standards or banners, but something in the way they drooped—like thin branches laden with heavy fruit—caused us to rein in our horses, to come to a stop on the narrow road.

Bayard squinted eastward, shielding his eyes with a gloved hand. He turned to me, his face pale.

"I cannot see what they are," he said, "but I have my suspicions."

Before I could ask, he started toward the dark, slanting needles ahead of us. The severed heads on the ends of the pikes had been dead some time. It was the horses who knew them first, snorting and rearing. The mules sat on the trail and refused to budge; only a strong Sir Ramiro and a firm riding crop got them going again.

I can't say that I blamed them. The dried and withered faces had sunken in upon the skulls. From the designs of the helmets—the kingfishers, the roses—I could tell that they once sat atop Solamnic shoulders.

"An old Nerakan strategy," Ramiro explained, guiding his skittish animal around the first of the pikes. "A sign to your enemies to come no farther."

"Have they been set here long?" Alfric asked apprehensively.

Ramiro did not answer as we filed along the path, winding between the grim warnings. But when his hand moved to the hilt of his sword, it was sign enough.

Perhaps the mist around us was thicker than we had thought. Perhaps knowing we had crossed into the mouth of the old Chaktamir Pass, scene of bloody history both noble and best forgotten, had set our thoughts to wandering. But none of these reasons could explain the castle and its sudden appearance.

It was as though the mist solidified, that at one moment the fog began to take on the substance of stone.

Startled, Alfric brought his horse to a sudden stop, sliding in the frost and gravel. My mare and Brithelm's mule piled into the horse from behind, and Bayard had to move Valorous deftly aside to avoid the tangle of horse, mare, mule, and Pathwarden, all limbs and eyes, looking up to the heights of the castle.

"This looks familiar," Alfric ventured.

"Perhaps that's because it's drawn to the plans of Castle di Caela, boy," Sir Robert snapped.

So it was.

It stood, a big gray castle, a huge tower at each corner of its large, rectangular courtyard. As the last reddening light of the sun struck the flag on the tall southwest tower, our eyes were drawn by the play of red and black in the castle standard.

Sable scorpion statant on a field gules.

A black scorpion on a red flag. Simple and bloody and daunting.

"The Scorpion's Nest," Sir Robert breathed. "We're nearing the end of this."

Sir Ramiro and Sir Robert reined in their horses beside us.

"It is. As I live and breathe, it is. Castle di Caela, stone for stone!" Robert exclaimed.

"'Somehow those illusions have delivered him a castle,'" Bayard breathed, quoting something I should have remembered but could not. "How predictable of old Benedict, if Benedict it is, to model his castle, down to the very crenelations and to the mortar itself, upon the one castle he knows intimately, has known for over four hundred years."

"It is an outrage," Sir Robert stated.

"It is also not real, and therefore nothing to trouble yourself over, Robert," soothed old Ramiro.

"And easy to find our way around," Brithelm insisted. Everyone turned and looked at him.

He stood calmly amid the rocks, looking up at the castle as if he were a general taking stock of his siegecraft. He took his eyes from the castle and rested them on Sir Robert.

"Benedict's had his eye on Castle di Caela for centuries. He knows it intimately. It's no challenge for him to slip undetected through the halls of the keep, but we know Castle di Caela, too, and if the Scorpion's copy resembles it more than outwardly, that resemblance is to our advantage. That is, when we're inside."

Thinking of the swamp and its illusions, I hurled a rock toward the walls ahead of me and heard it clatter against the stonework.

Solid, this time.

"You mean we're going in?" Alfric whimpered, glancing behind him down the trail.

"Hush, Alfric," snapped Sir Ramiro. "We're at his damned gates, after all."

A flutter of wings and the soft gurgling sound of pigeons descended from the wall off to our left. Over there, somewhere near the main gate of the castle, the huge birds, purple and glistening with a dirty metallic shine, were coming to light on the battlements.

There was movement, then a dim outcry from somewhere within the walls.

Bayard drew his sword, and the other two Knights did likewise. Alfric ducked behind his horse and drew his menacing long knife.

Bayard turned to me.

"You, too," he admonished softly. "It's about to begin."

I drew my sword.

* * * * *

Begin it did, in a new and unexpected form.

I had been prepared for satyrs, for some other half-human, half-beast arrangement such as the Scorpion seemed fond of throwing against his enemies—minotaurs, perhaps, or even the lizard men of whom legends had arisen lately.

But not prepared for centaurs.

We had dismounted because of the steep climb, and we were leading our horses toward the castle gate. Then it opened, and two of the creatures issued forth, lumbering unsteadily, almost drunkenly toward us over the rocks and the incline. I wondered for a moment about the truth of the old proverbs about centaurs and wine.

Then the smell that reached me stopped my wondering entirely. It was a smell of neither wine nor spirits, but of mold and dried vegetation and decay. The smell of a swamp—but the smell of a deeper decay beneath all that moss and mud and vallenwood and cedar—the smell when dead flesh, left exposed to the air and the moisture and the unseasonably warm autumn days, begins to rot.

"Walking dead!" Sir Robert exclaimed. "Spit into the sunlight by Chemosh!" He stepped toward them warily, followed by Bayard, then Ramiro.

I waved my knife as menacingly as I could, though I had no idea what earthly good a piece of cutlery would do against creatures of such size.

A whistling sound arose from their throats, as though they mocked the act of breathing or had forgotten how to breathe.

They were now close enough that I could see the wounds. *Who saw them fall, Kallites and Elemon.* I remembered Agion's story.

Riddled with arrows as though they had walked through a gathering of archers.

Who saw them fall.

Still in the side of the larger—Kallites or Elemon? I could not remember the details of the tale—arrows were imbedded to the nock, to the feathers. With the smaller it was as though the arrows—feather and shaft entirely—grew from his chest and shoulders.

My companions raised their swords as the centaurs stumbled blindly into their midst, flailing with their huge arms and the clubs they carried.

The larger centaur struck Sir Robert a heavy blow with its forearm. The old man was knocked off his feet and tumbled into a cursing heap at the side of the trail. At that moment Enid di Caela almost came into her inheritance, for the big creature reared, preparing to bring his front hooves crashing down on Sir Robert.

I rushed toward Sir Robert, knife drawn.

Bayard, however, slipped behind the centaur before it noticed—indeed, before I had noticed—and hamstrung the creature with a blinding swipe of the sword. The big thing tottered and fell over on its side, struggled to right itself. It was only a second before Bayard's sword flashed once again, and the big centaur's head rolled several yards down the slanting trail.

Ramiro had that strange fat man's grace—the quickness and agility you never expect in someone his size. He went for the smaller centaur and circled it like an immense and

deadly fencing master, sword extended in front of him. His
first serious lunge struck home on the stumbling, ungainly
centaur.

Which did not fall.

Which hissed, widened its dull black eyes, and climbed
down the blade toward Ramiro. It climbed until the blade
burst through its back and it had Ramiro in its fetid, crush-
ing embrace.

But its arms were not long enough to encircle the big
Knight, much less crush him. Quickly Ramiro shrugged
away his attacker and dislodged his sword with the sound of
a knife drawn through a rotten melon. Then he spun quickly, putting all his considerable weight behind his sword.

The blow was so clean that the centaur's head came down
upon its shoulders and wobbled there for a moment before
toppling off.

The air about us lay stilled and foul.

Sir Robert groaned and creaked as Brithelm helped him
up from the roadside. Ramiro and Bayard sheathed their
swords, standing over their fallen enemies. And something
sniffled in the road behind us, curled into a dark heap.

"Alfric?" Bayard called.

"Alfric?"

But there was no answer. My brother lay clenched and
shivering in a pile of gravel, covered by a blanket. Bayard
looked back at me.

"Alfric?" I began, with no better results.

"Get control of yourself!" Sir Robert ordered, shaking
himself from Brithelm's grasp and striding toward my veiled
brother. Robert di Caela was never one for charity.

"Maybe," Alfric stated flatly, eyes still tightly shut, "this
rescue business has got out of hand."

"That's absurd, Alfric," Bayard said calmly.

"Absurd and treacherous," Ramiro muttered, as he turned
and lumbered toward Alfric.

"Come now, Alfric," I joined in. "How do you think Enid
would take this hysteria?" At which he burrowed even more
deeply into the blanket, shivering even more fiercely, as if
caught up in a strange and deadly fever. Brithelm rested his
hand on Alfric's shoulder.

Ramiro stepped forward, dealing a swift kick to the knot of blanket and brother. Alfric grunted, whimpered, and curled into a tighter ball.

Now it was Sir Robert's turn, and we all dreaded it.

"Alfric. Son."

No response. Sir Robert sighed.

"Alfric, if you don't come out from hiding this minute, you'll have to answer to this."

If anything outweighed Alfric's fear, it was his curiosity. He peered from beneath the blankets and saw Sir Robert holding a sword.

In no time, Alfric was out of the blanket quickly, and we all started toward the gates of the castle, Sir Robert whispering to Brithelm a judgment that the wind picked up and carried down to us as we followed them.

"It is a fortunate thing that your brother came when called. A few minutes more of this disobedience and I should have been forced to kill him."

Sir Robert followed that with a threatening glance back at Alfric, who had begun to shiver a little once more. Sir Robert turned to face the castle ahead of him, and his shoulders shook in turn.

But from where I walked, it looked like the shaking of laughter, a pleasant relief after a long afternoon of sorrow.

* * * * *

It was at that moment that Agion stumbled out through the gate. At first both Bayard and I cried out joyously, sure that we had somehow been mistaken during that sad time in the Vingaard Mountains, that the trident through his great heart and the humble little funeral had all taken place in a nightmare we now only dimly remembered as we saw our friend weave toward us.

We rejoiced until we saw the look in his eyes.

The dullness, the flatness. The look of the dead, beyond caring or recall.

Agion weaved slowly toward Bayard, club raised in his swollen, yellowed hand. Bayard stood his ground, drew his sword, and raised it.

Then lowered his weapon as the centaur drew near him.

"Bayard! It's no longer Agion!" I shouted.

But my protector stood there motionless, his sword at his side. The centaur stopped in front of him and slowly, mechanically raised its heavy club.

I do not know how I got to Bayard's side. Brithelm said later that he had never seen me move so quickly, and don't forget he had seen me in flight many times about the moat house. Whatever the circumstances, the next thing I knew I was between Bayard and Agion, facing the dead centaur.

"No! Agion! It's Bayard! It's Galen!" I shouted, waving my arms.

For a moment the dull, flat eyes softened. But only for a moment, as the steely hardness of death returned, and the Agion-thing raised its club, hissed, and prepared to bring both of us into its darkened world.

The moment of delay was enough. Sir Robert, battered and sore though he might be, was not entirely disabled—as we discovered when he rushed between me and the centaur, deflecting the downward stroke of the club with the flat of the ancient di Caela sword. Then, turning the sword above his head in a time-honored, brisk Solamnic fencing maneuver, he brought it up and over, slicing neatly through the bloated neck of Agion.

Everything went away. I was deep in black nothingness, and though I may have dreamed while I lay unconscious on the ground in the Chaktamir Pass, I do not remember dreaming.

I remember only the waking, Bayard shaking me back into light and cold and pain, and into a sadness I did not recognize for a moment—a sadness I could not place until I saw the centaur bodies and remembered.

"As you said," Bayard soothed, helping me to my feet, "it was no longer Agion."

"And yet . . . for a moment there, I thought it was Agion, thought that despite death and what the Scorpion had wrought, our old friend stayed his hand," I murmured.

"Perhaps he did, lad," Sir Robert replied softly. "And let it encourage us, for it shows that the Scorpion's power does not go on forever."

"That some things," Brithelm added softly, "are stronger

than death."

We paused in silence for a moment.

Sir Robert pointed toward the open gate.

And two by two we walked toward its menacing arch.

*   *   *   *   *

Through a curtain of driving snow, through the hovering mist, they appeared—the shadows of men, crouched, shambling, almost apelike in their movements. Though the forms were dim behind us and beside us, I could tell they were carrying weapons; the slim shadows of curved Nerakan swords lay in their shadowy hands. The cold air around us drummed with groans and inhuman cries.

It was as though someone were smothering an army.

Bayard drew his sword and started for the heart of the shadows, but Brithelm grabbed his arm.

"Sir Bayard, your duty lies in the castle—a task none but you can perform. For who knows but that the Lady Enid faces horrors that make ours seem light?"

"B-but . . . ," Bayard began.

"Into the castle, sir, and may the gods speed you." Brithelm smiled serenely, confidently. An arrow flew out of the mist and clattered on the stony ground beside him.

"By Paladine, you'll not stand against an army alone, lad!" bellowed Sir Ramiro. "Give me an armed enemy any day, rather than the cloudy hocus-pocus you'll find in that house of mirrors there. Bring 'em on, dead or alive! I'll be watching your back, Brithelm!"

Ramiro drew his sword, pushed me toward Bayard, and took his place beside my calm, clerical brother. Bayard grabbed my arm and pulled me, struggling, onto the drawbridge, Alfric and Sir Robert following closely behind us.

As we crossed the bridge toward the gate looming dark in front of us, Bayard leaned into me and whispered, "Don't worry, son."

We looked back upon my brother, the man of peace, bearing weapons among mist-covered stones. Beside him stood that hulking, merry man, Ramiro, whose enormous shield was raised over both of them to guard against the arching arrows.

"I trust we shall see them both again, Galen. Accidents avoid them."

Suddenly a red light shot from Brithelm's hand and buried itself in the shadowy forms in front of him. A loud shriek tore through the mist, and the army stopped in its tracks, hovering some distance away from our little rear guard.

"Damn!" I heard Ramiro rumble before I lost his voice in the mist and the outcry of shadowy soldiers. "Everywhere you look, this damnable sleight of hand! What does it take for a man to find sensible company?" And he laughed heartily, shaking his shield in front of the gibbering soldiers.

* * * * *

From that point on, the laughter faded. We passed first under the great arch of the castle gate. The courtyard itself seemed dreamed up, half-remembered from images of Castle di Caela and built with an eye to the floor plans only. The buildings were the same shape and size, rising from the same points within the courtyard.

That is, as far as I could see. For at the far reaches of the courtyard, the towers and shops and stables—the battlements themselves—were lost behind mists, or dissolved into mists. Sometimes a wall would be there, then seemed to be there no longer, as though it were solid or insubstantial, depending on a gust of wind or the intensity of the snow.

I was possessed of the uncanny feeling that the builder had it right only by blueprint. The keep and the towers and the other structures looked hollow, made up for visitors.

Whether it was from the mist or from some darker intention, the ground seemed to appear in front of us as we crossed toward the bailey. We dismounted at once, letting the horses go where they would in the confines of the courtyard. They would be safe, no doubt, and perhaps unnecessary from this time on.

Behind us, outside the walls, screams arose out of the fog. For a moment Bayard paused, turned, and prepared to go back. Then he muttered "Enid," grabbed me by the arm, and virtually lifted me above the mist as the horses galloped off. Together, slowly, we tested our first few steps, then picked up the pace to catch Sir Robert and Alfric, who had sprinted on ahead of us. We overtook them at the door of the keep.

Which, unlike the gate, was locked. Sir Robert had tried it once, twice, and now was pacing, stomping and blustering, while Alfric used Father's sword in an idiotic attempt to pry open the door.

"Out of the way!" Bayard shouted, and Alfric, accustomed to scrambling out of everyone's way, did so with surprising ease and grace. Bayard took four steps and leaped toward the door, giving it a resounding kick.

The door shivered but neither broke nor dislodged. Bayard bounced off the thick oak and clattered to the ground where he lay winded and dazed. Behind us and around us, the courtyard seemed to come to life. From somewhere in the mists I could hear heavy movement, the creak of leather and of metal, and the grumble of something large stirring and breathing. It was beginning to move our way.

Bayard labored to his feet with help from Sir Robert and prepared to rush the door again. Alfric moved quickly beside me and tugged at my sleeve.

"There's something out there, Brother, and I expect it has designs on us by now."

I agreed and said, "We'd better distract Sir Bayard before he injures himself, and then find a window to gain entry. Whatever lies in store for us is not through that door, evidently."

Bayard crashed against the door in question, then lay motionless beside it before beginning once more the painful struggle to his feet. The sounds—the snuffling, the movement of armor—grew nearer, and huge, horned things now hovered dark at the edge of the mist.

"Demons!" Alfric exclaimed.

"Men of Neraka," Sir Robert corrected, grabbing my eldest brother, "dressed in their ceremonial minotaur helmets, calling on Kiri-Jolith to scatter their enemies. And some time dead from the smell of them. Pick up your sword. They're coming this way. Quickly, around the side of the keep. If I'm not mistaken, there will be windows there."

We understood well enough, and the four of us started off toward where we hoped devoutly would be windows, Sir Robert clanking in the lead and Alfric no less noisy right behind him. I followed the two of them, blending in and out of the mist as quietly as one of Mariel di Caela's cats, and Bayard hobbled along at the rear, sword drawn.

It was evident by the time we reached the topiary and the chamber window that the Nerakan soldiers—or whatever they were—had gained ground on us. At first, thinking they were upon us, we drew our weapons as we turned the corner of the keep wall and saw horned figures in the garden by the window. But those were only shrubbery in the shape of owls, and we relaxed but a moment before we could hear, through the mists beyond the garden, the sound of snuffling and steady movement.

"Keep going around the wall!" Alfric urged. "They'll catch us here for sure! There must be other windows! You should know, Sir Robert!"

"Oh, there are other windows," Sir Robert mused calmly, "but none on this side of the keep that we can reach. Just listen; ahead of us, along the wall, is the same sound we have been running from since first we heard it. Whether it is armed men, or monsters, living or dead, we should prepare to take them here. The last thing they'll expect is a fight, so that is precisely what we'll give them."

So we stood there, looking at one another, Pathwardens and Brightblades and di Caelas.

All of a sudden the garden crashed and crackled with the sound of something huge, and the sound of breathing and snuffling increased into low rumbling, with an occasional bellow, as the rotten throats tried forgetfully the bull-cry of the Nerakan warriors.

The enemy approached us through the topiary, sometimes pushing aside the shrubbery with the sound of twigs snapping, of leaves crumpling, sometimes grunting as they staggered into the boles of trees. They were like the walls of the castle in the mist: forming, dissolving, then reforming. But continuing to move toward us.

"Galen!" Bayard snapped. "Can you reach the window from my shoulders?"

Reach the window? Desert my companions?

Desert my companions? What kind of Solamnic notions had infected me, that I should condemn myself for seeking the safest prospect available? Had I been listening to myself when I answered, I might well have heard that Solamnic self-righteous little quiver in my voice.

"I shall try, sir, if you see a further purpose in my doing so."

"Up on my shoulders, then," Bayard hissed urgently. "When you're inside, find your way back to that front door and unlatch it. That should be easy enough. The halls and the rooms inside should be the image of the di Caela keep, just as the keep is from the outside."

"I know, sir. But, for Huma's lance-wielding sake, what if—"

"You'd be no more dead there than you would be here."

Not the most encouraging of prospects. There or here. But Bayard was quite serene about the whole business.

"Take heart and climb atop my shoulders."

I did, and surprisingly, it was a short jump to the window, which somehow seemed lower than Enid's window at the di Caela keep. I leaped, clutched the sill, and pulled myself over. The room in front of me was dark.

Behind me I heard Alfric pleading with Bayard, heard Bayard respond that, no, Alfric was far too heavy for such acrobatics and that besides, they needed him for the battle that was sure to come.

"Now stop whining and face the garden," Sir Robert chimed in. "They'll come from that direction first, or I'm no tactician."

I set my dagger on the sill, stood in the darkened room, then looked behind me and below me once more, down to where Bayard stood, sword at the ready, looking up.

"We'll try to fight our way back around to the door," he murmured.

"Good luck to you, sir," I offered.

"Hurry," he shot back, then smiled and winked at me—a most unSolamnic gesture.

"The weasel's luck to you, lad. Which as I gather, has not been bad yet."

Without stopping to think—as I should have—I plunged into the unlit room.

I made two steps only, and then sunk to my knees in the

dark floor. I cried out for Bayard, but stifled the cry when I heard it echoing down the halls of the keep, heard the sound of shouting and the clash of weapons outside the window—sounds that seemed so far away.

I sunk farther, and thought of the quagmires in the Coastlund Swamp. I was sinking into the heart of the Scorpion, I figured. I flailed my arms around the floor of the chamber, striking solid stone at arm's length, nearly as far from me as I could reach. Breasting through the nothingness like a swimmer in a dark, thick pool of something more solid than water, more liquid than the ground around him, I finally gained purchase on the floor and pulled myself up, out of the morass, discovering to my surprise, that I was entirely dry.

"What is this?" I whispered, touching the floor in front of me to assure that no other pits had been set in the chambers. My hand brushed against a hurricane lamp, fully intact but lying on its side.

Picking up the lamp, I fumbled in my pocket for a tinderbox, coming up with gloves only. I swore a stable groom's curse and pressed on in the general direction of the door—or where Enid's door was set in the corresponding room in Castle di Caela. Like a monstrous crab I scuttled across the dark floor, groping at the floor beside me for other places in the room where things were not quite solid.

I found the door by the light that escaped from beneath it. The hall outside was eerily torchlit, but otherwise the image of the halls of Castle di Caela. Yet, on second look, it was not quite the image. Some small, unidentifiable thing was missing.

Not five cautious steps down the hall, it occurred to me. Mechanical birds. The birds Enid had wound up and hated through the otherwise pampered days of her childhood.

For the halls of the Scorpion's Nest were silent.

I sat, pondering the corridor ahead of me and behind me, and noticed at points that the walls were swirling as though tiny whirlpools, scarcely the size of a man's fist, were embedded in them as some kind of bizarre ornament. The whirlpools turned hypnotically clockwise, as gray as the surrounding stones but liquid in texture and shimmering like liquid as they caught and reflected the torchlight.

Walls that, like the floors, could swallow you entirely.

I backed away from them and seated myself in the center of the corridor, those spiraling flaws in the wall at a safe arm's length.

I breathed heavily, the sound of the sigh racing down the corridor ahead of me, where it mingled with another distant sound, strangely and irritatingly familiar.

The sound of whirring and chirping.

So there was one, at least.

* * * * *

It was just curiosity, a nosiness about other people's houses and furnishings and decorations, that led me to follow the sound of the mechanical bird. That and the knowledge that the sound came from the direction of the great landing, below which was the main entrance to the keep— the door Bayard had charged me with unlocking.

Relying on my memories of the keep's exterior, it was not hard to remember where I was. Down the hall straight ahead of me, eyes carefully fixed on the floor to avoid stepping into one of those whirlpools of liquid stone, I picked up a larger, wider hall. This large hall led straight to the landing, and I rested my hands carefully on the banister before I trusted it to support my weight.

Down this hall I went and turned right, into a hall of statuary. Which contained marble di Caelas, but none I had seen commemorated in Sir Robert's palace.

Instead, it was the family in all its darkest moments.

For here was Mariel di Caela, reclining on a marble divan, marble cats at her throat, her eyes, her breast. It was even more gruesome because it was so white, so smooth.

And Denis di Caela, bearing a marble rat in a marble cage. Not to mention Simon di Caela, basking contentedly forever like a huge white iguana.

It was almost obscene.

Presiding over the lot of them was another statue I had never seen—that of a man hooded and seated on a skeletal throne, sculptured scorpions twisting over the arms of the chair and the man himself.

Old Benedict di Caela, enthroned in the dark of brothers' negligence.

I moved past the door that would have been Dannelle's in a safer world I recalled most fondly, most despairingly. I continued down the hall to the right, sidestepping a quagmire, then again to the left, then right again until I faced the hallway, where, to my right, the siege of Ergoth raged silently and motionlessly, forever, in paint upon the wall.

At the end of that hall, the mechanical bird was grinding and singing, grinding and singing again.

When the bird paused, I heard voices. Two of them, both raised in anger, coming from the door opposite the mural.

The door which, in Castle di Caela, had led to the balcony overlooking the great hall.

I opened the door a crack, saw darkness, and smelled expensive cloth and the slight whiff of decay. Beyond that was darkness and, more clearly now, I could hear voices.

One was sweet and high and melodious, one low and melodious and deadly.

Enid and the Scorpion.

Obviously, they were not getting along.

* * * * *

I stood not six feet from a set of curtains that resembled those of the Castle di Caela, right down to the velvet and the stitchery—as much as I could tell in the gray dimness of the balcony I was on. Beyond those curtains the voices rose and ebbed in the old duet of argument.

I closed the door behind me.

"Remember, you are my prisoner, my dear." The Scorpion's voice rose coldly, menacingly.

Enid, bless her soul, was not intimidated in the least.

"You cannot have this arrangement both ways, Cousin Benedict. Either I am your hostage, and therefore you should keep me in confinement under lock and key, as is the custom with hostages, or I am the singular, although reluctant, object of your affections, in which case you are no more dear to me than those clicking vermin outside the door."

"What if I were to untie you, Lady Enid?" The Scorpion's

voice slipped back into its old ways—smooth and honeyed and terribly inviting. "If I do so, will you look on me with any . . . greater regard?"

Slowly I creeped toward the opening in the curtains, drawn by the faint crack of light. I stirred the floor with my hands, remembering my adventures in the chambers and on the landing, remembering Alfric's tumble from a balcony where stone was stone and curtains were curtains.

Her answer came as I touched the cloth and began to part the heavy velvet ever so slightly. Enid's voice swelled even louder, riding a wave of scorn and amusement.

"Oh, Benedict, Benedict. You could untie me and grant me full run of your castle, and I would still regard you with indifference. I would, however, appreciate the favor, and I might ask Sir Robert to be a little less severe with you when he comes to rescue me."

She was bluffing the Scorpion, bluffing him well and considerably. I looked through the curtains and saw the both of them.

Enid was seated in a straight-backed wooden chair, all blond and brown-eyed and surpassing beautiful. Also fearless and surpassing angry.

Across from her sat old Benedict—the Scorpion of my apprehensions and nightmares—crouched and hooded on his skeletal throne, which looked strangely smaller, strangely more flimsy, less menacing.

"Sir Robert! Sir Robert!" the Scorpion called mockingly. "My dear, your father is a blustering, reckless fool."

"Which is why you had to steal his daughter, rather than confront him directly," Enid answered merrily, ironically.

"You think he will come and rescue you. Oh, yes, Lady Enid, he will walk into the arms of my soldiers, into the arrows and the daggers of the long dead men of Neraka— the 'generations from the grass,' as the prophecy calls them. He will feel the Scorpion's sting, my sweet one."

The Scorpion leaned back on his throne and laughed richly, venomously. From the folds of his robe he drew something that shone, something that glittered, and he began to speak as he held the pendulum to the light, swinging it back and forth like a cheap carnival hypnotist.

I did not notice the swirling gray stone near the railing of the balcony, and it was all I could do to grab the curtain as I fell through it. My stifled cry of alarm was not stifled enough. Both Enid and the Scorpion looked up at me from their seats in the great hall.

For the first time, I saw clearly that Enid's hands were tied to the arms of her chair. And the eyes of the Scorpion glowed red, glowed blue, glowed white.

"Welcome, Weasel," he purred, clutching the arms of his throne with a grip that whitened his knuckles. "We were just getting ready to . . . discuss you."

CHAPTER 19

"We can always discuss this later, if you'd like," I offered, but the Scorpion was having none of it. He leaned forward on his throne, his eyes spiraling though all the colors of fire until they took on the white of the fire's very center.

"I think I have no further need of you," he snarled, his voice stripped of its deadly music, become something harsh and remotely human. We were in his country now, where he had no more need of masks.

He pointed at the floor below me, the golden pendant dangling from his long, pale index finger.

The spot of floor to which he pointed began to turn, twist, and glitter, much like the walls and floors of the corridors through which I had passed. But this vortex was black, not the slate gray of the walls and the other floors.

I squinted and looked closer.

A blanket of scorpions covered the floor beneath me. They flickered and twisted in the torchlight, poisonous tails aloft. To fall into their midst would make you pray on the way down that the fall itself would kill you.

Slowly, ever so carefully, I tried to pull myself up the curtain and over the railing of the balcony, praying to Gilean, to Mishakal, to whatever god or goddess came to mind for a strongly woven fabric in my hands, for careful carpentry on the railing and no more illusions where I was headed. The mechanical bird chattered again in the hall outside.

I sighed and whispered to myself, "Now just climb up and tunnel your way out of here, Weasel."

Then I saw the giant scorpion, its black scales shimmering, its sharp tail raised, as it began a slow climb down the curtain, clutching the hem and the stitchery on its way toward my hands.

Things like this compose your worst nightmares. I reached for the railing, only to have my hand pass through it as though it were made of smoke.

There was nothing of substance to serve as a lifeline. I let myself down the curtain as far as I could, hand over hand like I was descending a rope. Then I thought of the boiling throng of creatures below me and stopped where I was, not daring to move down any farther, lest I run out of curtain.

Still the giant scorpion approached me, its black tail raised and its delicate legs dancing over the soft drapery.

"Get away!" I hissed. The thing paused, tail turning in the air like a black leaf catching moisture or sunlight, then hopped threateningly in my direction before pausing ironically on a gold tassel not a yard from my hands.

"Such heroism!" the Scorpion drawled ironically. "A creature not a tenth your size, and you shy from him as though he were . . . poison?" His laughter rose into a piercing howl; the scorpions below me churned more frantically, and Enid covered her ears.

"You're not known for picking the fair fight yourself, Benedict!" Enid shouted angrily. She was saying something more, but her words warred with his laughter and lost.

Finally, when the laughter subsided, Benedict looked up at me. With a strange, demented tenderness he smiled, but I could see his glowing eyes sink farther and farther into their sockets, and the framework of the skull emerging from the pale, yellowed skin.

"You did me good service once, did you not, Galen Pathwarden?"

The verminous thing above me paused in its descent, as its master spoke. "As reward for your service, little Weasel, you shall live longer than all your friends."

Enid shot an angry glance at me, reminded, no doubt, of the stories of my betrayals.

I looked remorseful and shrugged, or at least as much as I could while hanging from a drapery.

Her anger softened. Helplessly we stared at one another. Helplessly I dangled. Above me and below me, the chittering poisonous things awaited their orders. I was left in wicked suspension.

Dimly through the halls, I could hear someone pounding at the door—the door I had tried to get to, to open. The Scorpion cupped his hand to his ear, ironically.

"We have visitors, my dear! Don't get up. I'll answer the door!" he exclaimed, then burst once again into laughter. "It should be my father-in-law, if I am not mistaken."

He turned to me, his eyes glowing.

"And I am never mistaken. For after your verbal gymnastics, your long nights with poetry and history and Solamnic lore, it is I who broke the code of the prophecy, not Bayard, who nursed it for a lifetime, nor Sir Robert, who pondered it like his father did and his father before him.

"I like to think that a little bit of . . . the bardic soul resides within me," he mused, and leaned back on his throne exultantly.

"If it does, Uncle Benedict, I'd wager it is lonely," Enid retorted.

"Silence, child," Benedict commanded softly, almost soothingly. "For your . . . bridal time is nigh."

From the folds of his robe he drew a dagger. It shimmered in the off-yellow light of the hall as he placed it delicately on the arm of his throne. Just as he did, the door to the Great

Hall shivered and burst from its hinges.

Bayard and Sir Robert stood in the doorway, swords drawn. Sir Robert's left hand was tangled in Alfric's hair, which he had used as a rein to guide my reluctant brother to the spot. Alfric puffed and whimpered.

"Welcome," the Scorpion intoned ominously. "I have awaited you, Bayard Brightblade. And you . . . Sir Robert.

"There is time—not much time, but time enough—to take up our quarrel of four centuries. But first, let us cover a wound more freshly opened, a factional dispute of scarcely thirty years back."

He held out his hands, palms up, and raised them slowly above his head. Its chain entwined in the fingers of his left hand, the pendulum dangled and glittered.

"Let my friends resume their quarrel . . . where your high-and-mighty Order fancies it has put all quarrel to rest," he pronounced casually. "Let 'generations from the grass arise and lay the curse aside.'"

Beneath me the scorpions began to scatter, the floor of the hall to shake and crack.

When the attention of its master turned elsewhere, my enemy from above resumed his scrambling descent.

"Stop right there!" I threatened, trying to sound menacing, then clamping my mouth shut in the realization that the creature might be following the sound of my voice. I reached into the mist for my belt and the knife that hung . . .

Did *not* hang.

I remembered the windowsill through which I had entered this castle, the glitter of iron in the light of the red moon. My dagger was conveniently three corridors away, forgotten on a windowsill beyond my reach.

In vain I fumbled through my pockets for anything sharp or heavy. At last my desperate hand rested on something rough, thick, and leathery.

"The gloves!" I hissed, and the scorpion creeped down the curtain, now within a foot of my one clinging hand.

I slipped on a glove, using one hand and my mouth in a movement that, given other circumstances, I'd have dismissed as acrobatic if not downright impossible. Agility had always been my strong suit, and the suit was stretched to its limit of strength there at the end of the Scorpion's curtains.

The merchant who had sold them to me had boasted of the gloves' sturdiness, that indeed they could "stand up to a knife if they were called to do so, young sir."

As the scorpion tested the fabric not six inches from my hand, its jointed leg strumming the rough embroidery, I reached forward and grabbed the creature with my gloved hand, gripping it as hard as I could.

I heard the sound of its skeleton crackle and felt something breaking in the padded palm of my hand. The lethal tail wound its way out of my grip from between my fingers, arched and plunged harmlessly time and again into the thick, resilient leather.

For once, a merchant had not lied.

I hurled the remnants of the creature from me and watched them fall in fragments to the floor of the hall.

Which was now erupting around my friends.

Through the mist and the rocks and the floor, a battalion was rising, breaking through stone and tile. Some wore minotaur helmets, the sign of the Nerakan soldier then and now. All were armed with the feared scimitars and the half-moon shield of the Western Corps, the branch of the army that had fallen to Enric Stormhold—and to my father— thirty years back at the Battle of Chaktamir.

As the Scorpion watched calmly from his seat in the hall, his soldiers climbed out of the ground and onto their feet, trudging toward Bayard and Robert and Alfric. Moss and earth and ordure dripped from their hair, and the ivory of the bones lay bare through the yellowed, mottled flesh. The smell was that of a slaughterhouse long abandoned.

Alfric wrenched away from Sir Robert, leaving a handful of red hair behind him, and sprang out the door in an instant, only to come back shamefacedly when other noises arose from the hall—the smothered, almost bleating battle-cry of more undead soldiers.

I started my ascent of the curtain, checked for purchase on the balcony, and found a solid spot after an endless minute of pawing the air with my foot. But from that height I was powerless to help as the numbers grew against us.

Bayard and Sir Robert stood back to back so that

between the two of them, they could see the entire hall and the outlying corridor. Alfric tried vainly to sandwich himself between them, but was elbowed away with the warning from Sir Robert, "Stand your own ground, boy! We need even the sorriest of swords at this pass!"

Alfric whimpered and drew his sword. Steadily the Nerakan soldiers closed in on my companions.

Meanwhile, the Scorpion rose from his throne, walked to Enid's chair, and very calmly began to untie her wrists from the armrests. Though she was obviously unnerved by the creatures the Scorpion had called from out of the ground, she was not about to swoon or scream. Instead, she fetched a blow to her captor's chest that sent him staggering backward, and only a viper-quick grab at the girl kept her from escaping.

"Come with me," the Scorpion said, as he dragged the struggling Enid back toward his pedestal, where the dagger sat waiting on the arm of his throne. A murmuring sea of black scorpions converged upon them, parting to form a pathway from one chair to the other.

"Up on the pedestal, my dear," he urged.

It was then—too late, I feared, but nonetheless swiftly— that Bayard Brightblade began to cut his own path through the men of Neraka. Often urgency shackles the hand of the swordsman, but it brought Bayard to life, to a blinding swiftness. Five Nerakans fell to his sword in an instant, and it was all that Sir Robert could do to follow in the wake of the younger Knight. Alfric in turn followed Sir Robert, his face blanched, his own blade shaking in his extended hand.

All outcry, all the moans and bellows ceased. The hall was silent except for the shuffling of long-dead feet, the skittering of scorpions, and the sound of Bayard's sword striking continually, wetly home.

It was as though the Nerakans were lining up for execution. But halfway through the undead soldiers, Bayard's path slowed, as bodies heaped upon and against bodies, as the Nerakans began to mill in front of him, as they fell back into one another and were buoyed and carried by those who approached the battle from behind them. They shrank back from him as though even having passed through death, they were still daunted by this harrowing, bright champion in front of them.

Walled off from Bayard by his legion of moving, decaying flesh, the Scorpion raised his knife.

"Wait!" I shouted, and my voice piped embarrassingly thin and shrill in the large hall. Bayard's sword stilled, and Sir Robert stood stiffly behind him, his hand stretched toward the Scorpion in silent anguish. The Nerakan soldiers lowered their weapons and stared stupidly, lifelessly at their leader standing on the platform.

For a moment the Scorpion paused. The red light of his eyes flickered as he glanced up to me.

I began once again to burrow in words, to bargain for time, hoping devoutly that Bayard would think of something violent and heroic before I ran out of breath and argument.

"You think you have that prophecy figured as neat as a recipe, with no line left unexplained and unmanaged?"

I glanced at Bayard, who was looking at me, sword raised overhead.

Move, Bayard. Move quickly, like a striking snake. Let's see a little Solamnic velocity in this nest of scorpions!

So I thought and hoped, but Bayard did not move. And the Scorpion's dagger stayed poised above Enid as I spoke.

"What if you're wrong, Benedict? After all, you've proven that Bayard misread the prophecy entirely. As did Sir Robert, evidently. So what if you did, too? What if that little piece of doggerel has squirmed away from all three of you—Bayard, Robert, and Benedict—and there's another solution to all this rhyme and foreboding?

"After all, you kill the bride but the line doesn't end. Sir Robert can father more children, more di Caelas to wrestle you down each time you trundle back to claim your inheritance."

"Which is why I brought her here, fool!" the Scorpion proclaimed. "Now all the di Caelas are under my roof, and the line ends where they do!"

"Perhaps. Or perhaps not," I answered triumphantly. Another invention had occured to me, and for all I knew it stood just as good a chance of being true as any story, poem, or prophecy I had heard so far. For as my thoughts raced, they had settled on lamplight in a window, on a pale arm waving.

"Have you heard of Dannelle di Caela, sir?"

The hand holding the dagger wavered. Bayard started for the platform, but the Scorpion wheeled and, clutching Enid to him, brought the dagger to her throat. Again the creatures at his feet began to chitter and mill.

"Stand back, Solamnic! Prophecy or no, if you come any nearer, I'll send this girl to Hiddukel!"

"Regardless, 'a girl succeeds to all,' Benedict," I urged. "For if you kill Enid, who will be Sir Robert's heir but Dannelle di Caela?"

"No," the Scorpion said quietly. He grasped Enid so tightly that she cried out, startling him. For a moment he lost his grip on the girl, and she wriggled free of his encircling arm.

Now, Enid di Caela was her father's daughter—no helpless damsel in distress. She fetched the Scorpion a sound kick in the leg that sent him stumbling to the center of the platform, where he clutched the arm of his throne to regain his balance.

A moment's stumble was all she needed. Enid slipped through the milling Nerakans and into her father's arms, as Bayard stepped quickly between her and the Scorpion's ghastly army.

"Kill her!" the Scorpion shrieked, pointing a bony finger at the escaping Enid, but it was too late. The girl had returned to the protection of Bayard Brightblade, who put four Nerakans to the sword with movements so quick that the blade even ceased to blur and became invisible, and only the swarm of bodies between him and the Scorpion allowed the scoundrel to rush toward the far door of the great hall, surrounded by his clattering black attendants.

I whooped and started down the curtain again, still slowly, testing the cloth for strength and for vermin in the folds.

For a moment it looked as though the Scorpion would escape. Bayard pushed one more Nerakan to the floor, ducked the slash of another's scimitar, and beheaded a third with a quick, flashing movement of his sword arm. Sir Robert, after parrying a slow thrust from a Nerakan scimitar, severed the hand that held it. The undead soldier dropped to his knees and Alfric, who had been hiding behind Enid when the battle resumed, slipped in behind the half-fallen Nerakan and stabbed him in the back.

But even more quickly than the Knights moved through his undead protectors, the Scorpion made his way toward the door and freedom. His cloak wrapped around him, he moved with the silent grace of an enormous nocturnal bird, the door not ten feet in front of him now.

Then as though he had conjured them with a wave of that mysterious crystal, in that very doorway stood Ramiro and Brithelm.

Both were bedraggled and tattered—a little worse for wear from their struggle in the pass—but neither was about to give way to the thing they had come so far to hunt down. Sword drawn, Ramiro stepped through the door and approached old Benedict from one side, while Bayard cut a path toward him from another.

The Scorpion raised his pendulum, and hundreds of small beasts, their sharp tails poised for the fatal sting, scurried toward Sir Ramiro.

A red light tumbled from Brithelm's hands, and the floor of the room was awash with an unearthly fire that bathed the creatures and set them burning. There on the floor between my brother and their dark-hooded commander the scorpions twisted, contorted, and crackled.

Then they began to sting each other.

Slowly the red fire faded from about the charred, spidery remains of the scorpions. And I heard my brother speaking in quiet mourning.

"I am sorry. Even to such as you, I am sorry."

The Scorpion backed away. Still, he remained undaunted. Cautiously he backed to a corner, his red eyes taking in the hall. Once again he raised his hands, and again the ground began to tremble and boil.

"Oh, but it is not over, fools and Solamnics and more fools," he crowed. "We are gathered together—all of us beneath this roof of rock and cloud and fable—to bring an end to this prophecy, this wondering. No Dannelle di Caelas! The fate of the house is decided here! For remember the prophecy says that: 'Generations from the grass/will rise and lay the curse aside.' You have seen but the first generation. Now suffer the second!"

Slowly, more armed men clambered out of the swirling ground, leaving churned earth and moss and yellowed, tattered cloth behind them. The first arm bursting through the floor carried with it the shield of the House of Stormhold.

I stayed where I was, halfway down the dangling curtain.

"Yes, Bayard Brightblade!" Benedict shouted, his voice shrilling as the long-dead Solamnic Knights staggered to their feet, reaching into the swirl of cloud and earth below them to draw forth their weapons. "The men of Neraka join hands with these from your ancient order! Death is the leveler, all faction and race and country put aside in the long and abiding hatred for the living!"

The dead Solamnics righted themselves, more than a hundred strong. Clumsily, listlessly, they proffered their swords in the time-honored salute of the Order. By their gray and decaying hands it was scarcely recognizable—almost a mockery.

Bayard lowered his sword in dismay. All of the rest, even Sir Ramiro and Sir Robert, shrank from the earth-covered Knights, from the bandages and the smell.

* * * * *

Death may well be the leveler, but what was it that Brithelm said? *Some things are stronger than death?*

With a cry almost in unison, a dry, papery yell that despite its dryness, despite its fragility, shook the things in the Scorpion's hall, the Solamnic dead raised their swords and charged.

Straight at the waiting men of Neraka.

Through all these decades of death and oblivion, they had awakened to defend against a Nerakan assault. Some things, indeed, were stronger than death, among them the ancient oath, *Est Sularus oth Mithas*—my honor is my life—in the breathless breathing of each dry-voiced Knight.

It was as though time, too, had held its breath for a generation, and with a sudden, terrible gasp breathed again.

"No!" cried the Scorpion as, despite his best plans and

orders, the ancient armies again locked weapons. "You are commanded—"

But there was no time to speak, for Bayard Brightblade was hurtling toward him through the dozens of skirmishes that had erupted in the hall. From his black robe the Scorpion drew a sword whose blade was a dark blue steel. It glittered as black as onyx in the yellowed light of the room, and no sooner had he raised it than Bayard's great blade came crashing down upon it, driving Benedict to his knees.

They locked blades there for a moment, Bayard resting all his muscle and weight on the sword beneath him, the Scorpion pushing up with the bristling strength of a dozen men, the pendulum swinging wildly from his left hand as he brought it, too, to the pommel of the sword in a frantic attempt to stop Bayard's unyielding push downward. They poised at the far corner of the room in a violent balance, and for a moment the bright blade forced the dark one back, the silvery glint of Bayard's hundred-year-old sword inching closer and closer to the face of the enemy.

With a cry and a sudden, powerful movement, the Scorpion pushed Bayard away. Bayard tumbled backward toward the Scorpion's throne, and the dark-robed villain followed, his eyes glowing with a blue-white light, the pendulum bright in his lowered left hand, his black-edged weapon raised triumphantly in his right. Around him from the dark recesses of the room came the scratching sound of more of his little monsters scrambling to join him.

Feeling like a child's toy on a string, I shinnied a little farther up the curtain and called to Bayard, "The pendulum!"

He showed no sign of hearing me, struggling as he was to get to his feet in his extremely heavy armor. But he had heard, evidently.

In dodging the downward stroke of the Scorpion's sword, Bayard brought his own blade up and, flashing through the air, cleanly through the Scorpion's left wrist.

The hand skittered across the floor, writhing like a scorpion or spider, the chain of the pendulum tangled about its fingers. The Scorpion shrieked and held up the stump of his left arm, then toppled backward onto the hundreds of verminous creatures he had summoned from the darkness.

With the pendulum now gone, they descended on him blindly and hungrily. Benedict screamed, shuddered, and was lost in the clicking, rattling convergence of scorpions, in the plunging of hundreds and hundreds of venomous stingers.

Light then shot through the walls of the room, as the gray swirls of cloud dissolved in sunlight, evaporating to brisk air and a bare mountain pass that then began to shake and crumble.

The Scorpion's Nest was a ruin. What little remained of the stones in the castle—the skeleton of an ancient foundation, of a wall or two, of flights of stairs that led to nowhere—tottered and began to fall.

An old wall collapsed toward Enid and Sir Robert, and would have no doubt crushed the life from both of them had not Sir Robert raised his great Solamnic shield. Stone and mortar tumbled against ancient metal . . .

And the metal held.

All around us and below us the ground was opening, roiling, heaving, as though we had walked into the focus of an earthquake so violent, so widespread that it might well be the Cataclysm come again, transforming the surface of Krynn in its wreckage. Bayard stepped to the platform where the Scorpion's throne, once bone white and tall and menacing, had burst into pieces.

Bayard whistled, and Valorous, true to his name, came galloping out of a notch in the rocks, followed by the other horses. The big stallion was calm, obedient, but those who followed him were balanced at the edge of panic, frothing and snorting and rolling their eyes. When the ground had begun to shake and the rocks to fall, they reverted to instinct and followed the herd master—the lead stallion who, thankfully, had remained impressively composed. Only one horse and the mules, willful to the end, were left to the earthquake.

Into that turning earth the dead men walked or tumbled. Back to the quiet they went, into the peace that each of them, Nerakan or Solamnic, had earned for himself at dreadful cost a generation before. The land closed over them and continued to churn and boil as my companions did what they could to calm their horses, mount, and begin to ride.

* * * * *

"Bayard!" I shouted as he swept Enid up onto Valorous. The lady safe beside him, he was arranging the safety of the others. No room, then, on Valorous.

My brothers were doubled up on Brithelm's horse, Alfric's mule having vanished somewhere. With a flick of his glove to the horse's rump, Bayard set the two older Pathwardens west at a full gallop, over the shifting gravel and rock toward safety, followed closely by Sir Ramiro, burden enough for my little pack mare, which was bearing up beneath him.

"Jump, boy!" Sir Robert called up to me, rising in his stirrups atop a skittish Estrella, as the balcony from which I dangled like a crystal in a pendulum began to sway, snap, and teeter dangerously.

"Not too close, Sir Robert!" shouted Bayard. "It's likely to fall at any moment! Swing out on the curtain, Galen! Swing out to Sir Robert!" The tough old Knight opened his arms and nodded urgently. I began to swing on the curtain, going higher and higher as the balcony above me began to weave.

Back and forth, back and forth I flew, until at the sound of something falling behind me, I let go and tumbled through the air, a flying weasel on an aerial route to Sir Robert di Caela, whom I trusted to catch me and carry me out of the chaos, safely into the lowlands.

I had not figured on Estrella, who, spooked by yet another tremor beneath her hooves, skipped nervously forward at the worst of all possible moments. Sir Robert reached back desperately, but his mare had moved too far.

The ground surged rockily up to meet me. So did the darkness.

EPILOGUE

Head injuries are strange things, as Bayard could have told me from his time in the Vingaard Mountains. So my memories are spotty as to what happened after the fall of the Scorpion's Nest. Indeed, by the time my memory became certain, we were back in Castle di Caela and preparations were underway for the betrothal banquet.

But here is what happened, as best I can put it together from Bayard's accounts, from what Alfric told me grudgingly, from what is reliable in Brithelm's account, and from my scattered memories.

When the Scorpion fell to the floor of the hall and was covered by his mindlessly stinging creatures, when the castle began to collapse, we rushed to do what we had set out to do back at Castle di Caela—to escape the destruction of the

Scorpion and return to safety the girl on whom all prophecy hinged.

The rocks of Chaktamir tumbled into the gap, covering Scorpion and scorpions, the Nest, and all of the dead—Nerakans and Solamnics, all at peace again. It was there that we rested, and Sir Robert, who had tucked me under his arm like a rolled-up carpet, lowered me, unconscious, into the waiting arms of Brithelm and Enid.

Enid. I would have blushed in embarrassed delight had I been conscious to do so. But Enid dropped me all of a sudden, with a little cry of dismay that was the first thing I heard when the fall awakened me. Sir Ramiro was thrashing Alfric within an inch of his life, there in the peaceful foothills of Estwilde. Though they had agreed upon Bayard's heroism in the taking of the Scorpion's Nest, their argument as to who might receive second laurels had passed apparently from merely ill-spirited to downright aggressive.

Both were puffing from exhaustion and rage, and they were red from embarrassment, when Enid herself pulled them apart.

There followed a long round of revivals, of reconciliations. And soon, Alfric and Sir Robert were to their feet. Or so I am told. I still wobbled and fell to the ground, babbling about centaurs and the customs of drowning, and asking for my dice.

We were out of the mountains before I recalled leaving the little red prophets somewhere in the rough country around me. No doubt they are buried to this day amid rubble and rock, somewhere in the foothills of Estwilde.

I asked Bayard to pause and help me look for the Calantina dice, but he would have nothing to do with "such foolishness," saying I had outgrown playthings and false prophecy.

I was inclined to agree. I have no particular need of the future, though my hands still itch for the red dice and the wooden verses that, even if they did not explain the things that came to pass, provided an explanation into which you could fit those things and feel better.

I have put prophecy aside and, for the moment, scheming.

* * * * *

The sparks that we all expected would fly between Bayard and Enid finally began on the long road back to Castle di Caela. Sparks were also flying between Sir Ramiro and Alfric. My brother's bluster and boasting had not worn well on the old Knight after so many miles. Indeed, Sir Robert's diplomacy was called upon at the very gates of Castle di Caela, when Sir Ramiro pushed Alfric from his horse and into the moat for the sole reason that my eldest brother had "a face that deserved pushing into a moat."

He went on to maintain that Alfric's face would look better perched on a pike atop the battlements.

Alfric scarcely survived being fished from the water, and as soon as his armor had dried, he was on his way back to Coastlund, dreaming, I am sure, of the view from a pike. He whimpered a bit at the prospect of returning to Father bearing the now-battered armor and weaponry he had filched from the moat house, no doubt having caused the old man to comb the countryside and drag the swamp in his eldest son's absence, fearing that abduction, drowning, or just plain foolishness had lost him an heir.

The reception would not be warm.

My relief at Alfric's going was mixed with sadness, for Brithelm went with him, and I lost the companionship of my favored brother as well. Brithelm was to ride with Alfric as far as the Coastlund Swamp, where he intended to stop and set up the hermitage he had longed for during the dangerous times in which we hunted down the Scorpion.

But when my brothers had crossed the mountains and descended onto the plains of my home country, they found out—to nobody's real surprise, actually—that the Coastlund Swamp had vanished.

Centaurs and peasants agreed on the account: that gradually, tree by tree and vine by tendril, the swamp had shrunk and shrunk until all that was left was a curious house on stilts, miles from anywhere and still stinking of goat and decay and something, the centaurs claimed, a little more unsettling than even those disagreeable smells. So Brithelm escorted his elder brother all the way back to the moat house, where he spent a few days smoothing the path with Father, who, as I had suspected, was none too pleased with Alfric.

That mission done, Brithelm headed east once more, where he settled amid the huge stone structures in the Vingaard Mountains where Bayard, Agion, and I had passed the night and I had first heard of the prophecy in the *Book of Vinas Solamnus*.

Though, for the life of me, I have never been able to find my way to the spot where Brithelm has set up his hermitage, and though Bayard has sworn never to give directions to that spot, I am confident that my brother is safe and in good hands—a little abstract and foolish, perhaps, but safe and reliable should times of trouble come again.

Times of trouble, I understand, have come and gone at the moat house. After imprisoning Alfric for a brief and miserable sentence, Father once more has released him, and is riding him daily in the performance of squirely duties. Alfric has no time, I hear, to torture the servants or to sneak wine into his room, and I have it on good authority that Gileandos has burst into flames only once since my brother's return, and that because he had caught the sleeve of his robe in the fire of his homemade laboratory distillery. Alfric was not blamed for the accident.

I, for once, had the perfect alibi. I was miles away in Solamnia.

Who knows, Alfric may change his ways and become a reasonably presentable squire. A few years from now, when I am a Knight and in need of someone to curry my horse and polish my sword and armor, I may ride up to Coastlund and talk to Father about taking on his eldest son and heir for the job. I have no objections to a squire who's pushing thirty—I can forgive many things, even a certain slowness in learning.

What's more, being my squire would be especially galling to Brother dear.

It may surprise you that I have set my cap toward Knighthood, with all the terrible things I've said and thought about the Order. Well, I'm doing so because I have no real choice if I'm to inherit the considerable property I'll receive as a reward.

Castle di Caela and all its holdings.

For you see, after the banquet tonight, and the ceremonies, I shall be Galen Pathwarden Brightblade, adopted son and heir of Sir Bayard Brightblade.

At the turn of the month, after another banquet and other ceremonies even longer and more boring than these, I shall be Galen Pathwarden di Caela Brightblade, when Stepfather and Stepmother are wed at last.

* * * * *

The courtship was shy, almost ridiculous at first, since both Bayard and Enid had been accustomed to letting prophecy and family history govern their lives and hadn't the first idea about how to woo each other.

Bayard even tried to enlist my help in writing a courtship song to Enid. That lasted until I explained to him how effective my poetry had been on the night Alfric pursued his romantic fortunes. Bayard decided I was bad luck, and consulted me no more on matters of the heart.

Nonetheless, awkward though it may have been, the two fell in love. Scarcely a week had passed back at Castle di Caela, when "the troth was plighted," as the saying goes, and Sir Robert and Bayard began to make plans for the wedding. I caught Dannelle looking foolishly in my direction, so I moved my quarters into what I called Lady Mariel's Cat Tower, as far away from the marital line of fire as possible.

Yet I didn't see where it would hurt to escort Dannelle to the marital banquet, to let the poor girl see the apple of her eye decked out in Solamnic finery. Especially since I had almost sold her up the river when I dangled her name in front of the Scorpion to confuse his rather dramatic intentions.

After all, in the weeks to come, we would be in-laws, Dannelle and I, and it would not do for in-laws to hide from each other as they have been doing these last few weeks in the castle.

What's more, she is an ivory, bright-eyed thing. If it is nothing bridal, I expect I can shoulder the burden.

*   *   *   *   *

Two hours remain before I put on that robe of red and yellow, the colors of my new family, and march, like I saw so many Knights marching that night so long ago, through the great dining hall of Castle di Caela.

Downstairs they are preparing for it. You can hear out my open door the ringing of cutlery and the clatter of plates being set on the great hall's oaken tables. It is a night of ceremony, of celebration that approaches. It is a night of banquets.

I look forward to it devoutly.

But if anyone comes to my quarters beforehand, bearing proposals or bribes or promises or threats or offers of any kind, I shall say, "No, thank you, I am trying to quit that business."

I have stretched my luck and my story as far as I can.

Elminster:
The Making of a Mage

Ed Greenwood

From the creator of the FORGOTTEN REALMS® world comes the epic story of the Realms' greatest wizard!

Elminster. No other wizard wields such power. No other wizard has lived as long. No other book tells you the story of his origins. Born into humble circumstances, Elminster begins his life of magic in an odd way – by fleeing from it. When his village and his family are destroyed by a being of sorcerous might, young Elminster eschews the arcane arts. Instead, he becomes a journeyman warrior and embarks on a mission of revenge . . . until his destiny turns in on itself and he embraces the magic he once despised.

COMING FALL/WINTER '94

The Ogre's Pact

Book One in the new Twilight Giants Trilogy by Troy Denning, *New York Times* best-selling author

When ogres kidnap Brianna of Hartwick, her father forbids his knights to rescue her. Only a brash peasant, who covets Brianna's hand, has the courage to ignore the duke's orders. To Tavis's surprise, slaying the ogres is the easiest part . . . the challenge has only begun!

ISBN 1-56076-891-6

Realms of Infamy

The incredible companion volume to the *Realms of Valor* anthology

From the secret annals of Realms history come never-before-published tales of villains – Artemis Entreri, Manshoon of Zhentil Keep, Elaith Craulnober, and many others – told by your favorite authors: R. A. Salvatore, Ed Greenwood, Troy Denning, Elaine Cunningham, and others.

ISBN 1-56076-911-4

DragonLance® Saga

THE HISTORIC SAGA OF THE DWARVEN CLANS

Dwarven Nations Trilogy

Dan Parkinson

The Covenant of the Forge   **Volume One**
As the drums of Balladine thunder forth, calling humans to trade
with the dwarves of Thorin, Grayfen, a human struck by the magic of
the Graystone, infiltrates the dwarven stronghold, determined to
annihilate the dwarves and steal their treasure.   ISBN 1-56076-558-5

Hammer and Axe   **Volume Two**
The dwarven clans unite against the threat of encroaching humans
and create the fortress of Thorbardin. But old rivalries are not easily
forgotten, and the resulting political intrigue brings about
catastrophic change.   ISBN 1-56076-627-1

The Swordsheath Scroll   **Volume Three**
Despite the stubborn courage of the dwarves, the Wilderness War
ends as a no-win. The Swordsheath Scroll is signed, and the dwarves
join the elves of Qualinesti to build a symbol of peace among the
races: Pax Tharkas.   ISBN 1-56076-686-7

DragonLance® Saga

The sweeping saga of honor, courage, and
companions begins with . . .

The Chronicles Trilogy

By *The New York Times* best-selling authors
Margaret Weis & Tracy Hickman

Dragons of Autumn Twilight
Volume One
Dragons have returned to Krynn with a vengeance.
An unlikely band of heroes embarks on a perilous
quest for the legendary *Dragonlance!*

ISBN 0-88038-173-6

Dragons of Winter Night
Volume Two
The adventure continues . . . Treachery,
intrigue, and despair threaten to overcome
the Heroes of the Lance in their epic quest!

ISBN 0-88038-174-4

Dragons of Spring Dawning
Volume Three
Hope dawns with the coming of spring, but then
the heroes find themselves in a titanic battle
against Takhisis, Queen of Darkness!

ISBN 0-88038-175-2